THE
NO
WORLD
CONCERTO

nally published in Spanish as *Concierto del No Mundo* by
Editorial Acantilado, Barcelona, 2006

Library of Congress Cataloging-in-Publication Data
is available.
ISBN: 978-1-56478-861-0

Partially funded by a grant from the Illinois Arts Council,
a state agency

This work has been published with a subsidy from the
Directorate General of Books, Archives and Libraries of the
Spanish Ministry of Culture

www.dalkeyarchive.com

Cover: design and composition by Mikhail Iliatov

Printed on permanent/durable acid-free paper

THE
NO
WORLD
CONCERTO

A. G. PORTA

TRANSLATED BY
DARREN KOOLMAN AND
RHETT MCNEIL

WITH A PREFACE BY DARREN KOOLMAN

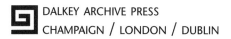 DALKEY ARCHIVE PRESS
CHAMPAIGN / LONDON / DUBLIN

Translator's Preface

Translating *The No World Concerto* was a difficult and pleasurable experience, much of the pleasure deriving from the difficulty, which always holds a fascination for those among us who enjoy reading books that not only move us but that, according to Blake, "rouze the faculties to act." An ambitious novelist, A. G. Porta is not content to take the approach of many contemporary writers who presume to subvert the literary tradition by ignoring it. Take his prize-winning debut, *Consejos de un discípulo de Morrison a un fanático de Joyce* (Advice from a Morrison Disciple to a Joycean Fanatic, 1984), which he wrote in collaboration with his friend, Roberto Bolaño: a highly ambitious, playfully irreverent novel about two bank-robbing lovers, Angel and Ana, who rebel against their parents and society by trying to steal enough money to realize their dream of starting a new life in Paris. Angel has a penchant for poetry, Ana for psychopathy. Angel wants to write a great novel about his moony protagonist, Dedalus, Ana wants to torture and murder as many people as possible. Both fancy themselves artists competing with rival criminals who are stealing all the headlines. Neither truly believes their personal ambitions or plan to escape to Paris will ever come to fruition. Despite the novel taking a decade to write, Porta and Bolaño were the ones who stole the headlines when they won the Ámbito Literario Prize in 1984, with many critics predicting a great follow-up from both writers. But whereas Bolaño quickly responded with a solo effort, *Monsieur Pain*, Porta entered a literary silence that lasted almost fifteen years.

During this time, Porta was earning his living as an editor of educational textbooks, spending much of his leisure time, according to Bolaño, obsessing over Joyce. Bolaño later joked that he remembered him "[writing or collecting] random sentences from *Ulysses* with which he assembled poems that he called readymades, à la Duchamp. Some were very good." Although Porta had seriously considered giving up fiction writing for good, he clearly hadn't stopped writing, because he eventually broke his long silence with three books in relatively quick succession: *Braudel por Braudel* (Braudel on Braudel, 1999), *El peso del aire* (The Weight of the Air, 2001), and *Singapur* (Singapore, 2003), all of which were applauded by the majority of critics and ignored in equal measure by the public.

His next effort, *Concierto del No Mundo* (*The No World Concerto*, 2006), features some of the characters from his previous three novels. But, besides retaining the same beguilingly simple prose style and metatextual construction, it is markedly more ambitious than any of his previous works. Ostensibly the story of an old screenwriter's struggle to finish his script, and his relationship with a former student—a female piano prodigy referred to only as "the girl"—who is similarly struggling to write her own novel, it is a bewildering superposition of tales within tales that often blend seamlessly into one another, and at many times confound readers' attempts to determine whether it is Porta, the screenwriter, or the girl they're reading at any given moment. As with his first novel, the book is haunted by the ghost of Joyce, and again like that novel, there is the *folie à deux* relationship of two ambitious characters intent on escaping their situation. But whereas the Porta-Bolaño world is one of violence and sweaty-balled erudition, entering the No World is like entering an M. C. Escher lithograph. Added to this difficulty is the author's pervasive use of epithets instead of proper names for designating characters, cities, historical figures, books, music, etc. Paris, for example, is called "the neighboring country's capital"; the composer, Schoenberg, is referred to as "the father of twelve-tone composition"; and Méliès, the film director, may or may not be the "the inventor of the cinematic spectacle" who's buried in a "famous" cemetery Porta doesn't name.

Besides the many other cinematic, musical, and philosophical allusions in the book, what most concerns the characters—and the author through his characters—is literature. Both the screenwriter and the girl are obsessed by great writers like Shakespeare, Cervantes, Joyce, and Proust, among others, although Porta, of course, refuses to name them, choosing instead to refer to Joyce, for example, by the unwieldy epithet, "The author that revolutionized twentieth-century literature." Such evasive insistence could be a playful prank to keep the reader guessing, or it could be the author's indirect way of contending with these literary giants, as if not naming them might be a kind of desacralization.

All in all, Porta's approach is undoubtedly risky, but he's not so niggardly as to refuse to supply the reader with clues. In a sense, therefore, the reader becomes a kind of detective, and feels—as the screenwriter feels when writing his script—that if she follows all the clues, she'll be able to figure out the mystery behind this postmodern mystery play (or screenplay), a process the screenwriter compares with reconstructing the scene of a crime. Thus, the screenwriter's doubts at the beginning of the novel mirror the reader's. Each must navigate through this shadowy otherworld until all—or not quite all—is finally revealed.

Doubts, confusions, are indeed what Porta himself had experienced while writing the novel, for it was only after five complete revisions that it arrived at its present form. Even when he won the prestigious Café Gijón Prize in 2005, the novel wasn't in its final version, still bearing the early title *Cazadores de los No Mundos* (Seekers of No Worlds), and having an old guitarist as its protagonist instead of a screenwriter. Nonetheless, one gets the impression that even if he'd been cast as a biochemist or a ballet dancer, his obsessions would still have been with writers—as they would for the girl, who sees writing not only as a means of escaping into a No World but of liberation from her enthrallment to the piano on which her mother forces her to practice. The definitive title of this novel may only be incidental—whether or not it's "just" the tale of an uninspired screenwriter conceived structurally as a bastardization of Wittgenstein and Schoenberg, it's certainly not a musical concerto. And yet, it is undoubtedly a work of art. So, in calling his novel *The No World Concerto*, perhaps A. G. Porta was only reinforcing what Walter Pater famously said about all such endeavors: that they constantly aspire to the condition of music.

I'd like to thank the author, A. G. Porta, for writing this wonderful novel which was such a delight to translate; my fellow-translator, Rhett McNeil, for beginning a process that it was my privilege to complete; John O'Brien, for entrusting me with the task of doing so; and Jeremy M. Davies and the staff at Dalkey Archive Press, for helping so greatly to improve what I believed only an adequate translation.

Darren Koolman, 2012

THE
NO
WORLD
CONCERTO

To Joel, for his No World

1. The world is all that is the case.

5.123 If a god creates a world in which certain propositions are true, then by that very act he also creates a world in which all the propositions that follow from them come true.

LUDWIG WITTGENSTEIN, *Tractatus Logico-Philosophicus*

55. So is the *hypothesis* possible, that all the things around us don't exist? Would that not be like the hypothesis of our having miscalculated in all our calculations?

75. Would this be correct: If I merely believed wrongly that there is a table here in front of me, this might still be a mistake; but if I believe wrongly that I have seen this table, or one like it, every day for several months past, and have regularly used it, that isn't a mistake?

LUDWIG WITTGENSTEIN, *On Certainty*

The screenwriter stands with his luggage, facing the hotel, having just gotten out of a taxi, thinking he ought to know, or at least have a good idea, how the story he intends to write is going to end. He's certainly seen better hotels than this, but today he can't afford to pay for one, because he no longer gets the advances he used to, and he's lost a well-paying job teaching literature at a school for gifted kids. Now, all he's left are some savings and a miserable pension, and he doesn't know how long they're going to last, for life in the neighboring country's capital is so much more expensive than the city he just left. He remembers when he was young and distinguished, back when he was working in the movies, back in the days when he didn't have to teach. It is noon, on August 1st, when the taxi leaves him standing at the hotel's entrance, motionless, as if afraid to confront his destiny, wincing at the small, grimy windows of the dreary façade, at the weather-beaten awning covering part of the sidewalk, thinking he's seen better hotels than this one, wondering if anyone alive can recall its last renovation. After spending a few moments gathering his thoughts, he gathers his belongings, taking the portable typewriter in one hand, his cane in the other—against which he leans to offset his imbalance—and wobbles through the front door, keeping the corner of his eye fixed on the luggage he leaves on the sidewalk as he stumbles toward the reception desk. There are no bellhops in sight, and the receptionist talks on the telephone, watching him insouciantly as he clumsily lugs in his bags. He doesn't know how many days he'll stay. He thinks a few. Once in his room on the fourth floor, he briefly inspects the facilities, a diminutive bathroom and a mini-kitchen converted from a storage closet. He then sits on one of the beds and checks if the telephone is working. He promised his wife he'd call her every day; several times a day in fact, so he dials the number and waits, takes a good look around the room, noting the arrangement of the furniture, two beds and a writing desk, until he hears the fifth ring and hangs up. Still seated, he looks at a mirror on the wall, searches for the kitchen's reflection, which his position and viewing angle prevent him from finding, so he looks out the window instead. He thinks he'll have to move the desk a few inches if he wants to take advantage of the natural light. He takes a small diary from his jacket pocket and searches for a phone number, dials it, waits, but again there's no answer. After the voicemail prompt, he gives the details of his change of address then lies back on the bed for an ample stretch. He decides to sleep on the bed nearest the writing desk; the other, beside the window, will serve as a makeshift table for his bags and research material. He gets up to move the desk a few inches before setting up his workstation. He fiddles quite a while with the typewriter, for it must be in the perfect position. On one side of it, he places a couple of books, some index cards, and a few loose pages—both typewritten and scribbled on with pencil; on the other side, a carefully squared-off stack of blank paper. After arranging everything meticulously and standing back to admire his accomplishment, he goes over to the window to look down on the street below. He notes that the sidewalks are quite spacious, zooms in on the occasional passerby—many returning home from work, a few with bags of groceries—scans over to the other side of the street where some people are waiting for a bus, and finally pans upward to survey the building opposite. While looking in one of the windows, he surprises a woman folding children's laundry when she looks up and accidentally meets his eyes. He smiles, but she quickly looks away. No matter, he forgives her. She must deal with these situations everyday. Besides, she doesn't even know him. He turns to look at the typewriter, the books, the mountain of paper, but hesitates. Perhaps, he thinks, he shouldn't get ahead of himself. After all, fools rush in where angels fear to tread. Ideas should be given time to germinate. So he decides to freshen up and go for a walk instead. Although he's been to the neighboring country's capital before, he'd still like to do some exploring, to take a walk along the riverbank, and relax in the park on one the benches beside the pond. His limp affects his progress, but he thinks slow progress has its advantages. On reaching the river, he decides to follow its course while appreciating the view of the opposite bank, with its rows of houses, amusing himself by wondering about the people behind each window, living out their lives inscrutably, recalling, as he always does when in this mood, a certain movie in which an angel is able to hear other people's voices, not only when they speak, but also when they think, the spoken and unspoken thoughts of everyone on Earth. He stops at the railing to look out on the wharf, at the boats full of tourists, the barges full of cargo, before deciding to continue on to an old bookstore where, years before, he remembers buying his first collection of screenplays. The bookseller, who looks a hundred years old, is propped in a chair in the middle of the store—a book in one hand, a cup of tea in the other—not acknowledging the screenwriter, who imagines him dying in that same chair with the same cup of tea in his hand, since he presumes booksellers never retire. He buys nothing, doesn't want to disturb him, rob him of what little time he has left. Instead, he waits until he reaches the boulevard, and buys a newspaper at one of the kiosks. Although he thinks they're mostly a waste of time, sometimes they can be troves of great ideas. After dining at a restaurant next to the botanical gardens, he decides to head for the pond to see if the children there still sail their little toy boats. He recalls the day he went there with his son, when he sat down on one of the benches to have a rest and watch him play, and perhaps to do as he does now, reminisce. He sees some parents are doing the same with their children, young fathers and mothers, although his eyes are only for the mothers. He thinks they're pretty. He tries to make eye contact while riffling through a newspaper he's already read, but none of them answer his gaze. He soon forgets all about them though, adapts to his surroundings, diffuses himself among the other strangers present—the parents and children, the various tourists—until he finally believes he has possession of the place, and then returns to the hotel alone.

That evening, the screenwriter prepares to begin his work. He positions himself before the typewriter, the books, the mountain of paper, and a little notebook filled with plans, snatches of dialogue, and notes on the story's structure. Before beginning, he removes his glasses to massage his eyes, relaxes them on the middle distance, and then considers what he wants to say. He'd like to be original, but at his age, ambition has given way to disillusion. He'd be happy to produce a decent script. Before even touching the typewriter, he decides to make a cup of coffee, so he shuffles with the help of his cane toward the mini-kitchen, which is half obscured on the other side of the room. He lights a cigarette and smiles contentedly, glad that he has his own kitchen—not that his limp is an issue, but at least he doesn't have to stray too far to get a cup of coffee. He looks out the window and notices the woman across the street, whose movements he'd been following earlier that afternoon. He noted then that she was setting the table. Now he can see her serving dinner to some brats he assumes are her sons. After looking for a husband and not finding one, the screenwriter concludes there isn't one. He starts entertaining the notion of inviting her to dinner, but then quickly reproaches himself. Who says there isn't a husband? From a distance she looks quite pretty—young, the way he likes them. She's not going anywhere, he tells himself, and he has all the time in the world to seduce her. He leaves his vantage point by the window and retreats to the kitchen and the solace of a murmuring kettle. While pouring a cup, he fantasizes about their first encounter, imagining her likely negative reaction, before consoling himself by thinking she'll have the time to get to know him better. He returns to his desk and works for a while, if an activity that produces no results can be called work. First, he attributes his lack of inspiration on his taking an overlong break; then, he blames it on his sitting too long at the desk thinking, waiting for the *ipsissima verba* to fall into his lap. He removes his glasses and relaxes his eyes on the view outside the window, on the traffic lights in the street below, the glow from the windows in the building opposite, the numinous halo above the cityscape, until suddenly, a knock on the door restores him to his senses.

He wasn't expecting her. The reason, perhaps, is that he'd only just arrived in the capital. The real reason: he didn't want to delude himself. She floats over the threshold like a ghost and ambles through the room, pausing in front of the writing desk. She rests her hand on his typewriter momentarily and glances around, examining all four corners of the screenwriter's new abode, before going to the window and peeking through a chink in the curtain—which she quickly pulls shut, and then declares she's being followed. She's not certain of course, nothing is certain in this life, but she's had this feeling for days now. She sits on the edge of one of the beds. She can't stay long, the rehearsal lasted longer than she expected. She came to this country's capital to be part of a youth orchestra called the Little Sinfonietta, and to record the *5 Pieces for piano* by a famous composer of twelve-tone music. Although she's a celebrated pianist, her real obsession is writing. But she rarely has the time for what she considers to be her true calling, and even when she finds the time, she's unable to concentrate, due to her chronic suspicions of being followed, so her work in progress remains at an impasse. She came to see his new room, to examine the desk where the screenwriter will ply his trade. He watches her silently, longingly. He'd give anything to make her stay the whole night, to feel her body's warmth next to his, to be safe in the cocoon of their desire, and then the tender moment afterward when she would rest her head upon his breast, and tangle his graying chest hair between her fingers. But she seems nervous, and the screenwriter suspects she's taken caffeine pills to help her stay awake. The sex is strange when she's too wired, he thinks, she has no patience, just wants to get it over with as quickly and as roughly as possible. They say little, although, occasionally, they mention the voices she hears, and her impression that they pronounce her name with a "ka" sound. Voices from another world, not like the ones the screenwriter hears, or like the movie he recalls; they don't speak with the accent of his inner voice, nor do they sound like the voice she affects when reciting the twenty-one poems of that other twelve-tone composition, and though they call out to her, they're not human voices, and who knows what it is they want to say, or why they pronounce her name with a "ka." He watches her as she paces around the room. They begin to discuss literature, particularly the most revolutionary writer of the twentieth century. Sometimes I have trouble following you, she says. His work still impresses her, although the novelty has long since worn off. Perhaps it's because he always changes his approach, the standard that defines his whole idea of literature, and therefore hers, is never quite the same. It's too dry. No, she can't quite put her finger on it. Luckily, the novel came with a reader's guide, although it did little to help her penetrate its difficulty, and this, paradoxically, is what has made the novel famous. Maybe the thing that jars you the most in a novel is when it's not clear if the narrator or one of the characters is speaking, so the reader mistakes the narrator for one of the characters or one of the characters for the narrator, something the novelist has no control over, and hence both chance and contingency are given literary form, allowing for a multiplicity of possible narrative voices and possible characters that can all be confounded together in an infinite number of possible scenarios, without the reader knowing where they came from or where they're going, without her knowing more, perhaps, than their names. The reader may be taken aback at first, but after a few pages, sometimes by degrees, sometimes spontaneously, she begins at last to grasp what's going on. The screenwriter doesn't see the danger in reading other writers' works, except in getting too involved in them, in overly assimilating, imitating, which stymies one's developing a distinctive style. The girl spots the silhouette of someone waiting on the street below. She imagines a detective, or maybe a jealous lover keeping tabs on his fiancée; it could even be a spy or a policeman. He thinks she's too young to talk about developing a personal style. Perhaps, in all her sixteen years, she's read very little.

9

Perhaps she isn't familiar enough with the spectrum of different styles and languages that constitute his literary world. But the screenwriter is fully aware of his own shortcomings. To be a writer requires more than just desire, one has to want it more than anything else in the world. She made a promise to herself. Her musical talent wouldn't interfere with her writing, despite her making little progress on her *No World*, the work she writes and rewrites, having never progressed beyond twenty pages, saying something always prompts her to start over, to change the theme, the diction, even the structure. The screenwriter thinks youth ideal for self-discovery, the waiting ends when one finds one's true vocation. This may not apply to the pianist, but it certainly does to the writer. It's a game they play, in which sometimes he plays the tutor, sometimes the lover. He gives her advice on reading, tells her to focus on the twentieth century's most revolutionary writer, but he also recommends the great dramatist of the late sixteenth and early seventeenth centuries, whose works he insists have set the standard for everything written after them. She must read as widely as possible to cultivate a proper sense of what will stand the test of time. But being selective is not naïve reductionism, he says. The alternative is to read many more books than is feasible in a single lifetime, and of the making of books there is no end. So the girl reads everything he recommends, between each visit, each of her rehearsals, and each abortive attempt at her *No World*. But I don't see the point, she complains. He says young women today are spread too thinly between school and extra-curricular distractions to develop as artists, especially the so-called musical prodigies. She kisses his forehead. There was a message from the Principal on my mom's answering machine, she says, referring to the Principal of the school at which the screenwriter taught. It was from a week ago, ten days at most—before he embarked on his trip. He looks into her eyes; she delays, smiling mischievously, getting ready to leave, until the moment of her exit when she says, But don't worry, I deleted it.

The screenwriter forgets all about the woman in the building opposite, and her sons, who must have finished their dinner by now. Only the girl occupies his thoughts. He imagines her in a theater, sitting on a stool in the middle of a stage, surrounded by five other members of the Little Sinfonietta, reciting the same stanza over and over. The rehearsal might have gone quite differently of course, but this is how he likes to imagine her. He feels incapable of writing now. He needs her to be near him, speaking to him, for when she speaks, he takes what she says as dictation, which is why she's the protagonist of his script, but he also wants to keep her close-by, to prolong the time he has with her, a time during which he no longer feels the ache of her absence, a time that seems to contract with each visit. He writes his characters' initials on a blank page, with line strokes of varying thickness radiating from each, representing all manner of links and associations. He organizes himself and tries to gather his thoughts, but all he can think about is the girl's next visit. He goes to the window and looks down on the fading rush hour, the traffic lights, and the windows above the sidewalk across the street. He makes out the light of a TV in the darkness of the woman's apartment, and he imagines her children seated before it as she's washing the dishes in the kitchen. Although it's past their bedtime, he makes allowances for their staying up so late since it's vacation time. When he returns to his seat, it doesn't take long before he's fantasizing again, before he's affecting industry by jotting a few halfhearted notes on a card now and then. Some of his characters are gifted musicians. He's well acquainted with the type: the girl, the young orchestra conductor, and the brilliant composer and accompanist for the Little Sinfonietta had all been his students once. The Scholastic Institute at which he taught wouldn't settle for second best. The screenwriter thinks his movie is structured in concentric layers like an onion, but when his spirits are low, and he can't concentrate, he finds it impossible to distinguish between the layers. Maybe he's just tired, he thinks, attempting to justify abandoning his desk and going to bed. But he stays seated for a while longer, thinking of the layers, incomplete, indistinguishable, trying to cut the onion, bleary-eyed, purblind, until he finally gives up. Again, he removes his glasses to massage his eyes, to relax them on the middle distance beyond the window. The woman in the building opposite has turned out the lights and he stares into the darkness of her window. He's procrastinating. He thinks about the onion again. Then the girl—she's probably tired by now, at the point of sleep, but still burning with ambition all the same, still determined to be a writer who'll accomplish great things. He wonders about the voices in her head, always calling out to her, never silent, and about her persecution complex—like her ambition—ever restless. A thing of little consequence to others, perhaps, but for the screenwriter, at least, it's a beginning.

He sleeps badly, erratically, waking in the night repeatedly, until the new day's reveille breaks in through the curtain cracks, prompting him to get out of bed. It's early. In August, he always rises early. He draws the curtains and opens the window, taking a quick look at the building opposite. Nothing. No movement on the street below either. The city still slumbers. This makes the screenwriter think of his wife. He promised to call her several times a day, to sustain, rejuvenate her memory of him. He's already lost track, but he does remember yesterday was the last time he called. Something in the pit of his stomach goads him to pick up to phone and dial the number. No reply. Feeling a chill, he goes to the window. The drone of vehicles waiting at the traffic lights below tells him the city is stirring. He closes the window to shut out the noise, and takes a seat beside the telephone. Again, he calls his wife; again, he lets it ring five times before hanging up. Then he repeats the process again. She never answers. He cracks a smile as if the ritual induces a pleasurable frisson. Remember me? he mutters into receiver, biting his bottom lip. After hanging up for the last time, he grabs his glasses and returns to the writing desk, takes out a few index cards and scans them a while, reviewing his notes on the plot from the beginning: the girl practicing endlessly at the piano, her rehearsals with the Little Sinfonietta, her writings, her nightly visits. He imagines her thinking of him—thinking of him waiting for her, sitting at his desk in a modest room in a flophouse most piano starlets like her would avoid. After sleeping a little more, he wakes up hungry. He checks the time. He goes into the bathroom and eyes himself in the mirror for a while. Then he starts scrupulously combing his hair. He feels young, despite his age, no one could ever guess his age. In the hallway, the doors to some of the other rooms are open. He sees a maid pushing a vacuum, flanked by a massif of dirty towels. She says hello, he simply nods his head. Her blue uniform is unbuttoned at the crotch, but since he doesn't find her attractive anyway, he looks away. He heads for the canteen musing over the girl, imagines the realia she deems indispensable: the satchel in which she keeps her sheet music, the books he recommends, her diary, and the notebooks in which she works on her mag-

13

num opus. It's probably an idea he jotted elsewhere, but he imagines the young orchestra conductor saying something along the lines of: Supposing twelve-tone music had never been invented. The screenwriter scribbles it in his notebook just in case, setting it off from the rest of the page, and takes a seat at the table. No need for more detail, the suggestion of the phrase is all he needs to recover the whole idea. Now, he imagines the girl writing in her diary, gasping for an afflatus, groping after an elusive plot so she can finally continue her story, and the screenwriter squirms under this reminder of himself. When she finishes giving the concerts, he'll ask her to run away with him, he thinks, to go with him as far away as possible, to the other side of the world if need be, to a city where the cost of living could be covered by a pension check, where they could live off the earnings from his screenplays, the novels the girl will write under his aegis, and maybe even the proceeds of a piano recital or two: a beautiful thought, but the reverie makes him lose his train of thought. Still, the idea's now safely ensconced in his pocket. How different it would be, having breakfast with her, looking out at the sea: a different life; a different world. This neighboring country, this capital city, is only a hitching post—he thinks, trying to reassure himself—a momentary detour from his path to a better life. After breakfast and reading a newspaper in the discommodious hotel lobby, he decides to stretch his legs by joining the pedestrians outside. He heads first to the pond, then to a kiosk located at the point where the boulevards intersect, and purchases a broadsheet from his native country. He's unable to read while limping, so he stands aside and skims over some of the headlines. Then he tucks it under his arm and limps down the hill toward the café in the plaza. The waitress is attractive. He smiles, she doesn't seem to notice. So he lights a cigarette and finishes going over the headlines. While waiting to be served, he takes a look around the plaza and suddenly recalls the phrase he noted down during breakfast. He recites it a couple of times under his breath, and decides to build on it before it dissipates. The action takes place on stage in a small, empty theater. Near the end of the rehearsal, as the girl sees her father take a seat in the front row, the screenwriter puts in the mouth of the young conductor the words: Supposing twelve-tone music had never been invented. The brilliant composer, barely paying attention as he collects the tiny music boxes from the young musicians, eventually suggests that another, similar, genre of music would exist in its place, but under another name. It's a possibility, says the young conductor wearily, half-engrossed in his own thoughts. The girl grabs her satchel and steps down from the stage. As he enters the theater, her father takes a look around to get a sense of the place. He hopes the dreary surroundings, the darkness, the empty seats are only due to the orchestra's still being in rehearsal, not a foreboding of the concerts ahead. He wanted to be there for the whole rehearsal, but he arrived late. Still, at least he managed to catch the last few notes as he walked in the door. The precocious youngsters are putting away their instruments. The young conductor greets the girl's father, as does the brilliant composer. Both seem to be on familiar terms with him. They slowly exit the theater together. The girl wonders why her father showed up. He's never attended a rehearsal before, and she doubts he'd be interested in a work whose chief protagonist is a clown. But she doubts even more that he'd be interested in her. She explains to him part of their repertoire. It's a new version of an old composition, she says, so fresh it could be mistaken for an original piece, entitled *Dress Rehearsal for Voice and Music Boxes*. He's not very interested. He happened to be visiting the neighboring country's capital on business; his presence is a coincidence, that's all. The screenwriter considers the situation as presented, and asks himself why a father wouldn't take more of an interest in his own daughter. He doesn't seem the least bit concerned she might end up in the arms of an unscrupulous roué, he thinks, referring to the young conductor of the orchestra. For some reason, the young conductor's come to embody the screenwriter's notion of lubricity and perversion. All fathers must think like this. After all, the world is full of these kinds of people, and although they're precocious, the young musicians of the orchestra are still kids—dressed in their uniforms, heading for the minibus that will return them to their dorms. We were looking for a place with a foosball table, she says, referring to the conductor, the composer, and herself, who have a puckish streak, unlike the others. In reality, they don't even know if foosball bars exist here in the neighboring country's capital. Her father excuses himself, says he must go, for there are people waiting for him elsewhere, and he's already running late. Let's suppose twelve-tone music had never been invented, the young conductor is overheard declaiming, no serialism, or any of that stuff. For he wants to know if music with aleatoric elements, or whatever one wishes to call them, could have been conceived at any other time. The brilliant composer doesn't respond. He seems lost in thought, as if he's immersed in his mysterious creative process, playing the part of the genius, the brilliant one, the wunderkind that they all imagine him to be. The other two don't respond either. What do you think? The conductor asks, directing his question at the girl. That it couldn't have existed at any other time, she says. They walk a few meters in the opposite direction to her father, who's parked his car a little farther ahead. Night falls, and the screenwriter observes the scene from afar, he sees them poorly lit under a streetlight whose brightness has yet to overtake the dimming twilight. The girl takes a few steps away from her friends and tells her father good-bye. Putting her right arm around him, she feels a revolver at his side and asks him jokingly if he's on duty, though she's well aware he's not a policeman or anything of the sort. He smiles in a routine manner that could be interpreted to mean anything, and she returns to her friends as he makes his way up the street— thinking, perhaps, that the twelve-tone experiment was a failure, and wondering why anyone would want to repeat it. He saw you, says the girl reprovingly, addressing the brilliant composer, who's in the process of rolling a joint. Your dad probably knows more about this stuff than we do, he says, but the girl doesn't want her father getting too close. She doesn't want him interfering in her life.

I hear voices, the girl confesses. I think they come from another world. The young conductor asks her how she can be sure. How does she know the voices aren't just inside her head? But she's utterly convinced of it, and that should be proof enough, it seems. The young conductor says no one can know if something exists in and of itself outside the mind. Maybe you don't exist except in my head, he says. The world doesn't truly exist, interjects the brilliant composer, who then asks them to consider whether the entity that has created everything, that is imagining their existence, is of limited extension—if it takes up space somewhere—or whether it's infinite. They're not even voices from this world, insists the girl, they're from a false world, a No World created by some alien consciousness. The brilliant composer's symphony touches on this, she says, while really thinking about her own work in progress—the *No*

World she writes and rewrites without ever getting anywhere; the *No World* that's always expanding inside her, ever ripening, while never reaching maturity. There is a language that reaches out into the cosmos, with which we could communicate with beings from another galaxy. That language is music. How can she know they're not actually the voices of the great musicians? Suppose the great musicians had never really existed. At times, it seems they're only playing games. But then they'd say life itself is a game. The young conductor says it's all the same, speculating about what would've happened if twelve-tone serialism had never been invented, or if the great musicians had never been born: the point is the music *was* invented, the musicians *were* born. And these things happened because they had to. The screenwriter imagines the young conductor's voice off-screen, as the camera zooms in from a panoramic view of the city toward a dingy little bar with a foosball table—like one of those gambling dens in the movies, fumid and fusty, manned by local ruffians playing pool. Similarly, says the young conductor, youth exists in every age because it has to. The girl and the brilliant composer remain silent as he concludes his monologue, and the camera stops zooming once all three are together in the frame, their hands gripping the bars running through the tiny foosball players, the funk of smoke and alcohol pervading a setting unsuited for formalist debates and metaphysical colloquies. The two guys are wearing the Scholastic Institute's regulation uniform, comprised of a navy-blue blazer, gray pants, a white shirt, and a necktie. The girl, on the other hand, likes to think she's different, since she's considered a rising star of the piano world, and although she attends the same school, believes she can dress however she likes, and it so happens she likes to dress in white. The young orchestra conductor takes aim, maneuvering his defensive line, before spinning the bar violently, projecting the ball up the table. If the great musicians were never born, he says, other musicians would be revered in their place. The brilliant composer reproves him for sounding like a broken record, for he's merely repeating something he's stated several times before.

It is night. The young conductor is rolling a joint and wants to know if the girl will write a libretto about making love in her mother's bed. She can try, but all she really wants to do is get her novel back on track. Her cell phone rings, she moves her index finger to her lips, indicating that the conductor should remain silent. Her mother is off on her travels, but she'll be back for the concerts, and this, the girl presumes, is why she's calling . . . the young orchestra conductor nibbles on the girl's toes and then continues up her leg, putting the joint between his lips, from which he takes a final drag before proffering it to the girl. During the hand-off, he teases her by blowing the smoke in her face. But she ignores him and takes a long drag of the joint as her mother begins the interrogation. First she asks if the phone call had woken the girl up. No. She was reading the greatest dramatist who ever lived. A genius, she says. Her mother tends to disregard what her daughter is reading, no matter who the writer is, or how great he happens to be. She cares only about her career as a pianist. The girl talks about the reading material her literature teacher gave her. But haven't you already completed that course? Yes, but this is supplementary reading. You've already told him you want to be a writer, haven't you. The girl changes the subject and asks if her mother has managed to track down her cousin. Her mother's spent a long time trying to locate a certain cousin who went missing in the neighboring country's capital years before. No, she answers curtly and hangs up. That's new, the girl thinks. Her mother usually ignores her questions. An answer is progress. The girl and the young conductor are reading W's magnum opus. He wants to know if she'll write a libretto based on W and his work. Later that night, the dramatist visits her in a dream. It seems he wants to explain to her the secrets of his craft. He teaches by demonstration, his words accompanied by gesticulations, like a magician threading his hands through the air while uttering incantations, who creates a world and measures its just circumference, who molds his characters and gives them the breath of life. He talks about their diversity, each an individual, a separate creation. He mentions his audience, and the girl seizes on this with curiosity, because she wants to know if it plays a major part in the creation of his works. But he suddenly starts speaking another language, and she despairs that she will only get to hear but not understand his answer. She turns, in her dream, to the young conductor, and begs him to take some notes. But then she wakes up, and sees the young conductor is no longer by her side. She gets out of the bed to go look for him and finds him in the living room, sitting naked in an armchair watching TV, with a glass of beer in his hand. On the screen, a pornographic actress anxiously tongues an inordinately erect penis before putting it into her mouth. The girl stands beside the piano looking on, silently. How old would you say she is? the conductor asks without turning. The girl doesn't know. Perhaps thirty-something, she answers indecisively. There's something about mature women, he says, still not taking his eyes off the screen, and lets a few seconds go by before adding, it's as if they exude more confidence or something. The male actor then penetrates the actress, thrusting slowly at first, then faster, before settling into a regular rhythm. The girl says she feels the same way about older men, but she's not sure if it's for the same reason. The girl doesn't realize the conductor has an erection until he stands up. He brings her to the armchair and sits her facing backwards in his lap, penetrating her from behind, his eyes remaining fixed on the screen almost every moment. He even starts thrusting in time with the actor, and the girl feels he's only using her to imagine having sex with a thirty-something porn star. She tells him about her dream, about the dramatist's visitation, that she believes he was going to reveal to her the secrets of his dramaturgy. The young conductor isn't listening. Mature women really turn me on, he says. You'll find lots of mature women in his plays, she says. Then she continues by telling him about the point in the dream when the dramatist began speaking another language. The young conductor asks her if people ever have sex in sixteenth-century plays. She doesn't answer. He imagines they'd look exactly like the girl's mother, who's peering down at them from a photograph next to the TV. Your mother turns me on, he says while squeezing her. The girl jumps off and tells him to go to hell. She heads for the bathroom, turning only once, but just in time to see the young conductor cum in his glass of beer. The couple on-screen appears to be only getting started.

The screenwriter works all afternoon but is unable to produce a single line. It's been years since he's written a screenplay, and now he's trying to rediscover his voice. Bewildered, he asks himself what advice he'd give if he were one of his students. He thinks he'd suggest sticking to his guns, not abandoning the idea too soon. It's quite like the notion of a certain bishop centuries ago who said nothing exists outside the mind. The screenwriter hasn't done the research, it's just something he remembers hearing somewhere, and perhaps he has the wording all wrong. His students wouldn't care about the wording in any case. The point is not to give up on a promising idea too readily. Like twelve-tone music. After all, deep down, it's just another method, a different approach to musical performance and composition. And, although the screenwriter thinks his method a little erratic, he'd like to achieve similar distinction in his writing. His writing hasn't always been erratic, but he reassures himself that the change isn't because of his age. The problem is his current situation. He no longer has the freedom he used to have. The screenwriter grows more anxious with each passing hour, scribbling over and over, supposing twelve-tone music was never invented. But he can't stop thinking about the girl, whose imminent arrival he nervously anticipates. After dining on some fruit, he opens the windows to rest his feet on the ledge as he finishes his coffee and decides to roll a joint. He notes the evening temperature is pleasantly mild. The lights in the building opposite are going on and off like a switchboard, and although it happens completely at random, the screenwriter watches in amazement, as if something extraordinary was going on, something with purpose and meaning. The effect is hypnotic, soothing: a symphony of color, he'd say, if he wasn't more interested in catching sight of anything resembling a female figure in one of the windows. Then he looks down at the empty street. Maybe she won't show up, he thinks. He can't expect an assignation every night. But he wants to make love to her tonight. He turns off the lamp and watches the play of light and shade on the building across the street, the subtle grayish nuances between them, as his eyes adjust to the room's obscurity. He sees everything more clearly, but nothing new. And yet, the fresh evening air has a calming effect, so he decides to lie down and have a rest that before long turns into a nap. He wakes up in the middle of the night covered in sweat. He dreamed about the woman in the building across the street. Her light had suddenly come on, and he couldn't help staring as she drifted naked past the window. He watched and waited for some seconds in case she walked past the window again, but her light went out, and with that, he felt the thread of his story was lost. What a stupid dream, he thinks. It should never have caused him to break out in a sweat. He washes his face then goes to the window and parts the curtains. Although it's dark, he sees the building clearly, illumined by the lampposts on the streets below and the apartments whose lights are still on. He carefully counts these apartments and notes their position, promising himself to check if the same ones have their lights on every night. But what's the point? he wonders, knowing how feeble an excuse he'd give: curiosity, something to do for the sake of doing, something to ease his anxiety. Unable to sleep, he decides to call his wife. After waiting for five rings, he hangs up indifferently. Then he asks himself why he agreed to write the screenplay. Money. The word money keeps cropping up. But it makes the world go round, he says aloud while staring at the ceiling. It's not that he feels incapable of writing the script, but the other characters—those musicians—only matter to him in relation to the girl. He remembers when things were different, when he was young and ambitious, back when he was only starting out as a screenwriter. He reflects on an old cliché: he may have been poor, but at least he was happy; a sad cliché reinforced by the false belief that wealth and security will one day compensate the loss of youth and felicity. The fact is he's just as poor now as he was back then. Every so often, an old friend will take pity on him and allow him to assist on a project—to revise some greenhorn's script, or write dialogue for an older character, which a young writer may find difficult or even impossible to do. This tends to happen when a script doesn't have a single interesting scene. So a producer decides that adding more dialogue should solve the problem. Of course, this is the same as beating a dead pony. As long as the scene's interesting enough, it doesn't really matter what the characters are saying. On the other hand, the screenwriter counts himself lucky he still has the strength to write, or at least believes he has, and that his producer friends still have confidence in him. But how could he not have strength to write? He's a professional, after all. And he acts like a professional too, even when he's forced to listen to these tedious musical pieces, which lack anything resembling classical harmony and seem to go on interminably. He writes in his notebook: According to the girl, the twelve chromatic intervals into which a scale is divided are used indiscriminately in the atonal system, with no single tone predominating. If he could adapt these ideas to his screenplay, a very different movie could emerge. He goes back to the bed and rests his head on the pillow. Yes, maybe he could create something new, although he suspects practically everything's been said already. But he may still come away from the project with something interesting to tell his students—if he ever has students again, that is. Is he really interested in the girl's talent? He can't deceive himself: besides the screenplay, all he cares about is her body. Or is it her company? Or the hope of a new life?

It's Wednesday, in the middle of the night. She's still afraid they're following her, so the girl drops in on the screenwriter when he least expects it. She reminds him she's going through a white phase: her wardrobe has only generic white pants and

T-shirts. The screenwriter almost forgot this detail. She refuses to wear anything else. Maybe he read it in a previous draft of her novel, or heard it when she read to him from her diary. She says brand-name clothing is a thing of the past for her; she only wears white canvas shoes with the labels and shoelaces removed. She's shed her regard for fashion and conformity, she says, trying to sound convincing. They don't matter anymore. She then expresses her concern about her favorite soccer player, who's taken an extended vacation and will miss the next big game. The screenwriter feigns his surprise, for he's already read about it in the newspaper. It's been a long time since she last kicked a ball herself. Soccer's one of many hobbies she sacrificed for the sake of her music and for writing. Schools for gifted kids tend to encourage their students to discriminate between subjects that are worthy of study and those they deem to be trivial. Nevertheless, the girl never stopped supporting her favorite soccer team. What would you do if you were his coach? she asks the screenwriter. He knows he'd have fired him, but he doesn't dare say it. Instead, he dodges the question by asking her what she thinks her father would do. She mulls it over. Why are you interested in my father? There's something intriguing about him, he says. She smiles. But who is my father? she wonders as he watches her expectantly. My father is someone whose business dealings have made him very rich in a very short space of time, someone who never takes time off, except for a few days here and there during the course of a year. But she has no idea what he does with his time, what his line of work is. No one does. Like her, he wanted to be a writer when he was younger, but he didn't have the conviction, the perseverance necessary to become one in the end. On the other hand, he shows enormous dedication when it comes to reading that great swan song of nineteenth-century fiction, a book written by a novelist and cartographer of memory who turned jealousy into an aesthetic of stolen time. This is one of the reasons she has no qualms about telling her father she wants to be a writer, she says, although the screenwriter knows she'd hardly have any trouble telling the whole world. And yet, he's the very model of an absentee father. Her mother's the same, despite being the one who takes care of her. The girl knows her mother would rather take care of a successful company. But as for her father: he takes little interest in his daughter's life, especially since the separation, and he only follows her career as a pianist from a distance. He still frequently asks about her training for the soccer team, as if every time he receives the same answer, he cheerfully eradicates it from his memory. A light goes on across the street; the screenwriter can't help glancing over. A naked woman passes by a window. He's afraid of losing the thread of the girl's story, but he keeps looking in case she walks past again. She doesn't, and the light goes off. From his spot next to the writing desk, he watches the girl stretched out on one of the two beds—naked, her eyes closed, talking to him as if she was orating, as if she was reciting a passage from her book, a book she's unable to write. Isn't he worried about who you might be sleeping with? the screenwriter asks insistently. No, he doesn't care about that. He doesn't care about his daughter falling into the arms of an unscrupulous roué, the screenwriter muses. But all fathers should be worried about this. After all, the world's filled with those kinds of people.

The screenwriter's schedule is all over the place: perhaps the principles of atonality have begun sinking in. He'd been working from dawn until late in the morning then went to the kiosk to buy a newspaper from his native country. Now, he's sitting at the café in the plaza. He gets the impression that, here in the neighboring country's capital, there are people who spend all day in the cafés—some reading their newspapers, others who bring their offices to the tables along the sidewalk. The waitress continues ignoring him, so the screenwriter takes his notebook from his jacket pocket. He also utilizes the café as a temporary office, although he drinks his coffee while he works, unlike some others, who only work while drinking their coffee. After considering the difference between these two options, he asks himself if he'd be able to make the café his permanent workplace. It'd be cheaper than renting an office or an apartment. He takes a look around. Maybe he'd feel uncomfortable, be distracted by all the noise and bustle. A few meters in front of his table, a guy is unloading bottled drinks from a truck; a little farther on, he sees a dry-cleaner's van, and beyond that, a girl in uniform cleaning the fountain in the center of the plaza. There's no doubting it, he'd never be able to concentrate here. He can only do so now because of the one idea that happens to be preoccupying him. Supposing twelve-tone music was never invented, the girl says to her father, what do you think would exist in its place? He doesn't know what to say, why would anyone care about such things? The girl's fingers putter aimlessly along the piano keys, as if probing for something new and original. She's abandoned her piano practice and seems to be having a hard time keeping the conversation going. The screenwriter is trying to pin down the father accurately, but his character's elusive. In summary, he seems to be a man who no longer believes in anything or anyone; a character who, over a long period of time, has given up a lot of ground, bottled up his pride, suppressed his ideas, compromised his principles, become passionless, and were he pressed to admit a belief in anything at all, he'd say it was money. Now that he's rich, maybe he's becoming regretful; maybe the past is beginning to catch up with him. The screenwriter scribbles the idea in his notebook, although he doesn't know whether he'll end up using it. Perhaps it's time to lay the groundwork. McGregor speaking, he writes down in a flurry. For some reason, the girl answers a phone call intended for her father. And so the stranger introduces himself: McGregor speaking. The screenwriter closes the notebook, sighs contentedly, and asks the waitress for the check, giving her one of his very best smiles. She continues ignoring him. She'll come around yet, he tells himself, and leaves a generous tip. You've no idea who you're dealing with, he murmurs as he gets up to leave, and pushes the chair back in its place.

The screenwriter returns late from his morning stroll. His body clock is off because he stayed up working until the early hours of the morning. After buying his country's newspaper on the corner of the boulevard, he drank coffee at the café in the plaza, went for a stroll along the river, and dined in the afternoon. Now, he takes a short break before sitting at his desk to resume writing. He thinks about the young orchestra conductor and the brilliant composer, characters that should feature more prominently. But something always thwarts him when he sets out to concentrate on them. He opens the window and glances unconsciously at the building across the street. The days are becoming repetitive, each one resembling the next, and it occurs to him that maybe his characters should perceive the passage of days similarly. He has a god's eye view of the sunset, of the people passing in the street below, and he wonders about the girl, about what she may be doing at this moment. Maybe she's at a rehearsal; maybe she's reading the philosopher W with the young conductor of the orchestra. Or perhaps they're kissing. Or perhaps she's kissing someone else entirely. For the screenwriter, the thought of the girl kissing someone else is arousing. He sees her neglecting her piano practice to work on her novel instead, scribbling away fervidly, and is reminded of himself when he was young, back when he first set out to become a screenwriter, when he too would neglect anything and everything for the sake of his work. Things haven't turned out great for him, not as great as he expects they will for the girl. He's written some good screenplays for movies that passed in and out of the cinema without notice, but he's also written some truly awful screenplays, ones he'd like to forget, for movies that passed in and out of the cinema without notice. The woman in the building opposite passes her window; he raises his arm to attract her attention. He has no idea what he'll say to her, but he's come to regard her as something of an old acquaintance. But she doesn't see him, and he lowers his arm. He's had some success with women, he thinks. His marriage may have been a disaster, but he's had some success with other women. The screenwriter is sitting on his bed staring at the telephone. It takes a concerted effort to resist the impulse to call his wife. He distracts himself with the newspaper, goes over the personals, and reads the articles he'd been saving for later that evening. The screenplay once more obtrudes upon his thinking, but he turns the page, determined to concentrate on his reading. There's a photo the girl will get a kick out of, he tells himself: the star of her favorite soccer team on some distant beach doing tricks with a ball to impress a bevy of onlookers. He's done pretty okay with women, he muses to himself in another lapse of concentration, because the type of work he does confers on him a certain intellectual cachet. He believes himself reasonably attractive, but he knows this alone isn't enough. So he puts on airs, affects a cerebral pose to appear more interesting than he is. He puts the newspaper to one side, lies back on the bed, and looks at the ceiling. He knows what it is to be a failure. He'd liked to have experienced success, to know what it feels like to triumph at something. What does it mean to be a winner? He can't define it without reference to money and women. Years before, he'd have been able to sublimate his belief, qualify it by succeeding at various other things, but at his age, he can no longer deceive himself. Most people want success, but only a few ever manage it, because only a few people have the necessary strength, the self-confidence—indeed, the necessary selfishness—besides so many other qualities, to succeed; qualities the screenwriter sees in the young orchestra conductor, a character he's yet to fully develop, but who's shown indications of being someone who knows exactly what he wants, the kind of person who could go far in the music world, or in any world he chooses for that matter. He sees him as a winner, a precocious young man with a talent for bringing together disparate notions, and with a gift for getting along well with others. The future abounds with opportunities for such a character. A pity his role is so small, almost an extra compared with the girl's. And yet, he must worry about success as well, about money, which will probably come much later for him, when he's no longer young, after years of dragging himself on and off stages, having become jaded with women, and can only vaguely remember his salad days. What does it mean to be a winner? It only intimidates the girl—her fear of mediocrity, of writing like everyone else, of becoming complacent, selling out for fame . . . but she's already famous. Perhaps she doesn't appreciate it since it happened so soon; or perhaps the piano's become a

millstone around her neck. Maybe if she wasn't so well known
. . . the truth is he doesn't know what it means to be a winner.
Maybe luck has something to do with it, he finally says, as his
eyes begin to close, not wanting to see himself as the loser of
a long-distance race he began so long ago.

Her skin, he thinks while caressing her arm, examining every
fine blonde hair, delicate as down, looks so young in the light
of the bedside lamp. Her delicate skin, he thinks while envisioning her in a tuxedo, or perhaps just wearing the jacket,
double-breasted but unbuttoned, with a bowtie around her
neck; her mother's high-heel shoes, which are clearly too big
for her, the only other item of clothing covering her naked
body as she stands before him, aloof and domineering, despite
being only a girl. Thus the screenwriter imagines her, repent-
ing his decision to get rid of his camera equipment, not that
he could realize his vision onstage in the little theater where
they rehearse, let alone the church in which they're going to
perform their concerts. He caresses her delicate skin. What
does No World mean? he asks her. She answers without blink-
ing, without taking her eyes off the ceiling: it means a reality
existing parallel to ours, a reality that's essentially the same
as ours, but seen through a different lens. A No World, she
clarifies, exists in another dimension. The screenwriter wants
to know if she still thinks about him. She usually gives a vague
answer tending toward an affirmative, as if telling a white lie
to conceal a dark truth, in order to protect his feelings, while
he knows he's playing the role of the jealous old fool to a T, a
fool who can't conceal his jealousy, who can't prevent himself
interrogating her, who can't abide not knowing everything
about her, because perhaps he feels his life with her is something of a miracle, and he needs her reassurance that it's real,

he needs her to tell him that she loves him. Just a little bit? he suggests to her. Even if it's only a little bit, he hears himself whispering softly. Then silence. The two of them lie motionless on the sheets. She confesses that whenever she makes love to the young orchestra conductor, she thinks of him. A cold chill runs through his body. The girl doesn't notice this reaction, although she knows the effect her words have on him, this old teacher who is waiting for the least gesture, even a hint of acquiescence on her part, any sense that she might be willing to run away with him, as far away as possible, to that new life which exists only in his mind; this old teacher who listens patiently to her paranoid ravings about the shadows that pursue her, and about her unhealthy obsession with writing; this old screenwriter who entertains her wild speculations about the nonexistence of the world—only a dream, she says, drifting in the immensity of space—a poor old man who listens to her every word, who only wants to hear her say she loves him, who asks her, intimidated, gently holding her hand, as she allows some seconds of doubt to pass, then tells him, in a deliberately irresolute tone, that she does, she loves him. Is this another white lie? he asks. No, she says, pausing to let in more doubt, it isn't. The old man closes his eyes; she climbs out of the bed to get dressed; he responds by stretching out his hand, his eyes still closed, as if wanting a last touch of her skin, his arm—the stretch sustained for some seconds before failing, before falling on the sheets—reaching weakly after her. Will you come back? he asks her. I always do, she says, I've never stopped coming back. The conversation ends without her saying another word, not even good-bye; not slamming the door, closing it gently behind her, as he stays motionless, his eyes still closed, dreaming of her delicate skin, remembering her words, the sound of her voice. Then the usual fluttering in his stomach: he's not sure if he can bear only having the memory of her. He repeats the question again and again, does she love him; will it be forever? He gets up and goes to the window. This time, he doesn't look at the building opposite but at something down on the street, something that doesn't exist as yet. There's a man on a corner watching him from the shadows, trying to go unnoticed, but the screenwriter doesn't see, his eyes clouded, searching for a girl in white, he doesn't want to see anything unless it's decked in white. He sits at his desk, whispers the words that cause him so much anguish, will you come back? tears welling up in his eyes, blearing all color and shape, as the whisper drifts over the blank page and typewriter, then out through the window, and into the immensity of space.

At night, the clack and plink of the typewriter punctures the silence of the room. The screenwriter fingers the keys, listening to the dull staccato rhythm. There's a kind of silence, he writes, that is adorned by the sound of gentle breathing, the susurrus of two bodies ruffling the sheets, leaving their warm impressions on a bed. The screenwriter stops typing to look at the bed, to search for these impressions, for the recollection of how her skin felt, as if the sheets could preserve, even fossilize, every pore, every soft, downy follicle of hair, her blonde hair, which he wants to photograph, enlarge, and examine under a microscope. He removes his glasses, deftly cleans them with a handkerchief, and resumes his puttering on the keyboard. His writing is disjointed, haphazard, and perhaps, normally, he wouldn't feel so inclined to write after having sex, but the élan within him impels him to keep going. The scene is set in the hotel with the English name. The screenwriter thinks about placing it at the start of the film. He can almost see it, the movie beginning, and the opening credits superimposed upon images of the hotel. A kind of prelude of sorts, to establish the mood and setting, the time period in which the story takes place, before introducing the girl and her mother. The viewer sees a group of porters completing the transfer of a grand piano from the service entrance to a large suite. These images are intercut with shots of the girl's mother, dressed conservatively in a pantsuit and a pair of modest heels, instructing hotel employees to make space in the middle of a large living room. Seated to one side, and out of the way, an older man quietly watches the scene, perhaps in puzzlement at what's going on around him. The girl, wearing white jeans, a white T-shirt, and white canvas sneakers with the laces removed, walks slowly behind the piano, which the porters are trundling down the hallway. Once it's in place in the living room, the porters remove the protective padding. Their departure cues the older man, who stands up, leaves his jacket on the chair, and approaches the piano with a tuning key. The mother instructs the hotel employees to take her luggage to the car. There hasn't been any dialogue yet; in fact, nothing more has been said than a word or a phrase to underscore the visuals. Starting now, the soundtrack will consist of discordant notes being pounded on the piano by the tuner, each note emphasized, to give the impression of something on the verge of becoming a melody, while mother and daughter say good-bye at the hotel's entrance. It's a procedure they've gone through dozens of times, having never had much to say to one another. This scene takes place before the one in which the father goes to see the girl in the little theater; perhaps a few days beforehand, and in the morning. The girl's mother watches attentively as they deposit her bags in the trunk of her convertible. She then looks out at the traffic and notes that it seems to be picking up. As she climbs into the sports car, she says her daughter's name, pronouncing it with a "ka." Why would she pronounce it with a "ka"? Because the girl hears everyone pronounce it with a "ka" instead of a "k." It's a clue. Something so subtle she can't share it with anyone else, because no one can understand it but her. Her mother looks at her over the rim of her sunglasses and tells her to stop talking nonsense. She then turns the ignition and looks in the rearview mirror, imprecates mildly at the traffic, and slowly pulls away, lifting her hand to wave good-bye as the car accelerates and mingles with the sea of other vehicles. "Ka" or "k": is it so hard to tell the difference? The girl watches from the sidewalk until the convertible becomes indistinguishable, like a drop in the sea, and asks herself what could be so important that her mother had to go on another trip. Sometimes she says she goes searching for her missing cousin, Dedalus, as if, after all these years, finding him is still one of her chief concerns. While waiting for the elevator, the girl remembers his story. She's never told anyone about him. She may have mentioned to some friends that her mother has a remarkable cousin, but she didn't go into any details. If the brilliant composer knew his story, she muses, he'd probably dedicate one of his compositions to him. She could write a novel about him, a young man who went to the neighboring country's capital years before, and was never heard from again. He fled to escape prosecution, she recalls. But after everything her mother's told her, the girl believes the truth will never be known. His story features many deaths, a shooting, and even a femme fatale. The piano tuner corrects the instrument's pitch, pounding on the keys, which emit a plangent sound, as if giving a mournfully slow rendition of the *5 Pieces for piano*. A couple of novelists had already written about those unfortunate events, although the girl would've taken a different approach to them. In the elevator, she thinks she may be able to write her own version of his story some day, maybe as a sequel to the book she's currently working on. But first she has to get that one written. She's never believed her mother's little jaunts indicated any sort of development in the cousin's story; she simply leaves every time under the pretext of a search she's never undertaken. The excuse is an old one for the girl, who's certain her mother's real motive for absconding has more to do with expensive clothes and lovers, and perhaps, if she can fit it in, a little business on the side. She's never told anyone about him, but perhaps she'll tell the young conductor and brilliant composer—who'll probably dedicate one of his compositions to him. Back in the living room, the girl asks the piano tuner to adjust the hammers and pedals for a particular composition. She's experimented in the past with prepared pianos, putting various objects into the strings to modify the timbre of the instrument. But it seems the man isn't quite finished yet. It's as though he is taking advantage of his duties as a tuner and performing his own plangent rendition of the *5 Pieces for piano*. He's taken long enough already, but he seems to want to make the process even slower, to let the music reverberate, to produce something unique, a sound that hasn't been heard before, as a gift to all posterity, a message to be transmitted to the cosmos. The girl—his only audience—decides to leave him to his task and sits down to her diary. She writes that they pronounce her name with a "ka"; that this makes her feel odd; that she's tried to figure out why they do it, but hasn't gotten anywhere yet.

It's night. The young conductor of the orchestra licks the gummed edge of a rolling paper to complete a joint. He wants to know if the girl could write a libretto for an opera about

aliens and life in other galaxies: a dirge on the ultimate fate
of humanity, he says, set on an ordinary day, to underscore
our species' insignificance—its nonexistence, almost—for
when placed in the context of a universe of infinite space and
illimitable time, what's a single person, a single day? In other
words, let it be a lament for the imminent death of all civilizations, with perhaps a few references to the philosophy of
W. The girl would rather write a libretto about having sex in
her mother's bed; she's saving the bigger ideas for her novel.
When her cell phone rings, she raises her finger to her lips,
indicating to the conductor that he should keep quiet. As they
talk, the conductor nibbles on the girl's toes and continues
up her leg, putting the joint between his lips, from which he
takes a final drag before passing it to her. She inhales deeply
and responds naturally to her mother's questions. The mother
wants to know if the phone call woke her up. It didn't, because
she was reading one of her favorite science-fiction novels. It's
about someone who spends his whole life trying to make contact with extraterrestrials, she lies, alluding to one of her own
ideas about someone who travels around the world setting up
satellites that can transmit and receive encrypted messages.
Her mother doesn't respond. He establishes a global network
that he controls from one location, where he sits and waits
patiently for news from other galaxies. The mother wishes her
daughter would make better use of her time, by practicing
piano, for example, because all she really cares about is her
daughter's career as a pianist. Later, the girl and the young
conductor make love. Perhaps there's no need to set up a
network of satellites, he says, still brooding on extraterrestrial
matters. Perhaps the aliens are right here among us.

In the morning, before freshening up, the screenwriter decides to keep working on the screenplay. He can't wait for the girl to arrive later that night to tell another story, because he needs another injection of inspiration. The hours go by agonizingly slow, although writing helps him while away the time. Enduring the passage of a long day, he says to himself, is like crossing a desert. But he'd rather keep moving than sit on the sand and wait to die. In his story, the Little Sinfonietta is still rehearsing the program they're going to perform in the church. He clearly remembers it—located right in front of the writers' café—, although there are dozens of cafés in the capital that bear such a name, places where hundreds of writers of every era, both famous and obscure, once sat. Meanwhile, the rehearsal takes place onstage in a small theater, where the young conductor directs the Little Sinfonietta to repeat, over and over, each movement of the composition. Most importantly, it's the stage where the girl is singing, or speaking almost, a confusing and disturbing series of verses that give the impression they were inspired by a strange vision or hallucination, or the effects of a psychotropic pill. The screenwriter then moves to another scene, where the girl is drinking in the lounge of a fashionable bar. The brilliant composer asks her if she knows the guy on the other side of the room who seems unable to take his eyes off her. She waits until he looks away to examine his features carefully. His face seems familiar, but she can't quite place him. Bad taste, says the brilliant composer laughing. If that guy's your type, then you've got seriously bad taste, he repeats. You don't often see guys that old in a place like this, he adds, but I suppose it really doesn't matter. You see strange things everywhere these days. The brilliant composer apprehends all things in terms of twelve-tone music, and adheres to his conviction that every note should be made available to the composer and be used without prejudice, that every relationship between them should be conceived on a basis of equality and not of subordination. So, by extension, the guy could approach the girl and ask her to go out on a date this very night. They could even sleep together. We might do an opera about it, says the young conductor as he joins them at the bar. He can already see the music-video version: a sleazy and sordid setting, with a song and lyrics that tell the story of a guy who accidentally winds up in a trendy bar and wants a nice young girl to rescue him from his insecurity, to take him somewhere else, a place where they can dance the bolero together, or something like that.

The screenwriter takes a look out the window. An ambiguous dawn: it has yet to define itself against the horizon. He places his glasses on the table and stands up. He needs to take a break. He lights a cigarette, takes a sip of water, and prepares the coffee. Perhaps he's found what he's looking for: a scene that will grab an audience's attention. He considers the new character he's added: someone who could end up being central, or peripheral; who could feature throughout the story, or vanish at any moment—he doesn't know yet; with a face not unfamiliar to the girl, although she can't quite place it. He takes another look out the window. Still, it's only a subplot. It's early, and his neighbors haven't gotten out of bed yet. He showers and goes down to the canteen for breakfast. He doesn't read the newspaper afterward in the lobby, as is customary, but decides to go back to his room and continue working. The girl sleeps badly and rises late. She jots a few notes in a notebook, scribbles the outlines of conversations, and drafts some possible beginnings to impossible chapters. Then she answers a phone call. McGregor speaking, says the voice on the other end, which then asks for the girl's father.

He's not staying in this hotel, she says. A while later, after ordering breakfast to her room, she practices the *5 Pieces for piano* and then some parts of the *No World Symphony*, the brilliant young composer's first opus, which she transcribed for piano and will be performing in her home city in a few days' time. That afternoon she goes to rehearsals. She uses the hotel's chauffeur service, and amuses herself on the journey to the theater by trying to guess which pedestrians are aliens. First, she thinks, she must determine what features distinguish them from normal human beings. The chin perhaps, or the eyes, the ears, or maybe a special aura about them . . . While the driver parks the car, the girl notices, in the crowd, the guy she saw the night before in the trendy bar in town, the one who couldn't take his eyes off her. He's tall and dark, around her father's age, has a receding hairline, and is wearing a black suit. He's looking at the façade of the theater where the Little Sinfonietta rehearses, as if deciding whether or not to go inside. Then he turns and heads up the sidewalk, disappearing into the crowd. It seems he decided not. The screenwriter sketches some ideas about the possible relationship between this character and the girl. He can almost see him, like a ghost that's yet to finish manifesting itself. During the rehearsal, the girl finds it difficult to concentrate, still intrigued by the man she saw outside, whose face she can't quite place. The screenwriter feels comfortable leaving the story at this point. He fixes his hair in the bathroom mirror and picks out a jacket from the wardrobe—he'd feel naked without it, in spite of the heat—and, before long, he's cantering on the sidewalk, with his conscience clear and a spring in his limp, for having started the day so well. He decides to digress from his usual route and discovers a classical music store. The young woman who attends to him is kind and good-natured. She asks if he's looking for anything in particular. The screenwriter tells her he's writing a script about the father of twelve-tone composition, and asks if any of his works are available. The saleswoman turns out to be an expert on dodecaphony and she persuades the screenwriter to buy four compact discs—his most representative works, she says—and her attractiveness convinces him they're going to be a great help. He likes the way the way she pronounces "dodecaphonic" and, in a strange attempt to impress her, also buys one of the books she recommends. At the cash register, he smiles at her and she responds in kind. With his new purchases in hand, he decides to browse in the jazz section because he has a feeling the girl's father is a fan of the genre. The screenwriter is well enough acquainted with jazz to be able to cite a number of musicians off the top of his head, so instead of buying anything, he simply takes note of some works he's half-forgotten, and repeats them to himself as he heads for the exit. On reaching the door, however, he changes his mind and goes limping back to the saleswoman. From a distance, she looks pretty, he thinks, and has a decent body. He imagines her in a tuxedo jacket. The store uniform certainly puts a damper on her style. Maybe she's like the girl and prefers dressing completely in white. She may be a few years older than the girl, and quite a few pounds heavier, but the screenwriter's not going to give up on a potential hook-up over the matter of a few pounds. He asks her when she gets off work: he'd like her to tell him more about "dodecaphonic" music. After examining him top to toe, she says there's more than enough to learn from the merchandise he bought. I bet you'd do anything for a part in my movie, he mutters as he leaves, you just don't know it yet.

The screenwriter doesn't take the time to listen to the CDs, or leaf through the pages of the book, but he knows exactly what he's going to write. He'd already sketched it in his notebook. The girl is inside a bus-stop shelter, watching her two friends' silhouettes receding down the street. After the rehearsal, the girl sent the chauffeur back to the hotel; now, she's waiting for a bus, along with a couple of shopgirls and a salesman, the latter leaning against one of the columns of the shelter, bobbing his briefcase and smoking a cigarette. The girl gives the impression that she's all alone in the city. The screenwriter listens to her thoughts as if they were a voice-over. At times, she thinks, I act like such a fool. Thoughts like these usually result from one of her daily quarrels with the young conductor: quarrels about the performance, their new arrangement of the piece, anything and everything really. Right now, nothing is more important to the conductor than the upcoming performance in the church, and the rehearsals are critical—an opportunity, he'd say, to repeat certain passages over and over until a steady, automatic rhythm is achieved. Every now and again, they go over the brilliant composer's compositions: the *No World Symphony* and the clown's almost song, almost recitation, for which the chief difficulty is the proper synchronization of a number of music boxes. After the rehearsal, the girl tells them about the guy she's run into a couple of times, and the young conductor insists they write the opera for which he'd already conceived a music video, the one with a sleazy and sordid setting, and a song with lyrics that tell the story of a guy who accidentally winds up in a trendy bar and looks for a nice young girl to rescue him, to take him somewhere they can dance the bolero together, or something like that. The girl likes to think it's all a game. They go into one of the bars with foosball tables, but they don't concentrate on their playing, since they're engrossed in a discussion about musical tempo.

The brilliant composer proposes writing without a set meter so he doesn't have to deal with all the changes in tempo, as all the various mathematical combinations and permutations are bogging him down. It's late when she says good-bye to them at the bus stop, and leans against a column of the bus shelter, opposite a cigarette-smoking salesman, to watch them recede down the street. She can't remember the last time she rode a bus. Maybe she'll grab the first available taxi, or call the chauffeur at the hotel. Maybe she'll just go for a walk. She wouldn't mind the fresh air. As she considers what to do, she can't help taking a look around, in case she sees that familiar face, the guy she's seen so many times before in the city, whose face she can't quite place.

The screenwriter doesn't feel like cooking, nor is he in the mood to go to a restaurant. So he settles for some cheese and cold cuts while watching TV, before deciding to go to the café. He tries to recall if this is the first time he's left the hotel at night since he arrived. He's almost certain it is, but before he can reach certainty on the matter, he's already at the bottom of the hill, and his attention is diverted by the lights and bustle of the plaza. There's nowhere to sit in the café, which is now teeming with people holding desperately onto the hem of a vanishing day. It seems paradoxical to have walked through deserted streets and yet find there's not a single seat available on the terrace. Since he's in a good mood, however, he settles for a table inside, and looks around for the waitress. He figures she doesn't work nights, and resigns himself to being waited on by a trainee. The book he bought speaks at length about the composer of the *5 Pieces for piano*, which the girl is planning to both perform and record; a composer who dedicated himself to a never-ending search for new sounds, and so substituted conventional tonalities and scales for those in which no single note takes precedence, in which all are of equal importance. He closes the book and looks at his watch. He starts to feel a little anxious: by his reckoning, the girl could be coming to see him in a couple of hours. But the fact he's made some progress on his work today eases his disquiet. He knows, however, that this is only a transitory feeling, for nothing can guarantee tomorrow's peace of mind. Back in his hotel room, the hours go by slowly, and when the new day finally arrives, it seems to him as if an eternity has passed. It's Friday the fifth. The screenwriter puts the calendar next to the typewriter and limps over to the bathroom mirror to smooth out the bags under his eyes. The girl never showed up, and he sacrificed his hours of sleep for a nightlong vigil next to the window. The bags refuse to go away, and all he's accomplished in trying to smooth them out is make them a little redder. No matter. He grabs his notebook and index cards and deposits them in his jacket pocket then heads to the café in the plaza. On arriving, he sees there are only a half-dozen customers, and he knows this is one shift the waitress never misses. As she waits on the other tables, the screenwriter goes through his index cards and tries to imagine the circumstances that prevented the girl from visiting the previous night. Perhaps her mother's gotten back from her trip and she has to keep up appearances. This doesn't seem a likely excuse. Perhaps she felt particularly threatened by her pursuer, despite her not knowing if the pursuit is real, since the mere suspicion seems to be enough to cause her to retreat into seclusion. The screenwriter considers the possibility she spent the night with the young conductor of the orchestra. Perhaps he's suspected this all along, and he's just been ferreting for excuses to avoid the knowledge that he's just a jealous old man. The screenwriter decides to stop thinking about it and return to his index cards. There are a variety of cards, some devoted to character, for example, others to scenery, although he doesn't take detailed notes on them, normally writing his outlines in his notebooks and then copying them onto blank but paginated sheets of paper. He still has his idea about the onion, although he's beginning to think it's defunct. He wonders if it was ever of any use. There's no point second-guessing, he says to himself; at least these kinds of ideas allow you to keep moving forward. The waitress returns after serving another table. Their eyes meet, but she still doesn't smile. You don't know what you're missing, he mutters to himself, turning his attention back to the notebook and index cards. An ambiguous character, the girl's father; a man who got rich through some shady business dealings, unscrupulous, capable of suspending his most cherished principles for the guerdon of a quick buck, a man who knows and can deal with the fact that the world abides by sets of unwritten rules, a man who functions according to these rules, secretly, as though he were above the law and every other man-made institution. The only law is that of the jungle, thinks the screenwriter, a jungle lacquered by the lie of civilization. This could be a potential sketch of the girl's father, a character with traits not unfamiliar to the screenwriter.

"Today's Friday, and my father's in a bad mood," the girl writes in her diary, "and when he's like this, it's best to just leave him alone. He's a decent guy overall, but today he seems out of sorts. And it's not because it's Friday. Something else is on his mind." He'd spent half the morning talking on the phone to this McGregor person while the girl was practicing on the piano in the living room. Then he left. In the bar next to the little theater where she rehearses, the girl is in a bad mood. And it's not because it's Friday. It's because she'd rather be writing than drinking, although she knows she never gets anywhere with her writing. Some members of the Little Sinfonietta—the violinist, the clarinetist, and the cellist—are sitting at a table awaiting the arrival of another two. Some of the musicians are so young they have to be accompanied from their dorm to attend rehearsals. The girl could've stayed at the same dorm, but her mother thought she'd be more comfortable at the hotel with the English name, and that she'd have more time on her own to practice. The brilliant composer, seated next to her, wants to know why she's in a bad mood. She says she's lost, that she can't find the right approach, the right plot, the right whatever for her work in progress. The brilliant composer offers an impromptu solution: he suggests her *No World* should be autobiographical. As she noisily slurps the lees of her soft drink, the young conductor appears in the doorway surrounded by other young musicians. The girl doesn't want to write about herself. She doesn't believe her life is interesting enough to write about. The brilliant composer, on the other hand, believes quite the reverse.

Human beings have spent centuries trying to determine their place in the universe, and perhaps the search amounts to nothing more than an investigation into our origins. These are the matters that preoccupy the girl whenever she thinks about her work: that there might be extraterrestrials among us masquerading as humans; that these beings may not be aware they're aliens; that she may have an important role in the whole affair, but she's unable to determine what it is. Moreover, the possibility she may never find out drives her up the wall. Perhaps the Earth's atmosphere wiped her memory. Perhaps her mission is something far simpler, something related to music.

Hence, the gift with which she's been bestowed. Supposing twelve-tone music was never invented—no serialism, or any of it. But why a gift for music and not writing? she wonders. In a nearby library, the young conductor of the orchestra consults an encyclopedia and finds, under the entry "Ka," the description of a certain religious notion. He reads that Ka is the expression of a man's double, his vital force, a tutelary spirit or genius or guardian angel that's born at the same time and outlives him. Perhaps this Ka is my guardian angel, she says sarcastically, even though she doesn't know why she keeps hearing this sound on other people's lips, as if it were several voices speaking as one, a voice communicating to her from outer space. She thinks it could be a sign, a key to her finally understanding what her mission is on Earth. Or it could be nothing at all.

It takes a huge effort for the screenwriter to write a couple of pages. Moreover, he's certain he's described the same scene more than once. He gets up from his desk and searches in vain among his papers. The image of the library reminds him of the film in which people's voices are coming from off-screen. They're not like the ones the girl hears, for they sound like the voice of the multitudes speaking in unison, as if all humanity spoke with a single voice. It's a voice he's obsessed with, just as the girl's obsessed with voices pronouncing her name with a "ka." This tutelary spirit named Ka is none other than the angel who appears in the film. The screenwriter pauses to listen, as if trying to detect the voices himself. But all he hears is the groaning of a bed from the room next door where a couple's having sex. He abandons his desk and collapses in an armchair. He feels exhausted, but is certain he's found a guardian angel for the girl. Someone whose face she knows but cannot place, whose identity will eventually be made clear. The screenwriter sees him as a specter, someone who bears a tangential relationship to her, who crosses paths with her at specific moments in her life. There's a movie on TV, but the actors are talking too fast for him to understand the dialogue. He switches through the channels until he encounters an old classic he's seen before. Someone in the movie mentions the girl's name. Perhaps it's a sign. Then a noise in the hallway grabs his attention and he turns the TV off. Silence. He checks his watch. Too early to get his hopes up. He imagines the girl in her living room practicing the *5 Pieces for piano*. She practices them one at a time, memorizing and repeating each piece over and over, now and then scribbling something onto the score, for each performance is a separate creation, a unique collocation of sounds, no two are alike, and whenever she practices or rehearses, she always has this in mind. She experiments by slowing it down more and more until the notes seem almost lost, until they seem to float freely, independently of each other. At times, she changes her mind, due to her fluctuating moods, although perhaps the pills militate too much on her decision-making. The girl's finally made up her mind. She wants to perform the pieces more slowly, make them more sonorous, so they reverberate continuously, almost infinitely. At this tempo, the *5 Pieces* would take up a whole compact disc. She has more than enough time to practice anyway, since the recording session isn't until after the concerts are over. The screenwriter would like to be the cause of the girl's agitation, but he knows this could never be the case, because she's young and rebellious, ambitious and impatient . . . at least that's the reason he convinces himself of. He pictures her taking a walk near the hotel before returning home to write in her diary. Then he sees her answering a phone call from her mother, jotting down a symbol on the score that he doesn't understand, which possibly no one understands but her. He rereads the last few pages he's written, the ones describing the scene in the library and the ones relating to Ka—his nagging idea of a guardian angel that might help the girl understand herself. The girl thinks she may be abusing the pills the young conductor and brilliant composer are giving her. After leaving the bar alone, she walks down a couple of side streets until she finally encounters a taxi. She looks out at the city through the window, a hackneyed view, something she's seen countless times on TV—shots of the sidewalks, the buildings, and passersby from a camera inside a car. The screenwriter doesn't know where these thoughts are leading, but when he finds a thread he feels he has to follow it. Sometimes it leads somewhere, but mostly, it leads nowhere. Despite being tired, he decides to go for a walk along the river. The clouds are passing swiftly overhead as he leans against the railing of the bridge, watching the water moving slowly underneath, his story still buzzing inside him. But there are many unresolved questions. A sixteen-year-old girl, he reflects, is in continual conflict with her environment and herself. And there's also this peculiar rebel attitude, not typical of a teenager, which makes her so special. The screenwriter contemplates the view of the opposite bank. He likes cities with large rivers flowing through them, especially when they run through the old historical centers. There are no such rivers in his native city. Instead, there's a beach. What advice would a father give his daughter? He doesn't have an answer, and he wonders if it's a worthwhile question, an essential question. It doesn't matter; all he really wants to do is play around with some ideas. But what would a father say to a pianist daughter who'd rather to be a writer; a daughter who recites or sings—he doesn't really know—as part of a performance he thinks will only create a nightmarish atmosphere in the theater; a child prodigy who lives a hectic life and has peculiar friends and relatives, including himself? Musical intelligence is very different from other forms, the screenwriter thinks. Had she not been trained from a young age, she could have ended up like everybody else. But that's irrelevant now. The fact is she was trained, she is a prodigy. Some guys are flirting with a girl next to him. The screenwriter watches them attentively for a few moments. It's as if the young conductor has been erased from his mind, as if he never existed or had any relationship with the girl. Something's throwing him off, so he starts thinking about the father again, who in his youth might also have wanted to be a writer. He knows nothing more than what the girl has told him and just uses his years of experience to figure out the rest. Actually, nobody knows very much about the girl's father. What advice would he give her? He'd want his daughter to be successful. What father wouldn't? Is he happy? Maybe he's only pretending to be. They say being able to do this is the ultimate mark of success. And so the screenwriter begins to wonder about happiness, about success, about celebrity and wealth, and about whether happiness and stupidity go hand in hand. He thinks if the world's so screwed up that certain things are mistaken for others, what sort of books will the girl write? Not necessarily now, but in a few years time. What kind of life would such a father want for his daughter? The life of a concert pianist? A writer, maybe? The screenwriter realizes he's talking about himself, because he never knew what advice to give his own son. He doesn't even know what advice he'd give himself. If he thinks about his work, he gets lost in the details; if he thinks about his life, he ends up blaming his misfortune on the cards he's been dealt. Perhaps the girl's father has never entertained such thoughts. Perhaps the only thing to do with a girl like this is to protect her. But protect her from what? he wonders. From herself, responds a voice inside him. The screenwriter looks for his glasses in his jacket pocket. The girl goes to visit her father at his hotel, but finds he's gone out, so she decides to wait for him. She's surprised he's staying in such a dump, although she thinks it must be for a good reason. After waiting in the lobby a while, she decides to go outside and stretch her legs. The environs don't compare with those of the hotel with the English name. When she returns, she sees there's been a shift change at the reception desk, so she asks for the key to her father's room—doing so with such aplomb, the new receptionist doesn't hesitate to hand her the key. The screenwriter considers some other ways to get the girl up to her father's room. He writes them down, seated on a riverside bench, under a streetlamp. On the bed, she sees a pistol, a passport, some credit cards, together with some old folders filled with documents, but it's to the pistol the girl gravitates. She picks it up and examines it, gently caresses it, running her fingers along its grooves and edges, and also the butt. She finds it quite heavy. She holds it with both hands, aims it high and low, lining up her sight with one eye closed, and then pretends to draw it from a holster like a cowboy. She needs practice. In front of the bathroom mirror, she imitates the classic stance of a policeman aiming at a bad guy: squat, with legs apart, and aiming with both hands. Before putting it back on the bed, she holsters the gun in her pants, feeling the cold metal against the small of her back. Then she takes a look at the passport. She doesn't recognize the name, but the man in the picture is definitely her father. For a moment she thought she was in the wrong room. She slowly reads the name aloud. There are numerous credit cards with the same

51

name on them. The girl searches through the documents, all reports from the space agency about unidentified sightings. The girl is intrigued. She didn't know her father had access to such information. There are also photographs of some people posing beside what appear to be flying saucers. But they don't look like beings from outer space, and perhaps they're only witnesses who were photographed after giving their statements. There are also photographs of men in uniform, some wearing shirtsleeves and neckties, standing around a rectangular table inspecting a large map. Later on, when she's back in her room at the hotel with the English name, the girl writes her father's alias in one of her notebooks. She then tries but finds it difficult to get some rest, thinking about the guy whose face she can't quite place, and those provocative photographs, as if they're somehow calling to her, pronouncing her name with a "ka." It all has to mean something. There are no such things as coincidences. Perhaps her father's name, the one she knows him by, is also an alias. She says both names aloud repeatedly and tries to determine which one suits him best. When matched with his picture, the new name sounds strange at first but, little by little, she starts to get used to it. She then puts the notebook away. She has an interview with a journalist and a session with a photographer later, and she still has lots of work to do.

The screenwriter finds he must resist his tendency for writing stories with duplicitous characters, the kinds with fake identities that usually feature in police-procedural dramas or spy movies and that become hackneyed through overuse, for he's written about such characters before and he doesn't want a rehash. The girl's head is seething with information and she needs to relax. She decides to read something by this actor-dramatist the screenwriter recommended, a figure so central to the literary canon that everyone else seems to simply orbit around him, and so, according to the screenwriter, she could certainly learn a thing or two from him, assuming his greatness doesn't prove so daunting that the girl is intimidated into silence. Perhaps she should read something more to her taste, he thinks, science fiction, say, but the screenwriter would prefer it if, from the beginning, she was reading only those works that have set the standards of literature. After spending some time reading, she feels the urge to write, but is somehow unable. The most she can do is smudge a page or two of her notebook with a few brief notes. She's still wondering if the alias she discovered is in fact her father's real name. This produces in her an immense desire to reveal her discoveries to the young conductor of the orchestra, but he's already left with the other musicians. Maybe it's for the best. These kinds of secrets shouldn't be shared with anyone. Otherwise, she wouldn't have taken care to leave her father's room before he returned. Sometimes she feels she's imprisoned inside a tower of gold, a room with a piano in the center reminding her constantly of her inescapable fate to be always and only a concert pianist. This was probably her mother's intention anyway. The girl does some piano exercises while waiting for the journalist and photographer, both of whom eventually arrive at the same time. She receives them together while seated at the piano, answers the journalist's questions while allowing the photographer to gather some shots of her puttering at the piano keys. At night, she goes searching for the young conductor in all the usual haunts, particularly those bars that happen to have foosball tables. She eventually gives up on the idea of showing up suddenly and surprising him, and decides to just call him on the phone. When they finally meet up, they end up having an argument because she catches him hitting on another girl. Then, after some hours, when the storm has blown over, and the new day dawns serenely over the river, the screenwriter decides that the camera should track slowly through the morning mist before alighting on the three friends seated together on a bench, their voices becoming audible as the camera closes in on them. "The clown, in an ecstasy / drinks deeply from the holy chalice to soothe his unrest," they sing together in unison. A sad lyric, since all the poems the clown recites are sad and desperate. The girl, perhaps, would rather to be singing something else, as she stares vacantly past the opposite bank toward the horizon, her thoughts becalming themselves on a vanishing point in the distance. She should've gone to bed early. In a few short hours, she has to do a TV interview and then leave for a recital in her native city. She drank too much and took too many pills, and now she doesn't really know what it is she wants. She does like the twelve-tone world though, is passionate about it—although the screenwriter dismisses it as a passing fad—a world of pure contrast between dissonance and harmony, in which pleasure is derived merely by finding different ways of resolving the conflict. She sits with her shoes in hand on the bank's retaining wall reciting a poem, as if wishing to prolong the previous night's adventure. The humidity around the river could damage her vocal cords, but she's not thinking about her vocal chords right now. She recites in a style all her own, not in the soprano register, because she wants to surprise her audience. They certainly won't expect to see her, the virtuoso pianist, swap the piano for voice. Beside her, the brilliant composer is cleaning his glasses on his shirttail, while the young conductor of the orchestra paces up and down in his Institute's uniform, which he'd been wearing most of the night. He's had too much to drink, and insists on telling the girl about some last-minute changes to the *No World Symphony*. The girl isn't listening, though, being too tired and intoxicated to pay attention to his list of finicky alterations, not that she'd even remember or get the chance to rehearse them. She's no longer jealous, their argument ended some time ago; and, although it's the beginning of a new day, she feels as if the old one is still drawing to a close. The screenwriter sips the dregs of his glass and continues writing. He doesn't know what shape these last moments will eventually have, since they only take a few seconds to transpire. He writes whole paragraphs he'll probably cut from the final script, but he writes them anyway, because they give the story consistency, and because he's in the moment. He thinks about the significance of that nightmarish work in which a mendacious clown wanders about aimlessly, without purpose or direction. Maybe the girl feels the same, that she too has no purpose or direction, that she too only tells lies. He thinks about when they first began meeting up in secret, far from prying eyes. He'd like her to think about him, even momentarily, as she sits on that riverbank. Maybe she is, he tells himself, before immediately banishing the thought. She knows it's only part of a game. The screenwriter may not know the rules, but he supposes it's a game to which she and the young conductor have decided to dedicate their lives, per-haps the brilliant composer too. At times they're musicians, at other times hustlers or even aliens. Their whole life is part of a game. Sometimes, the screenwriter questions the girl about it, but her answers are always ambiguous. Maybe he's just jealous, feels powerless for not knowing what to do about it, for not even knowing whether the girl's desire to be a writer is also only part of a game.

The girl dreams she's surrounded by invisible aliens that talk to her incessantly. One of them talks about the planet and its destruction. It's hard to accept that something which took so much time and effort to build up could disappear in an instant. One supreme instant, the voice says, in which the world blows up and vanishes from sight. The girl looks around, disbelieving. She can't see them, but she knows the voices aren't lying. The thought then occurs to her that perhaps this has already happened, and that the world she knows is nothing but a transitory ripple in eternity's ocean, a ripple careening through space, perhaps a part of the expanding shock wave propelling outwards from that initial explosion. Maybe we're only information in a microchip, or in a machine that can recreate the past and fabricate the future. Maybe we're nothing at all, she says while smiling at the emptiness around her from which the alien voices seem to come. When the alarm sounds the next morning, she's hungover, and can barely remember her dream or her argument with the young conductor. It's going to be a long day, she thinks, as she opens the curtains and looks down on the city through the double-paned windows, which insulate her from the noise outside. She hears the distant muttering of her father in the living room talking on the phone. She can't utter a single word that doesn't set off the throbbing in her head, so she avoids him. The air conditioner has the temperature much too low and she starts shivering, although maybe her hangover's at fault, the alcohol and drugs having screwed up her body temperature. She takes a quick shower and then goes outside to breathe in the air and feel the pleasant warmth of the sun on her skin. But it seems the sun doesn't agree very well with hangovers, for the bright light almost cleaves her head in two, so she quickly retreats back inside. Her father's no longer on the phone and is sitting down reading a newspaper. Do you believe aliens really exist? she asks. The screenwriter's having a hard time with this father-daughter scene. After writing and rewriting, the dialogue is still unconvincing, so he ends up just jotting down the main idea: a scene in which they go over their flight schedules, the TV interview, and the concert in her native city. They also talk about topics of interest to the girl. As regards the aliens, her father says, if they're not around, it's because they don't exist. If they existed, she muses, there'd be an organization set up to prevent us from knowing anything about them.

The girl is practicing on the piano. In its first few measures, the brilliant composer's work flows clearly and smoothly, although a little farther on, it segues into a rough and discordant mishmash of notes. Someone told her it's mathematically perfect, but the girl pays no attention to the score or its mathematical properties, and focuses solely on the keys. She's performed the *No World Symphony* so often now that her fingers move without hesitation, and perhaps only a few people would notice that she's straying from the score and encroaching on new territory. Then she stops playing the piano, goes over to the table, and spreads out the sheet music for the clown's part in *Dress Rehearsal for Voice and Music Boxes*. She plays a cassette that reproduces the sound of the music boxes, and checks her reflection in the bathroom mirror before beginning the recitation. She notices the horrible bags under her eyes. She takes a pill from her pocket and swallows it with a sip of water. Maybe she needs two, just in case. She recites whole verses, forgets some others, while continuing to stare at herself in the mirror, perhaps looking for something she's been purposely ignoring until now. I shouldn't worry about anything, she sings, almost recites, putting her own words to the music.

Then she adds a deuteragonist to the scene: You shouldn't fight with the young conductor, she says to the reflection in the mirror. And try not to worry about the voices, about your future, your father or what his real name might be, not even about extraterrestrials or your writing. Bags under your eyes, she sneers with an actress's hammy delivery, beautiful teenage bags under your eyes. She can't help thinking of the screenwriter at this point. Maybe it's because he can relate to having bags under the eyes, unlike the young conductor of the orchestra. She goes back into her room and sits on her bed, trying to write while waiting for the pill to take effect. She could go in search of Cousin Dedalus, try to uncover his real story, because she doesn't believe what she's been told up until now. She calls her mother and asks about him, but this proves to be a mistake. Her mother doesn't like it when people ask about her cousin, and she assures the girl they've completely lost track of him. Why do you want to know? she asks. The girl wants to go in search of him but she doesn't know where to start looking. He more than likely changed his name, in which case there's nothing more to be said. She could just make it all up, as novelists do with their characters. But she already has her *No World*. So to speak. Since all she really has is the title. Writing is such an ordeal for her. Perhaps it would be easier if her book was based on a true story.

The girl spends a few hours canceling her appointments in the neighboring country's capital. She's ostensibly traveling to her native city for a TV interview and to perform a concert. In reality, her trip has taken on a new significance, because she's going in search of an image, a clue perhaps, some vestige of her lost cousin Dedalus. She signs some autographs at the airport while waiting in the VIP area. The next shot shows her alighting from a car in front of her home and asking the chauffeur to wait. We then see her walking around a spacious, luxurious apartment very few families could afford. The floor is completely empty, perhaps because the servants are on vacation. Then we see her looking through a photo album. There are pictures of the girl, her father and mother, and various other relatives and friends. She glances over the pictures one at a time, pausing at her favorite ones, the ones she links to pleasant memories: pictures of the garden of her old house; of her first attempts at playing the piano; of her father when he was younger. In a panoramic shot of a swimming pool, she's shown next to the brilliant composer, who was only known as the talented boy back then. She reckons it was taken about ten years earlier because they're only little kids. It's a charming photo: both their faces are covered in chocolate, and neither is wearing a school uniform. She remembers how strange he looked without a school uniform, without his navy-blue blazer, gray pants, white shirt, and necktie. There are also pictures of her mother when she was younger. She looks happy; much different from the way she looks today. While leafing through the album, the girl recites some verses from the piece they've entitled *Dress Rehearsal for Voice and Music Boxes*. She plays the clown, but uses her own lyrics, the ones that tell her not to care about her father's real name, or worry about herself; words that remind her not to fight with the young conductor, and to stop fretting about her writing. There's one photo she particularly detests, in which she's posing with a doll that was quite popular at the time, before she developed her aversion for dolls. All of a sudden, she finds what she was looking for: a snapshot of her cousin Dedalus, taken before he fled to the neighboring country's capital. He's posing on a pier she assumes is somewhere in her native city, and there's a boat behind him whose name she can't quite make out. He looks young in it, but the most striking thing about him is his face, it is the face of the man she keeps seeing in the neighboring country's capital. The man she saw sitting at the bar in the dance club, and standing in front of the theater where she rehearses. She's certain he's her cousin, only he looks a lot older now. The girl strains to read the name of the boat behind him, but gives up because she'd need a magnifying glass. Perhaps she's reading too much into it—that the boat betokens his intention to embark on a journey. There's also a passport-sized photo, and another of him sitting beside the girl's mother at some sort of family reunion. The screenwriter leaves his glasses on the desk and lights a cigarette, taking a deep drag as he fixes his gaze on the building across the street. He leans back in the chair and contemplates the unfeasibility of matching up the time it takes to show so many images with the speed at which the girl would tend to flip through the album. In any case, he should have enough time to show the most important ones. Perhaps he need only show a few. His likens his writing process to the way some painters work, marking off areas of the canvas before drawing their preliminary sketches, the figures gradually coming to life as they take on more definite features. He extinguishes his cigarette, puts his glasses back on, and turns toward the typewriter. For some reason, the girl's convinced there are no such things as coincidences, despite being unable to understand why she keeps running into the man she presumes is her cousin. She goes out to take a hurried look into her mother's study, ferreting frantically through her correspondence and the agendas she keeps in meticulous order, because the girl feels that the photographs are a testament of the past, reminding her of certain moments in her life, urging her to discover more. It's possible her cousin doesn't sign his correspondence with his own name or the pseudonym Dedalus, so she pays close attention to any letter with a sender or addressee she doesn't recognize. She's running out of time, so she starts focusing on specific dates. She answers a call on the landline. The chauffeur is getting nervous because they're going to be late. Some of the letters are quite strange. One is a donation request for an ostensibly noble cause, but the girl thinks it's probably a scam. But then she's suddenly taken aback by the following line: "Since our genetic code reveals that all living things have a common ancestry, it might lead one to believe that life on Earth was seeded by extraterrestrial engineers." She searches in vain for her mother's response. She gets the impression she's missing something crucial, but intuits she won't find anything else pertaining to her cousin, so decides to put an end to the investigation. Before leaving the apartment, she takes out a black dress from the back of a closet. She can't give a concert in a white T-shirt and jeans. She looks through the mail and listens to a message on the answering machine. Once again, the Principal of the Scholastic Institute wants to speak to the girl's mother. She erases the message.

The girl is speaking to her mother on her cell phone while waiting in the airport terminal. Her mother is annoyed, not only because her daughter was late for all her appointments, but her concert performance left a lot to be desired. How do you know? asks the girl. Who do you think they call when you don't show up on time? Who do you think they come crying to when your performance isn't up to scratch? The girl mumbles some excuses, saying at first that she went to the apartment to get in some last-minute practice on the piano and also to fetch her dress, but then she ends up admitting her real motive for going was to satisfy her curiosity in her mother's cousin. She can no longer hide from her the fact she's run into him. She's seen him twice already, she tells her mother, who doesn't believe her in the least. But she doesn't realize her daughter also went home to get some photographic confirmation. She asks her where and how she ended up seeing him, insisting it couldn't be their cousin but only someone who bears a passing resemblance. Why doesn't her mother believe her? In the following scene, she's back in the neighboring country's capital, and it will be obvious to the audience a few hours have passed since the girl's conversation with her mother. It begins in the middle of another conversation about which we know none of the preliminaries. It's around midnight, and the girl and her father are walking back to the hotel after dining at a nearby restaurant. They're talking about her future as a writer. She pouts with annoyance, because whenever he talks about her future, she can hear all his misgivings in his voice. Perhaps it's because he too wanted to be a writer when he was young. He no longer writes. He says there's no point; everything's already been said, more or less. By reading a certain number of books, one can see that every subject and style, every possible form that could ever exist has already been anticipated by someone else. Music, on the other hand, gives the performer a chance to recreate a chosen piece. According to him, there are only three reasons people write: for money, for fame, or to realize a deluded ambition to be original. So for which reason do you suppose I write? she asks her father. He shrugs his shoulders and maintains that routine expression on his face which could be interpreted to mean anything. Why can't he believe she could write as well as the novelist he admires so much, the one who wrote about jealousy and the passage of time? The girl aspires to be ranked with the Olympians, something her father doesn't even think her capable of dreaming about. She could try something unprecedented like writing a story without a theme. She'll do it, one of these days, but not now. In music, someone said it took years to be able to compose without a theme, and she doesn't feel prepared to try it in her writing. She'd like to construct a theory of atonality, but applied to literature: the dodecaphonic novel, but she doesn't dare mention it to her father. Come to think of it, her father is always hindering her ambitions. Not by erecting obstacles, as such, but he builds roads and bridges that lead nowhere. If their conversation were taking place in the hotel, the girl would go to her room, but walking back together, she just silently endures it. If she's managed to succeed as a concert pianist since the age of thirteen, why couldn't she be a writer at sixteen? She wonders if her precocity is limited to music. It's been a while since her father pronounced her name with a "ka." The girl sticks her fingers in her ears. Things aren't much different with her mother. She's always had a cold and distant relationship with her. She's like a corset, fitting her to a daily schedule, and the girl feels as uncomfortable talking to her about the future as she does with her father. Plus, her mother dismisses all literary fiction as complete nonsense. The girl thinks if her father was still writing, he'd only be doing it for the money. The screenwriter rereads the scene and wonders whether he should bore the audience with so much dialogue. Maybe he should make some cuts. He's still in doubt after rereading it several times, and ultimately chooses to postpone his decision. Perhaps he only wrote it for the girl. Once she's read it, he may decide to remove her from the story altogether. He needs a turning point though, something to move it in another direction. Why has everything already been said and written? he wonders. The same thought probably crossed the minds of the greatest writers, both of this century and the last, and of every century before that, all the way back to antiquity.

She's so tired, she could sleep for two days straight, so she decides to call him on the phone instead of visiting. He likes older women, she says, referring to the young conductor. That's why he always has a photo handy whenever we have sex—a photo of my mother, or some other woman. Sometimes he likes to have an older woman present. The screenwriter wants to know if the older woman joins in or just watches. The girl says she only watches. The screenwriter needs to know where, and under what circumstances. She's a hotel employee, the girl replies timidly. He wants to know every lurid detail. The woman watches while reading aloud random passages from the philosopher, W's, greatest work—something like "2.063 The sum-total of reality is the No World." The woman usually only watches and reads, but occasionally she lends a hand. Sometimes she's naked; sometimes she's dressed in her uniform. It all depends. Depends on what? pants the screenwriter. On how much she gets paid.

Sundays are strange, thinks the screenwriter, who'd rather every day was a Monday, Tuesday, or a Thursday, but never a Sunday. The silence on the streets bothers him, and all the closed stores only dampen his mood further. He puts on his navy-blue blazer and looks in the bathroom mirror. It may seem an odd quirk, but it's important for him to leave the jacket unbuttoned so it isn't pulled tightly around his waist, since his stomach has been growing outward for some time. At his age, most men have lost the svelte physique of their youth. In exchange for the loss though, he tells himself he's gained in stature, become more distinguished. He can't remember when he bought the jacket, but he doesn't feel the need to continually change his wardrobe in order to keep up with fashion. Nowadays it would take several seasons for his clothes to begin looking outmoded to him. He runs his fingers through his hair, which is still plentiful after all these years, more so than many younger men's, and he reckons that this, along with his deportment, is what makes him attractive to women. Moreover, his sage old professor's aura makes him respectable in the eyes of younger students, who've always perceived him as something of a bohemian. Maybe I'll teach again someday, thinks the screenwriter, amusing himself with the notion, assuming he ever reaches the paradisiacal destination to which he wants to travel with the girl. With his free hand, he touches his pocket to check he has his notebook, and then taps his cane against the floor. The carpet deadens the blows, as if deadening his thoughts. The only true paradises are the ones that are lost, he recalls. It's a phrase by the author who uses time as a lens, the actor and audience together, in an attempt to recover a world that all but disappears as soon as the actor leaves the stage, and the audience disperses. Not at all surprising coming from an asthmatic recluse who shut himself away in a room with cork-covered walls in order to prevent the outside world intruding; an ailing melancholic who drowned himself in the depths of solitude. Sundays are strange, the screenwriter thinks as he looks down on the street from his window. The woman in the building opposite must be up by now. He'd call her, if he had her number. There's no harm in striking up a friendly conversation with one's neighbors. Maybe he'll look it up in the phonebook one of these days. At the café in the plaza, he drinks his coffee, contemplating the way the neighborhood stretches away and disappears on the horizon. A couple of tourists are sitting in the bar on the other side of the fountain, next to a man about his own age, whom he's seen before. He's a regular who usually reads his paper there in the morning. If someone took a photograph of the two of them together, they'd capture a peculiar scene, a snapshot of two people who don't know what else to do to with their free time. Which reminds the screenwriter of the author the girl's father admires so much, of those long monologues wending their way through memories of former times, recalling the outdoor excursions and social gatherings of high society: a beautiful, distant epoch, which someone like the girl could scarcely appreciate. The girl would've been a wonderful success in the salons. She'd be doing what she already does in the concert halls. Although concerts are more impersonal, being beholden to sponsors, promoters, and impresarios instead of a single patron. At any rate, it's Sunday, and it takes a great effort for the screenwriter to get up and leave. He doesn't for a moment suspect the man on the other side of the fountain is anything other than an incorrigible reader like himself; he doesn't suspect, for example, that he might be following him; and even if he did, he'd never in a million years suspect the real motive. That the reason he's being followed is the girl.

True paradises are of the mind, he says aloud while strolling along the empty streets, past all the closed storefronts and other establishments, which give the neighborhood an eerie atmosphere. He'll have to head toward the city center if he wants to meet anyone. Even the bookstores are open on Sundays in that part of the city. He takes the metro and heads toward the noise and commotion of the city center, where he spends the afternoon roaming through empty, uninviting streets or darting through excessively crowded ones. He doesn't know the secret of why some streets are busy and others not. He looks around for potential exteriors for some of his scenes, but he doesn't find anything special, so he goes to the cinema archive where they're showing a movie by the director of the film in which an angel is able to hear other people's voices, not only when they speak, but also when they think, the spoken and unspoken thoughts of everyone on Earth. The featured film is a much earlier work, one that's held up well over the years, although the screenwriter finds the music the most striking thing about it. He'd almost forgotten how startling it actually is, and when the movie's finished, he leaves the theater humming the main theme. It has an unsettling rhythm, like something that's always approaching but never quite arrives. He'd like to use it in the *No World*. Is that what he'll call his script, *No World?* He'd never seriously considered it. Up till now, it didn't have a title, and he knows this one belongs to the girl. But he still has time to decide. Now, as he goes over the scenes in his head, it seems inevitable they'd be accompanied by the music he just heard. As night falls, he heads back. There's no place to sit at the café, which is once again thronging with tourists trying their best to prolong the late summer evening, so he passes it by, a little wearied from all his walking, and continues down the street until he reaches a pizzeria. He's not hungry, perhaps it's because he's so tired. But he resists the urge to go back to the hotel, orders a plate of food, and starts thinking about the girl. At his age, he doesn't need the extra calories. He needs only her. He'd like to be near her. He checks his watch automatically, as if to figure out how much time is left until he sees her, takes his notebook and pencil from his jacket pocket, and goes over some of his notes for a scene in which she appears with her father and the other musicians of the Little Sinfonietta.

The screenplay is quite inane really, but he's not watching the movie for the quality of its script. The only thing he wants to see in a porno is women fucking. He could spend hours watching the same scenes. One day, perhaps, his circumstances will force him to branch into the genre. He never used to think about the future the way he does now. His pension doesn't amount to much without the added remuneration from teaching. Goddamn money, he complains. Yes, he could do it, write proper screenplays for porn. But they don't pay for shit, he thinks, and he's heard it's really hard work, that they demand a script per day or something like that. He doesn't know if he could produce decent writing at that rate. He probably couldn't. It runs against his idea of the proper pacing needed for achieving quality work. He imagines the working method: arriving early on set; making up a script on the spot, preferably one that makes use of the set another group has just finished using; dashing it off, and presenting it to the waiting director. He's never worked like that. He's touched up another person's screenplay, extemporized new dialogue to satisfy the whim of a producer, but he's never started from scratch using someone else's set. He isn't sure he could improvise to that extent. I suppose you should just throw yourself into it, he says to himself. Once in the thick of it, you'll learn quickly enough. He can see himself sitting in a corner dashing off the final parts of a script while the actresses are drinking coffee and the director deliberates about how to conduct the day's shoot. The long and short of it is there's not much dialogue to write, and the actors have neither the time nor the acting skills to memorize and deliver their lines the way he'd want. It can't be much different from churning out scripts for TV shows, although in TV, writers tend to work in teams. The screenwriter considers the scene that's playing out on his TV set: an attractive, respectable-looking woman enters a shoe-repair shop, limping, shows the broken stiletto heel to the cobbler, and requests he fix it immediately. The screenwriter once toyed with the notion that his scripts punctuated different stages of his life; like his offspring, each child belonging to a different era, with its own individual memories, specific mental states, favorite colors, lovers . . . yet, for the line of work the screenwriter's considering, such complicated entities would have to be conceived on a daily basis—different sets, eras, mental states—a different lover every day?—how could he take stock of all that? Yet, he's still thinking about a possible career as a porno screenwriter: arriving early on set; making up a script on the spot that can employ the sets of other films; perhaps he'd come up with a story on his way to work, or while drinking coffee in the café on the corner; perhaps he'd have written one the night before, after sleeping with one of the actresses. There's a new idea running through the screenwriter's head that seems brilliant to him, and quite original, an idea to rival even the great dramatist's work, something he himself might have written had he lived at a different time. Amorous scenes between a king and queen talking at length about their eccentric son's future—about whether they'll end up having him murdered somewhere far from their kingdom—while they spank each other, revealing to the audience another side to the familiar story. He's even thought of the title he'd give to a series of such films: *Hidden Scenes from so-and-so's Work*. Or if he changed the author and work in question: *Leon Kowalski, the Hidden Years of a Replicant*. It would be a matter of putting false memories into the mind of a movie character, although of course it wouldn't make a difference if the memories were true or false. It's all the same in fiction. The screenwriter puts the matter aside for the moment and continues watching the TV. The lady has finally made her way to the back of the shoe-repair shop. Looking closely, one can clearly see a halo of light around her body. The screenwriter doesn't understand why no one else can see that she's an alien.

It is well after midnight, and the screenwriter is speculating about the No World. What does No World mean? It's not the first time he's asked the question. The girl no longer remembers the answer; that is, if she ever really had the answer. What *does* No World mean? she asks herself in turn. Where does a game lead to in the end? Perhaps it leads to the young orchestra conductor, the screenwriter thinks. For him, the girl's writing is very arid, too descriptive and plain, and he doesn't know how to encourage her without lying. They've just made love: slowly, at his pace. Sometimes they do it more energetically, the way she likes it, sometimes not. The screenwriter feels as if his soul has climbed up to heaven and is looking back on Earth. Lying on the bed next to the girl, looking pensive, he slides his left arm under her nape and just looks at her, examines her fringe of hair, short and flat against her brow, and so he delicately displaces it with his fingers. The early morning silence breezes in through the half-open windows. You'll end up preferring him to me, the screenwriter whispers, meaning the young conductor, speaking so softly his voice almost peters out entirely. No I won't, she says, the after-silence stretching out indefinitely. You'll want somebody younger, the screenwriter insists, holding his breath. He wants to know what will happen when he gets even older. What do you want to happen? she asks, her eyes glued to the ceiling. He shrugs his shoulders feebly, unable to answer her. There's a prolonged silence as she turns to look at him, unwavering, not moving a single muscle in her face. I've told you I'll always love you, she says. The screenwriter wishes he could believe her, that she'd promise her undying love, give her word to never abandon him. But then, in a moment of lucidity, he remembers that only desire matters, there can be no room for sentiment. They say old age vitiates desire. But he doesn't see it that way. His life is a torment, and he supposes it'll always be a torment: rest, repose, who'd want that? Maybe it's a different kind of desire, the desire for peace—more complex, but also more self-evident. Well, perhaps. She lights a joint and hands it to him, then gets up and starts dressing by the side of the bed. She puts her notebook in her satchel and takes a quick look outside, searching for the inconspicuous shadow that often lurks near the hotel's entrance. An hour has passed, maybe two, and the murmur of engines paused at the traffic lights is getting louder by the moment. The city's stirring. Don't go, he implores her as she heads to the door, his hand reaching weakly, vainly, for hers.

Sometimes she feels like a fool, writes the screenwriter in a margin of his notebook, listening to the girl's inner voice, which is torturing her with that idea. Sometimes she feels like the angel in the film, that she can hear other people's voices, not only when they speak, but also when they think, convinced she's eavesdropping on their most intimate thoughts and desires. During these moments, the screenwriter listens to the girl's inner voice, as plain as if it were a voiceover, saying it doesn't matter that she has exceptional talent, she's still a fool. She always feels this way after an argument with the young conductor. She knows she shouldn't allow herself be carried away by these jealous rages, but by the time she remembers this, it's already too late. As she gets dressed, the telephone rings, and

71

the young conductor, lying naked on the bed, answers it, his eyes remaining on the girl, engrossed by her body. Listening to what the young conductor's saying, she guesses that the caller is the brilliant composer. In fact, she'd have known by just listening to the young conductor's tone of voice. She wouldn't even need to use her sixth sense, which allows her to perceive all that's hidden around her, to hear other people's thoughts, detect when someone pronounces her name with a "ka." They're talking about irregular sound waves, which they both agree are harsh on the ears, about the difference between dissonance and consonance, about mathematics, acoustics, and all the rest of it. She takes the book by W from the nightstand and walks out, not forgetting to slam the door behind her. Maybe she's overreacting; maybe it's the pills; or maybe it's just her personality. "3.04 If a thought were correct a priori, it would be a thought whose possibility ensured its truth." She asks herself what this could mean. Possibly nothing. She walks the streets aimlessly, alone. She inadvertently overhears a conversation by a couple in a café. The man, reading his newspaper, lifts his head to pass a comment about the news. We really don't belong on this planet, he says solemnly. The woman nods in agreement, drops her cigarette to the ground, and crushes it under the sole of her shoe. The girl walks into a bookstore, passes several tables laden with books, not looking for anything in particular, but she thinks she should start reading other authors, besides the great dramatist and the genius who revolutionized twentieth-century literature. Once again, she gets lost wandering the streets before finding her way again, and decides to head for the bars with the foosball tables. She wouldn't mind challenging one of the players, or even joining someone else's team. She watches for a while, but they're too focused on the game to notice her. As for the screenwriter, Sunday passes by without his even noticing. He went for a walk by the river and then relaxed in the afternoon. He called his wife a couple of times, and watched TV as he waited for the girl. Later in the night, he typed up a scene he'd already written longhand, in which she has an argument with the young conductor and then wanders the streets aimlessly before heading for the bar with the foosball tables. All of a sudden the girl becomes anxious, believing someone's following her. Perhaps alien hunters have zeroed in on the voices she always hears. All they have to do is narrow the range of their sensors, adjust their frequency, and then it's only a matter of time before they get to her. The screenwriter turns off the light and looks over at the building opposite as he undresses for bed. He can't get the girl out of his head. Finally, though, his exhaustion overtakes him, and at precisely the moment he thinks he's discerned what direction the story will take, his lids give way, and he's lost in the oblivion of sleep.

It's cold for an August morning, and the low clouds are moving swiftly, threatening rain. Near the hotel, there's a second-hand clothes store, and the screenwriter decides to go inside and have a look around. He never used to think of buying anything in a place like this. It's true, these kinds of stores haven't always been around, he tells himself, but even if they had been, he'd never have entered one, much less bought anything inside. These days, however, if he needed some pants, a jacket, or possibly a new shirt, such a place could be his only port of call. Necessity can alter habits, he thinks. He's beginning to run low on money, and one of these days he'll have to phone the producer to request another advance. He walks down the aisle, past rows of shelves and clothing racks. He notices his leg hurts: a sign it's going to rain. He exits the store, spends a few moments looking in the window before walking down the street to board the metro. He isn't traveling far, but his limp makes it seem like a million miles. He should avoid the hotel where the girl's staying, that's a no-go area. Curiosity, however, overrides his better judgment. On getting off the metro, the wet street tells him it's been raining. He looks up at the sky, searching for any indication it might rain again. The air is still quite cool for early August. He returns his eyes to the ground and continues wearily on his way. He knows the girl is staying at one of the best hotels in the capital. Her mother always puts her up in it. It has an English name, and the doorman, dressed like an admiral, cheerily salutes him whenever he passes by. There's no one at his hotel to hold the door open or carry his bags, much less drive him to the café. Such are the differences between people who have everything and guys like him; palpable differences, which are never adequately described by the girl when she tries to give an account of them, differences which are only felt by him when he takes a stroll through her reality. But when they're in bed together, sharing ideas and feelings, these distances vanish, he thinks. Sometimes he asks himself if he isn't writing screenplays to live his life through his characters. The mind is filled with strange things, he reflects, content with this ambiguous response. But if this truly was his reason for writing, it would mean he's wasted his life. There are so many people who dedicate their efforts to doing something useful, he thinks, like making cars, refrigerators, knives, bread . . . while others are working in the dream industry. They don't make anything that's real; all they do is provide opportunities for people to dream their lives away by living in fictional realities that are depicted onscreen or in a book. It's no different than providing drugs, narcotics, to both divert and stupefy the public at the same time. In turn, he thinks, these creators of dreams, whether through screenplays or novels, are dreaming themselves in the act of writing, so it seems the lie goes full circle. He sits in one of the armchairs of the grand lobby that separates the hotel's café from its restaurant, picks up a menu, and goes over the prices—all outside his budget no doubt. He should've dedicated himself to something more remunerative. He might have a decent pension by now, or even be rich like the girl's parents. Instead he's wasted his time, he thinks, and has been unable to scrape together enough money to spend even a day in the least expensive room of this hotel. He orders a coffee, the cheapest option, although it costs as much as a full breakfast at his own hotel, lights a cigarette while taking his notebook and pencil from his jacket pocket, and describes in detail the movements of the barman. Then he describes the chairs, the carpet, the magnificent garden outside the windows, and the features of the hotel guests passing by. He wants to immerse himself in the places the girl frequents. For him, these guests are like extras in his film. He spends some time absorbing the full splendor of this place, and finds he can at last appreciate the pomp and circumstance surrounding the girl's concerts. The girl represents a financial investment. This kind of outlook shouldn't be scoffed at; after all, a concert pianist is essentially an industry on legs. A young waitress, impeccably dressed in a jacket and pink skirt, serves the screenwriter his cup of coffee. She smiles at him, unlike the waitress at the café in the plaza; to get a smile from her would be like drawing blood from a stone. This waitress's smile is natural, candid, sincere . . . The screenwriter's at a loss for other adjectives. He'd love to go on a date with her sometime, but somewhere far away from here. Of course, he doesn't even try asking her out. He knows it's not a good idea. Instead, he just reciprocates a smile and thanks her for her kindness. She's too young to be the waitress the girl was talking about; the one who recites random passages from the philosopher W's magnum opus while watching her and the young conductor having sex. To his right, sitting in one of the armchairs, a guy is chatting to a young woman. Both are dressed elegantly. They're more than likely talking about money, he thinks, some business deal perhaps, or maybe they're exchanging ideas about all the great sex they're going to have later, he thinks, again feeling a little dispirited. Their world is simply too far removed from his own. If a writer doesn't make enough money to lead this kind of life, he's better off choosing another career. The screenwriter is living proof. If he were young, and could start all over, he'd do something else. This is one of the reasons a writer or screenwriter will abandon literature or the cinema and dedicate his life to business, he thinks. There are real-world examples of this. They never again show the same interest in poetry, art, or whatever their métier may have been. If the girl gave up her career as a pianist to become a writer, it would be a kind of reversal of this scenario, though. As for him, it's too late for a career change. When he dies, he thinks, he will have wasted his life. He tries to think of an analogy, and can only come up a case of someone wasting a bumper-car ride, spinning around and around without ever moving from the starting point. He thinks of all the time not spent on furthering his career. Time wasted on attractive young students, or on grooming this or that shy starlet. If he ever returns to teaching, he promises to tell his students the truth about this dirty business: that all they can expect from becoming a writer is a life of frustration and staying in cheap hotels. To hell with writers and to hell with screenwriters, he declaims to himself through gritted teeth. He gets back down to work. He must get something done after spending an arm and a leg for the privilege of drinking a coffee at the hotel with the English name. What goes through the girl's mother's head when she's thinking about her daughter? Money, the screenwriter decides while looking through the windows at the magnificent garden outside. He wouldn't recognize the girl's mother if he ran into her, though. He doesn't remember ever having seen her, or the girl's father for that matter. They're the type of people who pay someone to take their children to school, like servants or bodyguards. The screenwriter thinks it immoral for parents to allow a stranger to take their young girl to school. In the distance he sees some patio umbrellas and white wooden tables on the freshly mown grass. Nobody's sitting outside because it's just rained. But it seems the rich prefer to eat indoors anyway. The screenwriter pays his bill and crumples the receipt into his pocket along with his notebook. He then leans on his cane to get to his feet, and wobbles slowly toward the door. He could manage a swifter exit, but he wants to enjoy this moment, prolong it, so he memorizes every step like a series of snapshots. As he passes the reception desk, some hotel employees greet him sympathetically. He'd say his age, his bearing, and his cane are all complicit in making him worthy of their deference.

They've called him a beacon, the creator of the modern world, and the inventor of the human. His characters are kings, princes, soldiers, clerks, impostors, witches, murderers, et al. He limns the whole spectrum of human society—the high and the low, the wicked and the good: specters of the No World, as the girl would say. He shows us heaven and hell exist within us and without, and teaches us that appearances can often be deceiving. The dramatist par excellence surpasses every other writer we know. His wit, energy, and scope of invention bespeak a man of illimitable intellect and boundless creative power. He's the greatest comedian, the most sublime tragedian of them all, and as someone once said of his characters, the secret to their depth, their humanity, is their ability to overhear themselves, and in doing so, to change. For all these reasons, therefore, he has to be read. In the end, he gave up poetry and the theater, dying three years later. Perhaps of unemployment. There are people who can't bear not having a job, the screenwriter says. Later, in the middle of the night, he asks the girl to read to him some fragments from her diary. She's thought about giving up writing; if she hasn't done so yet, it's because only in writing does she feel alive. She opens her diary and leafs through its pages, chooses a passage about her walk back to the foosball bars; then one about loneliness, about her feeling like she's a writer although she doesn't write; and another about the futility of trying to evade her extraterrestrial pursuers. The screenwriter listens to her voice, deems it firm, assured, if slightly monotonous, and looks at her face, the movement of her lips, the way her hands grip the diary. She once wrote that everything whirls around her at great speed, that her rehearsals are only a game, her writings only a game, even her life's only an elaborate game in which events seem to succeed each other with an inconceivable rapidity, all her arguments with her mother and the young conductor, all her disappointments in love, are just part of this elaborate game. She's written that everyone pronounces her name with a "ka," and that this is a way of giving meaning to something that has no meaning. It's like being on drugs all day, she thinks. Perhaps she's been searching high and low for the face of her cousin Dedalus. Perhaps she hopes to see him again. The screenwriter believes there are secrets we should keep to ourselves, that they shouldn't be confessed, except perhaps to a diary. The girl reads aloud, her head pillowed against his graying chest, speaking of her father, of the neighboring country's capital, and of herself. She feels more like a writer than ever, she says, and that she often imagines discovering her mother in flagrante with a secret lover. She turns on the TV and flips through the channels. On the news, there's talk of other places in the world where people don't know the game exists. She turns the TV off and goes to the piano. She wants to set her performance apart from everyone else's. Perhaps she's found a way to do so by slowing it down. But she can't really trust herself after taking so many pills—a strange distrust, since the young conductor insists the pills will enhance her emotional states, and raise the level of her performance to near genius, which will compensate for the foibles of youth and inexperience. There aren't too many hours left until concert at the church in front of the writers' café, and there isn't enough time for her to find a way to make her performance unique. After thinking about it, though, she believes she's already found a way, but the young conductor and brilliant composer aren't satisfied with it. Yet, she shouldn't doubt herself. She lies down naked at the foot of the bed and writes again until she falls asleep. She awakens to the faint light of dawn streaming in the window. She dreamed she was driving around in a yellow convertible, and she recalls how it gleamed, the way things only do in dreams, and the way it seemed to glide so smoothly, silently along through the outskirts of the city, with the young conductor in the driver's seat, and the brilliant composer sitting beside him, while she was in the backseat standing up, reciting a poem, playing the part of the cosmic clown. On the sidewalk, people had stopped to listen to her, and she saw the face of her cousin among them. She then asked the young conductor to stop the car, but it seemed as though the words never reached his ears, and Cousin Dedalus vanished among the pedestrians, who all dispersed, continuing on their way to nowhere in particular, dropping into the margins of her dream. It seems strange to her now that the car drove so smoothly, as if gliding over a thin layer of oil, strange that she noticed the one face among so many others. She'd like to decipher the meaning of the dream, but she can only guess that it must have something to do with the concerts and her obsession with finding her cousin. After a while, feeling a little weary, she stops reading from her diary and gets out of bed. The screenwriter smokes a joint as she gets dressed. Will you come back tomorrow? he asks. Tomorrow's opening night, she says. No it's not, he says, tomorrow's just a momentary blip in the boundless expanse of time; right now, tomorrow's but a barely perceived premonition in the brain—not a psychic premonition, but a forecast, as of the weather, and the weathergirl's frequently wrong. She takes the joint from between his fingers and takes a deep drag before returning it. She goes over to the window and opens the curtains to looks down on the deserted streets. What do you see? the screenwriter asks, the question half-muffled, his face half-buried in the pillow. She doesn't answer. She finds it difficult to describe the figure she sees lurking almost imperceptibly in the shadows. It's the same figure she sees every night, like having a recurring dream. Maybe she's only imagining it. Maybe it's nothing.

Still lying in bed, the screenwriter realizes he's commenced the same ritual as always: remaining in bed a long time, staring up at the ceiling, and listening to the sounds from the street below. He slept very little, and he suspects the girl is still floating around somewhere in his unconscious. He only vaguely recollects what he's written. He gets out of bed to freshen up, has a look at himself in the bathroom mirror, takes a deep breath, and makes his way down to the canteen. The elevator takes its time arriving. He gets the feeling he may be better off taking the stairs. He'd do it if it wasn't for his damned limp. He grips his cane impatiently and knocks it against the floor a couple of times, the strokes, muted by the carpet, rendering the act meaningless. He doesn't like the muffled thud, he says to himself, because it probably unleashed a cloud of dust mites that are now colonizing his socks and the hem of his pants. He passes some time in the lobby reading the newspaper. He reads something about a country too far away for him to care about, peruses the personal ads, and encounters an article about the queen of porn that says she's buried in one of the local cemeteries. He remembers there are many cinematic luminaries buried there: actors, actresses, directors, and of course people from other professions who neither matter nor warrant a visit. He went there once with a friend. He remembers her clearly: a woman with whom he was romantically involved some forty years before, and with whom he corresponded for quite some time. He reckons it's been a decade since he last heard from her. He doesn't recall the reason they went to the cemetery; he doesn't recall when they started writing to each other, or why their correspondence came to an end. There's a notice about the Little Sinfonietta's concert in the events section. The screenwriter hurriedly finishes his breakfast and heads out. A cemetery's quite a cinematic location. Maybe he'll be able to set some of his scenes there. On the way, he considers some of the possibilities for the location, but he struggles to focus, and his ideas seem to dissipate before assuming any definite shape. Near the entrance, a map points to the sites of celebrity graves. He makes a rough sketch of it in his notebook, marking the ones he plans to visit. The tomb of the inventor of the cinematic spectacle is nearby: although he doesn't consider him the most alluring figure, the screenwriter decides to pay him a visit nonetheless. He struggles up the hill with his limp, and then has a hard time finding the grave among so many anonymous ones in a sort of narrow embankment. The history of film is short, he thinks. The inventor of the cinematic spectacle died fifty-six years earlier, and his tomb is in a terrible state, not unlike all the others around it, facing the wall that separates the cemetery grounds from the street and the apartments on the other side. It seems sad and pitiful. He then wonders about people like himself, the kind who won't go down in history, who'll rest in unvisited tombs. He strikes his cane forcefully against the ground while making his way back to the main footpath. He's lost the strength that got him here, replaced it with sadness, and although he continues walking, he does so without a destination in mind, and soon begins to flag. Some small pebbles and rocks have been placed haphazardly, or so it seems, atop some of the gravestones. There are people leaving postcards or small scraps of paper with messages for the dead. A few are ambling casually among the graves, some may be family members, others tourists, and there's no telling about the rest. A woman reads while sitting on the tomb of a great writer. The screenwriter supposes it's one of that writer's great works, although he's too shy to approach her and corroborate his suspicion. He's tired from hobbling along under the hot sun, so he sits down in the shade beside a marble headstone and wipes his forehead with a handkerchief. This part of the cemetery is more modern. He reads on the tombstones the names and dates of some of the deceased. He could use them to conceive some fascinating stories: a young man dead at twenty-five, and then only a year later, the death, at forty-eight, of what appears to be his mother. It really makes you think.

After writing in the afternoon, the screenwriter rested a couple of hours. Then he took a shower, and awaited her arrival. He's had too much to drink, and his throat is raw from all the smoking. He's still stoned, and he can't help but keep staring out the window on the empty street below. It's almost dawn, and he suspects the girl is going to stand him up. He raises his eyes to look for his neighbor in the building across the street. It might be too late for her, or perhaps too early. Either way, she's probably asleep. Her window is black, empty. Maybe black actually signifies the opposite of empty. No matter. He scans the front of the building, then the shop windows on the lower floors: the real-estate agency on the corner, the bakery, the shop selling women's lingerie, and the shoe and handbag store that's closed for the August vacation. It doesn't matter, the girl isn't coming. The screenwriter assumes her mother returned from her trip. She wouldn't have missed the concert for anything in the world, especially after the poor performance the girl gave in her native city. Then she calls him. The concert went perfectly, she tells him on the phone, as if she were a journalist submitting a last-minute review. Before the performance, she paid tribute to the famous composer of dodecaphonic music, describing him as a teacher, an arranger of operettas, and a conductor of cabaret orchestras. His actual compositions took a backseat, and she gave them brief mention in her peroration, alluding mostly to his theory of harmony and his role as inventor of the twelve-tone method of composition. The girl has a curious fondness for odd composers, the screenwriter thinks to himself, forgetting momentarily that he's the one responsible for her predilections. It seems she only cares about extremes, and the possibility of encroaching on them, surpassing them, of transgressing the norm. Immediately following her introduction, she began the concert with the famous composer's *5 Pieces for piano*, a difficult work, both for the performer to execute and the auditor to appreciate, although the girl knew they'd applaud anyway, for the audience came mainly to catch sight of a celebrity, not to admire her pianissimo or to listen to her rendition of what most of them would've thought a baffling composition. The screenwriter listens in silence, transcribing her words as fast as he can. The scene will be hazy, subjective, quite involved, and he wants to be sure it accurately reflects the reality. He makes use of the program notes for ideas on how it might be filmed. Simple ideas, really, some shots of the girl seated at the piano, alone or with the orchestra, and then some others of her transformed into a clown. Vocals aren't her strong point, but she has the desired effect when playing the role of the cosmic clown. All she needs is a red nose, the kind that's held in place with a rubber band, a red speckle to contrast with her black and white tuxedo, and a nasal voice that sounds like a transmission from another galaxy, a voice reciting verses about a clown who wanders in the moonlight with a shiv in his hand. At this moment, the screenwriter listens to the very same piece from a CD, ensconced in his hotel room, sitting at his desk scribbling notes for scenes. The images he records are seen first by the girl, refracted first through the lenses of her eyes. Before leaving the presbytery, which was transformed for the Little Sinfonietta into a concert venue, the young orchestra conductor, the brilliant composer, and the girl wave to the audience with a practiced air of humility. The girl then removes the red nose from her pocket and tosses it to the crowd, whose applause continues unabated. They cheer as if for a pop star, and it suddenly dawns on her that now she'll have to repeat the same stunt every night, because she saw how their eyes gleamed when the photographers flashed in unison. Afterward, her mother shows up in the sacristy, a starlet's makeshift dressing room, and drives her away to attend a celebratory dinner with the concert organizers.

It's late the next time he speaks to her. The girl calls him from the ladies' room of a fashionable nightspot where the group's ended up. She's had a confrontation with the young conductor of the orchestra who was unhappy with her performance. The dispute then evolved into a jealous altercation, and the young conductor left with another girl. The screenwriter wants to know if she was beautiful. Very, she replies. The applause and admiration she receives from the public doesn't tally with the young conductor's animadversions. Moreover, the brilliant composer also takes issue with her interpretation of his *No World Symphony*. She says they're only jealous, and then she starts crying. Does she know the address, or at least the name of the place she's at? He could grab a taxi and come get her, come rescue her, he says. They could even make love right there in the ladies' room, if she wants, or in some secluded part of the building. But first he needs to know where she is. She stammers something through her sobs. She feels like a fool. Not an uncommon feeling for her. He tells her to leave the restroom and ask someone for the address. She promises to call him back. The screenwriter waits by the phone, drinking, lighting his next cigarette with the previous one, finishes that, lights another in the same manner, empties his glass, fills it again, thinks how long it's been, a minute, an hour perhaps, he can't tell exactly. He doesn't think she'll call. He doubts he'll be able get a taxi in his state. At last, the phone rings. Although muffled, he can hear the dance music blaring in the background. He wants to ask her where she is but struggles to articulate the question. The girl's voice is beginning to falter. She says she's in one of the rooms at the fashionable night-spot, a storeroom or office, she's not sure, and someone's there with her, a stranger. The screenwriter listens, hears her heavy breathing, her moaning, the occasional groans of the guy she's screwing. He doesn't dare say anything, ask anything, but only listens. He doubts she'd be able to respond to him anyway. They start screaming so loudly he can hear them when he holds the phone away from his ear. Afterward, he listens as the girl begins to argue with the guy; it only last a few seconds, but it seems to go on forever. Then someone slams a door. The screenwriter whispers her name, waits, whispers it again, then again. Then he yells her name. He doesn't know what else to do. Suddenly, at long last, the girl responds. He hit me, she says, and hangs up the phone.

It's a cool morning. According to the TV, the temperature has dropped to seventeen degrees Celsius. The screenwriter takes a look out the window. He didn't sleep well, and the girl's words are still ringing in his ears, the voice on the other end of the phone that said he hit me, and then nothing, silence. He turns the TV off. He hit me, the screenwriter says, unconsciously mouthing the words in front of the bathroom mirror as he washes up. He runs his fingers proudly through his hair, still thick after all these years. His mouth is dry. He fills a glass from the cold tap and drinks the water slowly, examining the saggy bags under his eyes. He decides to head for the café in the plaza, limping as always, repeating her words to himself, mouthing them unconsciously, even up to the point the waitress sets down his double espresso and a small cruet of milk on the table. He wishes it had been him who violated her instead of some stranger. Maybe it was one of the other teenagers, or one of the patrons of the Scholastic Institute. He notices he has an erection. Then he asks himself what sort of life he expected to lead in the neighboring country's capital: to be locked away with her in a hotel room perhaps, or a garret, old and derelict, where he could embark on a new adventure with her. No, that wasn't it. The scene of her being slapped in the storeroom or office of a fashionable bar is worth exploiting. At a table in a corner of the café, a young guy is working on his laptop. He's surrounded by a mountain of paper. For a moment, the screenwriter thinks he's a writer, perhaps a screenwriter like himself, but instead of notebooks and index cards, he sees what appear to be invoices and packing slips, so he looks away dismissively. The screenwriter still uses a portable typewriter—no longer state-of-the-art, as in its day—and a notebook he carries with him everywhere. He's too old to learn how to use a computer. Some accordion music is playing softly over the café's speakers. He uses little details like this to focus his thoughts when he finds it difficult to concentrate, a scatterbrain centering itself on something trivial. He needs to write the scene, but feels chagrined at his inability to do so. The girl's like that, he says to himself, surprised at her capacity to navigate between extremes of sluggish inactivity when feeling uninspired, and of rebellious excitability during a fit of passion. He doesn't know why she behaves like this, and he believes discovering the answer will tax the very limits—as he'd put it—of his comprehension. He writes half a dozen lines that help him forget about it, and having written something at last, his conscience eases, so he decides to go to the park he visited on his first day in town. On his way there, he indulges in an erotic daydream, and eventually decides to go into a lingerie store to buy a pair of sexy panties. Afterward, he continues his fantasizing en route to the park, imagining the girl wearing the panties he bought, masturbating in them, writhing, her body twisting into the kinds of positions only a contortionist could manage. He imagines himself watching her through a peephole. Once again he develops an erection, so he decides to sit down on a bench and allow some time to pass, his mind to wander, and his excitement to abate. In the park, he pays close attention to everything going on around him, since a few of his scenes are likely to take place there. Next to the wrought-iron fence separating the park from the avenue, there's a jogging path on which some young athletes are running, or maybe they're only amateurs decked out to look like accomplished athletes. Years before, when he was young, and regularly visited the neighboring country's capital, nobody jogged in the park. Perhaps the jogging path didn't even exist back then, he thinks. In fact, back in his day, nobody jogged at all, unless they were training to be athletes. On the top floor of the hotel with the English name, somewhat recovered from the previous night, the girl is running on a treadmill. She looks out through the windows at the city, at the river dividing it in two, at the approaching clouds above, and the diminutive creatures below who listen to her music and read about her in magazines. Sometimes, the young conductor or brilliant composer exercise along with her; occasionally, they all go running together in the woods nearby. The screenwriter doesn't really care who goes jogging where; he only thinks about what actors and actresses could play these roles. The girl ought to play herself, of course. No one could do it better. No one her age could perform those piano pieces the way she does, or even simulate her performances, her body language, her poise, the way she deliberates at every note before striking, the way she accents every note on striking, the way her hands engage and then withdraw from the keyboard. No one could recreate the voice she uses when reciting those poems in the guise of the cosmic clown. All of this runs through his mind as he ambles to the pond and takes a seat on one of the benches next to it. Perhaps he's writing a musical and doesn't know it yet. Half a dozen sailboats scud from one side to the other through the water, their captains steering them with long sticks from the pond's edge. A few ducks are soliciting food from some other park visitors. A guy who must be around thirty is mingling with some of the children, launching and recovering his own sailboat. The screenwriter believes this to be unacceptable behavior. People shouldn't be allowed on the pond with a sailboat once they pass a certain age, he thinks, although what really bothers him is that the man seems completely at ease, tripping nonchalantly around the pond, barefoot, while playing with his toy. There are tourists everywhere, some stop to watch the sailboats, sitting on the grass or lying in the sun, a few eventually moving off to explore the rest of the park. The screenwriter jots down a few notes before growing weary of the heat. He looks out on the water, the children, the sailboats, and at the guy he thinks should act his age. He puts his notebook in his jacket pocket and gets up to accost him. Do you know how many infectious diseases you could catch? he says to the guy, signaling at his bare feet with a flourish of his cane, inadvertently striking one of his toes. Slightly hurt and taken aback, the guy answers the screenwriter with a disconcerted look. You should be more careful, the screenwriter says contemptuously while turning away. The guy mutters something unintelligible behind his back before returning to the pond's edge, tripping nonchalantly around it, barefoot, and playing with his little toy.

The screenwriter dined at a restaurant on the island before making his way to the sidewalk café, where he now sits, trying to get down to some writing. The scene he's working on is set just before dawn. The girl and her mother are getting out of a limousine in front of the hotel with the English name. A doorman with an admiral's uniform holds the front door open for them. They go through without responding to his greeting. Next, we see the two of them talking in the large living area separating their bedrooms. The mother is standing at the window admiring the city lights, which appear to her to be emerging from under her feet and extending toward the horizon. They're talking about the neighboring country's capital. It reminds the girl of her native city, except it's perhaps ten times bigger. In front of the mirror, she sees a scratch on her face. Her mother goes over to examine it up close. It's nothing, says the girl dismissively. We then see a shot from outside of the building of the mother returning to the window. All cities have something in common, she says. The camera closes in on her face, her eyes, looking out at the world, or perhaps within, at herself. She's beautiful, photogenic, and could've played the lead role in any other film; that much will have been made clear after the first scene. As with her father, the girl doesn't know exactly what it is her mother does professionally. She knows only that she has a good job at an international company, that she's well connected, and that she has friends even in the remotest parts of the world. The girl's success as a pianist may in part be due to her mother's connections. A quick phone call or two may have been sufficient to arrange the Little Sinfonietta's performance at the church, for example. Such beneficence is perhaps typical for a woman of her station: helping to further the careers of talented kids whose families haven't the means of doing so. The girl has never met any of her mother's friends. But she presumes she has lovers, it's only that she's careful about not being seen with them. Her greatest love is definitely herself, though; and her greatest passion, being the one in charge. She only has an occasional and transitory interest in her daughter's professional life, which is usually disrupted when they have an argument and stop communicating—except, that is, by telephone, through the cleaning lady, or on the chalkboard in the kitchen. The girl again faces the mirror, watches her mother's reflection looking down at the city. How's it going with the young conductor? she asks in a blasé tone, her eyes meandering with the river.

The following morning, the girl is in a bad mood. She's just finished a phone call with the brilliant composer, who suggested they go jogging in the park. She dismissed the offer out of hand, and asked after the young conductor. He's with his latest conquest, more than likely, replies the brilliant composer in disgust. The girl finds it harder every day to concentrate, and she therefore keeps increasing the number of pills she takes. It's going to be a long day, she thinks. Earlier, she visited a children's hospital. Her mother was annoyed there were so few photographers there. After she got back, she practiced the *5 Pieces for piano*, and then went for a workout in the gym. Finally, after catching up on some reading in the hotel, she decided to go for a walk, and perhaps continue her reading outside. It's Wednesday, and the sunny weather is at variance with her mood. She's not hungry and doesn't intend to eat anytime soon, so she remains where she lies, reading on the riverbank. She can't grasp how this dramatist of the sixteenth and seventeenth centuries could've been so prolific and wide-ranging, how he could have written so much about so many subjects, created so many different characters. Maybe she lacks the intelligence to understand him, the talent to emulate him. Maybe she has nothing to say anyway. Maybe she's striving in vain to be a writer. She decides she must persist, that she should perhaps sit down and write for a few hours. She doesn't do so however, because she needs to do more thinking about her work. Although she knows it's easy to find excuses, to pass the time staring at reflections in the water, at the buildings on the opposite bank. The sun tickles her skin, and she closes her eyes to fantasize about becoming a prolific and wide-ranging author. It seems impossible, though. Even her fantasies don't stretch that far. And if she can't even finish a single chapter, how can she hope to emulate the famous dramatist? She walks to the other side of the island in the river, doing some window-shopping along the way. There's a little girl sitting in a garden, chewing on some flower petals. Her father hurries over to put a stop to it. She doesn't know why, but this reminds the girl of a conversation she overheard in a café. When she gets back to the hotel, she takes out her notebook and writes in a direct and unambiguous tone, "1. The No World is everything that is the case. 1.1 We are beings from another world. 1.2 The No World is falling to pieces. Its inhabitants are not from planet Earth." She believes such precepts would only be adopted by a rather singular character. One who hunts aliens. An alien that hunts aliens. An idea that's been exploited ad nauseam, she thinks, although in quite different storylines. The girl is trying to make her character unique: a guy who escapes to the City in Outer Space. The idea doesn't strike her as either good or bad; she just doesn't know what to do with it. But what if all the inhabitants of Earth actually came from another world? Yes, she feels her narrative could proceed along this line. It wouldn't be the main plot, but something running parallel to it: the story of a renegade alien hunter. The girl truly believes the Earth is just a colony occupied by beings from another planet, but whether it's true or not, it's still not an original idea. She's read some stuff about it before, although she doesn't remember reading any stories in which the Earth is a refuge for interplanetary immigrants—beings from another world, as she overheard in the café. She does remember similar stories depicted in the movies, in which aliens assume human form and commingle with us, but she can't think of any in which absolutely every-one on Earth is an alien. The girl realizes there's something interesting in this idea of people being unaware of their ori-gins. Some may hear strange voices in their heads, believing they're being called by a higher power. The way she hears her name pronounced with a "ka." When she writes, perhaps she's being actuated by some strange radiation emanating from a distant planet; perhaps it's her own home planet. But if this is the case, why does she have writer's block? The screen-writer smiles. He can't help thinking that such stories are ten a penny for most science-fiction writers. But the young must be allowed to discover the world for themselves. We mustn't forget that everyone's been young, that everyone's made mis-takes. For better or worse, the girl must continue working on her No World—with its extraterrestrial voices, its alien hunter who doesn't know he's an alien himself—to distract her and help mitigate her jealousy and hatred of the young conduc-tor, her growing hostility toward the brilliant composer—al-though, when she thinks about it, the brilliant composer isn't important enough to hate.

"1.3 Space is the ideal location for building the future. 1.31 Space can also be understood as the No World. 1.32 The No

World is the ideal location for building the future. 1.4 Notes on triggering a war in the City in Outer Space: loss of contact with Earth; lack of basic provisions; the inability to leave the City; fight for control of storehouses, warehouses, and grocery stores that are stocked with basic supplies, water, and fuel; a single survivor—aged, alone—wanders the streets of the desolate City in Outer Space, observing the universe from behind the windows of a control room in a military base, recording his memories of the old world, the place from which he came, his impressions of the new world, which he suspects is coming to an end, doing so as if he's writing his will; the only person who managed to survive the war; he can't trust his own mind, he says it plays tricks on him, but with nothing else to go on he records his impressions as they occur to him. He takes up a paperback edition of W, the margins of every page covered with notes, and picks a passage at random that appears near the very end: '6.54 He must transcend these initial propositions, and then he will see the No World aright.'"

In the hotel lobby, he collects the little tape recorder and cassette the girl has sent him. She's not coming tonight, so she sent him a recording of her voice instead. The screenwriter sits at his desk, smoking as he listens, with one arm resting on the typewriter. She's describing a scene in the small theater where the Little Sinfonietta rehearses. It's an interview, she says, for which some chairs have been arranged in a semicircle in front of a journalist. They're talking about being young and gifted, about how much hard work is required to achieve success, and about why they insist on championing such strange and unmelodic music. They then discuss the girl's surprising role in the piece about the clown: they mention her declamatory skills, her talent as an actress, and the journalist remarks that they're not accomplishments for which she's become well known. This leads to another question about hidden talent, the journalist asking her if there are any links between the brilliant composer's *No World Symphony* and the work he's heard she's writing. At this point, the recording cuts off then begins again with girl: "No World," she says suddenly, her voice intruding on the momentary silence, is one of those expressions like "Undead" or "Nonliving"—a play on words, or so to speak—something that derives its meaning through what it negates. Something that's known by understanding what it is not. The screenwriter wonders about this. He associates the term "undead" with something like "the living dead." He's not sure whether No World refers to a kind of resuscitated world resembling ours, or to a world that exists in another dimension. Perhaps it's really only a play on words, as she says. The screenwriter continues listening. She's been writing her work for quite a while, she lies, and always finds something wrong with it, something that impels her to start over, be it the characters, the plot, the narrative, although never the title. The title is always the same. Her work, she says, is about someone who's constantly on the run from something, be it extraterrestrials or even the world itself, by which she means this world, this planet. The girl says she writes about these things, about the world and all, because she's young, and since the young lack experience, they tend to write about stuff they're familiar with, the things they see around them everyday. The journalist then asks her in jest if she has many alien friends. I hear voices, she confesses, aware that it sounds like a cliché. She says they call her by name, except they mispronounce the first syllable, always saying "ka" instead of "k." It's difficult to explain, she adds. Then the recording cuts off again. Some moments later, it starts up with the girl describing what's going on around her. After he answers each question, she says, the young conductor always looks at my mother for signs of approval. He also hears an oracular statement whose context he assumes was lost the last time the recording cut off. He rewinds the tape again and again, but no matter how many times he hears the sentence, he can't quite understand it. "2.063 The sum-total of reality is the No World."

He needs to see her again, but he's not sure if she'll keep visiting him in the middle of the night. Something's changed. It could be the concerts she's to give every evening, or it could be that her mother's returned, and she's being forced to keep up appearances. After transcribing everything in the recordings, as if it were dialogue for a scene in his movie, the screenwriter decides to take a break. He scavenges the fridge and settles for a meal comprised of last night's leftovers. Then he lights a cigarette and turns to look for his neighbor in the building across the street. He doesn't see her: the window of her apartment is a rectangular void. He examines the front of the building. It's really composed of two buildings: one with balconies and the other with just windows. Most of the doors leading onto the balconies have blinds and there aren't any flowers outside. He scans the storefronts along the street: the real-estate agency on the corner, the lingerie store, the bakery, and the shoe and handbag store that's closed for the August vacation. The last store makes him think of his wife. He switches his thoughts back to the screenplay. The most important thing, he says, is the construction. The dialogue can be added later on. He might even get someone else to write it. He remembers the most important thing about planning a script is to know the ending before the beginning, to have a good idea of the storyline, and then to proceed by gradual steps toward that ending. Any other approach would be like running around in circles. Despite the fact he knows better, the screenwriter still tends to run around in circles. Perhaps though, he knows the end of his story better than he lets on. He moves away from the desk and sits on the bed next to the telephone. He dials his wife's number. In all the screenplays he's written up to this point, he's always had the same problem: giving enough weight and meaning to each dramatic moment—or, if he manages that, giving meaning and continuity to a series of moments, to a series of scenes, acts, and finally to the whole story. In times of crisis, it helps him to encapsulate the problem as just that. He listens until the fifth ring, then hangs up. He's surprised, but he would've liked her to answer this time. He returns to his surveillance of his neighbor's window. He'll go crazy if he doesn't see the girl. He flicks his cigarette butt into the darkness, grabs his coat, and goes downstairs to hail a cab. The girl's mother doesn't know him. They've never met because she's never accompanied her daughter to the Scholastic Institute. In the doorway of the church, he introduces himself as her literature teacher, telling her he's on vacation and was reading about the concerts in the local newspaper, so he decided to drop by and say hello. The girl's mother lets him through. He won't be allowed meet the musicians until after the concert, but he agrees to join her in the reserved seating area. During the girl's performance, the screenwriter occasionally jots in his notebook. He waits until the intermission to inform the girl's mother that he's writing a screenplay about talented young musicians. She thanks him for encouraging her daughter to read that actor cum dramatist cum impresario from the end of the sixteenth and beginning of seventeenth centuries whose works she now devours like a cormorant. The screenwriter chalks it up to his duties as a teacher, and justifies the girl's excesses by arguing that literature can take possession of the soul, has the power to render one positively demoniac. Her mother asks that he recommend another author now, as the girl's possession by this particular demon is taking its toll, She hints specifically at a contemporary of the dramatist, a novelist who lacked the use of one arm. The screenwriter applauds her choice, says there is much to be learned from him about the human condition: he writes about love and deceit, madness and sanity, dreams and wakefulness, life and death—the whole gamut basically—giving us a veritable portrait of the world. We take it for granted now, but no one had written about these things before, described them so exhaustively and in so much detail. People haven't changed much in the last three thousand years, and perhaps this writer's greatest accomplishment is that he managed to etch all our absurdities into a single novel, transformed all our frailties into a work of fiction. Despite his encomium, the screenwriter doesn't mention his reservations about this novelist's greatest work, for he doesn't want to contradict the mother, because, in fact, he believes the novelist's most famous protagonist is something of a wastrel—what with all his pointless wanderings about and endless searches for new adventures. Perhaps he feels slightly embarrassed about voicing such criticisms, considering some of the sillier aspects of his own script. But the screenwriter shrugs away his insecurity. His conversation with the mother has come to an end anyway, and his blushes have gone unnoticed. After the concert, the girl's mother takes the screenwriter to meet the musicians. The young orchestra conductor and brilliant composer greet him warmly. The girl, on the other hand, goes pale. He turns to look at the young men's smiling faces, and notes the contrast with her cold and distant aspect. The screenwriter gauges their reactions and starts wondering if the young men even knew he was in the neighboring country's capital. They discuss the concert, most notably the affect on the audience of a well-known pianist reciting verses in a clown suit. The girl is the star of the show, although she barely takes any notice of the fact. Maybe this is what captivates the audience, the screenwriter thinks. The discussion moves on to poetry, the kind that's subversive, irreverent, and needless to say, unrhymed, but which nonetheless has an energetic rhythm that sustains itself through the work. What a fine poet the clown's creator was! although he's completely unknown to the laity. They discuss experimentation, for which the brilliant composer has a stronger predilection than the rest. Composers, it would seem, have a natural bent for trailblazing, and true artists must experiment with new approaches, investigate new ways to advance their vision. Since the screenwriter was once a teacher at the Scholastic Institute, he knows a thing or two about music, about the importance of certain musical parameters such as volume, pitch, and tempo, and he tries discussing them with the brilliant composer whenever he has his ear. The composer complains about the difficulty of premiering a new work. The screenwriter proposes he imagine twelve-tone music was never invented—no serialism, or any of it. But the girl's mother interrupts the discussion by suggesting they all go to dinner. During the meal, the screenwriter continues taking notes, and accompanies the group afterward when they head to a trendy café. They are joined by some people that are unknown to the girl and the rest of the group as well. They're probably friends of the concert promoters, says her mother, unconcerned. Among them are patrons, musicians, variety acts, a hypnotist, and the young conductor's latest conquest. The girl waits until her mother's back is turned, then approaches the screenwriter. If you intrude on my life one more time, you'll never see me again. The hypnotist puts a young man into a trance—a circus performer who said he's been having trouble with one of the numbers in his show. She commands him to make no more mistakes, snaps him back to reality, and then requests he perform the routine. Although he doesn't have his equipment, he tries to improvise with some coffee spoons, performing a juggling act while blindfolded, which everyone applauds. The young conductor of the orchestra proposes the girl be hypnotized next, because she's under a lot of pressure to achieve great things in her life. The girl goes along with it, since everyone's laughing and having a good time. She tells the hypnotist she wants to be a great writer. So the hypnotist puts her in a trance, and while in that state, assures her and everyone present she's going to be a great writer. This in spite of the fact she's not yet written anything of note. The girl awakens and asks what happened. Nobody responds, except the young conductor who tells her she had a little fainting spell, nothing more.

By the early hours of the morning, there are only a few survivors from the previous night, and they continued drinking heavily long after the girl's mother left. At some point during the night, the screenwriter suggested the girl read S's sonnets, and that, instead of writing, she should study the piano works of B, H, M, or C. They say you run out of time, that after the age of twenty, if you haven't already mastered the whole repertoire, something will be lacking for the rest of your life. At some other point in the evening, the screenwriter told the girl about an early film by the director of the movie in which an angel can hear other people's voices. He wants to listen to the soundtrack of the film. The music is ideal for his screenplay. The brilliant composer, overhearing the conversation, proposes writing an original soundtrack to supplement the one the screenwriter's talking about. It would be a simple mathematical exercise, he says. Then the screenwriter gets the impression he must have lost consciousness for a moment, because when he comes to, the girl is no longer beside him. He must have dozed off. He checks his watch. It's gotten late. Too late to do anything, he says, without quite knowing what he means. He doubts she'll show up back at the hotel tonight, but what worries him the most is the possibility he ruined everything with his intrusion. A simple mathematical exercise, repeats the brilliant composer, his back against a wall at the other end of the table, his legs stretched out along the length of a bench. He's no longer talking about the soundtrack, though. The screenwriter stopped paying attention when he started thinking about the girl, or perhaps it's because he fell asleep. Each successive number in the series is the sum of the two that preceded it, the composer continues, and if you pick a number far enough along and divide it by the number immediately following it, the result approximates the golden ratio, or 1.618. If he hadn't had so much to drink, the screenwriter might be able to get his head around the compositional method the young man is talking about. He'd probably even ask a couple of questions, if only to be polite, but he's too tired, and the words aren't coming. Besides, who said he's even talking about a compositional method? The screenwriter has only ever heard the golden ratio spoken of with reference to architecture or painting. He decides to leave his queries for another day and, instead, feigns comprehension by nodding his head a couple of times, biding his time until the opportunity comes for him to leave without saying good-bye. The brilliant composer watches him as he skulks away, but maintains his decumbent position on the bench, too comfortable to move or even say good-bye himself, although, eventually, languidly, he raises his arm and mumbles good-bye, as if bidding farewell to a vanishing ghost. Then he takes a cough-syrup bottle filled with cognac from his pocket and empties it to the dregs. Maybe he's had too much to drink, the screenwriter hears someone say on exiting. They could be talking about him; they could be talking about the brilliant composer; either way, the screenwriter thinks, they're telling the truth. On his way back to the hotel, he writes a scene in which the girl and young conductor quarrel over her interpretations of the *5 Pieces for piano* and the *No World Symphony*. It's an argument provoked mainly by jealousy: his for the girl's fame, hers for the young conductor's philandering. It's the same one from last night, the brilliant composer assures the girl, referring to the young conductor's latest conquest, who's been stuck to his hip all night. Perhaps what's going on between the girl and young conductor of the orchestra is only a game, the screenwriter muses, as he imagines the girl back at the hotel with the English name, sitting alone in her room, restless, distrait, looking out the window, deep in thought perhaps, remembering the strange looks exchanged between the young conductor and her mother. He's finding it difficult to pin down the essentials of his story. He's certain it's because he drank too much. But if not today, he'll do it sooner or later, he promises himself. In an alcoholic haze, the screenwriter sees the girl and young conductor as being completely devoted to the game. After each of their battles, they probably keep a tally of all their victims, he thinks; perhaps by making notches in their instruments. The screenwriter thinks he might well be one of the girl's pawns, but he quickly sweeps the thought from his mind, unable to imagine he's merely the victim of a jealous tit-for-tat between young lovers. He turns to look at the streets below, dark, empty, on which he's still hoping the numinous figure of the girl will appear. Suddenly, he hears a taxi approaching; but it passes without slowing. He raises his eyes to the building across the street, sees only a rectangular void where he hoped to catch sight his neighbor. Then, as if for the first time, he examines the front of the building and notices, as if for the first time, there are in fact two different buildings. He looks at the storefronts again: the real estate agency on the corner, the bakery, the shop selling women's lingerie, and the shoe and handbag store that's closed for the August vacation. He thinks about his wife again; remembers the sexy panties he bought, which are lying idle in the back of the closet. But it doesn't matter, the girl isn't coming.

Nothing matters now except the writing. It's all she thinks about since being hypnotized. Nothing else in her life makes sense anymore, and she doesn't care how the change happened, what the trance did to her, because now not only does she know what she wants to do, she's determined to get it done. The act of writing has become an end in itself, despite the newspapers back in the screenwriter's native city acclaiming her success and that of the Little Sinfonietta, publishing loads of pictures, and giving her the kind of coverage usually accorded to more serious, newsworthy topics. The screenwriter knows that only a person with plenty of clout and lots of contacts could make that happen. His leg hurts, a sign it's going to rain. Even so, he ventures outside and heads for the National Museum of Modern Art. It starts raining, so he seeks shelter in a café. Some of the customers are reading, others conversing, a few are staring at the sidewalk being spattered by rain. The screenwriter thinks he'd be able to write if he were sitting in a café in the neighboring country's capital. He's thought this ever since he got home. Maybe the girl will also become one of those people who write in cafés. The windows are open here, allowing sparrows to flutter in and make themselves part of the décor, gadding about competing for crumbs left on the tables or whatever the customers let fall on the floor. If the girl was here, she'd sit beside the window and admire the Museum building, which the screenwriter thinks a singular structure; she'd probably throw crumbs at the sparrows too, while rambling on about the direction her life is going in, and perhaps mention the first chapter of her book or talk about her novel as a whole, with which she'll confess she's at last getting somewhere. Perhaps she'd write in her diary that she no longer doubts herself because, since being hypnotized, she feels as if the scales have fallen from her eyes and her literary objectives become completely clear. The screenwriter too thinks he knows where his story should go, but he still deliberates, goes over it again and again, before committing a single thought to paper. It seems the rain's died down, so he crosses the plaza and heads for the museum, limping slowly, so as not to slip and fall. The clouds are low, the wind cool and blustery. It might start raining again, he thinks while standing in the ticket line with a bunch of tourists, who flock to his native capital, attracted by its fame and allure. Once inside, he goes up to the floor where all the most important works are displayed. He exaggerates his limp, pauses before each painting, affecting a grave expression, while all he's really thinking about is his script. He wants to plan it out systematically but always struggles to keep the story's structure in mind long enough to commit it to paper. Occasionally, he gets distracted by the paintings, a few of which he finds totally bewildering. It's clear to him not everyone on Earth has the same taste in

Art, or anything else for that matter. His thoughts return to the script and the girl, whose daily routine has suffered an upheaval. Now, all she wants to do is write, anything else is a distraction. If she practices the piano at all, it's out of a sense of professional duty, or as preparation for an impending recording session. The screenwriter thinks of a scene he imagines will transpire later in the evening, beginning at the moment the girl arrives at the church in front of the writer's café. She's arriving late, the screenwriter thinks. That's the phrase he'll begin with, the phrase with which he'll start his recapitulation of that morning's events. He goes over to the museum café to sit on a balcony that offers a panoramic view of the lobby. She's arriving late, he thinks again. A few tables down, a guy is sitting with his legs resting on a chair. He's facing the other way, scooted up close to the railings, observing the constant procession of museumgoers entering and exiting the building. The screenwriter orders the daily special, about which the only thing special is its reasonable price. Then, before leaving, he strikes his cane hard against the floor and points it at the guy with his legs up. You're getting that chair dirty, he says. The man puts his feet on the ground, and the screenwriter turns away, smiling. She's arriving late, he repeats to himself, the phrase that will begin his next scene.

He slept longer than he intended, and when he woke up, he waited, as if he had nothing better to do, and now that she's finally with him, he just looks at her, stares at her from his little nook beside the window, as if the fact that she's now there justified all the waiting. Blindfolded, kneeling on the bed, the girl plays with herself, rubs herself through her panties, pushing them into herself, her body writhing slowly, trembling, her other arm softly grazing a nipple, as she continues mas-

105

turbating, doubled over with pleasure, manipulating the fine silk between her legs, each movement of her hand eliciting a spasm. She bites her lip. Her blindfold prevents her from seeing the screenwriter, who's looking through a crack in the curtains at the darkness of his neighbor's window. How grateful he would be, grateful to God and all the angels in heaven, if the woman suddenly appeared. He'd fling open the curtains, as if to reveal a stage, on which the girl lies naked on his bed, masturbating for his own private delectation, and perhaps that of his neighbor, as long as she consented to play the voyeur. But the darkness in the window doesn't change, so he goes over to the girl, who senses his approach, and the screenwriter, unable to bridle his lust, tears off her panties and buries his face in them. Before long, come the tremors, the earthquakes, and then the world collapsing beneath them.

The only true paradises are the ones we lose. Or perhaps they're the ones we imagine. Time and space don't exist outside the mind, and after all, nothingness is the girl's favorite topic of discussion, if only during those brief intervals when she feels at ease—safe from her extraterrestrial stalkers. There's an infinitesimally small point, a point so small we'd probably need a magnifying glass, or something more powerful like an electron microscope to see it, and even then it would probably be undetectable. This is the point from which everything begins. But being undetectable, perhaps we have to trust in its existence by a leap of faith. What really matters though is not the object in itself, whether it exists objectively, so to speak, but the fact we can perceive it at all, and perception, being subjective, is as multifarious as the number of people that comprise the human race. So external reality, as any one of us perceives it, must be considered only one among many realities. Only the girl can hear the difference between "ka" and "k"; only she knows the world isn't real, that it's only a projection from a single point, the thoughtlet of a single mind, or—as she calls it—the big bang. In his world, the screenwriter finds it difficult to understand nothingness, whether it's true to say "nothing" exists, or that "nothing" does not exist. He's read something about it before. There is no difference, the girl explains, because neither is real, neither the infinitesimally small point before the big bang, nor the big bang itself. The truth is they're a fabrication—a metaphor conceived by the mind to account for and makes sense of its own existence. The screenwriter seems to be thinking about something else she's said. The official version, the one you read in the textbooks, is just as hard to accept, she declares: that nothingness is a miniscule point of departure loaded with matter, and that from this point the whole universe arose. If there really was nothing there, wouldn't it be just as plausible to say this miniscule point was loaded with thought? The discussion ends. A minute passes, perhaps an hour. Every now and then, the screenwriter looks into the girl's eyes, focusing on some point in space reflected there. The girl eventually rouses herself from semi-consciousness, as if returning from some distant region in space, climbs out of the bed, and gets dressed. Do you know my father's been to the church? she asks, half-yawning. She draws open the curtains and looks out the window, scanning the streets for the shadow that persistently stalks her. He doesn't come to hear me play, she says while lighting a joint. People change, he says while reaching to partake of a drag. Well, maybe, she says while proffering him one.

She's going to be late. She spent most of the day writing before going for a long walk in the city, wandering here and there, not sticking to a specified route, because the only thing on her mind was writing. As always, she's going to be late for rehearsals. With the church closed to the public, the young conductor's going over some final details with the other musicians, reviewing some tricky passages they haven't been performing very well the past few days. Then the girl's mother arrives and reads some reviews to them from the city's major newspapers to them. She glosses over any negative comments and gushes about the critics' unanimous praise, about the length of the queues outside the church, which she says exceeded everyone's expectations. The girl's surprised her mother kept this news from them until now. There will be even more coverage because of this, she predicts, more critical acclaim, and many more lucrative offers. This is a turning point in all your careers. The girl's mother is always talking business. Even when she seems to be discussing music, she's thinking business. The girl peeks out to watch the people taking their seats. Although they don't say it, the girl knows perfectly well what the young orchestra conductor and brilliant composer want in life: an opportunity to triumph on the stage, to alter the course of modern music, to be thought revolutionaries by future generations who'll speak of their influence in terms what came before and what came after them: ambition is as old as life itself—as old as desire. And the girl's desire is to be a writer. She turns from the audience toward her two colleagues. Perhaps it's an innocent question, perhaps it's a part of the game, but she wants to know what she should do about her literary ambitions. Nothing, they say. Just focus on the music, play the piano, maybe you could write librettos for the brilliant composer. The girl believes they should be the ones writing librettos for her. She's the only star among them. But she shouldn't be worrying about this now, all this squabbling and pointless rivalry, when there's a concert to perform. The young conductor says accidental elements should be included in the music, for, although submerged, they form part of a unity in which each decision, each act, has intended and unintended repercussions, but the unintended shouldn't be eliminated because they're accidental, because everything works together toward the same end, which is to evoke the one meaning, one image, one thought that encapsulates the work. Just like in the game. The girl believes this can be accomplished only in two things: fiction or insanity. She wonders if this kind of thinking will prevent their ever playing foosball together again, or being happy the way they used to be: used to be, she can barely remember it now. Maybe he's just being sensational, has all her mother's talk of marketing and promotion on the brain. All the girl wants to do is go back to her hotel room and write. About what she doesn't know, she just wants to write. She peeks out at the audience again. There are people of all ages. Some are fans, others came to see what the fuss is about, but they all want to be wowed by the precocious young musicians, and by the girl, the starlet. Children whose parents hope they will emulate her sit upright in their seats, waiting excitedly, and the girl smiles sardonically at the prospect of one of them succeeding her. She recognizes a couple of familiar faces in the first row, including the young conductor's latest conquest. The brilliant composer remarks on the Little Sinfonietta's popularity. Maybe they didn't come just to see the clown's nose, he sneers, but are actually interested in the music.

While waving to the audience at the end of the second part, the girl spots her father sitting next to a pillar. It's strange. He usually doesn't attend her concerts, especially when they're abroad. The girl spends the intermission debating whether or not to go out and talk to him. Then someone announces the third part is about to begin. It's the part in which she sings, or recites almost, a confusing and disturbing series of verses which give the impression they were inspired by a strange vision or hallucination, or the effects of a psychotropic pill: at least according to a modern interpretation. During her recitation, the girl looks out at the auditorium, her voice, enveloping, bewitching the audience, creates an atmosphere of unease. Dressed as a clown brandishing a bloody knife, wandering in a desolate landscape covered in craters, it's not quite clear what she's looking at exactly, because she seems completely focused on the lyrics she's reciting, a seemingly interminable series of lyrics. Perhaps she's looking for her father in the audience, or maybe, unconsciously, for the young conductor's latest conquest, who hasn't left his side in days. The girl's won over the crowd, and she gets the impression the performance has gone as well or better than on previous nights. There are even people outside on the plaza who couldn't get in. After the concert, the girl takes her father to the writer's café opposite the church. He's going to be in the neighboring country's capital for longer than he expected. I needed a vacation, he tells her. A vacation? she asks, detecting a lie. Well maybe it's also something to do with work, he admits. They sit at the bar and discuss the concert program together, keeping well away from the other musicians, especially the young conductor and his latest conquest, who are sitting at a table in the back with the girl's mother. The girl's father can't make heads or tails of the repertoire, but he deduces from the audience's reaction and the critical reception that there must be something to it. He finds it odd she performs in a clown suit. What did you imagine the concert would be like? she asks him. But he doesn't know, he's never seen this side of her before, he's only ever thought of her as a pianist. Is there really an audience for this kind of music? Are other musicians the only ones who attend these kinds of concerts? Is this the kind of music musicians are writing nowadays? The girl points out the fact that many parents have brought their pianist children to see her play so they can follow her example. Maybe it's all the publicity that attracts them, all the hype, a false image created by the newspapers. They move on to other subjects, both of them endeavoring to avoid an argument: she not mentioning her recent literary afflatus, he putting his friendliest side forward—this being his daughter's special night; she not admitting the real reason the night was special—that her father finally showed up; and he not realizing his daughter feels this way, or perhaps choosing to ignore it. A woman approaches the girl and asks her to sign a concert stub. Her father says he's staying in a hotel in front of the Grand Central Station. Maybe he'll visit her again another day. As he leaves, he pauses at the doorway to say good-bye. She goes over and kisses him, embraces him. She would've liked to go to dinner, to be rescued from the nightmare awaiting her back inside. Are you on duty? she asks, noticing the bulge on his hip. He smiles in a routine manner that could be interpreted in any way, with an expression that could be said to express absolutely nothing.

The screenwriter doesn't think he's forgotten anything important. He extinguishes his cigarette and takes a deep breath, puts his glasses on the desk next to the typewriter, leans back and closes his eyes. He allows some time to pass by, enough to accommodate a daydream, before opening them again to examine a few photos of the girl. He took them a while back, well before his trip to the neighboring country's capital. He goes through them slowly one by one, scrutinizing every detail. ONE: a photo of the girl posing nude, seated at the piano. A classic pose and well captured. TWO: a photo of the girl posing nude with her arms crossed standing next to the piano. Perhaps it's the way the light hits her face, or the way she's standing—a pose he's seen her enact when fully-clothed—or the music she played that day, the notes that still resound in his ear, but he doesn't know, can't determine what it is that makes this photograph so special to him. THREE: a photo of the girl posing nude, stretched out on the piano. Her white skin contrasts exquisitely with the black lacquered finish on the instrument. FOUR: a photo of the girl posing nude, blindfolded, clenching in her teeth one end of a piece of ribbon, which passes between her legs and up along her back; the other end in her hands, clutched tightly above her head. FIVE: a photo of the girl posing nude, a piece of ribbon around her neck, which passes between her legs, tying her wrists behind her back. SIX: a photo of the girl posing nude, standing in the tub, holding a vessel over her head which she tips slightly, letting a trickle of water fall on her face. Also in the picture, seen from behind, is her old teacher, naked, kneeling on the ground, passing a sponge over her body. SEVEN: a photo of the girl posing nude in front of a large canvas on which she's painting with a thick brush; beside her are two bottles of paint, one blue, one yellow. There's paint everywhere—on the ground as much as on the canvas, and all over the girl's body, especially her arms and legs. She's covering every inch of the canvas with writing—disconnected phrases about nothingness, "ka," space and time, and so on. They're fine photographs, the screenwriter thinks as he goes through them. They may be a little crude, and perhaps a professional could tell at a glance they're the work of an amateur, but they're still quite good. He had a famous photographer in mind when he took them, one who's well-known for his images of domineering women, always depicting them as being cold and aloof. The girl couldn't pull it off though, she needs a few more years on her, but there's something about her attitude, the look in her eyes, which suggests she has the potential. Maybe that's her strength. He regrets not taking a photo of her wearing the tuxedo, the silken black necktie, and her mother's high heel shoes, the latter perhaps a little too big for her. A photograph in which she's almost nude, he thinks, but not quite.

Do you know what I think about before I fall asleep? the girl asks on the other end of the telephone. He doesn't know. Aliens, she says. The screenwriter looks at his watch. Only an hour before he goes to bed, but he likes listening to her voice. The girl can't sleep. She feels she should be writing, despite the fact she's not getting anywhere with it. Instead, she records her ideas and impressions, filling whole pages of her notebook. Inspiration is impending, so close she can almost touch it, and she can't possibly go to sleep until she does. So she decides to go over everything again: the plot, the argument, the characters, their attributes, every detail and all the links between them. She hasn't assimilated enough to begin writing yet: the details of her story must be fully digested first, fully incorporated, as it were, for they must become a part of her. The screenwriter listens to her patiently. Why extra-terrestrials? he asks himself. It's neither new nor original. Though her idea is as original as things get, he thinks, referring the girl's notion that every living thing on Earth is an alien but doesn't know it. The screenwriter's annoyed at having to waste so much time discussing sci-fi hokum; it's a genre no one takes seriously. Literature shouldn't be divided into genres anyway, he thinks. There should only be good books and bad books. Science fiction! he grumbles to himself, as the dawn starts peeping timorously into the room. If these beings exist in another galaxy, continues the girl, they'd have to travel faster than the speed of light, since it takes thousands of years for light to reach us even from the nearest star. Who knows, perhaps these beings experience time differently, perhaps a thousand years isn't such a long time for them, and covering such distances may in fact be commonplace. They've probably found a way to move freely through the universe, perhaps by using a doorway or portal, like in the movies, portals connecting far-flung regions of the cosmos through wormholes tunneled in the fabric of space-time. In the movies, they call it a gateway to the stars, or something like that.

He slept the whole morning, and needed a couple of coffees to bring him out of his stupor. Then he collected his clothes from the laundry place: in the neighboring country's capital, the price of even getting one's laundry done is extortionate. He should try harder to stick to his schedule, whatever the circumstances, no matter how tempting the opportunity to deviate from it. He goes to his desk and tries to get down to work. He let himself get carried away, almost to the point of believing the girl's idea that a universe full of extraterrestrials emerged from a single miniscule point. But she doesn't imagine just one universe, one point of origin, but many, existing in parallel—stories, some unique, some with alternate beginnings and endings, even some that don't have a beginning or an ending at all, that don't have a continuous narrative or identifiable characters, for the literary fashion is always changing, and who knows, perhaps the number of parallel universes is infinite. The screenwriter sets this conundrum aside for the time being, and considers another problem. Perhaps he should've made the girl older. Some of the scenes he's describing won't be suitable on film. Not that he's going to rewrite them. Any concessions made for the sake of convenience or to resolve contradictions in the story would make him a liar and a copout. He needs the tender inexperience, the raw sexuality of someone young, very young in fact. He switches on the TV. Three people are having a discussion about television as a medium for quality programming. A fourth person, who must be the moderator, asks them if quality is even possible on TV. Being old gives you a new perspective on things, the screenwriter thinks. The same controversies tend to arise again and again. This debate has been going on since moving pictures were invented. Depending on his mood, he could argue quite well for either position. He's done so in the past. He's inclined to believe quality isn't possible, but right now, since he's sitting in front of the TV, he doesn't mind suspending his disbelief, along with his inclination toward debate for its own sake. The discussion doesn't really matter to him anyway. Perhaps it's because he's only an old curmudgeon at heart, someone with no real convictions; and perhaps this is because of the way he's lived his life. He thinks about this, but can't ascertain where exactly he went wrong, what led him to become so cynical. Nevertheless, he knows it's true. He switches through the channels. Nothing worth watching. He looks at his watch. Too early for porn. So he turns off the TV and returns to the typewriter. Those disputes about quality, artistic merit, arise again and again, in each generation. No thinking person can avoid them, including the girl. Although, at the moment, she only thinks about one thing, her one desire in life, perhaps it's an illusion, unreachable, something so close she can almost touch it, but perhaps it will always be out of reach. She feels like a writer. Being hypnotized instilled an inexorable belief in her. "2.223 To determine if a No World is true or false one must compare it with reality. 2.224 Reality doesn't exist." She revisits the idea of aliens from another planet being unaware of their origins. They came from their mothers' wombs. This fact alone precludes their ever learning the truth about what they really are, and where they really come from. It's the most extraordinary way to protect a secret. To live their whole lives and never be cured of an unwitting blindness, a disease they don't even know they have. It's not likely to be the Earth's atmosphere that caused them to forget, something she's already considered, but rather a kind of innate programming. But why make them forget? For their own protection. But protection from what? From something she can't even begin to fathom. Is there a planet in the universe called Ka? "6.5 If the No World provides questions, it also provides answers." There is a girl with heightened perceptions who intuits that something isn't right. It's undoubtedly a defect in her programming. This girl has a peculiar feeling her name isn't her real name, in the same way her father's name isn't really his. Sometimes, she hears people pronouncing it differently, wrongly; at other times, disembodied voices do so. The phenomenon is so bewildering she can't share her thoughts with anyone, because no one else understands what's going on. She hears them pronounce her name with the letter k, but the difference is subtle when her name is pronounced with a "ka" instead of a "k" sound. And there's the rub. "4. The thought is the significant proposition." It seems a crazy person has introduced herself into the novel. She feels strange when she writes "ka," not knowing if it refers to her name or the name of a distant planet. She stops writing and forces herself to think. She couldn't say how many times she's begun writing only to subsequently destroy what she'd written. Now she writes every day, it doesn't matter what. Perhaps it's something about the mission she's been entrusted with, to penetrate the mystery of "ka" or "k." She knows she's a writer. She's heard it said that practice and experience lead to inspiration. *No World* could be the story of an old professor, an alien hunter, who fled from his hometown and settled in the City in Outer Space. It's also the story of Cousin Dedalus, at least what she's written so far, because she's still afraid to tackle the next part, and would rather take her mind off it and focus on another character. He could be old, as old as the screenwriter, she tells herself, but from whom or what could this character be running? From himself perhaps, or his wife, maybe some people from his hometown. Another alien, she eventually decides, but one who isn't aware he's an alien. Slowly, the screenwriter considers the possible options. He used to describe the writing of a screenplay as the reverse of a police investigation. Now he's trying to remember why. Probably because there's no difference between the acts of constructing a fictional story from memory and imagination, and reconstructing a crime scene from evidence, at least in the way the mind operates. The screenwriter imagines a voiceover reciting some of the girl's work, an ideal way to present her writings if he spreads her narration evenly through the script. If he begins with a voiceover, he should use it again periodically throughout the movie, to remind the audience who's telling the story. Of course, the character telling the story is the girl, and her voice reminds us of the special way she views the world. She continues writing about the alien hunter who fled to the City in Outer Space. A guy who could be her Cousin Dedalus, except much older, perhaps the screenwriter himself, her old literature teacher, except this one teaches philosophy. He went there to reinvent himself, start his life over, even though he isn't as reliant on place to do so, on being situated somewhere, having a home, as most people are. Then there's the idea that

117

nothing exists outside the mind, that there's no external reality, that everything is conceived in the imagination: a hypothesis that allows each individual mind to create its own world, its own universe, from scratch. The kinds of minds that are unable to determine their own origins, she says to herself, minds that tend to sublimate their uncertainty in works of fiction, a book about people who don't know they're aliens, for example. This uncertainty could simply be the whim of a creator. To what end, though? she asks herself. Why create worlds at all, why populate them with characters, imbue them with intelligence, make them think they're alive? And why only one creator, a single being that's responsible for the existence of everything else, that regards everything else as its own possession? Let's suppose nothing around us really exists. Could each of these characters' minds then falsely conceive of millions of other minds, each of them unique, each of them believing itself to be central? Could each of these independent minds organize themselves into a system of networks, each node of which is somehow self-created, self-imagined, and yet at the center of everything? Could each of these minds believe they are God? Yes, replies a voice inside her. They could.

The screenwriter stops typing and turns toward the building across the street. He's not looking at anything in particular, for his thoughts are elsewhere. He wonders if he'll ever see through the onion layers of his screenplay, and if his idea of superposing different stories together in one script—one of them real, the rest fictitious, but keeping the viewer guessing which is which—could make for a decent movie, and if there's someone out there who could even bring such a concept to the big screen. He doubts such a person exists today, a professional reminiscent of one of the greats from a bygone era. By his reckoning, the greatest difficulty is in preventing one narrative predominating over the rest. But his thinking has lately become disjointed and diffuse. It's been days since he thought about McGregor, the strange voice that one day asked to speak to the girl's father, a voice which could be that of her guardian angel from the planet Ka, an angel like the one in the movie who can hear other people's voices, perhaps those of everyone on Earth. He thinks it's amazing because it's such a recent movie too, not belonging to the golden age, when movies of true quality were de rigueur—before they lost their soul, as he'd say. The girl would say the voices are responsible for his seeing the movie in this way, he thinks. And that they've influenced many other things besides. It's time for a change, to find a turning point. The screenwriter fetches his index cards and searches through the headings for "McGregor." It's not good for a character to disappear from a story for so long.

The Little Sinfonietta has extended its run of performances by a week, which will include a tour of the provinces. It's also emerged that a record company has expressed an interest in signing them. The girl listens to the news indifferently. She already has a contract with another label, and the provincial cities don't matter very much to her. In fact, neither do the capital cities of the world. The Little Sinfonietta has some important decisions to make in the coming hours. The girl won't be involved. She doesn't care what they decide. Her future is writing. This is no longer a game, but a serious business, she hears her mother say, admonishing the younger musicians. A game: It's as if she's tapped into the girl's private thoughts on the matter, and also those of the young conductor and brilliant composer. The game was a secret. Until now, only the three of them were privy to it. The girl's eyes flit to the young conductor. She stares fixedly at him, waiting for a reaction to what her mother said, but he acts as if nothing's changed. It's all a game. Only one step further, that's all it's going to take, just one step. But the girl's mother isn't going to hold their hands anymore. It's not her job. They should elect a representative, a manager, to handle their affairs. Later, during a tumultuous business dinner, they discuss contracts, albums, and the subject of fame, the responsibilities involved—about which they interrogate the girl, for she's experienced it, asking about her travels, how many celebrities she knows. She doesn't answer. To break an awkward silence, someone inquires whether one becomes more famous after death. There are cemeteries that are only famous for the people buried in them, opines one of the more recent additions to their group. In any major city, it's easy to find a cemetery teeming with illustrious dead, but this is especially true in the neighboring country's capital, where the cemeteries have become major tourist attractions, providing maps to the tombs of their famous occupants, the more notable graves bearing a plaque with a brief biography. The girl considers visiting one of these cemeteries. She asks if there's one near the hotel. No one answers. It seems they didn't hear the question, or perhaps they're giving her reticence tit for tat. Nonetheless, the new arrival starts listing the names of some famous writers buried in a particular cemetery. It's decided. She'll go. In one of the nightclubs where the group often stays until the early hours of the morning, the young conductor of the orchestra is chatting away, beleaguered by a bunch of admirers. The girl spends the whole night sitting beside her mother. Maybe she ought to visit one of those graveyards, and sit beside the graves writing elegies under the moonlight. What's preoccupying you? asks her mother. The girl shrugs her shoulders. Nothing, nothing at all. But she immediately changes her attitude and suggests a visit to the cemetery. To pay tribute to those great authors who, in their work, still manage to address our present age. Stop talking nonsense! her mother scolded her. Do you know the time? the girl asks, watching the young conductor dancing in a corner with his latest conquest. She then searches for the rest of the group, to recruit some volunteers to accompany her on an impromptu visit to the graveyard. Each will write a poem about a dead novelist, and a novel about a dead poet, excepting the young conductor and his conquest, who can dance on top of the tombs. Perhaps they'll even dance over their own graves, she thinks, smiling. She looks everywhere for them, but it seems the pair have now disappeared. I'm leaving, whispers the girl to her mother, under the watchful eyes of some other members of the group who are getting ready to exclude themselves from an incursion on the cemetery, with some moving stealthily off, fearing they may be dragged there against their will. Her mother gives her a hug and asks her to speak openly with her. She is her mother, after all. The girl rises from the sofa, her eyes on the dance floor, lost in a haze of dry ice. You should consider yourself lucky, her mother rebukes her. You should consider yourself an idiot, mutters the girl.

It's a pity neither the dramatist of the late sixteenth and early seventeenth centuries nor the writer who revolutionized twentieth-century literature are buried in the neighboring country's capital. What an opportunity it would be to sit beside their tombs, only feet away from where their bodies lay, and read their works aloud. The girl is wandering the streets in search of a taxi to take her back to the hotel. She doesn't find one, so she continues on foot along a wide avenue where, from a distance, she spots the young conductor and his latest conquest entering a nightclub. So she decides to enter as well, if for no other reason than to spoil their party. She sits at the bar, drinking lugubriously, at first mixing the contents of a cough-syrup bottle into a soft drink and then just drinking straight from the bottle. Although the bill won't reflect it, she's already drunk far too much alcohol, even for her. Nevertheless, she still thinks she can bring her plan to fruition. A black guy is dancing alone in the middle of the dance floor, so she moves into range in order to be able to make eye contact with him. Half distracted, the young conductor watches the proceedings with a sideways glance, trying to conceal a slight grin. The girl starts chatting with the black guy. He has doubts, suspects an ulterior motive. She takes his hand and leads him away from the dance floor. Do you have any condoms? she asks him. The black guy nods affirmatively, patting his side pocket. They lock themselves in one of the booths. She drops a pill, offers one to him, and then tells him to unbutton his pants. She wants to see if it's true what they say about black men. She then jerks him off with both hands before telling him to take her from behind, which he does, fondling her breasts under her white dress, thrusting slowly at first, and then picking up speed. He asks for her name. She doesn't understand why he wants to know her name. He says he just wants to know. She hesitates; then says her name is Ka. Ka? he exclaims. She tells him to stop talking. She wants to fuck, not have a conversation. The young conductor is still smiling when he sees her emerging from the back of the nightclub, offering the black guy her hand, flat, as if wanting him to read her future—this guy who just left a condom inside her—a future that should promise nothing but success. Then she walks past the young conductor, hand in hand with the black guy. Is this how you intend to improve your performance? she hears him ask behind her back.

She decides to skip her appointment with the screenwriter. She can't afford to waste any more time, she needs to write. She tiptoes in, so as not to awaken her mother. Luckily, there's a large living space separating their bedrooms. Her head's spinning, but she's looking forward to waking up in the morning and practicing her new magisterial interpretation of the *5 Pieces for piano*. But then she checks her enthusiasm, reminded that there's nothing magisterial about her current situation. She thinks about her writing, about not wasting any more time, for if the actor cum dramatist cum impresario of the late sixteenth and early seventeenth centuries was as prolific as he was, she must strive to be prolific too. Not that she valorizes quantity over quality, but she has no qualms about starting a new phase in her life this very day, about finally sitting down to begin her magnum opus, a work destined to be considered among the pinnacles of world literature. She reads a passage from another great work, a play by the dramatist, in which the protagonist, while in a cemetery, is presented with the skull of a man he knew. By contrast, the twentieth-century writer who revolutionized literature speaks of metempsychosis. She's read that the word signifies the transmigration of souls, which corresponds with her own idea of beings on Earth that don't realize they're aliens. She's drunk, and perhaps still under the influence of those pills, which would explain why she thinks she's now having a vision. An unclear vision, mind you, one she'd have difficulty putting into words. But there it is. She writes in her notebook: "*No World*. Chapter One." She's lost count of how many times she's written these same words, although now she thinks she's onto something. After a while, she finds herself writing about the usual things.

There has to be a good reason for migrating to another planet. The girl's researched various motives, but none were satisfactory: beings whose existence and that of their whole civilization depends upon their finding another planet to settle on, having exhausted the resources of their own; beings who are running away from other beings; beings with imperialistic motives; beings who want to plunder other planets for resources. She asks herself if there's anything novel about her characters being the unwitting colonists of another planet, being born there and subsequently losing all contact with their home, their past, all memory of their origins; and of having, at most, only a few chosen ones among them with the ability to hear strange voices now and then. She remembers reading somewhere that life on Earth was seeded by extraterrestrials. Why her, why is she able to intuit the truth? Is there really a fissure, a point of entry to a forgotten past, which only the chosen ones have access to? If someone from a distant planet wanted to make contact with the inhabitants of Earth, they'd choose the most sensible place. "3.41 This is the logical place. 3.411 The geometrical and the logical coincide in one place." The girl draws up a list of possible contact zones: cathedrals, stadiums, railway stations, airports, skyscrapers . . . in other words, places where large numbers of people gather. Why not a less crowded place? Because the alien hunter would surely target these places in order to interrupt any attempt to communicate, sever any link to the home planet. It's possible that what he does is forbidden, but at the same time, there are certain inhabitants of Earth who'd condone his actions, for they wouldn't tolerate aliens living among them. Some time passes, and the new day announces its arrival, dappling some flecks of light on the girl's face as she lies fast asleep on the bed, her notebook having fallen on the floor. On awakening, she remembers what she'd written the previous night about beings from another world, but then the image of the young conductor dancing with his latest conquest pops into her head. Maybe she dreamed it. She starts breathing heavily, urging herself to control her emotions, but just when she believes herself at ease, something triggers a new panic. She gets out of the bed, wanting to know the time, guessing it must be late, very late. It's midday in fact, and she hasn't written a thing, and she won't be able to write anything now either, because she's dying of a hangover. A noise in the background like an engine running monopolizes her attention. She takes the notebook from the floor. She's having a hard time focusing on nearby objects and is unable to read what she wrote during the night. After examining the pages more closely, however, she feels gratified at having written so much: not only did she fill many pages, but the handwriting on those pages is very small. Her mother left a note on the piano. She'll see her at the church tonight. The girl hurriedly dresses, almost stumbling, and runs out the door to grab a taxi. She directs the driver to take her to the place where the young musicians are staying. She finds that the brilliant composer appears to have lost his mind, or perhaps he's taken a few too many of those pills, because all he's doing is repeating the same phrase again and again, over one of his compositions playing in the background. Disturbing the peace, changing what happened before, changing what happens within, he exults repeatedly. From the door, the girl notes the deplorable condition of the rooms he shares with the young conductor of the orchestra. The latter hasn't slept in his bed, the only one that's still made up—a pristine monument to a night of lovemaking with his latest conquest. It's the vanguard's duty to be unsettling, to disturb the peace, to alter musical convention note by note, declaims the composer. Next to his bed, a computer and tape recorder are playing a piece of music he's programmed: thudding noises, the occasional sound of breaking glass, the din of an approaching tornado. Apparently, it's the sound of foosball balls going down a tube. He's entitled the piece *game 1-3-3-4*, a reference to the arrangement of the players on a foosball table. That sound is only the groundwork for the piece. Disturbing the peace, changing what happened before . . . he repeats, saying he intends to write an opera to explain what it all means. The girl has a massive hangover. Standing in this rat's nest is taking an enormous toll on her, although the brilliant composer looks an even more pitiful sight than she. The whole idea of his project seems utter nonsense. Perhaps if he incorporated some piano passages to consolidate the medley of different sounds, it might be more comprehensible. She asks herself why she believes this, but at the moment she doesn't want to think about the reasons, probably because she knows it's to do with a silly personal bias, or a jealousy so pronounced, so nettlesome, it could bring on a rash. The brilliant composer has strewn the whole place—including his bed, the nightstand, the chairs, and floor—with newspaper clippings and pages of sheet music. The clippings are all about the Little Sinfonietta. He's hopped up on those pills, she thinks. The most common of the clippings is a photo of the girl throwing her clown's nose into the audience, which became quite a popular image in the newspapers. The pages of sheet music are covered variously with letters, numbers, straight lines, circles, and other geometrical shapes; nowhere does there appear a conventional symbol of notation. If he's with his latest conquest, is there a chance he's disturbing someone else's peace? asks the composer, snickering, as he stretches himself out on the young conductor's pristine bed, beckoning her to follow.

You could write a manifesto about sex and infidelity, about having sex with his best friend in his own bed. The girl shuts the door and leaves. It doesn't matter what the brilliant composer says, does, or even thinks, says the girl to herself, because he's no one. But it isn't yet the time to tell this no one she intends to quit the Little Sinfonietta. On her way back to the hotel, she wonders how to broach the issue when the time does come.

Minutes go by, maybe hours. She's copied the first chapter of her *No World* and summarized the contents of her notebook on sheets of paper bearing the hotel's letterhead, all of which she requested be delivered to the screenwriter. Then she rehearsed the *5 Pieces for piano*, and performed a number of exercises to keep her skill at peak level. She had trouble concentrating, but she forced herself to complete all the exercises. It was something of a farewell. She knows there's a before and after the decision she's made, but no backing down from it. All she has left to do are the recordings, which she'll bequeath to posterity, and that'll be the end of her career as a musician. After laboring through the exercises, she collects her books, her sheet music, and other related material from her work desk, on her nightstand, and in the bathroom. In a few hours, the young conductor and the members of the Little Sinfonietta will decide whether or not they want to work with the new manager the girl's mother will introduce to them, perhaps dreaming of all she vouchsafed them if they followed her advice. The girl, on the other hand, who's all but abandoned her musical aspirations, is wondering whether or not to go to the meeting at all. She flings open her wardrobes and hurriedly packs her bags, fantasizing about her future as a writer. She calls the screenwriter to find out if he's received the first chapter of her novel yet, and the summary of what she's written in her diary. The screenwriter confirms he got them, that he's already read them. He waits for the girl to ask his opinion. But she doesn't care what he thinks. Perhaps she thinks it's too soon for him to have an opinion. Perhaps it's because she tells him there will be a major twist later. She then calls reception to collect her bags and asks them to get her a taxi. She'll talk to her mother later in the church. She won't see her until around the time of the concert anyway. She tells the driver to take her to the hotel in front of the Grand Central Station, the same one in which her father is staying. When she arrives in the lobby, the receptionist says there are no rooms available. She says she's staying in the same room as her father. The receptionist goes through the list of all the guests and doesn't find her father's name among them. The girl tries calling him, but his phone is either out of range or turned off. She'd swear this is the hotel. The girl asks if there's a room under someone else's name, remembering the pseudonym she saw on her father's other passport, but there's no one by that name either. Then she recalls McGregor, that friendly voice she's frequently heard on the phone asking to speak with her father. What about McGregor, she says. Is there someone called McGregor staying here? Yes, the receptionist responds, there is a McGregor staying with us. The screenwriter watches himself in the mirror, asks himself why, at his age, he's still surprised by the old maxim, money is power. He imagines the girl's peremptory attitude in picking up the phone and demanding they send a bellhop to collect her luggage, and someone else to deliver an envelope to his own hotel. Money is power, he murmurs on leaving the bathroom and returning to his writing desk. He remembers the girl's plan to write about an old professor cum alien hunter who has fled to the City in Outer Space, a free port far away from Earth in which a gateway into paradise is located, a paradise somewhere else in the universe, far away. This man can no longer be the missing cousin Dedalus. He seems to have more in common with the screenwriter than anyone else. In the City in Outer Space, the alien hunter, who doesn't know he's an alien himself, is attempting to start his life over. Not that the place matters all that much, writes the girl, because he's searching for something unknown to him: the reason why he fled there in the first place. Perhaps the girl should write about these preliminaries, give an account of his flight from his homeland. In the story there is a female student. The girl resists using the letter k to name this character. K or Ka? The oft repeated question. She's not the protagonist, this character, but she'll be an important part of the scaffolding propping the protagonist up. The scenes before his flight to the City in Outer Space pass quickly. What interests her most is the person he becomes years later—the alien hunter, aged and alone, the sole survivor of a devastating war, the sole inhabitant of a desolate city out in the nether regions of space. He can see the scene so clearly, like a recent memory, with the same intricacy as the design in the headboard of his bed, at which he happens to be looking, against which he's frequently struck his pate while making love to the girl. "1.21 Love can be the case or not the case, while everything else remains the same. Or perhaps it's not love, but something else, writes the female student, resting her back against a cushion. He blindly reaches for his cigarette lighter on the bedside table, his fingers probing the glass surface. On grasping it, he lights the cigarette and leaves it perched between his lips, blowing a mouthful of smoke toward the ceiling. Faintly, in the background, he hears the radio playing some classical music. The camera is moving slowly to one side until the old philosophy professor enters the shot, where it stops, maintaining an angle that captures the action as it unfolds. The man is much older than her, almost geriatric. She's just a girl. Does it matter what it is, he says. She plucks the cigarette from between his fingers, takes a drag, returns it, and gets out of the bed to get dressed. If it's not love and not nothing, then perhaps it's an illness, he continues without looking at her. Cut to a close-up of his face, keeping the female student out of focus in the background."

According to the newspaper, the soccer team the girl supports has lost a pre-season friendly match, and the star player still hasn't returned. The screenwriter takes a walk by the river and crosses one of the bridges. All he can think about is his script. Reading the girl's first chapter was like pulling on a thread that unraveled a skein of ideas. He stops now and then beside a lamppost or illumined window to take a rest and jot a few notes. She waits for her father in the hotel lobby. Waiting can be good. It makes the mind aware of its surroundings, puts it in tune with the smallest of details. Later it spurs recollection, then thought, reading then writing, as an attempt to reconstruct that environment from a farrago of impressions, none of which are perfectly recalled, and even if they were, it would take the labor of ages to record them all. The girl could probably recall ten, maybe twelve of these details. So the mind must navigate the maelstrom by latching onto a few things at a time, otherwise it won't be able to remember or think, to read or write, or even to exist at all. So, in choosing the details on which to focus, the mind takes part in its own creation, a unique creation, for no two minds agree on what details to take in. And it's also a continuous creation, for what's important today may be forgotten tomorrow. Nothing that continually creates itself can disappear, so long as it goes on existing through other beings, other characters—the number of which can be infinite, like a saga that goes on developing forever, a movie that never ends. There may only be so many actors, but there are many characters to play, and perhaps each actor changes roles continually, removing one mask, donning another. And each time a new character is born, the process starts again from scratch. Characters cannot procreate and pass on their accumulated experience. And the setting must remain the same, the *mise-en-scène* of an unrelenting pilgrimage: actors in their masks, stalking like ants around a globe that can never change, or not until . . . she was going to say until its obliteration, its annihilation. Who knows, thinks the girl as she sits on the sofa in the lobby of the hotel in front of the Grand Central Station. It's getting late, so she abandons the thought and leaves to perform at the concert. When she gets back, she takes her place on the sofa and waits for her father to return. There's been no sign of McGregor either. But she continues waiting in the lobby, careless of the passing hours. She writes about the No World, adds an entry to her diary, then reads the writer who revolutionized twentieth-century literature and the dramatist who set the literary standard for everyone who came after him. The former writer's novel describes the events of a single day, encompassing all its minutiae, as an inventory of quotidian experience—the city novel par excellence, a city through which consciousness flows as a river, carrying with it all its news, gossip, trade, men and women—flowing relentlessly in and out of the city, in and out of the protagonist's mind, in and out of life. Some readers had said they felt as though they'd lived a whole lifetime in reading about that single day. There's a chapter the girl especially likes. It's probably because it takes place in a library, or because it's about the dramatist who set the literary standard for everyone. Or perhaps it's because of the voices, the various voices that claim to have discovered the dramatist's greatest secret, as if they'd traveled back in time to eavesdrop on a backstage confession, voices that say he wasn't the son but the father, not the prince but the murdered king, the husband betrayed by his queen, or as some of them say, the man betrayed by his own two brothers. Occasionally, the girl is assailed by doubt and tries calling her father, but his phone is either out of range or turned off, so she just leaves another message and hangs up. When he does arrive, he'll find her asleep on the sofa in the lobby, having waited patiently for his return.

His works weren't published in his lifetime, at least under his own name, and there isn't a single surviving manuscript. Some have expressed doubts concerning the authorship of his works; some have questioned whether the author even existed. So thinks the screenwriter on entering an establishment that seems a cross between a dance club and a gay bar, but with the better qualities of both. He has an idea. It's something relating to what the girl said when she was upset with the young conductor and brilliant composer—and with the whole world, it seemed—and she mentioned something to do with subversive talent. He orders a drink and leans against the bar, watching the middle-aged couples dancing. He can't imagine the girl's father coming here to look for a young woman to party with. He'd more likely solicit her services by telephone: young, female undergraduate offers her services to mature executive. Besides, the music's so loud the screenwriter doubts her father would stay here longer than a minute. He'd more than likely take his young college chick to a local jazz joint, while his daughter takes refuge in a café—one of the modern ones, all chic and swanky, the kind that only cater to exclusive clientele. But then the screenwriter reconsiders. Perhaps she'd choose to take refuge in a foosball bar instead, as long as it isn't one frequented by the young conductor and brilliant composer. He lights a cigarette and begins reimagining his surroundings, taking as his cue an image from a movie in which a white jazz singer performs nightly in a club that caters mainly to blacks. In a similar place, although more upscale, the girl's father is leaning against the bar, sipping a cocktail and talking about jazz with the college chick. Neither one is an expert, although they can each name about twenty musicians in the genre. The chick admits her superficial knowledge of jazz, but then advertises her knowledge of literature and classical music. None of her clients have ever brought her to a jazz club before. It's usually a business dinner, some dancing, and—although she doesn't say it—a bed at an expensive hotel. Her cultural awareness and educated mien are but a front to make clients believe they have something in common with her, that she's classy, sophisticated, not just a hooker they've paid good money to sleep with. The girl's father doesn't give a damn what the others do on their dates with her. In the dimly lit lounge, the screenwriter's eyes are gleaming, his nostrils flaring as he leers at some of the women. None appear to be available. All couples. So he's left to imagine how it might have gone had he approached one of them. He looks at the cane by his side. They don't know what they're missing, he thinks sullenly. It's late in the night when he approaches a black prostitute loitering under the flickering neon lights of a sex shop. He hasn't seen the girl in two days, and he doesn't expect she'll be showing up tonight.

He gets back well after midnight, half drunk. The receptionist hands him the key along with an envelope. Without waiting to get to his room, he tears open the envelope there in the lobby, and extracts a card. On it, the girl has written that she's at the hotel where her father is staying, feeling a little discomfited, because it's one of those middling hotels in front of the Grand Central Station. It isn't like her father to stay in such a dump. And she says, moreover, that his room's registered under another name. The screenwriter doesn't find this news terribly important; he doesn't even consider it news, having read about it already in the girl's work. Also in the envelope is another chapter of her *No World*. She had written it while waiting for her father in the hotel lobby. The screenwriter imagines her there, sitting on a sofa, and then himself arriving instead of her father, in the early hours of the morning, to find her sleeping there, then carrying her up to his room. The screenwriter has his own reasons for feeling sad, one of which could be that no one was waiting for him here. But loneliness has its counterpart, he thinks, summoning the image of the prostitute under the flickering lights. Loneliness has its solace. He sits down on a sofa in the lobby and keeps reading—a counterpart to the girl who sat on another lobby's sofa to write down what he now reads. The receptionist, who in this hotel shares the duties of a doorman, looks at him askance, but the screenwriter doesn't care what he may be thinking, because the admiral at the hotel with the English name never once raised an eyebrow at his behavior. The girl has written a scene in which the old philosophy professor, jaded in the desolate City in Outer Space, recalls the existence of a set of photographic plates. He plans to use them to locate extraterrestrials because, according to him, the images they yield reveal them as surrounded by a halo of light. Right now, though, he's not looking for any extraterrestrials, and neither does he try to uncover his female student's hidden past. Beside a white canvas covering a wall, she stands naked. She stoops to gather some paint from a bucket at her feet, and smears it on the whiteness of the canvas, on the whiteness of her flesh. She writes her disconnected phrases about the No World, incomprehensible clauses about twelve-tone music—for dodecaphony is the means by which to communicate with beings from far-flung galaxies: something that should be of interest to an alien hunter, which is to say her teacher, who always photographs her—fixing her posture, directing her every gesture. "2.221 What the No World represents is its sense. 2.225 The No World does not exist a priori. How would I go about finding them? mouths the old professor to himself, referring to the aliens, as he stares out of one of the only intact windows left in the City in Outer Space, a vantage point that offers him a view of the stars. He's forgotten how old he is. He doubts the validity of his propositions. He can't be sure if his mind's playing tricks on him. He can only be sure of the sound of the machine that wakes him every morning and announces the beginning of a new day, although there's nothing to distinguish one day from the next. All that remain are his memories of her, and of his wish to escape with her to a paradise in outer space, something that couldn't happen—neither on this world nor the last, and never in this life. How would I go about finding them? inquires a voice in his head, a voice in his memory, while trying to capture all her nakedness as she smears it on the whiteness of the canvass."

Back in his room, the screenwriter barely has the energy to read let alone write. Nonetheless, he gathers whatever reserves he has and sits down at the typewriter to record his version of

135

the facts. He doesn't need much, maybe half a dozen lines, an adumbration of the main idea will do. She's arriving late, as always, and for the same reason she always arrives late: she was writing. In one of the lounges at the hotel with the English name, a guy is on his feet talking aloud as if addressing a grand assembly. Seated around him, the girl sees the parents of some of the gifted students, the young conductor of the orchestra, the brilliant composer, her mother, and a man she's never met. The guy stops talking for a moment in order to be introduced, after which he begs the girl to take a seat. We've only just started, he says. Then he launches into a screed about increasing the number of performances, making compromises, working hard, and having a winning mentality: in other words, all the things that maximize income. The girl must've missed the part about the music—or maybe it's implicit, she mutters wryly to herself: something so important it needn't be mentioned. Perhaps the music is implicit in the contracts too. At last, he mentions some other musicians, invoking them as exemplars, and then other large-scale orchestras—some well known, others not. Then he introduces the man she's never met. It is he who'll take the reigns and lead the Little Sinfonietta during its transition, he who'll deal with any problems that may arise. The man speaks gravely, adopting the same tone as her mother when she said that what they're doing is serious business; it can no longer be treated as a game. The young conductor and brilliant composer are prepared to make a pact with the devil, if this proves necessary to their aims. Like her, they're also interested in the gateways connecting different regions in time and space, although they only care about being remembered by posterity, about ensuring that decades or even centuries from now their names will glow like embers in the all-consuming ash. Poor fools, she thinks, the only name that can breast the relentless tide of passing eons is Ka, and it will be done through literature, and through an exceptional recording of the *5 Pieces for piano*, despite contemporary critics calling the interpretation too slow. There won't be a trace left of any of these mediocrities. It will be as if they never existed. Will she be known as Ka or K? The girl excuses herself, implying an urgent need to visit the lady's room, but once in the lobby, she continues onto the street, and has no intention of returning.

Late in the morning, the screenwriter is still asleep. He drank too much, and went to bed late, immersed as he was in the drafts of some scenes, bothered by the second act during which the audience is bound to yawn with boredom, because the story starts lagging, digressing, which will give them the impression the writer has lost the plot. On awakening, he feels confused, and decides to stay in bed and kill some more time in the curtained gloom. Sundays are strange, he muses with displeasure; he'd rather it was any other day but Sunday. When he finally gets up, he drains the half bottle of water he left in the fridge, then gets ready to go out and look for a place to have breakfast. He buys a newspaper at a kiosk where the boulevards intersect, and then limps to the café, with the help of his cane. Once seated on the terrace, he looks around for the waitress who often serves him, but he remembers she doesn't work on Sundays. Her replacement is an older woman, possibly an acquaintance of the owner. It could be the owner herself, as she's not wearing a uniform, although the way people dress nowadays, you never can tell. After going over the headlines, he folds the newspaper and leaves it on the table, puts away his glasses, and waits for someone to serve him. Once his coffee arrives, he lights a cigarette and tries to focus on his script. But he's too distracted by all the movement and noise around him, so he ends up just watching the people strolling around the plaza—seeing them as if through a mist, going about their business—some leisurely, others dutifully, their attitude made plain by their expression and gait, their business remaining a mystery. In the neighboring country's capital, the women are beautiful, and the screenwriter thinks they have a characteristic style of makeup and dress. Of course, the black prostitute is an exception. But, then, although this may be her native city, her roots are in the former colonies. The screenwriter seems noticeably relaxed, his breathing slow, regular; or, depending on how you see it, labored, sluggish—for he may be too relaxed, he may even be at the point of sleep. He likes the black prostitute because she doesn't wear makeup. He hadn't thought about it before. He likes her for other reasons too, but this one never occurred to him. Without makeup, a face seems clean to him, somehow, immaculate, even a face as black as the prostitute's. He doesn't feel pressed to go back to the hotel, so he orders another coffee, lights another cigarette, and leans back in his chair. Then he starts thinking about the girl. He wonders where she'll have gone after ducking out of the meeting. She probably needs to exorcise her demons. He imagines her wandering the streets of the neighboring country's capital until she remembers her intention to visit one of the cemeteries, and she decides to hail a taxi. There are many to choose from, so perhaps the driver brought her to the nearest one, or perhaps he knows the cemetery the girl's talking about, the one where all the writers are buried. At the entrance, there's a map showing the routes to their graves. She reads it briefly and makes a rough sketch of it in her notebook. It won't be difficult to find them, since the graves are arranged in numerical rows, which are separated by wide avenues. Near the entrance, is the tomb of the inventor of the cinematic spectacle. Although he's not a writer, she decides to pay him a visit anyway. The girl climbs a hillock between some graves that are shaded by trees. She thinks of the alien hunter from her novel, sees him exploring a cemetery in the City in Outer Space, but there are no illustrious dead, no famous writers or artists buried there. There were only a few of them left even during the war, but as the dead kept piling up, they had to be disinterred in order to make room, and then reburied, as it were, in outer space. Before leaving the cemetery in the City in Outer Space, the old professor of philosophy, hunter of aliens, spares a thought for those lifeless bodies drifting through the cosmos, even identifies with them, for they are his predecessors, and he pays tribute to them by reading some poems and extracts from their works. Perhaps what he feels is the old world calling to him, the world he despises, the world from which he came, although he doesn't know it, or perhaps he's just desperate to understand the voices in his head, voices of half-forgotten memories. He's given up searching for aliens, since he thinks he's all alone. He's yet to receive any news from Earth. All he knows is that the war broke out shortly after communications with Earth ceased. He's occasionally explored the other side of the city, and found nothing there but desolation and ruin. But he's grown used to the face of destruction, a landscape devastated by war, full of battle-scarred buildings ripe for demolition. Although he's never encountered anyone in these parts, he's still cautious, for he has yet to explore the entire city, and he doesn't know what may be lurking in the shadows. And then, he always hears the same music playing—eerie, slow piano music, accompanied by the almost imperceptible hum of the machines releasing oxygen into the city, music that's only

139

interrupted by a voice regularly announcing the time and date. He's not certain if these figures tally with those on Earth, and he doesn't bother trying to work out his age from them. The girl stops ruminating to add a reminder to her notes on the City in Outer Space that cemeteries should be added to the list of places where contact can be made with aliens communicating from Earth. They're not the safe kinds of places where large numbers of people gather, like airports or cathedrals, but they may attract a smaller number, the ones who like to set themselves apart from the multitude, who consider themselves different, special. The girl thinks about the kinds of people who might visit the inventor of the cinematic spectacle's tomb. She supposes film critics, historians of cinema, directors certainly, perhaps the occasional actor or screenwriter. Maybe even a photographer. Then her mind wanders again, now backward in time, into the memories of an old runaway who doesn't recall his flight from another world, a time long before the war, back when people barely knew what space was, back when he wanted to establish himself as a photographer, having practiced it his whole life and become a dab hand, acquiring an impressive palette of different styles, many for the express purpose of unmasking extraterrestrials. They have a peculiar halo, he recalls. He's really a professor of philosophy, but he's become sufficiently adept at photography to make it his métier. He offers his services to forensic laboratories, weddings, baptisms, exhibitions, conferences, and even erotic magazines. He places ads in newspapers, and is offered a deal by a guy who wants him to photograph some children beside a garden pond playing with specially designed sailboats. The girl wonders how they simulate wind in the City in Outer Space. Perhaps the old philosophy professor could earn a living taking pictures of the space dead, cataloguing them.

Daguerreotypes are currently in fashion again. They produce certain effects that aren't possible with modern methods. It's possible one of the earliest forms of photography will yield the first ever image of an alien. It may even be the only method that reveals their particular halo. If he knew any other alien hunters, he'd offer them his services too. Wherever he goes, he always leaves the telephone number of the space hotel he's staying in. The screenwriter smiles in a self-satisfied way for being the one who gave the girl this idea. He finishes his coffee, crushes the cigarette in the ashtray, and has a look around. When he feels he's come back to Earth, he goes for a walk by the river and then crosses a bridge onto one of the islands. He's always had a fondness for the smallest of them— now a haven for the wealthy, although he once stayed in a shabby hotel on its main thoroughfare; subsequent development led to a rise in its real-estate value, which means he can barely afford to walk up a side street now. He goes into a bookstore and looks with curiosity at some of the titles on the table of new releases. Then he decides to spend the rest of the time before the store closes browsing the other shelves. He's pleased he's able to find an open bookstore in the neighboring country's capital on a Sunday, and in the city center, of all places. He checks his watch. It's late, he reflects. He got out of bed late, and he's still a little drowsy. He doesn't want to eat at a restaurant on the island and then have to walk all the way back to the hotel. He's traversed such distances before, but only by walking very slowly because of his limp, and by stopping now and then under the pretext of having a cigarette, but really to catch his breath and recover his strength. Now he'd prefer to just take a taxi. Unfortunately, he has a bad feeling he's running out of cash, and will have to forgo certain luxuries for the time being—like taxis or paying women for sex. When he eventually does get back, he sees his room's been tidied in his absence. He pulls open the curtains and looks at his neighbor's apartment. Empty. No sign of the children playing, or of his neighbor painting their little toy soldiers. He wonders if he'll wake up late again tomorrow and lose another day. He starts feeling a little depressed at the thought because he knows how badly it affects his concentration. He even starts wondering if he'll ever be able to concentrate again. He tries to banish the negative thought, but it keeps popping into his head. He even starts wondering if, in the event he never writes another line, he'd be able to find another job. Although he had various jobs when he was younger, he didn't acquire any useful skills. He's spent almost his whole life teaching and writing scripts. He remembers as a kid he did an internship working in an office, but the whole experience came to nothing, and he hasn't worked in an office since. Besides, at his age, no one would hire him as an intern. Maybe he could supplement his pension by getting a job as a resident caretaker, or perhaps a night watchman in a seedy hotel. Or possibly a waiter, he thinks. He won't even consider a job as a photographer, because he refuses to let himself be confounded with a mere literary creation, that old philosophy professor the girl is writing about. Perhaps he'd enjoy working as a waiter. He's waited tables before, he remembers, many years before, shortly after his internship in fact. The screenwriter needs the fingers of both hands to count all the different jobs he's had in his life. He couldn't stomach working at any of them now, though, especially the jobs of his early youth. Who'd hire a cripple anyway? The image of himself carrying a briefcase and going around billing customers makes him shudder. He wouldn't have the energy to go hobbling from office to office with his cane. Besides, nowadays, everyone pays their bills electronically, through a bank, unlike when he was an intern. He hasn't a clue really, so he'll just have to make do with his script. He remembers giving advice to the kids of some friends and acquaintances who had aspirations of becoming writers, screenwriters, or film directors. He told them to work at several different jobs, to never hold one down for longer than six months, because then they'll have lots of experiences to draw upon later when they come to write. Now he thinks that this advice is total bullshit. Why did all those kids want to be writers and directors anyway? It came from breathing the same air as their parents, clearly. Perhaps it's the same for the children of soldiers and athletes, he thinks, all wanting to be soldiers and athletes like Mom and Dad. What became of his own son? What advice did he give him? This causes the screenwriter to think of the girl's father. He gives advice to his daughter as he would a multinational company. He knows he's written something like this before. Maybe he shouldn't use the simile again. The screenwriter likes to think of himself as a fugitive, except no one has come looking for him yet. He abandons the thought. All in good time. He sits in his chair and grabs the newspaper. If he's lucky, there may be something he can crib for his screenplay. Although it doesn't matter very much if there isn't. He's too tired to write, so he may as well see what's going on in the world. After reading the headlines and personals, he puts the newspaper down. Only bad news, as always; and there's nothing in the personals to suggest a secret meeting of chosen ones is being arranged. The police are holding two guys who were found with a stash of plutonium. There's no news about the star of the soccer team the girl supports. He takes a look outside. The street-lights are flickering on. They remind him of the day he's wasted, give him the impression he's spent it in front of the

TV, not watching anything in particular, just flicking through the channels to alleviate boredom. After honoring his daily promise to call his wife, he decides to allay his professional conscience by going over a scene that's been nagging at him. He decides to write it out, since he thinks he's found a suitable place for it in the script. It's set in the morning in the girl's father's hotel room. Sundays are strange, thinks the screenwriter, passing a hand over his unshaven cheek. At least he's no longer tired. He may find an idea in some corner of his brain that will stimulate his writing. It's nearing midday, and the father is shaving in the bathroom. The girl has returned from her strange excursion to the cemetery. The bathroom door is open and she talks to her father from the jamb. She fears there'll never be an end to all the concerts, all the interviews, that there'll never be a break from doing one radio show after another, and never a rest from the endless traveling. A world from which she rarely has the opportunity to escape— something she must remedy soon, or it may take over her life. Perhaps it already has, she says, and she's sick to death of it. Her father nods his head without saying a word, carefully shaving under his nose, but he seems to have heard what she said, and perhaps for the first time in his life, sympathized with what she said. She wants to be a writer, not a piano prodigy who travels the world filling auditoriums. She no longer wants to be part of the Little Sinfonietta that will shortly be selling itself out, abandoning its position at the vanguard of music to become a mere spectacle, a troupe of traveling musicians negotiating for TV contracts, making albums that put a premium on virtuosity and vulgar showing-off instead of music, who perform every night in a different city, in a different amphitheater, all with one and only one end in mind: money. The girl's father throws her a sideways glance as he carefully negotiates the blade down his cheek, his eyes flitting back to the mirror as he finishes the task, then downward as he cleans the blade under the cold running tap.

It's not true that everything's been said and written. The problem is, as time goes by, and bevies of writers come and go, there's less and less scope for even the greatest among them to be truly original. It's not going to be easy writing a dodecaphonic novel, thinks the screenwriter, especially if it's a first book. The mingling in a text of words and sentences that lack all restriction, in terms of concinnity and arrangement on the page, may lead to something quite beautiful, but there's also the risk of creating something grotesque. Structurally, he thinks the novel has too much in common with what the Serialists did many years before. And whether it turns out to be beautiful or grotesque, the idea behind it still won't be original.

How long can a person survive without food or water if they're tied to a bed and gagged? wonders the screenwriter before getting down to work. That night, in the church, it appears the girl performed her best interpretation yet of the *5 Pieces for piano*. It's as if her decision to abandon music gave her a more devil-may-care attitude in these last performances, and liberated her from the exigencies of having to stick slavishly to the score. Now she's performing the recitation part of the show, and once again seems to be surpassing herself. The clown's nose is like an extra appendage, so convincing is she in the role. And her delivery is magnificent. Now it's not just her voice but her whole personality that's become one with the cosmic clown. Now it's the girl herself that wanders through a desolate landscape pitted with craters, carrying a bloody dagger in her hands. The young conductor of the orchestra can scarcely believe his eyes, and neither can the rest of the people in the audience. After the concert, they follow their usual ritual of going to the cafés and trendy nightspots of the neighboring country's capital. On the way, they're joined by some people unknown to her and rest of the group. They're probably friends of the new manager, says her mother, unconcerned. As usual, they're also joined by someone who was sent by the promoters to attend to them during the night. The young conductor is dancing with his latest conquest, and the brilliant composer, having met a famous make-up artist, is hoping the grown-ups are going to be getting seriously drunk and so leave them alone. The girl's mother has been waiting for an opportunity to speak with her daughter. She wants to elaborate on the note she gave her, and to give her a chance to explain why she left in the middle of the meeting, and why she's been hanging around her father. She doesn't understand her daughter's sudden need to write, or why she thinks time spent on music is time lost on writing. She wants to have a serious discussion with her. But the girl would rather discuss it another time, and she leaves before the night's even begun. Back at the hotel, the girl is alone in her father's room, writing. She writes longhand first, and then transcribes what she's written on her father's laptop. "2.012 In logic nothing is accidental. Close-up of the female student seated at a small white desk organizing her notebooks. The camera slowly zooms out to reveal her in the middle of a classroom just before the lesson begins, surrounded by students still taking their seats. A collective murmur redoubles as the room gradually fills up. The scene takes place long before the old professor cum alien hunter flees to the City in Outer Space, where he'll probably finish setting himself up as a photographer." The girl stops writing for a moment. She doesn't know why she's narrating things as though she's writing a screenplay, or why she's enumerating her propositions as though this were a philosophical treatise. She hadn't given the least thought to these details before, perhaps because she didn't believe them very important then. She continues: "We picture no facts to ourselves. Some students are seated around the female student, while others are standing, chattering, using up the moments before class begins. 2.211 For the few that pay attention, there is no logical distinction between a no picture and what it depicts. Still immersed in her notes, a student with a freckled face stands in front of her desk and pronounces her name with a 'ka.' The female student looks up with a surly expression on account of being disturbed. I've been waiting, he says reproaching but timidly. I wasn't sure you'd show up, she says, her eyes returning to the notebook. He remains in front of her a few moments, staring at her silently, awkwardly, his growing discomfort becoming apparent. Unable to think of anything to say, he turns and goes to his seat on the other side of the room. 2.22 What a no picture represents it represents independently of its truth or falsity, by means of its pictorial form. A few minutes later, the old professor of philosophy shows up. He's the same old guy that in another scene will be seen in bed next to the girl, the same old guy who's already been described as an alien hunter." The girl wrote "the girl" when she should've written "the female student," although of course the female student is in fact a girl herself. "The murmur in the room dies down as the professor removes his coat. He looks around the room for the female student. On seeing her, he feels reassured and is ready to begin the lesson. He takes a booklet from his jacket pocket and spends a few moments scanning it, in order to remind himself where he left off the last time." The girl

147

stops to inquire into her current state of mind, and whether it's influencing what she's writing. No, she hasn't got the time to waste investigating the whys of things. She's writing, and that's all that matters. The pills have enhanced her powers of concentration, but perhaps they've also put her in a state of sustained agitation. Perhaps she's taken too many to be writing on. Yet, in this state, she can focus on several things at once. She hears her father's footsteps in the corridor. She can never predict his comings and goings. He enters and mumbles a perfunctory greeting, as if his mind's on other matters. She doesn't respond, but continues writing—her mood exalted, her thinking expansive—believing she's found the inspiration that's been lacking until now, the thread of the story that's been eluding her. She's writing the alien hunter's backstory, the life he had before fleeing to the City in Outer Space. Perhaps he flees because chasing aliens is forbidden at home. No, it won't be like Cousin Dedalus's story, the girl tells her father, because the character's an old guy, an alien hunter and philosophy professor who's having a relationship with one of his female students. She points out that, although the story's fictitious, she really believes an alien civilization has colonized the Earth, and that she's finally discovered the reason behind it all. The girl then decides to shut herself in the bathroom so she can continue writing undisturbed. The girl's father stands perplexed, not saying a word, having hardly uttered a sound since his arrival, as he watches her shut the bathroom door behind her.

In the morning, the screenwriter takes a seat in front of the typewriter and casts a couple of glances out the window before beginning. He wants to work on a scene in which the girl and mother are alone. Besides tying up some loose ends, he wants to show the kind of relationship that can exist between two women—in this case, a mother and daughter—which he believes is best revealed when they're alone. Until now, every scene in which they've appeared together has been brief, their interaction brusque and tense, and they've always been surrounded by an entourage. The mother is a strong character who feels she has the prerogative to talk about anything she wants with her daughter. Perhaps this has already been hinted at, but the screenwriter would like a highly charged dramatic encounter between the two to bring the point home. It's set in the morning. The screenwriter types forcefully, his fingers almost rebounding from the keys, the sound of piano music playing in his head. The girl is practicing in the room at the hotel with the English name. Her mother sits in one of the chairs, listening with enjoyment, thinking that all may not be lost. Beforehand, the girl had carefully placed some objects on the piano strings to distort the sound—some metal clips, a few pieces of her mother's jewelry, and even a copy of the philosopher W's greatest work, and then played, imagining how it would sound on a recording. The girl prolongs the practice session in order to avoid going out shopping afterward with her mother. She feels they have nothing in common. Nonetheless, in the very next shot we see them in the street together quarreling over some trivial matter. Perhaps it's because the girl insists on wearing her chosen livery of a white shirt and trousers, which her mother detests, thinking it unbecoming a celebrated pianist. She tells her to go back and change; such attire may be suitable for other people, but not someone who moves in her social circle, someone who's regularly accosted by strangers in the street asking for autographs, and who may report back to other strangers, perhaps even to the newspapers, the strange fashion statement she seems to be making. Such things can make or break a reputation. Right now she's quite popular, her mother says, but it won't last if she carries on like this. The world isn't the kind of place the girl imagines it is. The mother then changes the subject and starts talking about music while scanning potential purchases in the shopwindows. They didn't have far to travel. The hotel with the English name is located in one of the more fashionable streets in the neighboring country's capital, where one can find various stores only a few meters from each other selling all the major brands. They've often walked these streets together and the girl knows them like the back of her hand. There's nothing strange about wanting to shop on streets where only luxury and elegance are found, or that her mother should expect to find such streets in the neighboring country's capital, a city that cultivates a perception of itself as being the bastion of haute couture, and although the girl's mother blindly adheres to her own fixed standard of elegance, she admits that only here, in the neighboring country's capital, can the highest standard be found. Luckily, there's a fresh breeze and the temperature's low. The mother is curious about her old literature teacher. Do you know what his screenplay's about? she asks. No, he hasn't told me anything about it, says the girl. Then her mother starts singing the praises of the Little Sinfonietta's new manager. The young conductor and brilliant composer speak highly of him, she says. It's the best thing that could've happened. It hasn't been easy up till now, especially with all this twelve-tone music and experimentation, but things will be different from now on. The girl listens, silently. The screenwriter continues typing furiously, fleshing out the mother's character. She stops to point out a lovely dress on display in a shopwindow. The girl pays no attention. The woman in the building opposite the screenwriter's hotel lifts her blinds and looks up at the sky, as if to determine the kind of day she's going to face. Aping her, the screenwriter looks up as well. Weather forecast: sunny all day. He looks at her window again, but his neighbor's disappeared inside. Then he looks at his watch. He ought to freshen up before going down for breakfast. But he figures he still has another half hour. He adjusts his glasses, rereads the last few sentences, and continues typing. We see the pair leaving one store and immediately entering another. The girl takes a deep breath before pushing the door and hearing yet another jingle. Her mother looks at an outfit, checks the quality of the fabric, the label, the size, and, without looking at the girl, asks for her opinion. But instead of waiting for an answer, she goes off to consult one of the saleswomen. The girl's mother gets treated like a regular in almost every store they visit, which is only right, for she is indeed a regular, and it's the way her mother expects to be treated. She acts as if she buys everything on impulse, but in truth, she plans every purchase, since she's mentally created a shopping list beforehand. She refuses to write it down, because she wouldn't be caught dead with a shopping list in her hands. Next, she pauses in front of a jewelry store and points out a ring and pair of earrings in the display. The screenwriter wonders how a mother could be so blind as not to realize that her daughter doesn't give a damn about jewelry. You should've stayed until the end of the meeting, she says suddenly. Given your experience, your input might've been invaluable. The saleswoman solemnly processes toward them carrying the earrings on a garish salver. The mother hopes they'll bring out some of her daughter's more positive qualities, although the girl doesn't know which qualities they might be or how exactly the earrings will help. I'm not interested in your kind of fashion, the girl says, trying not to be too abrupt. Besides, I didn't come along to watch you to go shopping for a pair of earrings. You have to find some way of filling that emptiness inside you, her mother insists, and by the way, you wear your hair far too short. Next, the two of them are seen standing on a sidewalk, struggling to hold all their shopping bags. The girl takes a couple of hesitant steps toward her mother, as if to ask something; her mother, perceiving this, interrupts her and suggests they talk about it over dinner. But the girl has other plans, all of them to do with her writing. Her mother doesn't listen, or pretends not to listen, but then jumps in by saying she doesn't understand this sudden impulse to start writing potboilers for the masses. She doesn't understand why the girl writes at all. She doesn't see that her daughter takes it very seriously, that she couldn't give a damn about the masses. There are people who live for it, breathe for it, would even die for it, but her mother paints every writer with the same brush, dismisses them all as mere fabulists and tellers of tall tales. If you were writing about something practical, an idea that might be of use to humanity . . . I'm sorry, her mother says, I know there's a certain prestige in being a writer, but if you stop to think about it, you'd eventually agree the pursuit is vain and impractical. What's the point in reading stories about things that never even happened, about people who never existed? The girl was born with exceptional musical talent; that's what she should be trying her best to foster, not wasting her time on something for which she may not even have an aptitude. So that's that, thinks the girl sarcastically, I'd better give it up. Her mother pleads with her to reconsider abandoning her music, and suggests they discuss it over dinner. She has a table reserved at the restaurant back at the hotel. But the girl doesn't want to wait until dinner, so she just tells her mother flatly that she won't be going on tour with the Little Sinfonietta, before walking away without saying good-bye. She heads for the hotel in front of the Grand Central Station—a hotel where she won't be greeted at the door by a smiling admiral, a hotel where there are no bellhops to help you with your luggage, a hotel where no one's even heard of a thing called room service, a hotel where her father happens to be staying. She's finished with the piano and the Little Sinfonietta. I'm starting a new life! she proclaims loudly, boldly, in the street, once out of her mother's earshot, satisfied she's finally taken the first step, glad to have had the opportunity to be honest. I'm starting a new life! she says again, ignoring the astonished looks of passersby. All she has left to do is tie up some loose ends, fulfill a few outstanding commitments, and she'll be ready to start that new life, ready to dedicate every hour of every day to this vain and impractical pursuit. The life of a writer! she says again, loudly, boldly, ignoring the astonished looks of passersby.

Not only don't they help you with your luggage, you have share a table in the canteen with strangers. One of the guests forgets his room key and a map of the city at the table where the screenwriter is sitting. A tourist, no doubt. Good day, he says before scuttling off to the buffet. The screenwriter nods with propriety, but without looking, as he bites down on a piece of bread. Lost in thought. The tourist returns with a plate of croissants, a selection of jams, and a glass of orange juice, placing them on the plastic tablecloth as he takes a seat. At the adjacent table, a couple of middle-aged women are chattering about their husbands. The screenwriter imagines the husbands are still in bed: they were all probably out late exploring the city. Or perhaps they don't exist. They could be deceased, or perhaps they were invented so these women would have something to talk about at breakfast. Even if they do exist, the screenwriter's sure these women would exaggerate their husbands' attributes and achievements. They could even be describing completely different people from the ones they left snoring upstairs. A good idea for another script, he thinks, smiling with self-congratulation: two women traveling around the world together, telling each other fables about their nonexistent husbands. What might the ramifications be if their children found out, or their real husbands? They might assume they're living double lives. Tourists: they're a breed of their own. Where would they go, what places would they visit? he thinks. Then he murmurs: Everywhere. Before long, he starts losing interest in the two women. Once he looks away from their table, the idea for a new script seems to float away. He listens to the voices coming from the other tables. There's always a crowd in the canteen when he comes down late to breakfast. It's not his fault, he thinks. The screenplay determines his circadian rhythm. Are you a writer? comes a voice from the other side of the table. The screenwriter lifts his eyes. It dawns on him that he's passed this man frequently in the corridor. He delays in responding. The tourist explains his presumption by confessing that he's often heard the sound of a typewriter coming from his room—not that he minds; in fact, he's glad to know there's a writer hard at work in the room next door. It's a romantic image, he says, that of the writer clacking away at his opus, with a cigarette perched on his bottom lip. You have to have something quite special about you to be a writer, he says. He admits he couldn't write to save his life. He doesn't know why, he just couldn't. I'm a screenwriter, the screenwriter finally replies.

While the screenwriter is spending some time in the lobby

going over the day's newspapers, the receptionist signals to him from the counter, waving an envelope. It's a similar envelope to the ones the girl sent him before. He asks who delivered it. A young girl, says the receptionist. Damn it! he grumbles. She must have come when he was having breakfast. The receptionist could have alerted him. She points to the exit. I'm afraid it's like my own mailbox at home, she says. Any correspondence is left in a box outside. The screenwriter strikes his cane against the foot of the counter, turns, and flounces out onto the street. He looks everywhere, but there's no sign of her. She's gone. He goes back inside, dragging his feet and cane behind him, not noticing the receptionist's quizzical expression following his melancholy gait, not giving a damn now for the newspapers he'd intended to finish reading. Now only the envelope matters, which he grasps tightly while he waits for the elevator to arrive. Once in his room, he goes to his desk and opens the envelope. There's only a single page, and not much written on it. She talks about her father's room at the hotel in front of the Grand Central Station, describing it as his center of operations. No one told her this, she writes, but it wouldn't take a genius to figure it out: the evidence is everywhere—on his laptop, his cell phone, his fax machine, and even in the paper tray of the printer. Her father and an associate have rented a couple of rooms that gives them a good view of the Grand Central Station. She still hasn't figured out why they keep going there, but she doesn't spend too much time thinking about it, since it would distract her from her writing. Who cares what her father and his associate are up to? thinks the screenwriter. Most of what he reads on the page he already knows about. But then he thinks again. Of course *she* cares about what her father gets up to. Maybe she doesn't quite know how to say it—why she cares, that is

—but if she thinks hard enough, searches diligently enough in her memory banks, the answer will come, and the words she needs will surely follow suit.

The screenwriter continues making progress, at times seeming more industrious than the girl. He's now working on a scene he planned before breakfast. The girl is sitting down to a sandwich and refreshment at a downtown café. She takes her notebook from her pocket and goes over some of her notes. I'm starting a new life, she writes: the life of a writer. Unable to contain her jubilation, she looks around her timidly, in case someone might see her stupid grin. Then she thinks of her mother. Perhaps she went too far with her. She should be more accommodating, let her mother get used to the idea of the girl as a writer. After all, she takes it for granted her daughter will pursue a career she doesn't want, that she has a certain control over the girl's future, and is determined to tie her to the piano stool for life. Of course, this all has to change. So why does she feel so guilty? All she did was defend her own convictions. She always feels exactly the same after fighting with the young conductor. She leaves the café and heads for the cathedral. Cathedrals and large churches are perfect places for channeling extraterrestrial energy. The nearest cathedral is next to the island. It's basically a tourist trap. All the same, a structure like that could only have been erected for one reason and that's as a place for making contact. The inhabitants of Earth spent centuries constructing these heaps as supreme manifestations of beauty, order, and sanctity, wholly suited as places for people to gather together to exchange ideas, to worship, and to pray. They still do so, hoping to make contact. With whom? Or what? They don't exactly know, but it doesn't matter, they gather anyway, as if driven by some primal instinct. On the other hand, if cathedrals and churches actually encourage a relaxation of this same instinct, they'd complicate the process by which beings from other galaxies choose with whom to make contact. The girl's concerned about knowing beforehand what building she should go to. What's the difference between them? she wonders. How does she go about making a choice?

As she stands before an imposing altar, the girl thinks again about those great buildings—receivers of signals from space—to which servants come to pay homage, channeling those signals and transmitting their own thoughts back again. There's a worldwide organization dedicated to this activity. What would her mother say about that? She's not going back on her decision. She won't take one step backward on the path she's chosen, not even for the sake of an apology. There will be time to make amends later. When she gets back to the hotel and enters the room, she sees her father has a visitor. It seems they weren't expecting her back so soon. A man of slender build, older than her father, sits on the sofa and looks at her over the rim of his glasses. He then stands up and offers her his hand. He's wearing a heavy, classically-cut suit. Perhaps it's too heavy for this time of year. My daughter, says her father to the man, without reversing the introduction. The man compliments the girl's beauty, says she looks very like her mother. He must be thinking of her mother when she was young, she thinks while forcing a smile. She hates when people point out their resemblance. She has the impression she's walked in on an important business meeting or something, so she politely excuses herself and goes down to the lobby to wait on the sofa. There, she takes out her diary and writes her first impressions of the old guy in the classically-cut suit, describing his clothes, his shoes, his politeness, his face—thin and kindly—his bushy eyebrows . . . Then she sees the two men leaving the hotel together and climbing into a limousine. So she, without knowing exactly why, hails a taxi and asks the driver to follow them. She would have liked to know their destination, to have found out more about the old guy, about her father, but the clumsy driver loses their trail, so she tells him to take her to the hotel with the English name instead. She noticed the limousine was just about identical to those belonging to that hotel. But on arriving, she sees no sign of the limousine, her father, or the old guy in the classically-cut suit. She asks the admiral at the door, but he doesn't remember seeing them. Perhaps he does know, and has been told to be discreet. The girl then figures she'll find her mother in the dining room. Perhaps she could ease some of the tension between them, persuade her that her future is in writing, not music. She could even ask her about the old guy in the classically-cut suit, who seems to be acquainted with her. She pauses outside the dining room. Suddenly, all thought of her mother is obscured behind a fractured image of her father. He's wearing that routine smile again, the one which could be interpreted to mean anything. Then the girl becomes disheartened. Because although she recognizes the image in her head as that of her father, she still doesn't know what kind of man, what kind of person he really is.

At this time in the afternoon, there's very little activity in the hotel with the English name. The girl is walking through the lobby—her eyes in the middle distance, fixed on nothing in particular. She looked for her mother in all her usual haunts—the garden, the dining room, the salon beside the café—but she couldn't find her anywhere, so she decided to go up to the room. If she doesn't feel inspired to write, she'll dedicate a few hours to piano practice. She knows perfectly well how the young conductor wants her to play—to stick to the score, emphasize every note—but she doesn't think the music sounds right performed this way, and they're both far too stubborn to ever come to a compromise. Nevertheless, when all's said and done, he isn't the one who's got a recording career to boast about. If she's going to give up the piano, then she wants to go out with a bang: indeed, her final recording will be the culmination of all her musical ambitions, and it will leave a lasting impression on all who hear it. So she doesn't need anyone telling her how to play. She's developed a characteristic style, and whatever the composition, future generations will immediately recognize the performer when they hear her unique interpretation of it. In her last recording, though, she's going to go beyond even her own characteristic style. As the elevator approaches, she takes a last look around the lobby and sees, at the reception desk, a man she's seen several times before. There are no such things as coincidences, she murmurs. The screenwriter sees the scene unfolding as follows: the girl approaches the man slowly, timidly at first, but accelerates, gets more assured, the closer she gets; meanwhile, behind her, the elevator door opens with no one inside, and remains still a moment, like a gaping mouth. If it had eyes, it would see the girl accosting a man wearing a dark gray summer suit, a blue linen shirt, unbuttoned at the top, and no tie. He looks about fifty, his thin face wizened by the years. He turns his head, and their eyes meet momentarily. He squints at her to see if he knows her, but then turns back to the desk after convincing himself he doesn't. The girl, on the other hand, doesn't slow her pace, but continues walking toward the man she knows as cousin Dedalus, who's waiting for the receptionist to hang up the phone and attend to him. Seeing him up close, she thinks he looks a little chubbier, but also more elegant, than he does in the old photos she's seen of him. Also, his hair's somewhat thinner, with some streaks of gray, but the most striking difference she notices is in his bearing, his apparent self-assuredness. Over the years, the girl's constructed a very different image of him based on her mother's photos of him, in which she remembers he looked disheveled, gawky, like a man lacking in confidence. Not anymore. He invites her to sit with him in the salon. His voice sounds familiar, but the girl doesn't want to waste time trying to remember when and where she heard it last. My Mom will be delighted to see you, she says. She tells him her mother's spent years searching for him and that she'll be overjoyed to have finally found him. But the cousin shows little enthusiasm about the prospect of meeting her mother, and seems more interested in getting to know the girl. He's never had the chance to meet a celebrated pianist, let alone a child prodigy. I've seen you before a few times around the city? says the girl. But I wasn't sure who you were. He looks at her, surprised. The girl knows she shouldn't put off telling her mother of this discovery, but getting the chance to talk to her cousin alone is too tempting, so she agrees to join him when he suggests they go for a walk. In the next shot, the two are shown strolling on a bridge, and it seems some time has passed, for they both look more relaxed in each other's company, chatting casually as they cross over to the other side of the river. She regales him with details about her performances with the Little Sinfonietta, and explains that it's called the Little Sinfonietta both because the number of musicians is small and because the musicians are all child prodigies; all, that is, except the young conductor. But he was quite precocious in his day. Then she tells him how much she wants to be a writer, repeating the same story she's told again and again to whoever will listen. She thinks getting started on her literary opus hinged on her finally making the momentous decision to abandon music and begin a new life. She would've liked to write the next part of her cousin's story but she didn't know how to begin. It's difficult, she admits, writing about someone she doesn't know. But perhaps now that she's finally met him . . . she's being sincere, opening up, because she feels she can confide in him. She's writing about the No World, she tells him: roughly speaking, it's a story about aliens who don't know they're aliens. Cousin Dedalus is reminded of Leon Kowalski, a replicant who appears in the opening scenes of a famous sci-fi movie. She didn't know who or what Leon Kowalski was when she came up with the story, although she's found out since. Her cousin thinks it resembles the idea in the sci-fi movie about replicants believing that false, implanted memories—memories extracted from other people's minds—are a genuine record of their own past experience. During the walk, he shows the girl houses where some of the greatest writers of the century once lived. The writer who revolutionized twentieth-century literature lived in this city for years, he tells her. His knowledge greatly enhances her perception of the neighboring country's capital. This must be an interesting route through the city for a writer, he says. She's flattered he refers to her as a writer. He hardly says anything about himself, and when he does, it's only because she's dragged the information out of him. He repeats to her something she already knows: that he adopted the sobriquet Dedalus because of his admiration for the writer who revolutionized literature; that from his youth, he's been signing his letters and anything else he writes with that name. But he says nothing about his life during his exile in the neighboring country's capital. The

161

girl mentions her mother's interest in finding out what happened to him. There's an awkward silence. Then the girl remembers Ka, her impression that some people pronounce her name with a "ka" sound, and that this could be the way it *should* be pronounced. He asks her how she can tell. She doesn't know how she can tell. You seem to have very acute senses, but listen, what's the difference between "ka" and "k"? She doesn't reply right away. He gets the impression he's delving into the secrets of a hidden order. Ka, she eventually says, is a tutelary spirit or genius or guardian angel who is born with us and who'll take care of us after we die. That's the definition I found in an encyclopedia. The cousin doesn't recall the idea being used by any other famous writer, but he likes it. A tutelary spirit or genius or guardian angel that looks after us, he repeats to himself, as if trying to memorize the definition. The screenwriter sees the scene as being a single, extended dolly shot, the camera in front of the two characters, receding as they advance, but always keeping the same distance away from them as they walk together and talk—the cousin looking here and there, the girl looking only at the cousin. The scene behind them changes continually, showing many different people walking with them, past them, in front of them, and many different buildings, streets, and bridges, which the viewer may recognize as belonging to the neighboring country's capital. The girl wants to know about his exile. She asks him if, after so many years, a person in exile might not get used to the condition, if it might not become routine. The writer who revolutionized twentieth-century literature was an ex-pat virtually his whole life, who styled himself an exile. Cousin Dedalus rejects the comparison. But is he not a writer too? she asks. He responds evasively. So she starts talking about her father, who would respond in a similar way if he was asked a similar question. The cousin becomes silent, looking straight ahead, seemingly lost in those same memories the girl is so determined to dredge up. Her father likes this novel about a guy obsessed with solitude, jealousy, and the passage of time, while her teacher has advised her to read the dramatist par excellence and the writer who revolutionized literature. The girl supposes her cousin would agree with her teacher, but to her surprise, he shows no preference for either option. Instead, he suggests she find her own path. They stop walking as he points to a building, saying one of the great female writers from the beginning of the twentieth century lived there. This city has always attracted great writers, he says, both male and female. Do you think your passion for writing is fugitive, like your father's, something that will cool over time? he asks. Not a chance in hell, she says. She's only one step away from finally abandoning the piano for the pen. He then asks her if she'd like him to accompany her to the concert tonight. She tells him her mother will be there. He excuses himself and says he just remembered he had a previous engagement. He won't have many more opportunities to hear her play live, she says. She's resolute about giving it all up for literature. He smiles. One day you'll have to tell me all about this No World, he says while walking away. She stands at a corner watching him, overjoyed at having had the opportunity to spend a few hours with her cousin Dedalus, that legendary member of her family about whom the girl has always wanted to write, a man who's spent years hiding from the authorities in the neighboring country's capital. Yet she can't stop thinking about his voice, about where she might've heard it before. And what was he doing in the hotel?

That night, she enters the writer's café in front of the church where the young conductor of the orchestra and brilliant composer are sitting at the back. They ignore her. There are no more disputes, just cold dismissals. This is a new feeling, this drifting away, as if being dragged out to sea by the current, farther and farther away from those who were once so close, who are now starting to become a memory. Perhaps their coldness is a new strategy, a part of their game. The young conductor's latest conquest is sitting next to him. They know, the girl thinks. Her mother must've told them that she won't be joining them on tour. She finds her mother sitting on a stool at the bar. You're late, she says. You're not going to believe it, says the girl emphatically, grinning with relish before exulting: I spent the afternoon with your cousin, Dedalus.

Her mother's attitude softens as she hears about the details of their encounter. She says nothing during her daughter's energetic narration, answers none of her cursory questions, just listens quietly, taking economical drags on her cigarette. The two women are sitting alone in the corner of the café. There are many people walking back and forth in the shot, but only we are privy to this one conversation. As she speaks, the girl is suddenly overcome by the same anxious feeling she gets when she hears those voices calling to her. Should she give her mother time to digest this news, to get used to the fact that it was her daughter who found him, the one who got the prize deer, so to speak, and not her? No, it must be something else. She looks straight into her mother's eyes. You knew exactly where he was, didn't you? In fact, I think you've known for years. Her mother breaks eye contact and looks elsewhere, a gesture the girl takes for assent; and although the smoke from her cigarette may be the real culprit as far as her refusal to put the matter into words, the truth seems about to transude from her mother's pores. Perhaps they were lovers. Why else would she keep his whereabouts a secret for so many years? Are you finished? asks her mother, who insists they end the conversation. Now it's the girl who doesn't answer. She can't think of anything to say that will prolong her victory. Her mother gets up from the stool, slinging her handbag over her shoulder. The screenwriter imagines a large handbag, matching a short, loose dress. You should focus on the concert, she advises the girl, before turning around and walking away.

The screenwriter is exhausted. He stands up and does a couple of laps of the room to wake himself up. Then he lights a cigarette, sits down again, and rereads the last page. He takes a hopeful look at the building opposite. Again, his neighbor's window is dark. She must have gone out. He goes to the mini-kitchen next to the door and pours himself a glass of water. Then he sits down on the sofa and turns on the TV. It seems something quite significant has happened, because all the channels are broadcasting the same news: they're all reporting the arrest of the most notorious terrorist in history—a man who, for twenty years perhaps, has been the world's most wanted fugitive. It seems they captured, or maybe kidnapped him in a faraway country and then brought him to the capital. The screenwriter doesn't understand why they went to all that trouble. Why they didn't just assassinate him. While watching, he half-consciously considers a few synonyms for assassinate: dispatch, murder, liquidate . . . no, assassinate is the best word.

She hasn't gone to bed yet. She's been writing in the bathroom since her father fell asleep. She doesn't know where it's going, but she's writing, and that's all that matters. Her meeting with Cousin Dedalus has again made her reconsider her story. The old philosophy professor could be replaced with the cousin. But after considering some options and writing some drafts that now are nestling in the wastebasket, she hasn't found a plausible way to do so. There's nothing new to write about really. All she did, in the end, was find him. She still knows as little about the man as she did before. So she still compensates for her ignorance by making things up based on the same prejudices and presumptions she already had about him. This isn't the way to start a book about Cousin Dedalus's life. She doesn't want ignorance and presumption to dictate the plot of her story. It might dictate everything else too. So she decided to stick with her original choice: the old professor cum alien hunter. At least, with him, she gets all her material firsthand. She's still describing the period immediately before his flight to the City in Outer Space, before he decides to establish himself as a photographer in some other part of the universe. "3.2 A thought can be expressed using simple signs. The professor watches the female student on the TV screen. She's standing in the middle of an empty room wearing a school uniform. All the walls are white, and the floor is covered over with a white sheet. The old guy's absorbed by the images on the screen. Occasionally, his voice is heard giving her instructions on how to undress, but mostly there's only silence, the soft whisper of movement as she takes off her clothes, the delicate rustle as they fall to the floor. Slowly, he says. Slowly . . . the uniform's an old one, and therefore a little snug. She first takes off her patent leather shoes, then she removes her skirt, and after unbuttoning her shirt, she turns her back to the camera and coyly removes her bra. She teases the camera, regardant, playing with her shirt, moistening with her tongue the area of fabric covering her nipples.

Then she knots the shirt around her waist. The old professor's voice bids her to pull the edges of her panties up. She obeys. But she does so slowly, teasingly, toying with both sides alternately, and pulling at the seams. Then the same voice bids her to pull the panties halfway down and leave them suspended between her thighs. Once again, she obeys. 3.203 Ka is the same sign as Ka. The female student's no longer on the TV screen, but beside the old professor, dressing after having had a shower. He asks her to sit and watch the video with him. It's late, she says. It doesn't matter how late it is, he says without taking his eyes off the screen. Just stay. Onscreen, the girl is on her knees, again wetting the parts of her shirt covering her nipples. She raises her breasts with both hands, and the voice of the professor bids her to start masturbating. Then the same voice bids her to urinate between her fingers. It seems like an eternity passes before she manages to squeeze out a few drops. They trickle down her thighs and onto the white sheet covering the floor. As she eases into a steady stream, the camera zooms in on the growing puddle. The old professor hears the door close, and he moves his eyes momentarily away from the screen, his mouth half-open, as if intending to say something, perhaps good-bye. But now it's too late even for good-byes, so his eyes return casually to the screen. A faint halo surrounds the female student's body. But the old professor, the out-of-practice alien hunter, either cannot or does not want to see it. Perhaps he's conditioned himself to see them only as they can be made to appear on his old daguerreotypes. 3.3 Only in daguerreotypes do extraterrestrials acquire true meaning. On the stairway, the female student thinks she just heard someone pronounce her name with a 'ka.'" The girl rereads what she's written and then types it up on the laptop. Now, whenever she writes in her father's hotel room, whether she does it in the bathroom or wherever, she always transcribes what she's done on his laptop. He doesn't know about this, of course, and she doesn't want to ask permission yet, in case he says no, because she hasn't got a laptop of her own. The screenwriter thinks it's a kind of fetish, this habit of typing up everything she writes, as if she's reluctant to let go of what she's done, to move forward and deal with what has yet to be done, to resist the temptation the relinquish the past, to resist the temptation to start all over again. The girl receives a phone call from the brilliant composer. Her father gets out of bed and stretches as he walks out onto the balcony to survey the Grand Central Station. The phone call is brief, formal—just letting her know the new rehearsal venue. She notes down the address in her diary. Then she collects her father's laptop from the bathroom and furtively, deftly, places it back on the table. She goes outside to ensure he didn't notice the sleight. But she needs a ruse—her encounter with cousin Dedalus. She notes the expression on his face. It's like the expression one prepares before receiving bad news. He turns to look at her. But his eyes seem not to see her. It's as if he's listening but is puzzling over something else. Just a chance encounter, he says once she finishes her account. Then silence. His expression is routine, the kind that could be interpreted to mean anything. Then one of his many cell phones rings. He goes inside to answer it. She hears him answer it by giving his name. He enters the bathroom and shuts the door. She hears nothing more. McGregor speaking, says the girl, imitating the voice she supposes is on the other line. Despite her suspicions, the girl wishes she knew for sure who was calling. She wishes she could hear what they are talking about. She's hardly a detective. A coincidence? There are no such things as coincidences, she says. There are no such things as chance encounters either.

It seems they lost no time finding a replacement. The girl watches them through the glass screen, chagrined. She didn't know the young conductor's latest conquest would be singing. In fact, the possibility never even entered her mind. She found the new rehearsal venue easily enough. Once inside the building, she walked along a corridor, looking into the other booths, some occupied, some not, which reminded her of the ones in her native city. On finding the booth the Little Sinfonietta were rehearsing in, she was shocked to see, through the glass screen, the latest conquest singing in her place—her voice almost imperceptible, distant, filtering into the corridor through the slots of the soundproof booth. The girl didn't know she could sing. Surely this means something, but what? A coincidence? They don't exist. Chance doesn't exist in logic, she thinks. She braces herself before entering, looks at them again through the glass screen. She can't tell by listening, but it looks like she's reciting some verses. It seems they lost no time in finding a replacement. They probably planned it all along, she thinks. She has to get over it and just accept the reality of the situation. There's no point in thinking about the hows and the whys. Whatever conclusion she arrives at will be painful. The girl enters the booth. She's not going on tour with them, so maybe now she can just disappear, she thinks, quietly and without a fuss, just as she planned. The latest conquest is a quick study. She's probably spent days practicing alone. The girl watches her carefully: she's beautiful, a little older than her. During his presentation, the young conductor says she studied at one of the musical conservatories in the neighboring country's capital. How lucky, he says while taking her hand, one of our biggest fans happens to be a soprano. Yeah, lucky, says the girl. She has a different musical background, but the young conductor says he's sure the conquest will learn quickly enough, because now they're going to be professionals, and everything they do will make the news—the girl's mother and their new manager will make sure of that. As such, the latest conquest will have to learn the Little Sinfonnieta's new motto. Marketing, it's all about marketing, the young conductor adds, inducting the orchestra's new member. His latest conquest feigns momentary indecision to disguise her inner jubilation.

It's just a coincidence, insists the young conductor. Until yesterday, no one knew she was a soprano. The girl listens, resting her elbows on the table of a dreary café. I'm not having another fight with you, he tells her. She doesn't believe him. He's being disarming because he's impatient to get to a meeting with his latest conquest. He has to teach her some of the Little Sinfonietta's repertoire before the tour. The girl looks away, dismissing what he says. She wonders if the conquest has also been learning how to play foosball. Wearily, she turns back to look at the conductor. As always, he's wearing the Scholastic Institute's regulation uniform, comprised of a navy-blue blazer, gray pants, white shirt, and necktie. The girl wonders how long into the meeting he'll manage to keep them on. The next scene takes place in a squalid apartment. On the street outside there's a neon sign flickering, phasing with an occasional breeze that parts the curtains of a window to reveal the young conductor of the orchestra lying in bed with the girl. It's a cliché, but the screenwriter decided to include this scene in order to show the sordid conditions in which they've made love. The young conductor licks the gummed edge of the paper skin of a joint he's rolling. He wants to know if the girl could write a libretto for an opera about a game, about a No World of parallel planes, where a female piano prodigy is trying to find an original way to interpret a difficult work, a prodigy who insists on using an impossible style, and who always contradicts the opinions of others. Of the people who love her, he adds. She knows he's being sarcastic, but she kisses his chest, mechanically, unfeelingly: a kiss good-bye. She wants to get out of this shit-hole. She has no intention of writing this or any other libretto. Things have changed. She tells him calmly, matter-of-factly, and without bitterness or anger. There's a silence. The young conductor looks at the ceiling, watches the light reflected there from the flickering sign outside. No, things aren't what they used to be, he says while lighting the joint. The world changes, people change. His words sound hollow, phatic, spoken to fill an emptiness, to break the silence. In the darkness of the bedroom, the girl's face flickers in and out of view with the blue light of the neon sign. Indeed, she says, but when you think about it, nothing stays the same. The young conductor mumbles an apology, the kind mumbled by someone who hardly ever apologizes, who only does so when someone he loves is threatening to leave him. But she doesn't care for his apology. She knows that, by the end of the week, the latest conquest will have taken her place—both in the Little Sinfonietta and the conductor's affections. Not that it matters. Not that anything matters to her now except writing. The philosopher W once wrote, "6.4 All propositions are of equal value." If she didn't know he was talking about something else, she'd say this proposition was false. She takes his magnum opus out from under her clothes to check that she remembered the line correctly. Then she puts the book safely in her satchel. Her thoughts drift elsewhere. She's been promising herself for days to get rid of the young conductor and brilliant composer. Getting rid of the brilliant composer shouldn't be a problem though. He's no one.

A death would make sense, thinks the screenwriter, as he finishes his cigarette and faces the building opposite. For once, though, his eyes aren't searching the darkness of his neighbor's window, but the darkness of the sky above it. A death would add suspense. He'd planned to involve the old guy in the classically-cut suit in some sort of shady affair. The girl's father is an expert in these dealings. He supposes the guy in the classically-cut suit is the one to kill off, but then he can't picture the circumstances under which it would happen. Not yet, at least. He can't see a single star in that cosmic dark from which they came. The aliens who don't know they're aliens. The screenwriter gives up the search and goes to the mini-kitchen. He lets the cold tap run a few seconds before filling his glass. A death would add an element of intrigue. But it doesn't have to be a death that provides this. He postpones his decision, takes a sip of water, and leaves the glass on the sink. After a minute or two, he's back in front of the typewriter. He can't just turn his mind off by flipping a switch. But doesn't he always say this when it happens to be on? The characters have independent lives. They make and break relationships, leave old paths to follow new ones. He thinks again about a possible death. The girl is on a path to a new life. In a moment, she'll discover her father's involved in something she hasn't yet considered, thinks the screenwriter, who's now rewriting a scene he isn't satisfied with. After hearing his stomach groan a fifth time, he decides to go to the café in the plaza and grab a sandwich. The waitress doesn't usually work nights, not that he's even thinking about her right now. He must consider the story's structure again. He feels rusty, like someone who's come back to do a job after a long absence. Still, he draws up a list of key characters. There's no such thing as gratuitousness in a movie—everything happens for a reason, exists for a reason.

He writes their names in the order he remembers them: the young conductor of the orchestra, the brilliant composer, the mother, the father, Cousin Dedalus, McGregor, the old guy in the classically-cut suit . . . who else? He thinks a few moments. He knows he's forgetting someone. He gives up. Besides, he's almost completely worn out after two days' almost uninterrupted writing. Once back in his room, he turns on the TV and lies back on the bed. He wonders if the girl will surprise him by showing up tonight. No. He doesn't want to get his hopes up. On the screen, the most notorious terrorist in history is appearing before the bench—his hands cuffed, dressed completely in white, smirking.

She's convinced they follow her. The feeling is always there, but for some reason, is more pronounced whenever she visits him. After finally managing to evade them, she goes to the window and peeps through a chink in the curtain just wide enough to see the dark, empty street below. They could be paparazzi, or a detective hired by her mother. They could be alien hunters who've found a way to detect her secret halo, who know her real name is Ka and, perhaps, that she came from a distant planet also called Ka. She has a feeling she's being watched, that strange eyes are scanning her every inch. The screenwriter's read somewhere that eyes have some sort of an effect on the objects they regard. Like the visual equivalent of echolocation used by bats. This is what produces our perception of distance, our consciousness of where an object or person really is, since it's only an image, an illusion that appears on our retinas. But this process must also have an effect on the person or object perceived, which is why the girl senses she's being watched, because she may have developed the ability to detect the movement of eyes on her body, by a kind of sixth sense. The screenwriter reads a series of descriptive passages the girl narrates in the third person. He reads slowly, sub-vocalizing the rhythm of each phrase, as if trying to uncover something new in the words, perhaps because he wants to estrange himself from what he wrote, as if he were in fact considering something she'd written herself: "3.31 I call any part of an image that characterizes its sense an expression (or a symbol). On the bed, the old alien hunter talks about youthful skin—dispassionately, as a dermatologist would, or so it would seem—while running his fingers slowly down her back and up her thighs and moving them stealthily toward her breasts. When he speaks about young women's skin, he has the air of an expert, and expatiates as if it was the most important topic in the world. The female student knows exactly what he's up to, but acts as if she doesn't, acts interested in his discourse—as if she's never heard anything so intriguing in all her young life—because she wants to seem innocent, inexperienced, for that's the way he likes to think she is. He wants to know if she's going out with someone. He must've asked her a dozen times by now, and every time her answer's been the same. Yes, she says again, knowing he wanted the other answer, knowing a No would put his mind at ease, and a Yes would only make him suffer. 3.313 In the limiting case, the image becomes a constant, the expression becomes a proposition. Now, in the City in Outer Space, the old professor shudders in recalling that moment. Now he writes only to record his memories. If anyone ever finds this great floating spaceship, this City adrift in Outer Space, they could reconstruct his life on Earth with his words, including his version of the war. He likes to dream of such an outcome to ease the passage of the years, to make sense of his life as a survivor alone in a desolate city, to make him believe the record of his experiences will not have been written in vain, whatever the number of intervening centuries. But he knows it's an absurd fantasy." The girl returns to the window to peer through the chink in the curtain. The screenwriter begs her to stay. She doesn't usually smoke, but this time it's she who lights a cigarette and puffs at the ceiling. I'll take care of you, she hears him promise. And you'll be able to write as much as you want, he says while moving a stack of paper away from his desk. She keeps looking out the window. There's a man down there at the corner—a guy she's seen before, standing in the very same place; at the very same time, perhaps. But the shadows are obscuring his features. It's probably just some guy waiting for someone. But then she remembers the time, and wonders who or what he'd be waiting for in the early hours of the morning. Maybe she didn't manage to evade her stalkers after all. Maybe her fate has already been determined and they're waiting for the right moment to move in on her. The screenwriter promises to protect her. What do you want more than anything else in the world? he asks her. She doesn't answer him, doesn't take her eyes off of the window. It's a stupid question. She's rich and already has everything he can offer and much more. Besides, what she wants more than anything else in the world no one can offer her. She must create it herself. The screenwriter suddenly feels distant from her, that he doesn't know anything about her. He doesn't know what else, besides writing, could possibly satisfy her. Outside the Institute, they've only ever been together in a dingy hotel room, or posing in a few random photographs. He tries for a moment to recall where else they might have been together. Of course, there was the night of the concert, the dinner afterward, and the running around the city with her and her retinue. But that doesn't count, he thinks. It wasn't a very good night. I'll teach you everything I know, he says, breaking the silence, the great writers, their works, everything. We can even read them aloud together—it'll be great—just promise you'll stay. She ignores his supplication and keeps looking coldly out the window at the man on the street corner. She doesn't even blink when the smoke rises up from the ashtray and drifts into her eyes, passing her face undisturbed, as if she were holding her breath, in case displacing the plume might give her away. You'll have nothing to do but write, he ventures. We'll just shut ourselves in this room forever. It will be our own little paradise.

It's quiet. The streets are deserted. The traffic lights are signaling in vain. The silhouette on the corner has abandoned its vigil and the girl is no longer peering through the curtains. The screenwriter's still begging her to stay with him, still promising he'll protect her. She doesn't see how this paradise of his could benefit her writing. He can't conceive of any paradise without her. But this could be fleeting. He may not feel the same way later on. He lowers his head and his eyes flit to the keys of the typewriter. Then the girl starts talking again, and seems like her old self. Why would a mind build an imaginary world around itself? she asks, referring to her idea of a whole world inhabited by beings who aren't aware they're from another planet. What role does such a mind play in the lives of these characters? What gives it the impression it's created a world at all? These are the questions that constantly run through her mind, the answers to which, like indefinite shapes, are always vague, although becoming more distinct with every passing day. Perhaps her work should deal only with this. The girl asks the screenwriter for another cigarette and lights it by the window. Let's imagine that nothing around us truly exists—that however much we believe what we see and touch is real, it's all in fact the creation of a single mind; that that mind is but a thoughtlet in one small corner of another, greater mind—the one that conceives the universe; and that the universe is but a thoughtlet in an even greater mind, and so on, ad infinitum. Is it physically possible, or even logically feasible, to have more than one universe? The screenwriter doesn't know. The girl expels a mouthful of smoke and asks: Does this cigarette exist? The smoke? "2.063 The sum-total of reality is the No World." A slight alteration of W's pronouncement. She goes back to her initial inquiry. She thinks the answer must be simple, because a thoughtlet is like a fundamental particle, and these constitute everything else in existence, everything a mind learns, and everything it imagines, are composed of these. And if it bodies forth a whole world, it must do so because it doesn't want to be alone. It's the only possible answer to the question. It's the only answer the girl can think of. Listening to her, the screenwriter starts thinking he should imagine his script not as a series of concentric layers like an onion, but of a series of parallel planes, each successive one subsumed in the next. So where should he situate the girl's watcher in the shadows? Should he exist in the same world in which she moves, or should he exist in the world she imagines? The plane she calls real, or the one she's created? He parodies an old controversy, but instead of mathematics, he asks himself whether it was the No World that was discovered or invented. Perhaps he should avoid philosophical polemics and stick to thinking about the story's subplots and themes, something better suited to a man of his trade. Nothing exists outside our minds—there is only intellectual curiosity, delusion, love. And aren't these the very things the movies try to capture?

He's inclined to believe the girl's lost her mind, if only temporarily, or that she's tired and this has impaired her reasoning, her thinking—he can't think of the right word. He's tired himself out. After all, she's only just left his room after staying up most of the night. For some reason she's obsessed with one of the least interesting elements of the plot, has warped it into something more important than it is. After arriving back at the hotel in front of the Grand Central Station, she found her father was out, which she thought suspicious, so she wrote something down that she says perfectly sums up her thinking on the matter. The screenwriter listens in the dark, his lights out, the girl's voice, on the other end of the line, seeming to emerge from the darkness. She's forgotten about the creations of her mind, including the shadow that stalks her in the night. He hears her voice plain and clear, although his dilated pupils are straining at the soft fletches of light filtering in through the curtains, as if to say we want more than this smattering of traffic light, lamplight, and moonlight—we hunger for a greater repast. But eyes can't speak, so all he can hear is the voice on the other end of the line, and only that occupies his thoughts. McGregor speaking, he thinks. Suddenly, as if she were reading his thoughts, she starts talking about that same associate of her father's, who, she says, as she only just discovered, is taking turns with him staying in the station. I think they're both hunters, she declares. They're pursuing a special kind of prey, but she hasn't yet discovered what it is.

Some time later, the screenwriter dreams the girl's father and this so-called McGregor emerge from the body of the old guy in the classically-cut suit. Then the two merge together and reincorporate him. The screenwriter awakens and writes a description of the dream while it's still fresh—as if trying to photograph a shadow that only moves in the night, returning to its sanctuary in the river at dawn. He's trying to remember where the dream was set, and thinks it took place in a city, but somewhere far from the neighboring country's capital. He turns off the light and goes back to sleep. He dreams of some things about which he's already written, and others about which he'd like to write, things he always fails to recall on awakening when they've returned to their sanctuary in his unconscious. Nevertheless, while still in bed, he goes over the note he wrote during the night. His handwriting is almost illegible, but it doesn't matter: he still remembers the dream—although a little less clearly—and what he manages to decipher from his notes supplements what he's forgotten. He gets out of bed and freshens up, has a look at himself in the bathroom mirror, takes a deep breath, and then heads down to the canteen for breakfast. The elevator takes its time arriving. He gets the feeling he may be better off taking the stairs. He'd do it, if it wasn't for his damned limp. He grips his cane impatiently and knocks it against the floor a couple of times, the strokes, muted by the carpet, rendering the act meaningless. He doesn't like those muffled thuds, he says to himself, because they probably unleashed a cloud of dust mites that are now colonizing his socks and the hem of his pants. Standing at the hotel's entrance, he looks outside and wonders if the world he sees is real or an invention of the mind. It's either one or the other, but it's still the same world that greets him every morning: the looming buildings, the rushing vehicles, the passing faces, that woman who lifts the shutters of the lingerie store. He decides to go out for breakfast instead of having it in the canteen. He heads to a kiosk, located at the point where the boulevards intersect, and buys a broadsheet from his native country and one from the neighboring one as well, before heading to a café on the small island in the river. It will take him about twenty minutes to get there, but he thinks the walk will do him good, the fresh air will do him good before he shuts himself away again. On arriving, he asks for a sandwich and coffee, and reads the news from his native country. The star of the soccer team the girl supports is still on vacation and hasn't made clear when he'll be rejoining his team. The coach is now threatening him with a fine and suspension, so the star player has announced to the press that he doesn't like being threatened. The same newspaper has a long article on the man who's considered the worst terrorist in history. After his sandwich, the screenwriter drinks his coffee and checks what movies are being advertised. He's especially interested in knowing which ones are showing in both cities. Only the big blockbusters, it seems. The movie business isn't what it used to be. They don't make quality films anymore. He's annoyed at himself for having such a trite opinion, but it comes from hearing similar comments expressed by many other people in the business. He'd liked to have worked with the truly great screenwriters—especially the ones from the golden age—to be numbered among them, to be considered great, or at least be remembered for having collaborated with them. When he was young, he'd hoped that one day he might be considered great, but nowadays, he has no such illusions. He hasn't the time or the energy he'd need to achieve greatness. But then he thinks of an exception to his rule—a movie whose screenwriter isn't from the golden age, a quite recent movie in fact, but one that he admires a lot, the one in which angels listen to other people's voices, perhaps those of everyone on Earth. He folds the newspapers and decides to stop thinking about it. Besides putting him in a bad mood, it's becoming a repetitive thought pattern, and this makes him feel uninspired. He takes out his notebook. There's something about the old guy in the classically-cut suit that's bothering him. But when he thinks about him in the context of the whole story, he finds himself wondering more about what it is the girl's father and the so-called McGregor are up to—why they take turns waiting in the Grand Central station, who or what it is they're waiting for. He notes down a few plausible hypotheses, nothing too outlandish, although he wants to keep an open mind. On the outdoor terrace of a bar, the girl's sitting down reading a newspaper while talking to her mother on her cell phone. She's expressing reluctance at the prospect of being interviewed by one of the neighboring country's leading newspapers, but her mother says she's coming to collect her to make sure she attends. The girl tells her the name of the bar she's at then looks around for a street plaque to tell her the name of the street it's on. She puts the cell phone away and goes through the headlines. News of the capture of the world's worst terrorist occupies the first few pages. There's no news about the star player of the soccer team she supports. It seems the neighboring country doesn't care about his refusal to come back from vacation. She turns one page, then another, and then, suddenly, she sees a picture of a familiar face. The screenwriter imagines the girl's puzzled expression, and then a shot of the page she's looking at, the photograph of the old guy in the classically-cut suit, and the caption that reads, "Well-Known Scientist Seriously Ill." The screenwriter wants to get the gist of the news across without worrying too much about the wording. So he summarizes the contents of the article telegraphically: World-renowned astrophysicist. Health declines sharply. Last twenty-four hours. Next to the article, a shaded box gives some information about his life. Apparently, the man she met in her father's hotel room is an expert researcher into the possibility of life in other galaxies, and a stalwart advocate of radio telescopes as a means of detecting intelligent life in space. The girl can't believe what she's reading and wonders whether she should pinch herself. This news couldn't be more exciting. She tears out the article and puts it between the pages of her diary as evidence, in case she ever doubts what she's just read. But then she checks her enthusiasm. This isn't exactly the windfall it seems to be, for although she's finally discovered the identity of the old guy in the classically-cut suit, she's done so at a point when his health's in serious decline. She's finally found someone to explain to her the reason there are so many churches and cathedrals scattered all over the planet, but that someone may in fact be on his deathbed. So the truth, like so many other things in her life so far, may be just out of reach. The next scene takes place in a taxi. Mother and daughter are sitting next to each other looking out their respective windows—not speaking to each other, the tension between them at breaking point. Finally, the mother asks what's going through the girl's mind. Nothing, she says. But, in reality, the girl's disgusted at being dragged away from her writing to sit through an interview with the young conductor and brilliant composer.

We cut to a scene in an office where the girl is sitting impatiently with the young conductor, brilliant composer, and her mother. The young conductor's latest conquest is also present, but at this point, there's nothing new in that. The office's glass walls make visible a large space where journalists, editors, and other employees are buzzing around like drones. The screenwriter pays without tipping, and makes his way back to the hotel, sticking to the narrow, winding streets that might otherwise be described as confining, labyrinthine, for he wants to empathize with the girl, confined in that office with people she dislikes. He walks slowly, leaning on his cane, the newspapers folded under his other arm, thinking about the girl, about the old guy in the classically-cut suit, the cathedrals, and the Little Sinfonietta, before deciding to stop at an ATM. He inserts the card and enters his PIN. He can't believe his balance; his account's almost empty. He takes out enough to survive on for the next few days, and then goes looking for a telephone booth. He wants to ask the producer for another advance, but no one answers the call. He checks the time. Perhaps he's gone out. He calls the office, but again no one answers. Most businesses are closed for vacation in August, but he decides to try again later. He hangs up and continues to the hotel. If the producer asks to see part of the script, he'll have to send him something more than sketches for a series of scenes. He'll have to structure them better, arrange them in a sequence, and type them up. When he reaches the hotel, he stands in front of it for a moment, remembering the far better hotels he's stayed in before. But duty presses him to forget about this. So he wobbles through the door and proceeds through the lobby, following the frayed track in the carpet that leads to the elevator. On entering his room, he wastes no time in sitting at the typewriter and cleaning up the scene where the girl finds out about the scientist's illness. Then he tries calling the producer again. He sits at the edge of the bed listening to the rings, until the phone cuts out and he puts it back on the hook. Then he grins mischievously, as a bad guy would in the movies, picks up the phone again, and calls his own house. He waits five rings before hanging up. He stops smiling, remembers the pressing duty he's already postponed too long, and returns to his post at the typewriter.

During the interview, the young conductor and brilliant composer act as if their partnership with the girl is destined to go on forever. The girl, on the other hand, is withdrawn, unable to get the article about the old guy in the classically-cut suit out of her head—a guy she discovered was a scientist, an astrophysicist and expert researcher into the possibility of life in other galaxies, a scientist who may in fact be on his deathbed. So she ignores all the questions, lets the others answer them. In fact, she doesn't participate in the interview at all. The interviewer is a music journalist with a special interest in the Little Sinfonietta, who happens to work for one of the neighboring country's leading newspapers. So, according to the girl's mother, the interview is crucial for promoting the tour. The young conductor of the orchestra says you can never be too young to be a conductor, a composer, or a performer. Then he says the individual roles aren't important in themselves, but that all three must work together if any one of them is to succeed. The girl observes the scene while listening to him sensationalize their story, a story like so many others, about a bunch of unruly kids who have a certain special something about them, a certain aura that sets them apart from other kids, other people. The kinds of kids who are sent to the Scholastic Institute so they can be with other special kids, other people who've been labeled exceptional, gifted. The term's been overused, even abused. What teenager doesn't believe he's going to change the world, that all his ideas are great, original? Everyone thinks they're special at our age, but the young conductor of the orchestra would like to believe that, in our case, it's a fact. So he affects a grandiosity and self-assurance to give the journalist a visible manifestation of the fact—rattling on about the avant-garde, about how we've been, at one time or another, Futurists, Dadaists, Surrealists, and even all three at once, since ours is perhaps the era when

184

the vanguard finally comes to fruition; blathering on about how we have the best of everything, the best age, the best education, the best future, the best opportunity to achieve success, even glory. The girl's eyes move from the young conductor to her mother, who knows he's exaggerating, but is nonetheless mesmerized by the future star's adept handling of the interview. Perhaps our time's finally come, she hears him say. Then the girl turns to look at the latest conquest, sitting over there, imitating the journalist's posture, his actions, taking her own notes. The journalist then asks the girl how she came up with the idea of throwing the clown's nose into the crowd. The girl is stumped. That was perhaps the only spontaneous moment of the entire concert. She eventually says she's getting sick of having to repeat the same performance over and over, like a ritual. It didn't seem authentic. The others look at her, stupefied. Anyway, there was an urgent need to bring in extra noses, since the first offering to the crowd set a standard for the rest of the performances, but she'd have preferred to do something different every night instead of ritualizing that one spontaneous act. She thinks, for example, that she could've done a performance wearing the jersey of the soccer team she supports, with her favorite player's name on the back. Then, after the concert, she'd exchange shirts with someone in the crowd. Number ten, she adds, a controversial player at the moment. The reporter isn't aware he's been in the news for refusing to return to training. Perhaps he doesn't even know who the player is. A controversial player for a controversial young woman, her mother must be thinking. There are other questions, but the girl stops paying attention because she feels that the group is just reaffirming its commitment to a future of exploitation, of doing what's expected of it, the same as so many young men and women in the past who were threatened

185

by their parents with disinheritance unless they abandoned their dreams, did what they were told, married who they were told to marry. No writer who's worth her salt would ever abandon her dreams for lucre. So she remains silent, happy to let the time run by until the end of the interview, thinking that it's all just part of a game—quite a pretentious one, but a game nonetheless. But just as all this is going through her mind, the journalist interrupts her rumination: I've read somewhere, or maybe someone told me, that you say you can hear voices: I don't mean like the one you're hearing now, of course, but voices from another world.

The screenwriter remembers he hasn't eaten, so he makes a couple of sandwiches and eats them at his desk while rereading some passages and taking notes. Once finished, he rests a while before freshening up and going out. He's still thinking about the girl's interview. Fucking spoiled brats, he thinks, annoyed at the kinds of kids who are given everything on a silver platter, who hardly do any work and still succeed, who achieve their dreams without breaking a sweat. He's well acquainted with the type. They were once his students. He grants that they're special, uncommonly talented, but talent isn't enough. There's no merit, no accomplishment, if it comes too easily, he thinks. He leans on his cane and starts limping toward the fountain in the center of the plaza. He prefers people like the girl's father, guys who had to struggle to achieve their goals, who had to kick down doors, not have them opened for them; the kinds of people who would lie, cheat, and steal, if necessary, to succeed. But then they have children, mollycoddled brats who are given the freedom to do whatever they wish, to cast aspersions on the world while playing musical games like dodecaphony, or whatever, who invent silly terms like "No World," who have parents that allow them to sulk through a very important interview, who didn't have to shed a drop of their own blood for the fortune they'll eventually inherit. Who've never experienced suffering, he concludes. What would he have written about if he didn't have this script about musical prodigies? The screenwriter contemplates the café terrace on the other side of the plaza. The barmaid notices him watching, but continues cleaning the table before hurrying back inside. What would he have written about if he was free to choose? He doesn't know. Maybe screenwriters were treated differently back in the golden age, had more freedom. The golden age, he repeats aloud, addressing the fountain. Might there be any truth to such myths? He likes to think so. At least it's something to believe in, periods in history far better than the present one, which the world won't see the like of again, something to look back on when there's nothing to look forward to. He wonders if, sometime in the future, there will be a golden age he'll be too old to appreciate, too set in his ways to understand, or too blind to even recognize. Where are the myths about today, for example? He smiles to himself. There can't be a golden age happening now. If a golden age stuck its head over the parapet, the marketplace would shoot it off. Maybe he's deceiving himself, maybe he's living in the middle of a golden age, and he's the only screenwriter everyone's ignoring, because he's considered unfashionable, unmarketable, by those who think he's only an old retiree who supplements his pension by teaching a bunch of brats, some of whom are not only gifted but rich—twice blessed, in other words—as if having one or the other isn't enough. Maybe he truly despises these kids, resents them. He doesn't want to think about it. He turns his attention to modern cinema, which he feels he knows less and less about every day. Perhaps it's because he hasn't been paying attention, or hasn't been keeping up, or whatever—he can't think of the right phrase. Perhaps his preoccupation with the past has caused him to fall behind, made him antiquated, and he hasn't the strength or desire to catch up. Besides, it would be an uncomfortable transition, to suddenly return to the present. He can't cope with sudden changes. Unlike the girl's father: an old agent asleep in bed who is suddenly awakened by a phone call, a knock on the door, or a gunshot, or something, and finds he has to immediately adapt to this alarming situation. It's an old movie cliché that's been used again and again, to good effect, over the years. The screenwriter doesn't want to think of himself as an old cliché that still has its uses. An out-of-shape soccer player, rather, that's lost his passion, his instinct for the game, and is consequently at the point of retiring. He'd liked to have written about two old detectives who come out of retirement to solve a cold case that's been obsessing them for years: men who live in the past, in their memories. It's an old idea, about which he couldn't even manage a first draft. Why? He doesn't know. He doesn't even know why he began thinking about those old detectives just now. If he hates these gifted kids so much, what is it he finds so enchanting about the girl? Not only is she rich, and a paragon among child prodigies, she's also famous: thrice blessed. He should hate her more than all the rest, but he doesn't, he isn't able. Is there only so much hatred one can harbor for a person before it somehow short-circuits? All he knows is it's a contradiction. He circumambulates the plaza. When he passes the café, he notices there aren't many customers, and he can't see the waitress, so he decides to pass it by. He needs to do some thinking anyway, and he prefers to walk while doing so, and he won't stop until he resolves the contradictions in his story, and he assumes they can all be resolved during a single stroll. Two retired detectives remembering the old days. An idea no one today would touch with a barge pole. But what about the guy who agreed to produce the screenplay he's writing now? Contradictions, he murmurs while walking to the hotel.

The screenwriter goes over the scene in which the girl discovers the guy in the classically-cut suit is in fact a seriously ill scientist. The girl reads about him in the newspaper as she waits for her mother to collect her for the interview. It seems a little different compared to the article she saved in her diary, so she goes to a kiosk to check what the other newspapers have to say. Her mind races as she riffles through the pages, wondering what this guy was doing with her father just before he fell ill. She doesn't expect the newspapers will tell her. Each newspaper sketches its own portrait of the man, although they all agree in one respect, that he's an old eccentric who, in recent years, had withdrawn almost completely from public life. The girl doesn't remember her article saying this. In fact, she thinks it said quite the reverse. The screenwriter senses the girl's fascination with the man: a fascination they share, although their thoughts hardly converge in any other way. The scene then blurs into three or four parts he can't quite distinguish. He looks at his watch. It's late, and he's sleepy. What's the girl doing right now? Perhaps sitting beside her mother in a taxi; or beside the young conductor in that small theater, wondering what would've become of them had twelve-tone music never been invented; or beside the brilliant composer, who repeats the same answer he already gave to the question, whatever it was. She could even be helping to train the new conquest, demonstrating for her on the piano in exchange for answers to personal questions. But whatever it is she happens to be doing, her thoughts are the same, for she's only thinking about those newspaper articles, and the strange feeling that's suddenly come over her. She used to unload her agitation on the young conductor and brilliant composer, but now that those relationships have ended, she feels alone, and has no one else in the world to confide in. She imagines being strong, capable of creating layers of protection against the unknown entities lurking in the shadows, entities she senses could leap out at any moment. She feels uncomfortable, has lost her focus. The church is full, as usual, but she doesn't see anyone she knows. It's a magnificent church, with a high belfry for communicating with other civilizations, although it looks far less imposing compared with the large cathedral towers. For an instant during her recital, she thinks she sees her cousin Dedalus flashing by, like lightning that was absorbed into the crowd, and she wonders whether she just imagined it, although she does remember inviting him on the day they met. She searches for her mother's face in the audience, who might be able to corroborate what she saw, but she can't find her in any of the tiers. Her thoughts turn again to the gravely ill scientist. The articles stress his condition has worsened, which means he must have already been sick when she met him. She'd have liked to talk to him about the cathedrals transmitting and receiving messages to and from space. One of the articles speculated on why he retired from public life and abandoned his cutting-edge research to become a recluse. Something prevents her from talking to her father about it—a gut feeling, or something like it, tells her not to do so. Others obtain an advantage over you if they know too much about what goes on in your life. She'll admit to any foibles he might deem typical of a teenager, and update him on the musical career he shows little interest in, but nothing more. There are no such things as coincidences, she says to herself, not knowing why she's said it again: a proposition that's become a platitude.

He can no longer stand the solitude. Once again, it seems, the girl won't be coming, and even the disturbing dream he had only hours before has now left him. She thinks they're following her, so she must be breaking her usual routines. She's probably sorry she can't make it. After primping himself in front of the mirror, he takes his jacket out of the closet. He'd feel naked without it. It's a sultry night, perhaps too warm to go cruising, but his desire burns even hotter. As he closes the door behind him, he smiles to himself. They say old age vitiates desire. His whole life he's been hearing such lies. As the elevator descends, he taps the floor with small impatient strokes, thinking he'd strike anyone in the street who got in his way. He'll restrain himself, though, because of his cultivation, his manners, his savoir-faire: the kinds of things they used to teach in school, which no one teaches anymore. Or perhaps the real reason he'll restrain himself is fear. He walks in the direction of the boulevards until he manages to hail a taxi, telling the driver to take him to the street where he first met the black prostitute. A few meters above the sex shop, he finds her leaning at the entrance to the stairway, as if she's been waiting for him. He greets her with a hug, tells her how miserable his life is, that he no longer understands the world, and that the world no longer understands him. She strokes his hair, and asks him about his work. She's asked him the same question before, but it doesn't matter, she knows why he came: to be disburdened, to be allowed to repeat the same story as before about himself, the same rant about the rest of the world, until he's satisfied, or until she can't bear to listen anymore. After telling her how he became a screenwriter, he starts talking about the old days, how they're invariably better than the new ones. Then he talks about the screenplay he's writing. Do you know why I called it *No World?* She has no idea. Because the world we're living in isn't real. It doesn't exist. You and I don't exist. Is that what you mean by No World? she asks. But the screenwriter isn't listening to her, or perhaps he doesn't want to be waylaid during a monologue, or perhaps he's still trying to figure out why the girl apposes those two words, what exactly she's referring to. So he ignores the prostitute's question because he doesn't know the answer himself. And it doesn't end there, he says, continuing as if she'd never asked it, there's also the matter of truth and falsity. Let's imagine nothing around us is real. The screenwriter pauses, allowing her time to conceive of the scenario, but the prostitute instead takes advantage of the pause to ask him if *No World* is the definitive title for his movie. He nods his head, says it's a title he borrowed, but then insists nothing is definitive in this life. She keens pityingly, combing his gray hair with her fingers.

The screenwriter thinks, or perhaps he's hoping against hope, that if he's more prudent with his spending, he'll manage to struggle out of the financial quandary he's in. In any case, a creditable screenwriter ought to know, or at least have a good idea, how to finish the story he proposes to write. He pays for breakfast and takes a long detour to the river on his way back to the hotel. Today's a good day, even his limp has relented somewhat, and he feels he can walk any distance with ease. He buys fruit, cheese, and hamburger buns, food that's easy to prepare, in case he doesn't feel like leaving his room again later when he's hungry. The newspapers are piling up on the bed. On their front pages, he's written notes such as: today, it rained; or, the heat was unbearable today; or, interesting article today on the star of that soccer team. He looks out the window at the building opposite, at the floor exactly level with his. It seems like an eternity since the woman showed her face. He's not happy with the phrase, "showed her face," and tries to think of another. "Made an appearance," perhaps. Today's newspaper has an article about the trafficking of radioactive material, another on the soccer star, who still hasn't said when he'll be returning to training, and another on the worst terrorist in history, whose lawyers have filed a lawsuit against the government for kidnapping their client on territory outside their jurisdiction. The screenwriter reads a long article about the general who succeeded in capturing him, the head of the team of lawyers who'll be defending him, and the judge who—assuming he's found guilty—will be sentencing him. The general is depicted as an agent provocateur, the perfect spy, a person no one's succeeded in photographing. The screenwriter puts this newspaper on top of the pile and lights a cigarette. The kind of work the girl's father might do, he says. He imagines him in the hotel in front of the Grand Central Station, doing whatever it is he does there—spying, monitoring. The screenwriter's beating around the bush. But the girl's notes aren't very clear about it either. Perhaps her father's been especially cautious around her, concealed his activities well, or perhaps she knows all and doesn't want anyone else to. He exhales some smoke while standing up, goes to the bedside table, and picks up the receiver. He dials the producer's number, listens to the rings, not counting, but murmuring to himself: money; another advance; I'd appreciate whatever you can give. Not asking for a specific amount makes his situation seem more desperate. Oh yes, it's a magnificent screenplay, reminiscent of those legendary scripts written during the golden age. Perhaps he shouldn't boast, he thinks while waiting for the phone to cut out—these aren't the words the producer wants to hear. No one believes in magnificent screenplays anymore. Of course he wants a perfect script, but "perfect" for the producer doesn't mean a work of art. It means a work that has all the qualities that betoken commercial success. That's what people today seem to mean by words like "great," "perfect," "magnificent," etc. And they all mean the same thing to the producer. So if the script is described as magnificent, it had better be with this understanding in mind. The screenwriter didn't notice the phone cutting out, or the fact he's gone on holding the phone notwithstanding. He hangs up and dials his home number. Fucking August, he complains. Like a Sunday protracted to the length of a whole month. A month when the world seems to come to a standstill, when no one does anything productive, when even eating may be thought a supererogation. If I hate Sundays, I fucking hate Augusts, he says while hanging up the telephone, and angrily crushing his cigarette in the ashtray.

She prepared her question carefully: concealed the question mark, transformed it into something subtler. Her father's busy putting his papers in order. She watches him, mentions she saw Cousin Dedalus in the crowd. He seems too distracted to notice she even said anything. So she just silently watches as he puts certain documents in order, perhaps the same documents she saw before: photographs and reports from the space agency relating to sightings of aliens and flying saucers. He holds up an old black and white snapshot of the scientist and some other people. He flips it over, sees "1st Hunter Brigade" clearly written on the back. He then puts it among some other

194

photographs, as if the title had revealed to him its proper classification. Although she's a little nervous, the girl feigns a lack of interest in what he's doing, and keeps talking about her cousin. Don't you think it's extraordinary I keep bumping into him? Her father asks her how she could've picked him out in the shadows of the dimly lit church, and from so far away too. She doesn't tell him about her sixth sense, that she's also detected *him* under similar circumstances. Her father continues working away, not paying much attention to her, so she turns to her diary. She plans to go snooping through his papers later on. Why didn't she do it earlier when she had the chance? The timing wasn't right. She grabs the newspaper and continues scouring through the articles. She's suddenly developed a great interest in the neighboring country's newspapers. She always reads the one she buys her father every morning in the lobby downstairs, and others she might see in any bars, cafés, or restaurants she happens to come across. Indeed, whatever else she might be doing, whether it's sitting down to eat or drink, taking notes for her novel, or simply relaxing, she always has a newspaper at hand. Her father wants to know why she doesn't buy all the newspapers together at the kiosk and stop all the running around. She doesn't answer but instead asks her own question, trying her best to conceal the question mark: Dad, what if all the churches and cathedrals were really centers for transmitting and receiving messages to and from space? Her father doesn't think it's a bad idea. She might be able to use it in her novel. The girl returns to the newspaper. She's looking for some news on the scientist. She has a bad feeling any news will be a confirmation of his death. But there's nothing about the scientist in today's papers. So the girl decides to go out and lock herself inside the rehearsal booth with the young conductor's latest conquest and help her with some of the pieces she's having trouble with; in fact, the very same pieces the girl performs as a clown. Afterward, back in the hotel, she continues her story about the female student, although it's not really her story at all, but that of the old professor of philosophy, the alien hunter who hasn't even got a license to hunt. The female student only represents an idea, albeit the main idea of the story. "2.221 What the no picture represents is its sense. The female student walks breezily along the street, unaware that the young guy she cold-shouldered back in class is following her, a potential witness of her assignation with the professor." The girl looks up from the computer screen. She catches her father watching her. But he quickly lowers his eyes to the newspaper. Who knows what's going on in his head? "2.222 The agreement or disagreement of its sense with reality constitutes its truth or falsity. After some time has elapsed—perhaps only a few hours or so, because the female student's classmate isn't a dolt, and was quick to figure out what was going on—the professor's wife receives an anonymous phone call. She hangs up, and sits down slowly—as if sinking, but hesitatingly—into an armchair, her expression transitioning as she sits, becoming forlorn; her open eyes letting fall two tears, unsynchronized, which run unevenly down her cheeks. It's not the first time her husband's cheated on her. He's been having affairs with women almost from the day they were married. Some were even close acquaintances. She wasn't expecting him to change. At his age, most people have learned to rein in their desires, to control their rage, moderate their passions, but with him, it seems, old habits die hard. It seems he's entered a strange phase in life, a desperate clinging onto what he imagines is slipping away—his youth, his vitality, his sexuality—and he overcompensates for the growing lack instead of rationing what's left, like most people. It's as if he believes it's his last winter, and wants to burn down the storehouse to experience a final day of summer. Now that she thinks about it, he's been acting strangely the past few months. But, then again, perhaps she's only thinking this because she's jealous. Maybe he's had enough of her. It could be as simple as that. Even so, for the woman, it's nothing new. What really disturbs her is the fact he's having a relationship with a minor: a student of the Academy. She doesn't know why, but she thinks there's something different about this one, despite the fact she's so young. She's probably not even the first teenager he's had. Maybe she's thinking as a mother would, imagining what she'd do if she discovered her daughter was having an affair with an older man—a much older man; a retired much older man who gives classes to supplement his pension." When her father finally goes out, the girl searches the hotel room for his documents. The room isn't very big, so it doesn't take her long to realize her father took them with him. She can't even begin to guess where he might have gone, or why he took the documents. She should've paid more attention. All she can do is lament another lost opportunity and return resignedly to her writing. Her vocation should preclude her being distracted by what goes on around her anyway. She considers the old professor's wife. "There's no doubt about it. What the anonymous voice just told her is the truth. But she hasn't decided what to do about it, so she's going to keep quiet. She won't even mention a word about it. 2.224 It is impossible to tell from the picture alone whether it is true or false. When the old professor finally gets home, he finds his wife taciturn, so he suspects something isn't right. She gives the excuse that she has a terrible headache. Later, in the kitchen, he resolves to break the silence by asking about her day." The elevator stops on the landing, and she hears the sound of McGregor's footsteps approaching in the corridor—slowing, hesitating as they pass the girl's door, before receding as they proceed toward his room. The girl listens as he secures the latch of his door, thinking about their inevitable meeting, a man with whom she's only ever exchanged a few words on the telephone. But she won't leave anything to chance. She's already let too many opportunities slip through her fingers, so she intends to plan the meeting exactly. She'll interrogate him about the cathedrals, railway stations, and airports. The idea of using cathedrals as meeting points isn't a bad one, but there wouldn't be any privacy. The young conductor thinks if aliens really are among us, maybe she should try arranging a meeting by putting an ad in a newspaper. She returns to her writing. She needs to persist if she's to continue making progress. She still has to consolidate the relationship between the female student and old professor—two beings from another galaxy. They must come from another galaxy. It wouldn't make sense if this wasn't the case.

At night, there are scarcely any tables available, but the screenwriter scours the café terrace and eventually manages to find one. So he sits down, and waits to be served. He still doesn't understand the significance of the aliens for the girl. He considers whether she herself might be an alien hunter. But there wouldn't be many female hunters, he speculates, before dismissing the idea completely. Yet another ideation about which she daily obsesses, like the voices she thinks she hears, or the shadow that stalks her at all hours of the night, or the necessity to write. He thinks about the scientist, his radio telescopes roving the heavens for signs of intelligent life. Unlike the scientist, the girl must think along different lines. He'd almost say in terms of a game. What if things could be done much more simply? If they were still among us, perhaps a simple announcement would suffice. The right announcement need only contain a few key words to be understood, perhaps in code, since it would be naïve to publicize communications directly. Maybe they'd use special magazines with a limited circulation instead of popular newspapers. But the girl needs to get to the bottom of some mysteries before committing to a rigorous search. She doesn't want to lose track by attacking on too many fronts simultaneously. She doesn't know if she'll be able to finish her book while doing recitals and preparing to record the *5 Pieces for piano.* If she incorporates her search for extraterrestrials and her attempts to make contact with them into her writing, she'll end up with a kind of detective novel. But she shouldn't blur the line between her real-world obsessions and the things she considers only fiction. Still, combining two endeavors in this way could save her some time and effort. The screenwriter now sees the waitress on the other side of the terrace and is surprised when she seems to notice him at almost the same moment. It's the first time she's held eye contact with him for longer than an instant. Perhaps it's a sign, a golden opportunity, he thinks, and yet the waitress continues avoiding his table. He knows by now she won't come to take his order unless he signals her, and it needn't be an elaborate gesture. Moments later, she approaches, and the screenwriter can't help himself: What time do you get off work, beautiful? She keeps walking, pretending she hasn't heard him. If only you knew what you were missing, he says aloud, while reaching for the packet of cigarettes in his pocket. You'd swear I was a goddamn alien . . . , he adds as he puts the filter between his lips.

He's seen it dozens of times in X-rated movies. Sometimes,

it's done with two men and a woman; sometimes, two women and a man; he's only rarely seen three men. Instead of hearing about it from the girl's lips, the screenwriter would rather be watching from behind a screen, or by applying his eye to a peephole. Even a photograph would be better than a verbal account of her sexual encounter with the young conductor and brilliant composer. She asks him to imagine her naked on her knees, straddling the young conductor, while the brilliant composer probes her from behind with his tongue. They begin slowly, gently, gradually becoming more frenetic, while their breathing gets heavier, their moans louder, until their movement, breathing, moaning, seem to synchronize, as if they were performing one of the brilliant composer's pieces, in which each has their own part to play, but all have the same end in mind. The girl plays with the young conductor's penis, occasionally putting it in her mouth, and the screenwriter imagines her doing so wildly, hungrily, as if her life depended on it. The brilliant composer maintains his position behind her, holding her legs with one hand, since she keeps moving about uncontrollably, while using his free hand to pleasure her. Finally, she gets on her back and lets the other two cum on her face. And thus the performance concludes. The screenwriter can't take any more. A mixture of love and anguish is causing his stomach to churn, and he feels like throwing up. He hasn't felt this sickness in years, he thinks, this pain. And yet, he searches her features, replaying in his head the scene she just described. The two of them lie back on the sheets. Weren't you fighting with them? he asks her. The girl says they were all drinking and taking drugs when it happened. Perhaps they were taking revenge on me, she speculates, although she says it without conviction.

The first thing he does in the morning is call the producer. Money, another advance, I'd appreciate whatever you can send, he keeps repeating to himself, as if every time he calls he needs to persuade himself of his desperate situation in order to sound more convincing. Oh it's a magnificent screenplay, he murmurs, I'd say it's as good as anything written in the golden age. Then, he changes his mind. His insecurity always causes him to change his mind. But he doesn't think the producer wants to hear about the golden age, and he doesn't want any magnificent screenplays either, unless, by "magnificent," the screenwriter means a guaranteed box-office hit. In fact, nothing would delight the producer more than talking about a potential box-office hit. The screenwriter knows he's gone through this scenario before, had the same thoughts about money and the producer the last time he tried to call him. He hangs up and goes down to have breakfast. Afterward, in the lobby, he's reading in the paper about a Nobel Prize winner who's died. The screenwriter doesn't recall ever reading his works. But there are so many great books that reading them all would leave him with little time to do anything else in life. After perusing the personal ads, he gets up and limps to the elevator. Damn leg, he grumbles on the way to his room, impatient to get back to his writing. Today, the girl's wearing sunglasses. It seems the circles around her eyes, which the screenwriter finds so endearing on a teenager's countenance, are now looking particularly bad to her. She'd prefer not to linger on the events of the past few days. She likes to think they were part of a game; that everything's part of a game; the game of the world, the universe perhaps, but a game nonetheless. She's repeated this same mantra ad nauseam. Everything's a game, life's a game. If nothing exists, or if nothing is true, then why not think of it as a game? Her theory's plausible. She could return to the hotel and speak with her father, offer to help him, but she has her own plans. She wanders the streets of the neighboring country's capital immersed in her usual thoughts about her novel, about her mother, and the young conductor . . . She should've gone to rehearsals but was too lazy. So she goes into a library instead, and walks past books of every sort, from well-thumbed new releases piled up on tables near the front, to dusty old classics on inconspicuous shelves in the back. She's baffled at not knowing any of the fashionable authors. Their new books are always announced with fanfare and tickertape, because in the neighboring country's capital, there are authors who sell in the hundreds of thousands. The girl has certainly not sold so many records. She wonders which contemporary authors she should read, how to separate the grain from the chaff. She's always avoided reading her contemporaries. But a writer should know the works of other writers, both old and new, develop a kinship with both the past and present. She doesn't recognize any of their names. Maybe it's a defense mechanism, a means of avoiding a contest with the living. It's easier if the opponent's already dead. She takes a book from a shelf and reads the beginning: "One summer afternoon Mrs. Oedipa Maas came home from a Tupperware party whose hostess had put perhaps too much kirsch . . ." Then she reads the beginning of another: "In the town there were two mutes, and they were always together." There's a writer whose name has a K or Ka, and he happens to be one of the most important writers of the century; who knows, perhaps the voices she hears are directing her on a literary path, pointing out new things for her to read, new approaches to writing, new perspectives on literature in general. This writer may in fact be an extraterrestrial. She checks a book with a photograph of him, but it must've been retouched, because she can't decide whether or not she sees a faint halo around him. She reads the beginnings of several more books before leaving the store and continuing on her way, a way without a particular end, for she hasn't one in mind—the way of a vagabond, in other words. A foosball bar would be an end, she thinks, but she can't think of any that are nearby. She starts walking in the direction of the river, but then changes her mind and turns back. Maybe she should just go to rehearsals after all, shut herself away in a rehearsal booth with the Little Sinfonietta and the young conductor's latest conquest. She doesn't know why she mentioned the group and the conquest as separate entities. It seems the girl still can't accept her as a member of the group, as she's yet to even set foot onstage. Perhaps she's more of a member than the girl at this point—or at any point for that matter, for the girl has never really conformed to the role of orchestra member. Being the concert starlet she is, perhaps she thinks she's different from the rest. Perhaps she didn't want them having too great an influence on her. She can't remember who was responsible for inducting her— her mother, the young conductor, or the brilliant composer: it was probably all of them, but she always felt that being an orchestra member stifled her individuality and creativity. The girl is at a counter writing a personal ad to be published in all the major newspapers. She has trouble with the text of the message, though, because it should be phrased in a way that disguises its meaning to all but the intended recipients, a code that only the aliens are able to decipher. She decides to leave it as simple as possible, and writes: "I hear voices. 1. The No World is all that is the case." Then she debates whether to sign it K. or Ka. She hears Ka instead of K, hears the differ- ence between them, perhaps it's a clue. She signs her name

203

Ka. At the exit, next to a window, a shadow tries passing her unnoticed. The girl walks into its path and the hairs on her arms bristle, detecting a presence. Suddenly, she has the feeling again of being followed. She decides, once and for all, to get to the bottom of the mystery, so she turns around and goes back to where she felt the presence. She then considers if it's ill advised to confront an unknown entity unarmed. But it doesn't matter. When she reaches the agency window, the unknown entity's already vanished. For how long has it been following her? she wonders as she heads for the next block to hail a taxi. The rehearsal space isn't far, but she asks the driver to take a detour. When she passes the classifieds office again, she can't help darting another glance at the window. A few meters further on, she sees cousin Dedalus strolling casually while reading a newspaper. She watches him, wondering if he'll catch sight of her. But he doesn't see her—or if he has seen her, he's doing a good job pretending he hasn't.

Near the hotel, there's a second-hand clothes store, and the screenwriter decides to go inside and have a look. He never used to think of buying anything in a place like this. It's true they haven't always been around, he tells himself, but even if they had been, he'd never have thought to enter one, much less buy anything inside. These days, however, if he needed some pants, a jacket, or possibly a new shirt, he might see it as an obligation. Necessity can alter habits, he thinks, remembering it's already his second visit. He doesn't even know why he's come into the store again, but it's clearly something to do with his financial situation. On emerging from between rows of hangers, he notices a sign announcing, in flawless calligraphy, the sale of second-hand clothing. He goes outside and looks in the display window for a moment. Then he hobbles to the nearest metro station. He's not traveling far, but at his pace, it would take forever. The screenwriter wants to see the Grand Central Station first hand, that curious place where the girl's father and his associate McGregor swap vigils, waiting interminably for who knows what. He wants to see the stake-out point, try to determine why they've chosen it. Perhaps he should avoid the place altogether though. He knows the territory is forbidden to him. But curiosity, as usual, overrides his better judgment. Sometimes, he wonders if he only writes scripts to live the lives of his characters, beings that only exist in his dreams, people he'd like to be. The mind is a strange thing, full of oddities, he says. According to the girl, nothing exists outside it. But to live the lives of characters that only exist in the mind is to waste one's life chasing chimeras. There are people that dedicate their lives to research; scientists, both great and minor, who work for the benefit and improvement of our species, whose discoveries are in fact useful. He tries to think of some examples: cars, refrigerators, knives, bread— food in general, he supposes . . . These people don't just make stuff up; they don't just fabricate a loaf of bread into exis- tence. Nonetheless, the screenwriter can't help thinking of all the bureaucracy and political skulduggery a scientist has to deal with before he can make these amenities available to the public. Then there are those who work in the dream indus- try. They don't deal with reality at all. The screenwriter real- izes this is the second time he's repeated this thought pattern, invoked ideas and images exactly as before. It must be some- thing to do with his age. Dreams, flashbacks, fantasies, chi- meras, that which isn't real, that which once was, that which cannot be, that which he wants to be. To live together with the girl, the greatest adventure of his life. From the steps of the station, he surveys the hotel balconies on the other side of the plaza where, he imagines, the girl and her father, and maybe even McGregor, when he's not in the station, can frequently be seen looking back. But then he thinks McGregor unlikely to be on the balcony, since he wants to avoid an encounter with the girl. The screenwriter has no way of telling which of the balconies is the girl's, so he heads inside and sits at one of the station cafés, near the platforms. After ordering a coffee, he takes his notebook and pencil from his jacket pocket and describes in detail various things going on around him, such as the way the people move, the difference between those who pass through the station regularly and those who don't, those who stride purposefully, their eyes fixed head, and those who look lost, who look left and right then stare at departure boards, scanning for numbers to tell them where they should go, who only deign to ask for directions as a last resort. He wants to immerse himself in those places frequented by the girl, her father, and her father's enigmatic associate. Right now, the people in the station are like the extras at the peripheries of the shot in which he occupies the center, contemplating everything going on around him. He wouldn't know the girl's father if he bumped into him. He doesn't remember ever having seen him, or the girl's mother for that matter. They're the type of people who get other people to take their children to school, like servants or bodyguards. The screenwriter thinks it's immoral for parents to let strangers take a young girl to school. Near him, some travelers are boarding a train. He pays his bill and crumples the receipt into his pocket along with his notebook. Then he leans on his cane to get to his feet and wobbles slowly toward the main door. Damn leg, he murmurs, as he descends the steps, and surveys again the balconies of the hotels facing the station.

It's Saturday, in the early hours of the morning. The girl gets back to the hotel in a bad mood. She feels like she's wasted valuable time with the Little Sinfonietta. Sometimes, she feels like a fool. It's usually when the young conductor's nearby. She's started fighting with him again. If he thinks she's going to change the way she plays, he's a bigger fool than her. The *5 Pieces for piano* and the *No World Symphony* are different compositions and they should be performed differently. Both the young conductor and the brilliant composer are wrong. She finds her father sitting in a chair, talking on the telephone. Judging by his tone, she guesses McGregor is on the line. One of his legs is resting on the bed, which is half-covered with newspapers and other documents, and on which two cell phones lie, waiting forever, it seems, for a call that never comes. At the head of the bed is a pistol inside a leather holster. It's not the gun her father usually carries. The girl knows this, of course. She likes to think of it as a game, guessing whose gun it is. Her father also passes the time playing games—whether in the hotel room waiting for a call, diverting himself with a newspaper or two, or in the station bar when he's on watch, scrutinizing the faces of people walking past. Life's full of these little games. It would be unbearable if this wasn't the case. If something goes wrong, the girl recalls, it only has meaning when it's considered part of a game. If she's said it once, she's said it a thousand times to the young conductor and brilliant composer, when they were still her friends. What is a game? she asks, as if to the female student. It's dark outside, although light from the plaza still reaches the balcony. If she turns out the light, her silhouette on the opposite wall stretches to the ceiling. It's never quiet here. It's too near the station. It doesn't matter, though, the girl's not tired. Not going to get some sleep? her father asks. But sleep's the last thing on her mind. She shakes her head, putting the possibility to bed, and goes to the laptop to write. "3.5 A propositional sign, applied and thought out, is a thought. 4. A thought is a proposition with a sense. The game isn't a true proposition, thinks the female student. The game is just another way of imposing meaning on something that has no meaning. It's like trying to perform the part of a certain character that could be the female student herself. To become that character in every sense, to breathe the same air, think the same thoughts, live every instant of one's life just as that character would. The female student feels she's an actress, and that she's playing a certain part. It's not theater, though, but a way of life. The character speaks with her voice, but it's as though she herself were something other than the character she embodies. She immerses herself in the character and identifies with her. Some people do this by gathering around tables and performing from a script. But for others, this isn't enough. They need a stage and props to help them bring a character to life. The female student, on the other hand, prefers to just live permanently in her role: on the metro, at the beach, even here, lying next to the old professor. One moment it's W, the next Ka. The game then acquires a dimension we didn't know it had. It's not that difficult to play, but the amount of pleasure and pain one derives from playing is potentially unlimited, she thinks. There are no pieces to move, no cards to be dealt, no dice that need to be rolled; all one need do is acknowledge that life is a game, and that everything is part of that game. To live such a life is to play." The girl comes out of her trance, leans back in the chair, and yawns. She looks over at her father, thinks about him and McGregor on their interminable vigils. Who are they waiting for? she wonders, before rephrasing, On whom do they wait? And going further, What type of game are they playing? And further still, what part does the scientist play in it? She doesn't have an answer for any of these questions. The girl will also have to play. What part does all their waiting play in the game?

On the café terrace, the screenwriter orders a coffee. It's raining, so he decides to sit beneath the awning and write. It's ten in the morning, and the street's almost empty. Perhaps it's only for the time being. He observes the activity around him, and over at the café on the other side of the plaza. Some people are walking with their umbrellas; others don't seem to mind getting wet. Summer rain's different, he thinks. Tepid rain doesn't bother them. Besides, many don't have far to go. Perhaps they're taking a shortcut through the plaza. How does he know this? He doesn't. He's guessing from their clothes, the way they're walking, the expressions on their faces, and he further guesses they might be going to get something to eat in one of the several sandwich shops and snack bars around . . . His leg's no longer bothering him, but he decides to stay under the awning along with all the tourists and wait for the rain to subside. The air is fresh; the noise of the rain against the pavement is pleasing to him. Yes, he'll spend the time writing. Once again, the image he focuses on before beginning is the girl's. The story is his own invention, but he knows he borrows heavily from the girl, from the stories she tells him, from the extracts of her novel she reads to him or that get delivered to his hotel, with commentaries scribbled in the margins, which he incorporates into his own narrative. It's dawn. The girl's looking out from the balcony, standing almost exactly where she was the previous night while observing the front of the Grand Central Station, as if deliberating whether or not to go there and search for whomever, or whatever, her father and his associate are waiting for. She goes inside and writes in her diary until the noise of the traffic and people outside grows to the point of distraction. At some point in the night, her father left, and took the laptop with him. He never gives her an explanation for his sudden disappearances, and she never has any idea where he goes. When he eventually returns, she notices more newspapers folded under his arm. He hangs his jacket on the back of a chair and leaves the laptop case to one side. He looks tired, as if he hasn't had a good night's sleep in days. He routinely asks the girl how her writing's going, because he thinks she likes it when he asks. But without waiting for a response, he lights a cigarette, lies back on the bed, and stares listlessly up at the ceiling. The girl takes stock of their relationship: a relationship at once strange and fascinating, she thinks, worthy of being written about, or depicted on the big screen. She doesn't know why, but she has a profound sense that she's living in one of those defining periods in history. Writing is beginning to dominate her life more and more, and now she finds herself at the cusp of an issue she hasn't dared to mention yet, but which she hoped would eventually be resolved. If she had to describe how her father is passing his time, she'd start by saying he waits. She doesn't know what for. He just waits—as ash falls on the bedspread, and he brushes it away with his hand; as he reads the occasional newspaper, or takes the occasional look around the room; as he occasionally ventures to the balcony to look at the Grand Central Station opposite, before coming back inside, somber, resigned, because all he can do is wait. He passes time like the screenwriter, in other words, who locks himself away in his room, and spends all day strapped to a writing desk, typing, in order to get nowhere with his script. The girl's father reads a newspaper, then another, and another. The kiosk in the station sells newspapers from all over the world. Occasionally, he picks up the tome of his favorite author—the one obsessed with jealousy and lost time. Appropriate for someone who has nothing else to do with his time but wait. At times, the girl is sitting near him writing in her diary, or typing away on the laptop. They hardly ever speak to one another, each engrossed by their own work. If words are exchanged at all, it's only on general terms, school, the concerts, the weather, and generally about her, never him— although she knows that he's only passing the time, that he and his colleague McGregor are waiting for something to happen, for someone to make an appearance, perhaps someone who will be arriving after a long journey, having come from somewhere far away, unaware two predators are lying in wait, planning an ambuscade. Who knows, perhaps it's another scientist. The girl delights in speculating about the possibilities, in writing about them in her diary, perhaps with a view to incorporating them in her novel. Indeed, she can't stop thinking and writing, especially when her father's in the room, for his presence renews her fascination. She doesn't think it trivial that the man in the classically-cut suit happens to know her mother. A seriously ill scientist, according to the newspapers, an acquaintance of her parents, and a longtime acquaintance at that, for he recognized in the girl's features the face of her mother when she was young. Occasionally, the girl's father receives a phone call from McGregor, and he always goes to the balcony to speak to him, looking down at the plaza, as if addressing him directly. But the girl knows this isn't possible. In her imagination, McGregor always calls from the station platforms when he's on his watch. Then, when her father hangs up, he just resumes waiting. The girl never asks him why. By now she has the good sense to know what not to ask. Occasionally he connects the laptop to the phone line and checks his emails; occasionally he even sends a few. Later on, the girl continues writing her story about the old professor of philosophy, the hunter of aliens who also spends his time holed up in various rooms around a desolate city, such as an abandoned control room, where he thinks about the past, looking through windows that offer him a view of the stars. And while she writes, we don't know if she's completely focused on her narrative, or distracted, throwing an occasional sidelong glance at her father, with the hope of exploring the laptop's classified files, and uncovering a trove of secrets. She's tried before of course, but every time the system demands a password, which every time she fails to guess, and so is left only to imagine what untold stories are waiting to be unlocked. She comes out of her trance, sees her father asleep on the bed, fully clothed, so she goes over to search through the newspapers for the strange announcement that caught her attention the day before.

She's lucky to have found, in writing, a viable replacement for her music, because this very night, the night of the latest conquest's live debut, the Little Sinfonietta will have discovered she's a natural replacement for the girl. They don't need her anymore, and they're fed up with all the fighting—so the brilliant composer told her before hanging up, which he also did before she had a chance to respond. Seconds later, she calls her mother to confirm the news. One of the Institute's most promising young pianists has been recruited in her place to perform the *5 Pieces for piano* and the *No World Symphony*. Now the girl hangs up brusquely. It seems the young conductor hasn't got the guts to tell her himself. When she thinks about it carefully—the fact that they've treated her like this without even recognizing it was she who abandoned them first—it leaves a bad taste in her mouth. These things happen. They made the decision based on what they thought was best for the orchestra. That said, after exchanging one currency for another, you always seem to end up with less than you expected. She writes in her diary that today is different from all the other days; that she's not as annoyed as she thought she'd be; that she feels as if a weight's been lifted from her shoulders; but she grants that the news may still be sinking in. She's finally finished with the Little Sinfonietta. And isn't this what she wanted in the first place?

Why did they cancel her performance of the *5 Pieces for piano*? She calls her mother, who advises her first to calm down, to be reasonable, and then to consider why they replaced her. She's shown herself to be quite distracted lately, even indifferent. To be ranked among the elite in the piano world, one can't afford to be distracted, and certainly not indifferent. Be reasonable? How can she be reasonable when her own mother, and representative, is taking the side of her adversaries? Why would she want a daughter who lacks character, who just acts the way she's expected to act? Is this the way they want her to perform too? She does a few turns around the room, trying her best to calm down. It's time to prove to herself she's a writer, to accept that what's happened isn't important, to prove she can shut herself away and dedicate all her energies to writing. She'd like to make more progress on her story about the wistful professor in the floating City in Outer Space, but she gets distracted thinking about her father. Like the screenwriter, she has the feeling she's repeating herself, that she keeps having the same thought patterns, as if there are no other subjects to think about. Maybe it comes from being bound in a nutshell. All she basically writes about are commonplaces, silence and solitude, reading and writing, hope and patience. Sometimes she talks to her father about writing, about her future literary work, but he always falls silent because they can never get past the same fundamental disagreement. Her father is essentially a skeptic, while she believes she can change the world, that her novel will revolutionize literature. In these instances, he remains quiet while she's at pains to make him understand. It's probably the voices that make her feel so sure of herself, the ones that show her the way, although her father believes it's just youthful audacity, the arrogance of ignorance, the fruits of inexperience. Frustrated by this reminder, the girl directs her thoughts elsewhere. She looks at her father, asleep on the bed, fully clothed, as if to be ready for an event that, sooner or later, is bound to occur; a sudden and alarming event that won't allow him even a minute's reprieve to get dressed. The act of waiting: one of those ideas on which she leans. As is her fascination with the astrophysicist who knows her mother; her fascination with her father and his associate, the patience they demonstrate day by day, hour by hour, waiting, for whom, for what? she asks herself again as she looks over at the Grand Central Station, as if the act of looking will yield an answer. She goes to the balcony, lights a cigarette, and smokes it while she broods. Then she returns to her seat in front of the laptop. At first she has trouble getting into her zone, but finding a good opening phrase is like guessing the correct password, which then opens up a portal to her *No World*. "2.225 There is ultimately but one true image. A reasonable time has elapsed, perhaps a couple of weeks, since the woman received the first anonymous call. Now she's having an argument with her husband. She tells him an anonymous caller told her all about his affair with the female student. He's defensive at first, insists the accusation is false, that it was made by a student, perhaps one who resented a poor grade. She's got no idea what these little brats are capable of, he says. Some may use their precocity for getting good grades; others for avenging the receipt of bad grades; but neither sort will exercise any restraint in their machinations toward achieving their goals. But when his wife shows him the photograph, the old professor has no choice but to fess up. He then gives a vain and thoughtless excuse, asking her if she's ever looked in the mirror and lamented becoming shriveled and old when the rest of the world seems flush with youthful skin. The woman locks herself in one of the rooms. He goes to the door and stands outside. He can hear her crying. Not that this bothers him as much as the photograph, and where it came from. He knows it's one he took himself, in which he and the female student are posing together. It's not especially lewd, but the two of them are lying naked on a bed whose sheets are completely white, looking at the camera, with a copy of W's magnum opus by their side. He's worried about how it got into his wife's hands—if it was the work of a detective who broke into his study and filched it. He approaches the door of the room in which she shut herself, asks her softly how she got the photograph—softly, to mollify her, but only in the hope of soliciting an answer. But she doesn't answer, she only sobs. After a while, he hears her snuffle that they were sent anonymously. The woman then emerges from the room, having seemingly regained her composure, and threatens to report him to the Academy where he teaches philosophy. You're finished! she screams energetically. They'll fire him. They'll put him in jail. She's tired of all his lies. She's tired of him. The old professor curses at her and slams the door violently. He doesn't even think to suspect the female student, that it was she who stole the picture from his study." The girl goes back over what she's written, slowly moving the cursor along to follow what she reads. The old professor lacks a sense of playfulness. If something goes wrong, he should think of it as a game. Everything's a game. Life is only a game. "Perhaps, years later, when the old professor is even older, he'll finally understand the mantra of 'it's all a game,' and even sound it repeatedly while remembering the female student and his wife, recalling the events that drove him to leave, to flee to the City in Outer Space. Alone, in a desolate floating metropolis, careening aimlessly through space, waiting for death, with nothing to do except read and reminisce, he'll be poring over W—flipping through a musty old copy he found in a library next door to a depot he was raiding for supplies—and while sitting in that library waiting for death, flipping through the pages of a musty old book, he'll finally understand the mantra. He won't know what year it is on Earth, how far from it he is, whether he's getting closer or moving farther and farther away from it. Sometimes, he'll go to the control room, or the government building, but he won't know what to do, where to start, so he'll think of the movies he saw back on Earth, the ones about the future, space travel, and all the rest, not that they'll be of any help. If he was to go back now, perhaps the girl will not have aged; perhaps he'll even get to hear her whisper in his ear again: Life, it's only a game." The girl gets up and walks nervously around the room. She looks outside, nothing: just the usual ebb and flow of people through the plaza. The screenwriter's situation now reminds her of her own, holed away in a room, writing and staring out the window. Still sitting on the café terrace, it occurs to him that the girl will not be able to suffer her seclusion much longer. She's too young to be waiting indefinitely for something that may not materialize. She thinks life's a game. Delight in the novelty of living like an anchorite soon enough gives way to despair. She should be practicing the piano, working on the new sound she dreams will blaze a musical trail around the globe, but she doesn't want to practice. She wants to avoid bumping into her mother. Perhaps she needs to take a break. Perhaps too much practice will negatively affect her performance on the recording. The screenwriter thinks it's a bad idea. Giving up practice might upset her peace of mind. Playing the piano used to relieve the stress of a busy schedule. She may not have appreciated it, but after all the classes at the Institute, the rehearsals and concerts, the arguments with her mother, the fights with the young conductor, the piano was a release for her. It's still raining, so the screenwriter thinks about the girl as she looks out the window. The cell phone rings. The brilliant composer is calling from a radio station where they've just given an interview. Since you couldn't come, you can listen, he says curtly. She hangs up without answering. Moments later, however, she goes into the bathroom, so as not to awaken her father, and tries tuning in.

The Little Sinfonietta has only a few concerts to go before embarking on their tour of the major cities and provinces. Later on, they plan to return and perform a few more concerts in the capital. The radio DJ announces the dates slowly, with a pause between each, which is to suggest he won't be repeating them. Then he asks what the difference is between the young conductor of the Little Sinfonietta and all the other young conductors on the scene. The brilliant composer answers for him, saying it's not only in the way he leads the orchestra, but in his manner of conducting, which has all the hallmarks of a great maestro, that sets him apart form the rest, and more besides, for he promises to one day surpass the great maestros as well. He illustrates his point by describing the way he conducts his *No World Symphony*. The DJ asks if after all the success, given their youth, there's any time left to have some fun. The young conductor answers this time, saying everything's a game, even this interview, and life itself. The girl thinks about abandoning this mantra once and for all, not because of an aversion to the idea motivating it, but because she wants to distance herself further from these so-called friends whom, lately, she's come to detest. She doesn't want anything she sees, hears, or even thinks about to remind her of their existence. A strange way to finally sever all association with them, she thinks, noting the contradiction in arriving at the resolution while listening to them being interviewed on the radio. The future is happening now, says the young conductor, and this is evident in the compositions of the brilliant composer. He then makes allowances for the ex-pianist turned writer. At this point, the listeners, and probably the whole world, are aware of her new obsession. It wouldn't surprise him if she signed a contract with some major book publisher, he says, despite the fact she's written nothing yet. Especially if her mother finally comes to terms with her change of vocation. The girl listens attentively. A moment of absurdity, she thinks. It's as if she's sitting there with them, or perhaps they know she's listening. Doubt leads her to think it might be an old pre-recorded interview from before there was any malice between them. But she quickly dismisses this, since she doesn't remember any such interview taking place. She looks at herself in the mirror. She's so accustomed to her reflection it's become invisible to her, although she still knows where her head is; what that head is thinking—that she doesn't care what they say; that she should forget about them, and think again about the vigil in the Grand Central Station. A writer shouldn't rely on inconsistent premises, she thinks, like her friends. Reality is different. If the young conductor really believes life's a game, he should

218

prove it or shut up about it—stop trumpeting it around like the latest fashion, trying to get noticed by inciting controversy. All the young conductor truly believes in is himself and his music. The girl still doesn't understand why he complimented her on the radio. She'd like to see it as a belated act of recognition. And yet, his being a musician, and her being a writer, gives them very different conceptions of the world. This is a valid argument. And what about the brilliant composer? What does he think about? She sees the little guy, seated with the rest of the group around a large oval table, wearing headphones, perhaps perched on a chair with several cushions so he can see the interviewer. She laughs, imagining the DJ's face moving swiftly between his script and the so-called brilliant kid, sitting on those cushions, swinging his legs above the floor, having to strain to reach the microphone. Nothing, the composer finally says, he believes in nothing because nothing's worth believing in. He sits back in his chair. I've read somewhere that you can hear voices, says the interviewer to her replacement, the latest conquest. Is it true that you said they're voices from another world? The girl can't breathe. It's if she just received a sucker punch to the stomach. The latest conquest says she was talking about voices that pronounce her name with a "ka." She doesn't know what this signifies yet, but she's working on it. The girl can't bear to continue listening, so she turns the radio off. Are they going to transform her replacement into a writer as well? Will they eventually cancel her performances too, and introduce her to another replacement, another impersonator, a plagiarist, an impostor? She dials the young conductor's number. She notices her father's pistol, half-hidden in one of the laptop case's compartments, so she reaches in and grips it tightly, angrily. She should go to the church and declare herself perfectly healthy and ready to perform the *5 Pieces for piano*. What they told the public is all lies. They canceled her performances out of their own personal interests. They really are all monsters, she thinks. They'll go out of their way to wreck her career—not only as a pianist, but as a writer too—to rob her of a future. The line's busy. She hangs up, breathing heavily, as if she's just finished a long-distance run. She swears to give up her mantra at some point in the future, but not yet. Not while she still needs it. If something goes wrong, she repeats, it's not that important, because it's only part of a game. Everything's a game. Life is only a game.

The screenwriter searches for the black prostitute he was with on Wednesday night, or perhaps he should say the early hours of Thursday morning. He searches first around the sex shop then walks a couple of blocks, but he doesn't see her. So he decides to go back and wait for her at the club. It's still the early afternoon, perhaps too early to go cruising, but he decides to stay a while. After ordering a gin and tonic and lighting a cigarette, he thinks about the girl's father. If the screenwriter was he, or at least had his money, he'd have the prostitute all to himself. She wouldn't have to go out soliciting anymore. Some women can smell money on a man. Prostitutes make a living with this talent. He rests his elbow on the bar and lets his eyes dart around the room, as if waiting for someone to show up. The women are all young, are all taken. The black prostitute will show up when he least expects it, he thinks, while crushing the butt in the ashtray. Or perhaps he's just hoping against hope she will. He hesitates to light the next cigarette, prestidigitates it between his fingers, as if waiting for someone to light it for him, but he soon bores of this game, and ends up lighting it himself. He spends a few more minutes looking at the bottles on the shelves, the lights, the stools, and the pattern on the carpet. Then he goes to take a sip from his glass, but only fishes up an ice cube. He decides against ordering another drink. He decides against finishing his cigarette. Instead, he just gets up and leaves, walks slowly out onto the street, and goes to wait for the prostitute at the sex shop, where he can rest his aching back against the shutter. He looks around at the other women, but none attract his interest. A blonde approaches him. She doesn't say she wants a light, but insinuates by brandishing an unlit cigarette, and thumbing an invisible lighter. He obliges her, and asks about her dark-skinned colleague. She says she hasn't seen her all day, and she returns to her post a few meters away. The screenwriter decides to enter the sex shop and have a look around, but he soon bores of this, and goes back outside to smoke another cigarette. Then he smokes another, and another, thinking all the time about the black prostitute, but it seems this isn't going to be his day, and no one else is even bothering to ask him for a light, so he finally decides to go. He thinks about the girl's father, who wouldn't have spent a minute waiting on that miserable street. He'd be lying on his bed in a plush hotel room talking on the phone, arranging an assignation with the college chick. He remembers seeing something similar in a movie, but he decides to use the idea anyway. After all, it's only a subplot. Do they really advertise college chicks as private escorts in the newspaper? Why not dispense with the scenario and think of another one? During McGregor's shift in the Grand Central Station, the girl's father and the chick are having dinner in a classy restaurant. They talk about all kinds of things, but the screenwriter hasn't yet decided what they are. The day they met, they spoke about jazz, but now he's not sure. Maybe they should've spoken about something else. He thinks about changing the dialogue. Then he thinks again. It's all the same, he says, the plan of the scene is perfect, so it really doesn't matter what they talk about. He returns to the restaurant. She's the same age as his daughter, thinks the father, maybe a couple of years older. Not that this bothers him in the slightest. In fact, he seems to like it. It makes him feel younger. And it doesn't even occur to him what they're doing might be wrong. The next shot takes place in a hotel room. A far more luxurious hotel than the ones the father habitually stays in. He sees a book peeking out of the chick's handbag, which is lying on the other side of the bed, whose title he can just about make out. He points to it, and she recites the beginning from memory. He asks her to account for the book's having made such an impression on her. She says she remembers because she makes a hobby of collecting and memorizing the beginnings of books, all of which she records in her notebook. If they meet up again, she promises to bring it with her. She further explains that the sentences she memorizes are all the openings of famous novels, and although she sometimes misremembers, mistakes certain words for others, she can always recall the general sense of the quotation. The father decides to challenge her—not only to test her claim, but to determine the quality of the novels she reads. He asks her to quote the beginning of a certain novel. She responds, "Stately, plump . . ." Satisfied, he challenges her with another. She says, "For a long time I used to go to bed early. Sometimes, when I had put out my candle, my eyes would close . . ." The girl's father is genuinely surprised that a young escort, basically a high-class hooker, can quote with ease the beginnings of two of the greatest novels ever written, and he's impressed that she was able to prove that she is indeed cultured, refined, sophisticated, just as she claimed. What would the author who was obsessed with jealousy and the passage of time think of a prostitute quoting his novel from memory? He'd no doubt be flattered, but the young college chick doesn't give the girl's father much time to think about it, because she's already quoting another: "One summer afternoon Mrs. Oedipa Maas came home from a Tupperware party whose hostess had put perhaps too much kirsch . . ." Do you know what that is? she asks. He says he doesn't know, or maybe he doesn't remember. That's how most novels begin, she replies, with the author not knowing, plagued by uncertainty. As she undresses, she recites a medley of openings passages: "I first met Dean not long after my wife and I split up." The girl's father suspects the young college chick wants to be a writer like his daughter, although he doesn't mention this. The chick's hair is short, styled to resemble an organized mess, according to the latest fashion. He doesn't want to know her age, in case she's younger than she looks. The screenwriter imagines her as young as possible without having a precise age in mind. What attracts him most about these little gamines is their youth, perhaps because they remind him of all the students he's slept with. He thinks of the girl's delicate skin, her wild hair, and tries to remember if his desire for these things only came after sleeping with her. He tries to think of the other students he was with, and all the women he picked up, whatever the asking price. He can't seem to remember their faces. Memory can be fragile in certain cases, he thinks. It doesn't matter to him whether the sex is free or paid for. Sex is sex. Besides, he thinks if he doesn't pay for it one way, he'll end up paying for it in another. His whole life has been a continuous drifting from woman to woman, an aimless floating from pier to pier, as a boat without oar or anchor, unable to come into the shallows and berth, to get close enough to learn more than perhaps a name. He could almost say he moves from one woman to the next as he does from one screenplay to the next. And this is how he remembers the past, for each screenplay is a climax in the chronicle of his life, each one reminds him of the state of mind he was in when he wrote it, whether he was happy or sad, in or out of love, if he was young and distinguished, or, as he is now, old and semi-retired—a part-time screenwriter who barely gets commissions anymore—whose life is an aimless drifting from pier to pier, unable to berth. He feels no one can fully understand this aspect of his biography but himself, or maybe someone like himself. He doesn't want to think about it anymore. The screenwriter returns to his story, and imagines the next shot being of the girl's father and the college chick making love on an elegant bed with gray satin sheets. Her firm, round breasts joggling rhythmically as she rides him, tempered only by his up-reaching hands, grasping them, caressing them. The screenwriter develops an erection as he writes. And then the college chick declaims at the top of her voice, "Stately, plump . . ." and "For a long time I used to go to bed early . . ." and occasionally groans, "Oedipa Maas" or "Tupperware." She may be only simulating the groans. At the end of the day, it doesn't matter. It's only a movie. The actress who plays her part will be simulating anyway.

The girl won't be coming tonight, and as on previous nights, the screenwriter won't be able to tolerate the loneliness of another evening spent anxiously watching his neighbor's window in the building across the street. Her light's on, but she refuses to be seen, or so it seems, and he's seriously planning to go knocking on her door. I'm a great admirer of your beauty, he imagines confessing to her. And since the day I first beheld you from afar, I've been bewitched by you, could barely forsake my window lest I be deprived of another glimpse of you, or even the chance to espy your silhouette. Pray, would you consider being the heroine of my movie, or even deign to be cast in a supporting role; or if not you, peradventure, consider lending me your silhouette, which is the shadow of perfection? Then he comes back to reality. He can't bear it anymore, the loneliness. It's like a weight bearing down on his chest. He needs to go outside to get some air, to find someone, anyone. The prostitute. Assuming he finds her. Hope against hope. He's been writing nonstop anyway and needs a break. There are a lot of people on the street where he usually sees her; prostitutes and guys like him approaching them for private discussions about asking price and terms and conditions. He remembers it's Saturday. He probably should've waited until tomorrow or Monday—days when there's less work, when she could dedicate more time to him. He searches first around the sex shop then walks a couple of blocks, but he doesn't see her. He thinks about paying one of the other hookers he sees walking up and down the sidewalk. If he meets the black prostitute again, he'll ask for her phone number. He goes into the club. He didn't call the producer today. It would've been impossible to reach him on a Saturday. He'll try calling again tomorrow. Either way, sooner or later, he'll have to answer the phone. The screenwriter takes a cigarette from the packet as she approaches him from behind. You were looking for me? He turns and is greeted by a familiar smile. One of her friends told her he was around. A messenger of the gods, he thinks while lighting a cigarette and taking a deep drag, feeling as if a weight's been lifted from his chest.

Sundays are horrible, thinks the girl, who seems to have contracted this distaste from the screenwriter. Her father got back late, stumbled to his bed, and fell asleep. The smell of cigarettes and alcohol, his only companion, made its presence known in every room. She gets dressed in the darkness and picks up the gun she found in the compartment of his laptop case. She waits until she's locked herself in the bathroom to take it out of its holster. She sees it's quite small, could easily be concealed on her person. She puts the holster to one side and tries to hide the pistol between her jeans and the small of her back. It's not very comfortable, and she'd have to wear a jacket to fully conceal it. But this doesn't matter right now. She removes it from her pants and examines it again, gently caresses it, running her fingers along its grooves and edges and handle too. It's not very heavy. She holds it with both hands, aims it high and low, lining up her sight with one eye closed, and then pretends to draw it from the holster like a cowboy. She needs practice. In front of the bathroom mirror, she imitates the classic stance of a policeman aiming at a bad guy: squat, with legs apart, aiming with both hands. It's reminiscent of a scene in a very famous movie, but the screenwriter wants to use it anyway, as an *homage*. He knows he's not writing a cinematic masterpiece, but he does wonder whether such scenes lack authenticity, whether the actor in this scene, for example, will be imitating a police officer or the actor in the famous movie who's imitating a police officer. The girl finally manages to conceal the gun properly behind her back. She looks at herself in the mirror, first from the front, then the side. Nothing to betray that she's armed. She dons a headscarf and a pair of dark sunglasses and checks there's nothing else about her that could give her away. No one would know it's me, she thinks. She feels the bulge of the gun and notes its weight. While on her way to one of the bars on the dock, she questions whether she's really carrying it for her own protection—in case she meets her stalker in the shadows, say. It's one of those somber days when darkling clouds cover every patch of sky, and the sun only rises with reluctance. She takes a seat in a corner from where she can monitor most of the vicinity, principally the entrance. She feels like an actress, or as if she's in the middle of a game, and that she could write a work of fiction about herself, an autobiographical novel. She orders a light breakfast and takes a newspaper from one of the tables. She searches through the classified ads to check if she's received a reply. But then she thinks it's still way too early for that. She reads through the headlines, occasionally glances at the traffic on the bridge over a river she can't see or hear, but which she's sure must still be there, giving the bridge a purpose. She sees the buildings on the opposite bank, notes the sky in the backdrop, the same miserable sky that's lowering this side of the river. Her phone rings. The brilliant composer reminds her that tonight will be her last opportunity to see them in the church. Last night went extremely well: they didn't miss her at all. The latest conquest was magnificent, and her other replacement, on the piano, could very well surpass her in the near future. It seems he never really liked the way the girl played. They'll always be grateful, he says, that she played a part in making the Little Sinfonietta famous. She laughs and hangs up. She doesn't want to give him the pleasure of knowing she's offended. Maybe she'll pay them a visit after all, she says, adjusting the weapon in the small of her back. She decides to go back to the hotel, but takes some precautions—is suspicious of the people behind her, on both sides of the street, and those who cross her path, in case one of them is following her, while also being vigilant in case her pursuer should suddenly come out from around a corner and ambush her. But the reality of the streets is very different. They are almost deserted, and all the stores are closed. Sundays are horrible, she thinks as she adjusts the weapon in the small of her back. Yes, one of these days, she thinks again, being reminded of her so-called friends, she'll pay them a visit. A gun denotes action, but the screenwriter wants to be sure it's used to greatest effect. If there's a gun, he thinks, sooner or later, there'll be a dead body.

Alone in the room, the girl is writing in her notebook, doing some literary exercises in observation—writing a series of short, descriptive vignettes—as she resolved to do whenever she wasn't making any progress with her novel, as a form of self-resuscitation. She describes the old hotel room she's staying in: how the balcony looks, shrouded by timeworn curtains, barely translucent with all the stains; the high, flaking ceilings raining plaster on the carpet; the walls, the wallpaper, once kitsch, now obscenely discolored; and finally, of course, the room's furnishings. She describes what she sees because she believes the exercises will hone her skills as a writer, and whenever she gets writer's block, she exercises. More of a writer every day, she thinks. On her father's nightstand are some jazz CDs, some magazines and newspapers, which partially cover the monumental tome of his favorite author—a man obsessed with jealousy, solitude, and the passage of time—and a paper on the social responsibilities of the scientist, as well as another about the search for life beyond our solar system. The latter outlines methods to search for life at every stage of evolution, from primitive to intelligent. The girl lies down on the bed in order to compare all these coincidences that seem to be mounting, to see if there's any relationship between them: the voices that pronounce her name with a "ka," the extraterrestrials both inside and outside her novel, the documentation her father keeps, the domes of countless cathedrals and churches that act as transmitter-receiver stations, the astrophysicist . . . she lies back on the bed with her arms crossed, her eyes screwed to the ceiling. Is there life out there? she asks. She knows there are dots to connect, but she can't seem to focus at the moment. She thinks about the gravely ill scientist again, who's not only a friend of her father's but seems to have been acquainted with her mother in her youth. What's her mother up to right now? she wonders. After some deliberation, she calls her. It doesn't take long before they're arguing over why she was axed by the Little Sinfonietta. Her mother repeats the same warning as the day before. Is it so hard for you to understand why it happened? she asks, you're too distracted, you've lost your focus. Then she asks if the girl's with her father. He's just gone out, she responds. What are you up to, then? her mother asks. I'm writing, she says. It's a piece of dialogue between two people who are struggling to keep a conversation going, and which ultimately ends in silence. Her mother gets the message and the phone call ends. The girl's annoyed whenever anything reminds her of the young conductor and brilliant composer. But then she thinks she should have the courage to leave. Leave who, what? Everything, she says in haste, as if the answer had erupted from the very depths of her. But it's no use. Running away from everything is like running away from nothing; and besides, she doesn't exactly know why it is she wants to run away at all. She can't imagine herself packing her bags then hailing a taxi to the airport. Before she even thinks about going anywhere, she must wait for a reply to her ad. It will surely come any day now. There are too many coincidences telling her that contact is imminent. She returns to her position on the bed, lying back with her arms crossed, her eyes screwed to the ceiling.

She's not getting into any taxi. She's not running away from any world. The young conductor pops into her head. If she did run away, at least she'd never have to see him again. She'll never have to think about him either. She then immediately contradicts herself by imagining a hypothetical dialogue between them. They're talking about her novel. How do they know they're aliens? he asks. She says they don't know. The question you should be asking is: How *don't* I know they're aliens? The young conductor says this is like asking how do we know what we see is real—that we're not just the product of inconceivably sophisticated software, or the creation of an over-arching consciousness, a part of a game created by that consciousness for its own amusement; a consciousness that some have called God? The girl closes her eyes. Once again, someone's trying to steal her thoughts. I'm sorry, she says, but I think you're just regurgitating something I've already said. The words have hardly left her mouth when, deep within, the girl hears the sound of a thousand voices speaking in unison, growing louder and louder, saying every idea in the world has been thought of, that there's nothing she'll ever conceive or imagine that hasn't been spoken of or written about before. Then the voices fall silent, and the conversation with the young conductor of the orchestra comes to an end. She won't be having these kinds of discussions again, she thinks. They're finished for good. An inner voice reminds her, "The clown, in an ecstasy, drinks deeply from the holy chalice, to heaven lifts up his entranced head . . ." Yes, they're finished for good, as is her friendship with the young conductor. They didn't miss her at all, said the brilliant composer. The statement could be the straw that breaks the camel's back. For a nobody, he certainly has a good way of gauging the situation. They didn't need her, she repeats. Perhaps she should pay them a visit. The girl dismisses the thought and concentrates on a single point on the ceiling. She doesn't want her imagination to wander. "3.11 The method of projection is to think of the sense of the No World." She writes about the old professor, says he only acquires full significance when he's thought of as part of a much bigger picture, as in that terrible image of him staring out through the windows of a control room at the vast emptiness of space. When her father gets back, tired after a long vigil in the station, they converse on a number of trivial topics, after which he asks her how the writing's going. It would be better to ask if she knew the beginnings of certain novels. But that would be expecting too much of him. She's content to just record them in her notebook. "One summer afternoon Mrs. Oedipa Maas came home from a Tupperware . . ." "Stately . . ." The girl decides to leave the room and go for something to eat—not knowing exactly where to go, or perhaps, unconsciously, she does know, but it won't occur to her until she reaches the lobby, when it will suddenly dawn on her, as if by chance, as if spontaneously—except it won't be by chance, for the knowledge has always been there in her unconscious, and it only needed the right moment, the right suggestion, to bubble up into her conscious mind, and perhaps entering the lobby was all the suggestion it needed. It's not the first time the thought occurred to her, she just hasn't dared follow through on it. She knows it's one of those things her father forbids her to do, although he doesn't say it directly, because he doesn't have to, and she doesn't ask, because she knows better, because his answer's implicit. The Grand Central Station looms imposingly before the girl, with its vaulted glass ceiling, its huge displays announcing the arrival and departure of trains, whether they'll be on schedule or delayed. It reminds the girl of an airport, although a gray, old, and filthy one. The place is crowded, and the girl suspects that all these people are getting back after a short weekend away somewhere. Even a train station knows Sundays are horrible, she thinks. She passes a kiosk on her way to a café in which, seated at the back, watching her as she enters, is the elusive cousin Dedalus. The girl can't help suspecting that Cousin Dedalus and McGregor are in fact the same person. That would explain why McGregor seems to want to avoid crossing paths with her, and why her father was so surprised when she told him she met Cousin Dedalus. She walks right past him, close enough to say hello, to sit down and interrogate him about the churches and cathedrals, those transmitters and receivers of intergalactic messages, but he turns his face as she passes, as if to avoid being seen by her, and she ends up sitting far away from him. The girl takes notes in her notebook. She wants to describe the behavior of someone who has nothing else to do with his time but wait. Wait for what? she wonders, still convinced the answer will mark a turning point—although she knows simply asking herself the question won't yield an answer. She finishes her meal without having thought of a single particular quality to distinguish Cousin Dedalus from McGregor. So what will she call him from now on, this Dedalus/McGregor? She looks around the station. She can't think of anything that makes him stand out from the crowd, and no one around her in the station is acting strangely—acting like someone who has nothing to do but wait—although she knows every single one of them has something about them that they don't want the rest of the world knowing. The girl thinks she'll never again be able to enter a train station without thinking about her father and his associate, the man she's now convinced is Cousin Dedalus. Perhaps she'll never be able to enter a train station again without thinking the way they do about the commuters—that some of them aren't really commuters at all.

He can't sleep. So he leaves the light off and gets up, moving through the darkness toward the window, and looks down at the street below. He then looks at the building opposite, then the bakery, the lingerie store, and the shoe and handbag store that's closed for the August vacation. Sundays are pointless, he thinks. Fortunately, he missed this one. He got back late from his assignation with the black prostitute and spent most of the day sleeping. He then got up and ate some leftovers from the fridge, drank lots of water to defuse his hangover, and even managed to write a little. He doesn't have the stamina for drinking he once had, but he can't help himself when he's around the black prostitute, or any prostitute for that matter. He finds he has to drink when he's around them. The girl's different though. He doesn't drink when he's with her. There's a car waiting in front of the hotel. Its droning engine is distracting him. The streets are dimly lit but he can still see the white envelope in the driver's hands. He gets dressed and goes down to the lobby, limps nervously with the help of his cane toward the receptionist, and asks if there's a letter for him. There is. He sits in the nearest chair and tears open the envelope. It's a scene in which the girl illustrates the connection between two different characters, the quality that brings them together, making them one. "4.1 Connections represent the existence and nonexistence of states of affairs. The female student is lying next to the window smoking. The old professor of philosophy is standing with his hands in his pockets on the other side of the room, thinking about his wife, who's threatening to report him to the Academy. He lights his own cigarette and starts walking back and forth in the room,

233

toward and away from her. There's a guilty silence between them. We should make love tonight, and not stop until we die, he says. She doesn't respond. He looks at the ground. She doesn't know whether he's being serious or ironic. Nobody can keep making love until they die, thinks the female student, smirking. She looks out onto the street. She's in a cynical mood. How can she die making love when she hasn't finished reading the philosopher W? The cigarette smoke bothers her. She waves her hand to dissipate the plumes moving toward her face. He wants to know if she still loves him, if he can at least count on that. The female student keeps looking out the window as if she hadn't heard the question, as if there was a guilty silence between them. I could easily dump her, he says. The female student shudders, but she tries to ignore his use of the word 'dump' to describe divorcing his wife. 4. A thought is a proposition with a sense." There are more pages, but the screenwriter decides to stop reading and return them to the envelope, which he folds in two, and puts in his jacket pocket. He stays seated, thinking a while, alone except for the receptionist—perhaps more a night watchman than receptionist. A couple of tourists ring the doorbell. So he plays the night watchman himself by letting them in and accompanying them to the elevator. Good evening, they say in passing, but the screenwriter doesn't answer; he just nods his head. Back behind the desk, the receptionist turns the radio on and lowers the volume until it's practically inaudible. I won't sleep now, the screenwriter says as he exits onto the street. The fresh air calms him, clears his lungs. He walks slowly in the direction of the river, the sound of his cane on the pavement echoing in the evening silence. As he approaches the bridge, he notices a dim light flickering under it. He gets closer, and sees a group of tramps sleeping around a candle. The screenwriter thinks the place resembles a campsite. There are cardboard boxes and rags piled up beside the piers. Sundays are vile, he keeps thinking, although he's not sure these poor guttersnipes would agree with him. It's probably a special day for them, a day when they receive alms from their parishes, or something. He laughs at the notion, turns, and begins the slow walk back to the hotel. Once in his room, he continues reading where he left off. "4.2 The sense of an accusation is its agreement with the possibilities of existence of states of affairs. The woman has followed through on her threats and reported the professor to the board of the Academy. The director considers an immediate dismissal, but decides to allow him to finish his classes, since the school vacation is drawing near, and at that point, the old professor's contract will be up. Of course, he won't be offered a new one, but the director's still anxious to avoid a scandal. Perhaps the female student's parents will agree to keep the matter under wraps. The director calls her mother twice, but no one's at home, so he leaves a message after the second attempt. He's never met her father, and he'd rather discuss the matter with someone he knows. He doesn't have his phone number anyway, he says aloud, as if to offer himself an excuse. A scandal will harm the Academy's image, he thinks. He needs time to plan ahead for damage control."

Early the next morning, the screenwriter finds himself beginning again the old ritual of doing nothing except lying on his back, staring at the ceiling, and listening to the noises outside. He only vaguely recalls last night's perambulation, the streets whose silence seemed to swallow the echoes of his cane, the candle beleaguered by vagrants, his tiredness, his finally falling into the bed and going asleep. Now, he wants to pick up the thread of the story. First, he wants to conjure, in his mind's eye, an image of the girl, and where he thinks she'll be that very moment, for in situating her, his feet find the ground on which he'll have to slog until he reaches the end of his story. He sees her in the hotel, writing in her diary while looking at the balcony. The screenwriter wonders if she has breakfast with her father. They're rarely in the same room together, but they must surely eat together on occasion, he thinks. He wonders what these two people, who can barely say more than a few words to one another other, would talk about if they had to sit together in the hotel café, or wherever else they might choose to go and eat, and endure each other's company for longer than it takes to exhaust the available small talk about school or the weather. He stands with the help of his cane and takes a look out the window, as if he's been entrusted with a mission to monitor his neighbor's movements in the building opposite. She seems to be deliberately avoiding him. He then looks at the lingerie store, at the people walking past it, to see who goes in, then at the stores that are closed for the August vacation, and at the people waiting at the bus stop. He concludes the world's still in its orbit. While shaving, he thinks of the girl's father sitting on a café terrace in front of the Grand Central Station. The girl, sitting at his side, asks him about the terrorist who's just been captured, and about whom all the newspapers are reporting. Her father would rather talk about the star of her favorite soccer team, a player who doesn't seem to want to rejoin his teammates; or perhaps he'd like to ask her why she's stopped practicing piano. But the girl is insistent, and she finally risks broaching the subject of Cousin Dedalus, a man who disappeared in the neighboring country's capital years ago, and for whom the police are still looking. What will the press say when they capture him? she asks. Her father looks over his newspaper at her. That has nothing to do with the terrorist, he says, as he folds the newspaper and puts it to one side. He then takes a sip of his coffee and fixes his eyes on his daughter. The screenwriter cleans his razor under the running tap and leaves it dripping to air-dry next to the soap. He then dries his face with a towel and examines the results in the mirror. His face refuses to accord with the image he has of himself. Not that he despises the reflection staring back at him, but it's not the face of the man he imagines himself to be. Alas, he's gotten used to it at this stage of his life. Suddenly he remembers the producer: a man who seems to be avoiding him. But he's running seriously short of funds, he thinks, so he decides once again to try calling him. Which he does, and yet again, there's no answer. He must be on vacation, he thinks. There's no other explanation. Either way, he'll have to prepare some material to send him. He can't ask for an advance without sending something. Where was I? the screenwriter wonders, sitting at the typewriter and scavenging through his papers. He left off at the station, where the girl and Cousin Dedalus/McGregor—he still doesn't know which name to keep—are sitting in the same café. The girl had been starting to feel the same as her father and cousin do during their long vigils. No it wasn't that, he thinks, recalling a more recent interaction. Before he called the producer, he happened on an interesting idea. He lights a cigarette. He knows he shouldn't be smoking before breakfast, but he's a little anxious, and the tobacco helps to calm him. He remembers exactly what it was, although he hasn't written it down yet. He notes it down quickly before it recedes into his unconscious. The girl's sitting on the terrace of a café in front of the Grand Central Station, having breakfast with her father. She'd like to know what the press will say when the police catch Cousin Dedalus. Her father says that has nothing to do with the terrorist, and takes a sip of coffee. Meanwhile, she's looking past him, perhaps at the steps outside the station, and she hears him say he doesn't want her interfering either with him or his associate while they're working. The girl looks at her father again, intending to demur, but the face she meets warns her against any rejoinder, against any demand for further explanation. He cautions her not to interfere in any of his affairs. He simply won't tolerate it. She nods reluctantly, again looking away, this time at the foyer she can see just inside the station. Affairs . . . she thinks, repeating her father's euphemism as she looks at the station's frontage. Don't even try interfering, he said. She tries to think what affairs he might mean: the vigils, the astrophysicist's illness, making contact with aliens? Are these the things he won't tolerate her interfering in?

He's left his clothes at the laundry. Now, he finds himself slogging uphill, leaning precariously on his cane, but once he reaches the end of the road, he can see the finish line, as it were, the seats and tables of the café in the plaza. The screenwriter limps slowly. There are days when he has to drag his leg like a dead weight, he thinks. It depends on the mood he's in when he wakes up. On crossing the finish line, he flumps into the nearest seat and looks out for the waitress, hoping she doesn't take too long. He puts both hands on the pommel of his cane and rests his chin there. But he immediately alters his posture, since he thinks that position makes him look older. He's seen people do it who look as if they've got one foot in the grave. Perhaps he does it because he's tired, he thinks. Watching the waitress serving a table not too far away seems to reinvigorate him. He then looks over at the plaza. He wishes he knew the names of the people he regularly crosses paths with, simple people with simple habits, he imagines: the girl who walks her dog, the pensioner on his way to buy groceries, the gardener . . . The waitress approaches. One day, we'll have to go on a date, he says. The girl's expression doesn't change; she doesn't even betray a slight grin. The usual? she asks, after an awkward silence. I'm bewitched by you, he continues, ignoring her question. Is it because I'm older than you? You know, maturity is indicative of experience . . . he says, beginning an apologia on the virtues of senescence. She quickly loses patience. The usual then, she says, turning around and leaving him mid-sentence. You've no idea what you're missing, he mutters, unfolding the newspaper. One of the detained terrorist's ex-girlfriends says the police have been harassing her for twenty years, and that the relationship ruined her life. The soccer player still hasn't returned. Sure you won't change your mind? he asks the waitress when she brings his coffee. After she stonewalls him a second time, he goes fumbling for his cigarettes in his jacket pocket, whereupon his fingers touch the envelope the girl sent him. He recalls that he hasn't read all she'd written. The Principal of the Institute in which he once taught had also tried to prevent a scandal, and the screenwriter wonders whether what he's reading is hitting too close to home. He lights a cigarette and removes the pages from the envelope. "4.3 The possibility of uncertainty does not mean that finally such a possibility exists or does not exist. Classes are over, and the director of the Academy is deliberating. He would like to avoid a scandal, but the old professor of philosophy simply can't continue teaching there. Do you know the female student's parents? the professor asks the director. He says he doesn't. Perhaps he doesn't care to after what's happened. The old professor asks if he can gather his things and leave. Deep down he knows that sooner or later her parents will find out. If some persona incognita managed to find

239

out, then surely it's only a matter of time. 4.4 An accusation is an expression of agreement. 4.41 The mere possibility of being accused is the condition of the truth and falsity of the accusation. The old professor leaves the Academy, incensed at his wife. It had to be she who betrayed him. He can't stand the thought of continuing to live under the same roof as that woman. For an instant, his alien hunter's instinct leads him to suspect both his wife and the director of the Academy come from another world. But he needs to find a photo of each to verify whether or not they have a special halo. 4.5 It now seems possible to give the most general propositional form. We can start all over, he says to the female student that night. We can begin a new life. Let's get out of here, run away together. What kind of new life do you propose? she asks. He can't answer. It's an idea he only just came up with—still inchoate, indefinite, something nebulous floating around his head—but he quickly improvises an answer, as one who divines the shape of a cloud in the sky, and suggests their life would be such that she could write while he gave classes at other academies. Write, murmurs the female student, sounding a little disenchanted. The old professor is talking about starting a new life in a city far away, perhaps somewhere in outer space. He'd even run away to the No World, if necessary, where they could lie together under an artificial palm tree, and make love on white sand imported from the tropics. He says they could read W and all the great classics together, and she'd get the opportunity to revolutionize the world of letters. All she needs is the daring, the audacity, to take the first step. The female student smiles. Maybe she will leave her mark on the world of letters; maybe future generations will judge her contribution in terms of what came before and what came after her, but it won't be with him. I can't leave now, she says apologetically. I've got commitments. He begs her to break away from them; to break away from everything, starting with her past. We can become new beings, he urges her, with an exuberance bordering on the pathetic. Free! The girl can't make such a decision in haste. She wants to write, she says, but she doesn't know if she'll be able to do so with him around. She also has musical commitments she can't simply forsake. She has several concerts to perform in one of those cities in space orbiting the Earth. She also wants to make an unforgettable recording of the *5 Pieces for piano* . . . Run away with me, he urges her again. But the female student knows it's not a matter of running anywhere with him, for he'll be going nowhere himself unless she goes with him. Just try to imagine we're there, she says consolingly. After all, this life, or any life you care to have, will only ever exist in your mind. There's nothing outside it. Besides, even if we did run away together, it wouldn't be long before he found us. Before who found us? he says, taken aback. My father."

Alone in the room, the girl tries to continue writing. Her father's on his vigil in the Grand Central Station, or perhaps he's somewhere else entirely, on a date, say, with the young college chick. The screenwriter is outraged her father doesn't look after her, as any half-decent father would, but that he'd rather be out dallying with a jumped-up prostitute. He can't care for his daughter at all, he can't love her, the screenwriter concludes. Alone in the room, the girl wonders whether the world seems so real because it's created by a single, immense, and unfathomable intelligence, or by many intelligences working collectively. Did a single consciousness create the world she lives in, or are there many consciousnesses, many different minds, responsible for its existence, and for the existence of each individual in the world—one for her, say, one for the screenwriter, another for her father? It may be that this scattering of minds, being held in a loose conjunction with billions of others, each of which believes itself the center around which the rest of them turn, is really a single powerful collective mind that purposely fractures itself into smaller pieces in order to exist more thoroughly, more intensely. Is that possible? Sometimes, the girl imagines a structure resembling a glass honeycomb, each of whose cells contains a separate brain. At other times, she imagines billions of small, cloudlike structures drifting aimlessly in infinite space. If nothing exists outside these minds, where in space are the minds themselves located? Perhaps it's more sensible to imagine either a loose collective of minds, or just a single mind, like her own, that creates itself and everything else around it. She remembers having reached this same conclusion before. She goes out onto the balcony. But in what material is this single or collective mind suspended? The girl doesn't quite understand it. She touches her hand, touches the balcony rail, closes and opens her eyes. Does the Grand Central Station really exist? And where are the aliens, or where is the so-called guardian angel the screenwriter keeps talking about? There must be something linking them, some secret connection between the voices, the aliens, and the guardian angel. She wonders how she can tell if those beings that are supposedly born with us, that then accompany us throughout our lives, listening to our voices, inner and outer, our conversations with others, with ourselves, beings that ultimately outlive us, but will preserve our memory after we die—she wonders how to tell if they're angels or aliens from outer space. How can a girl of sixteen believe in angels? It makes more sense to believe in extraterrestrials, she says while watching the traffic of people and vehicles in the plaza. And what if there's only one place in the whole world where we can make contact? She supposes something as important as that would have to be located in a city somewhere, and not some secret location in a rainforest, say, that no one can find. Besides, there are many places to hide in the city. The contact point could be in a bookstore by the river, for example, the kind that sells old books. Then she thinks, what if this actually turned out be the case? She touches her hand, touches the balcony rail, closes and opens her eyes. Does the Grand Central Station really exist? Is it another illusion? She suddenly has an empty feeling inside. Did you say something? she hears her father ask as he walks in the door.

That's probably it, says the girl to herself while sitting in a half-empty restaurant, still thinking about the old bookstore she imagined could be the place in which she finally makes contact with the aliens. From a distance, we wouldn't recognize her, but as we approached, we'd see it was the girl, and that she's undergone a significant transformation, cutting her hair quite short, and dying it metallic blonde. She's anxious, breathing quite heavily, filling her lungs with air, her veins and arteries with oxygen, and yet there remains an empty feeling inside her. Maybe she's just hungry and impatient for the food to arrive. At the table next to hers, a recently married couple is flirting. A little farther away, a husband and wife, with a daughter not yet old enough to walk, are having dessert. Some of the empty tables in the restaurant don't have a tablecloth or any such covering at all. One of the waiters is watching her intently. It's late, but if she must eat alone, the girl prefers the restaurant to be empty; the solitude is less overwhelming. She's always more lonely in a crowd. Nonetheless, the girl listens to people's true voices: the recently married couple's, the older couple's and their daughter's—voices they can't hear themselves, but which the girl hears clearly. She even listens to the voices of the people who were once sitting at the empty tables, people who've long since left. There's a movie in which we listen to other people's voices. These aren't like the ones the girl hears—which are like the voice of the multitudes speaking in unison, as if all humanity was speaking with a single voice. What does it signify? she wonders. Nothing happens by chance. They're voices informing her of a task, a mission she has to complete; whispers she'll eventually understand. So there's no need for her to lose heart. Sooner or later, it'll all start making sense. Suddenly, the recently married woman interrupts her musings to ask for an autograph. She just happened to have a magazine with a picture of the girl inside. It's better with a picture than on blank paper, the woman says. The girl signs it, but not without scanning the article first. She then apologizes for the delay, saying she hadn't been aware of its existence. The world must be conspiring against her. How did the woman recognize her even though she cut and dyed her hair? Should she start dining with sunglasses on? When her cell phone rings, the recently married couple and the couple with the daughter have long since left. On the other line, the brilliant composer is praising the design and acoustics of the concert hall in which the Little Sinfonietta are performing tonight. The girl isn't impressed either by the hall's architecture or the number of people it can accommodate. The brilliant composer is about to begin a short rehearsal, but he took the time to call her anyway—as if to say, look at what you're missing with all your silly scribbling. She listens in silence, considers an adequate response. Perhaps something like: Oh, but haven't you premiered in this or that concert hall yet? No?

Well, wait until you see it. It's far better than the one you're describing. If you ever perform there, don't forget to call me. Or maybe, instead of irony, she should wait until he's in mid-sentence then hang up on him. In the end, she decides against playing either card, chooses instead to listen, in case she needs the information to finish her novel. She also wants to find out how far his malice will stretch. He asks if she's planning to make her novel autobiographical, as he suggested she should do. The girl stops talking. She doesn't want him to know how she really feels. She'd gladly shoot him dead, but she pretends everything he says rolls off her as water off a duck's back, as if the interview she heard on the radio hadn't fazed her at all, as if she didn't mind the latest conquest pretending to be her, as if she wasn't enraged at her boasting about hearing voices and writing novels. No, she wouldn't stoop so low.

If nothing exists, writes the girl in her diary, the dead are nothing more than products of the imagination: a corollary of the theorem that a single mind is responsible for conceiving everything. And reinforced by the lemma: the single creative mind must somehow exist outside its creation. It must exist in another dimension. So why not bring the dead back to life? Why not create life in other galaxies? She has to think of a mechanism that connects aliens and the dead, nothing too simple, or others would've already thought of it. It has to be something like those gateways connecting far-flung regions of the cosmos, through which one could traverse vast distances of space and time. She can't rely too much on the personal ads in the newspaper. She once believed the *No World Symphony* was the place to have an encounter, a place from which she'd be transported to another world. She once believed they shared a common language with us, but she never managed to discover it. Not even the brilliant composer, with all his mathematical casuistry, and those compositions that are more like secret messages for cabals of code-breakers than music to delight a listener, no, not even he had managed to discover a common language between humans and aliens, between the living and the dead. He may not even believe that such a common language is possible. He may only believe in the game. Now the girl considers the possibility of a single creative consciousness again, wondering if, in her eagerness to know it better, she might begin by asking a completely different question. Would a mind that creates itself and everything else still have need of success and recognition? It would require a superhuman effort at self-deception.

Early the following morning, the screenwriter is browsing the shelves of a recently opened bookstore. In one of the aisles, he notices a mop inside a bucket of water and that portions of the floor are still wet. He also sees the owner, standing on a ladder, sorting the books on one of the shelves. The screenwriter's resisted the temptation to read any books on this trip because he wants to focus completely on his script. He hasn't changed his mind, but he has to check certain references, take some notes directly from primary sources. He also wants to double check some of the things the girl's father believes about the writer he refers to variously as the author of jealousy, the warder of cherished memories, and the master of the subordinate clause, because he needs to plan his next scene with the young college chick cum private escort. In it, the girl continues quoting the beginnings of books by renowned authors. The screenwriter hasn't actually read many of these books, but he thinks he knows which ones she'd choose. "One day, I was already old, in the entrance of a public place a man came up to me. He introduced himself and said, 'I've known you for years . . .'" Another novel she'd choose begins as follows: "He—for there could be no doubt of his sex, although the fashion of the time did something to disguise it . . ." The screenwriter continues browsing the shelves, selects another book that begins: "Early in 1880, in spite of a well-founded suspicion as to the advisability of perpetuating that race which has the sanction of the Lord and the disapproval of the people . . ." He doesn't recall it being so brilliant. If asked, he'd say he chose them for their fame, their canonicity, or something like that, but in reality, the only criteria that matter are his intuition and personal taste. When he's in a good mood, he always feels he hasn't given all of himself yet, that there's yet another book to write. Perhaps one day, he tells himself, he'll write a book based on the notes assembled from all his notebooks. A collage built up of many different pieces of books and scripts he's written over the years, revealing the secret, unpublished lives of his characters, and collating all his abortive ideas, as well as the brilliant ideas that never found their proper place. "In the town there were two mutes, and they were always together." He jots it down neatly in his notebook and returns the book to the shelf. Then he undergoes a change of mood, becomes glum, and no longer sees any sense in taking such detailed notes. No one will care about all this once the movie's made. A script, he tells himself, is nothing. Nothing but a tiny part of the huge process that brings a movie to the big screen; it's only an itemization of what will appear in the final product, and it's only the final product people care about. Why would anyone be remotely interested in these notes that won't even appear in the final script? Only the great directors and screenwriters from the past would take care to incorporate them into the movie, but these are the elect, and at his age, it's too late to be admitted into their ranks. "Once an angry man dragged his father along the ground through his own orchard . . ." He recognizes this one, not for having read the book, but because he's often quoted it in other contexts. The screenwriter's satisfied with the number of openings he's collected so he starts looking around for the exit. The bookseller gives him a few fleeting looks as he walks by, as if casting about in his mind to match this face with one of the writers he knows, for he must be a writer, since he's far too old to be a student, and the screenwriter slows his canter to a trot in order to allow enough time for the penny to drop. Two more writers, and then that's it, he says. So he diverts to another bookshelf and, before long, finds the first of the two: "The lie detector was asleep when he heard the telephone ringing . . ." And then the second: "On a January evening of the early seventies, Christine Nilsson was singing in *Faust* at the Academy of Music in New York . . ." The young college escort will have chosen some passages specifically for a game with the girl's father, who'll know them, and will try to name the books and authors. Others, though, will have been chosen specifically for their obscurity, and probably won't be recognized by anyone. The screenwriter grants, however, that after a few days, he himself will probably forget who the authors are, and will have to make due with attributing them to one of the two characters that speak them—the girl's father or the young college escort. He puts the notebook and pencil in his jacket pocket, picks up his cane—which he left leaning against a bookshelf—and goes looking for the main aisle that leads to the exit. On reaching the front of the store, he sees a number of tables on which the new releases have been arranged in small stacks. He reads some of the titles, perhaps considering one of them as a last inclusion. But he's really only doing so to linger, delay his exit, to give the bookseller a little more time to recognize him. Besides, it wouldn't be characteristic of the girl's father to remember the beginning of a recently published book. He doesn't find anything among the new releases that's worth including, but he does happen upon a book about the screenwriters of the golden age. He opens it and immediately recognizes some of the names. The author gives a brief biography of each and a summary of their contributions to cinema. There are also photographs of them—some are just passport-sized snapshots, some feature a given screenwriter posing next to a poster for the film they wrote, others show a screenwriter looking up from his desk in an office, and there are even a few of the screenwriter disporting on set with actors, directors, and other crew members. The screenwriter's surprised such a book exists, and he checks the blurb, the preface, and the introduction to see what criteria the author used to make his selection. His tastes are slightly different, but the screenwriter admires the selection nonetheless, especially considering it isn't an exhaustive list. While flipping through the book, he stops at the synopsis of a certain film. "The protagonist makes his living renting a boat to wealthy vacationers to go fishing offshore." He quickly reads a few more random passages before finally deciding to buy the book. He knows he can't afford it, but once again, desire overrides his better judgment—a desire that will make him feel guilty as soon as he leaves the bookshop. Who knows, it may come in useful one day, if he manages to get a university appointment as professor of screenwriting. It's an excuse as valid as any other.

It's been days since he visited the pond; since he sat on one of the benches to have a rest and admire the young mothers who bring their children there to play; since he saw their little sail-boats scudding on the water, driven by the lightest of breezes. But the benches are far, and it's getting quite late. The screenwriter is eating a sandwich in a small park, not far from the island in the river, and reading some passages from his new book. He pays no heed to the time, until he casually looks at his watch and is alerted of the fact he's let another day go by without having written a single line. He also forgot to call the producer, but resolves to do so as soon as he gets back to the hotel. During the walk, he notes his leg has improved over the course of the day, and before long, he finds himself standing at the reception desk collecting yet another envelope. He asks who delivered it, but the receptionist doesn't know, having just begun her shift. Distrait, the screenwriter moves away without a thank you or good-bye. He's sick of these people never being around when the girl's envelopes are delivered. Such incompetence is typical, universal in fact, and he can't stand it anymore, can't tolerate living in a world he believes to be defective—completely inadequate to a discerning mind, utterly detrimental to a brilliant one. He takes the elevator up to his room, sits at his desk, and begins reading. But suddenly, he remembers his livelihood depends on his making a certain phone call. He picks up the handset and dials the number. This time he's in luck, the producer's at home. They spend a few minutes exchanging pleasantries, talking about the August vacation. The producer says he's just gotten back from a distant retreat where he went to catch up on some work. The screenwriter takes his mention of work as an opportunity to tell him about his predicament. He then immediately reassures the producer by mentioning the magnificent script he's holding in his hands. But he's in urgent need of money, he says. The producer remains silent. The screenwriter then replies to that silence by insisting he's at a crucial juncture with the screenplay. After some persuasion, the producer finally acquiesces, and promises he'll speak to the accountant. But the screenwriter detects in his tone a tacit warning that this will be his last advance. The producer then fills him in about the time constraints under which this draft must be produced, about deadlines, and important dates relating to the shoot. But the screenwriter doesn't believe any of it. He thinks it's only a pro forma test, a mere convention, that he'd send the advance anyway. Perhaps he'd send it to pay back an old favor, or perhaps because they're old friends; the point is these are the reasons he'll continue sending advances, the reasons why the screenwriter refuses to heed the tacit warning. Would you consider making the girl the main protagonist? No, she's only his student. Yes, there are other students as well. And yes, all of them are gifted. After hanging up, the screenwriter feels like a weight's been lifted. He decides to pick up the phone and call his wife. He still doesn't know why he counts the rings, why he waits until the fifth one: just a meaningless habit perhaps, something to do while he waits so he doesn't have to think about anything. After the fifth ring, he hangs up. He then returns to his chair and starts reading the pages he collected at reception. It seems she sent him more passages about the City in Outer Space. "5.471 The general form of the No World is the essence of the No World. One day he sleeps in an area far from his old address, the next he sleeps in an area quite close to it. Or perhaps the reverse. He's long since lost track. Besides, he doesn't see the point of sleeping in the same bed every night if there's another one close-by. Even so, every now and then he still feels the urge to go back. Not for any special reason: there's nothing there he can't find in any other house in the city. He could move into a first-class hotel, even requisition the luxury suite, but for the moment he's happy playing the vagabond, content to sleep wherever his head happens to fall. If he does go back to the house he lived in, the bed he slept in, during the war, it won't be for any other reason than to feel at home. A purely sentimental motive. He's usually accompanied on his travels by the female student's music, which is transmitted from speakers located around the city—her recordings of twelve-tone piano music performed so slowly, with the pauses between notes so long, that the waiting becomes a kind of torment—now a note, then a silence, now another—the only interruption occurs on the hour, every hour, when a voice can be heard announcing the time and date. Sometimes, the old survivor recognizes some of the beds from having slept in them many years before. His only possessions are a tape recorder, a copy of W, and a gun. He doesn't expect to find any other survivors, especially after all this time, but he carries a gun because he can never be sure, and he doesn't really know what to expect in a city he's yet to fully explore. Moreover, he doesn't know when the fuel supplies are going to run out, when the solar powered generators or the machines supplying oxygen to the city will fail. He carries a gun for his protection, but he also carries it in the event the oxygen runs out, for then he intends to kill himself. To commit suicide and prevent a slow, torturous demise, or perhaps as an alternative to boredom, to despairing of ever being rescued, to the weariness of performing the same rituals every day, thinking the same thoughts every day, repeating the same day every day, or seeming to. The old professor feels hollow. He wishes things were like they used to be. As if the old days were timeless, renewable, could exist again in the present or the future. Lying in one of the beds he frequents, he remembers a time before he fled to the City in Outer Space, when the only thing he wanted in the world was to run away and disappear somewhere with the female student; somewhere far away from everything and everyone. He has a vivid memory of her smiling at him. It is a knowing smile, as if she's finally come to understand him, or perhaps as if she's always understood him. He's looking deep into her eyes, entranced, bewitched, because she's lavishing on him an expression he rarely gets to see—at once seductive and timorous, knowing and innocent, the things that draw him most to her, that caused him fall in love with her. He wants to run away with her, begin a new life somewhere else, somewhere far away where he could find a decent job, a place where the laws are in his favor, and where he could easily get a license and even make a living as an alien hunter. The female student remains silent. She has no intention of going anywhere with him. Let's leave, says the old professor. Run away with me. Run away? she asks. 5.5542 Is it really legitimate to ask the question 'What must be the case for the No World not to be the case?' The old professor is going to be reported by his wife to the director of the Academy. The female student thinks it's all just a game. Life's just a game. She could run away to that City in Outer Space where she has a number of concerts pending." The screenwriter sees perfectly the path the girl is taking in her novel, where it deviates from and where it comes back to his own life, and there's nothing he can do about it. He sees her alone in her room, reading then writing, editing her diary then typing away on her father's laptop, lying on her bed listening to music while looking outside through a gap in the curtains before indulging in a peripatetic jaunt around the room. The screenwriter eventually forgets about the role the girl assigned him in her novel. At this point, he shouldn't allow anything to distract him. The girl's boredom has become chronic from all the waiting. She could go for a walk, catch a movie, or take up a hobby, but she doesn't think there's anything worth doing in the neighboring country's capital except writing and trying to contact extraterrestrials. Nothing else interests her. She may try to find out what her father and Cousin McGregor are up to. She finally knows what to call him: by contracting the names, Cousin Dedalus and McGregor, Cousin McGregor was the obvious choice. She thinks about going home. But she knows she still has a commitment to fulfill, to record the *5 Pieces for piano*, her own unique interpretation, which she must leave behind so that posterity will remember who she was. Meanwhile, her father will be spending more time getting to know the young college chick. When not waiting in the hotel room, or on his vigil in the station, the girl's father always visits the young college chick. The girl believes her father works twenty-four hours a day. The contrast of the girl writing alone in the room with her father lying in bed with his throwaway girlfriend accents the many distances between them. The screenwriter gets up from his typewriter and goes to the kitchen. He lights a cigarette while waiting for the coffee to prepare. He doesn't feel like going to the café in the plaza. He opens the fridge to make sure there's enough food, decides to fix something with whatever he can find. Then he picks up the telephone and calls the black prostitute, asks her if she can come to the hotel. He wants her to be with him while he writes. It'll only be for a couple of hours, he says in an almost-whisper. On the other end, the prostitute is smiling as she reminds him that the price is higher if she travels. He tells her not to worry about the price, that her presence alone is bound to bring him luck. He then hangs up, and returns to his desk to resume writing . . . Alone in her father's hotel room, the girl is writing in her notebook, doing some literary exercises in observation—writing a series of short, descriptive vignettes—as she resolved to do whenever she wasn't making progress with her novel, as a form of self-resuscitation. She describes the old hotel room she's staying in: how the balcony looks, shrouded by timeworn curtains, barely translucent with all the stains; the high, flaking ceilings raining plaster on the carpet; the walls; the once kitsch, now obscenely discolored wallpaper; and finally, of course, the room's furnishings. She describes what she sees because she believes the exercises will hone her skills as a writer, and whenever she gets writer's block, she exercises. Then she decides to reads some of the writers the screenwriter recommended, perhaps as a nod to the gossamer thread still connecting them. On her father's nightstand, the jazz CDs, magazines, and newspapers continue to mount, but now completely cover the monumental work of his favorite author—warder of cherished memories, master of subordinate clauses. The screenwriter would relish explaining to the girl's father that his favorite author doesn't write about lost time at all, nor jealousy, nor any other subject he has defined him by, but of a world that disappears before his eyes, a world overwhelmed by change, by time's ineluctable progress, sometimes slow, sometimes rapid, always inconceivable, especially to those who lived in times past; explaining that his favorite author is nothing but a hoarder of memories, a starry-eyed futilitarian in search of a past he can never retrieve, and yet tries to nonetheless, for whatever reason, being unable to abandon his quest, perhaps because the guerdon's in the searching, in the writing about a world of refinement and bon ton, of frivolity and effeminacy, of waxen moustaches and scented handkerchiefs, a world that was his own, and could limn to the smallest detail, a world in which he believed, for there was none other to believe in. Of course, this is in stark contrast to the screenwriter, who doesn't write about his past, who couldn't bear the reprisal of so many bruised memories. The girl reads in a short introduction that, through the cumulative effect of describing many small and seemingly insignificant events, the author creates a magnificent crumbling mosaic of a world in crisis; that he seems to bask in the recollection of those who lived in that world, of hours that have long since tolled, epitomizing both in a plethora of fictive personalities; that we don't know if he confabulated his memories of early childhood, such memories being unreliable at best, or if he likewise supplemented his memories of youth and early adulthood; that perhaps his vision of a bootless world, empty and decadent, was only that, and vanished only from his own memory, and that his wistfulness, his yearning, is symptomatic of a man who'd have mourned the loss of any age, any time, because the only thing that truly vanishes is the self located there, located then, so the narrator interprets the end of his age as the end of the self, and the end of the self as end of the world entire.

Youth is that condition of being without a past; old age, of being without a future. For this reason, the screenwriter thinks the girl's character is ultimately uninteresting. He, on the other hand, has a surfeit of memories to draw upon, to crowd his horizons with, and yet he refuses to do so because these memories are mostly bad, mostly painful. So, content to languish in no-man's-land, his thoughts always revolve around the girl. She has no past to speak of, but strangely, neither does she seem to have a future. The glittering path to fame and fortune has abruptly vanished, and now a thick mist beclouds her horizon. The future has become for her a dream instead of a reality, a hope instead of a certainty, a squinting at some indiscernible offing. And yet, the girl still has a purpose, has an aim: why not write in such a way about the future? Perhaps in reading the author her father holds in highest esteem, the girl is learning something about herself. If someone considered to be unhealthy, once a salon wit, now a bedridden recluse who lacks the strength to write a serious novel, who never showed any sign of wanting to write one, who'd rather have cultivated good manners, who seemed to hold courtesy at a higher premium than celerity of thought; if such a man could successfully disguise his commitment to his craft, his belief in his vocation, and still produce a monumental masterpiece for the ages, why can't the girl? Youth is that condition of being without a past. Time is a dimension added to those of space, but this is not the sort of time that can be measured by a watch: it's the girl's own personal time, which is different. A tunnel could transport her to another instant, another day, another life. But the girl can't predict the future, and therefore, she cannot know that on the other side of the tunnel is only misery and desolation. The telephone rings, interrupting her musings. It's the brilliant composer calling to update her on the continued success of the Little Sinfonietta. Her replacements are outdoing her every day, he gloats. It seems he never liked the way she played. But he'll always be grateful, he says, that she played a part in making him a recognized composer. Right now, they're on their way to another capital, where everyone excitedly awaits their arrival. Are you still writing? he asks. She says yes. He says he thinks it's a result of the hypnosis. What do you mean hypnosis? It seems she doesn't even remember she was hypnotized. The hypnotist turned you into a writer, he assures her. It was from then that she began hitting false notes and missing beats in rehearsals and performances. She doesn't remember a thing. This is all just beacuse of his jealousy. One day she'll call him to account—him and the young conductor, whom she imagines is sitting right beside him, egging him on. The girl won't let anything he says upset her. She remembers that, in the end, the brilliant composer is nothing to her. He could drop off the earth and she'd forget he ever existed. Before hanging up, the girl asks him to name the people who were there that night. The screenwriter then improvises a scene in which the girl is in a writing frenzy, actuated by the material she's read about that author from a bygone era, the one her father reveres. She disconnects the phone, just in the case the brat composer decides to call again, telling herself that there's no limit to human wickedness. She doesn't feel like she's been hypnotized. She stops writing and gets up to stretch her legs, to do a couple of laps around the room. After a few moments, she takes her seat in front of the laptop, and continues: "5.5561 The limit also makes itself manifest in the totality of elementary images. He's sold all his belongings, but he wants to take one last photograph of her. He wants to take it before they come to take away the furniture, the computer, the camera, and the spotlights. Just one more, he begs her. Again, he wants her to be naked; again, wants to be the one who takes her clothes off. They're both used to it by now, of course, but this time is special, because it may in fact be the last. The girl gets in the bath, and the old professor produces a safety razor, which he uses, along with scissors, to trim her pubic area until it's practically hairless. He prefers it like this, thinks it looks perfect, almost angelic. He wants the camera to capture every single pore. After drying her with a towel, he goes down on her, kissing the warm pink flesh of her labia until she trembles. He wants to make love to her, but he decides to take the photograph first, because he knows he always gets his

258

best shots when overcome with desire. She's lets him take his photos, although she'd rather be talking about W, and the No World. 3.04 If a No World were correct a priori, it would be a No World whose possibility ensured its truth."

This last scene has turned the screenwriter on. So he goes looking for the envelope with the photographs and examines them one after the other. He remembers when the girl used to visit him all the time, back when she bowed to his every whim. Now, incomprehensibly, the nightly visitations have come to an end. A few months ago she wasn't afraid of anything or anyone. Because no one was following her, he sighs. He returns the photos to the envelope. If she came back—if he could believe, for even an instant, that she'd be visiting this very night . . . But then he remembers his appointment with the black prostitute. He goes to the kitchen to see if there's anything to offer by way of a drink. Nothing strong enough to tempt her. He goes down to the street to a store that's open until midnight. He's not worried about cash now that he's managed to secure an advance. He buys a couple of bottles of liquor and heads back to the hotel. On the way, he remembers the beginning to a novel everyone in the world must know: "I had a farm in Africa, at the foot of the Ngong Hills." It's definitely one the girl's father would recognize.

It's like trying to catch smoke in his hands, compiling all this information that's destined to disappear, that will at best form part of the film's subtext, probably: something existing below the waterline, the greater part of the iceberg. The prostitute takes a seat. He'd like to believe she knows what he's talking about. This stuff moves in parallel with the other stuff, the stuff that actually winds up on the screen. Well, not really on the screen, technically, because they aren't images, because the script is more about how the narrative gets told. The screenwriter isn't explaining it all very well. He's had too much to drink, and he's getting tongue-tied. He remembers the book about screenwriters and looks for a section that might explain better what a subplot is. When he finds what he's looking for, he reads it aloud slowly, to make sure she understands. The author writes that the subplot usually contains the most important elements of the main storyline, but that the protagonist isn't directly involved in it. Instead, a deuteragonist of the story becomes the hero of the subplot, with a supporting cast of major and minor characters. While the main plot advances the action of the story, subplots explore the main themes. He leaves the book on the nightstand. What he's trying to say is that it's a difficult sketching in all the different characters' stories while sticking to the essential idea of the screenplay. What he's trying to say is that he's only doing this because he's lost his bearings and is trying to find a way to end his story. What he's trying to say is that he's writing because he wants to express what it's like to truly be alone. What he's trying to say is that he knows there's nothing special about his predicament, and that the prostitute must hear the exact same story every single night of the week. She lies down beside him and watches him as he speaks, pretends to show interest in what he has to say. "I had a farm in Africa, at the foot of the Ngong Hills," he whispers while staring at the ceiling— seeing, instead of white plaster, an image of the girl kissing another man. He'd like to see who the man is; he'd like to be the one responsible for his existence, as he is with the characters he sketches on index cards. But the longer he looks, the more the man's face appears to be that of the young conductor, until, eventually, that's the only face he can see. The black prostitute looks at the clock. She thinks it's about time they got down to business. The screenwriter asks her how much she'll charge to stay the night. Not to have sex, not even to listen to him whine about his sad old life, but just to sleep next to him—only that—just so he can feel the warmth of her body next to his. She complains about the lack of air conditioning in the room. He suggests they leave the window open during the night. The prostitute kisses him on the cheek, then on the lips, before telling him the amount it'll cost. Although he can't afford it, the screenwriter thinks it's a reasonable price. Space and time, he wants to say, that's what distinguishes one scene from another. He thinks she brings him luck, so he tries to think of a sentence or two he can start up with again the next morning, something to ensure he doesn't stay up all night thinking about what he's going to write. "The girl returns to the hotel after a long walk and immediately gets to work. She must resolve the question of her hypnosis." It's not bad. He recites it to the black prostitute, who seductively whispers it back to him. Then they recite it together a couple of times, and he asks her to remember it when they awaken, because he's had too much to drink, and he's afraid he's going to forget it. The next morning, when he wakes up, he can't remember having fallen asleep. Then he tries but fails to remember exactly when the black prostitute left.

"The girl returns to the hotel after a long walk and immediately gets to work. She must resolve the question of her hypnosis." Sainted woman, thinks the screenwriter of the black prostitute, who used red lipstick to write the sentences on the bathroom mirror. He'd have had a hard time getting started, but now the words are flowing uninhibited. The same can't be said for the girl, who seems to have run aground on account of not knowing whether or not she was really hypnotized. After getting back to her father's hotel room, she lay down on the bed. She couldn't sleep, thinking about the hypnosis; and then later on, wasn't able to write more than a few miserable lines in her notebook. On the other bed, her father is lying back on a couple of pillows, reading the newspaper. The girl would like to know how long he's going to go on waiting, but when she asks him, he just shrugs his shoulders and continues reading. Now he's talking on one of the telephones, whispering so the girl doesn't hear, although he doesn't bother leaving the room. His eyes move around the hotel room as he listens, but fix on a particular point on the floor when he speaks. Occasionally, he seems to be looking straight at her, but is actually looking through her. At other times, he inspects his own reflection in the wardrobe mirror, running his hand through his hair once or twice. The girl hears him say something about money. Then there's a pause. The girl shrugs her shoulders and leaves her father to it. She starts wondering again about the alleged hypnotism, on what night it could've happened, and who might've been present. She takes a deep breath—something she seems to do a lot, these days—and goes into the bathroom so as not to be distracted by her father's phone call. She's unable to hide her preoccupation with his business, and she doesn't want her father to notice this. She's annoyed that the brilliant composer has managed to paralyze her work on the novel, although she's loath to admit he's the one responsible. She splashes some water on her face and stares at her reflection in the mirror. She's still getting used to her dyed hair. She puts on her sunglasses so her eyes don't betray her agitation. Then she stands perfectly still, not making a sound, and tries to eavesdrop on her father's conversation. She's used to him always whispering about business and such, but there's something different about this call. Perhaps she's beginning to figure things out. She doesn't close the bathroom door, because while she doesn't want her father knowing there's something wrong, that she may have been hypnotized, and that this is the only reason she's been writing all the time, neither does she want to pretend there's nothing wrong. She looks in the mirror again. Her expression is dour, sour, but she doesn't care. She leans against the sink and continues listening, continues looking at the reflection she doesn't recognize. She has no idea what he's talking about now because he's speaking another language. She tries brushing her hair behind her ears, but it's too short, so she finds it keeps returning to the same place. She then examines her roots, thinking she'll have to dye them too. Besides her identity, the metallic blonde will also conceal her few gray hairs. She wonders what she'll look like when she's old. Her father hangs up the phone. She dries her face with a towel, wondering about how to ascertain whether or not this alleged hypnosis took place. She knows the game's also part of her reality, that her relationships with the young conductor and brilliant composer, and even the screenwriter, are all directed by it. But she gets the feeling something's not as it should be, and perhaps now, for the first time, she's seriously considering where reality is located. Does it exist outside the mind? Always the same question. Sooner or later, in one form or another, the answer will be revealed to her. The idea has its charms, for if nothing exists outside the mind, or to put it another way, if everything that happens outside the mind is unreal, and whatever does exist depends solely on that mind's creative whim—then nothing has any meaning, and everything's just a game. Isn't this the same conclusion she arrived at before? The girl's thoughts are beginning to fold in on themselves, and she's feeling disoriented. She sits down. Her father's voice brings her back to reality. Reality? Hasn't she just formulated a valid argument negating it? All the same, she could say it's situated somewhere on another plane, or in a different dimension, although looking at a lie from another angle doesn't make it any less of a lie. Her father tells her the star of her favorite soccer team has finally returned, and is to face disciplinary action. The girl approaches him. The words "disciplinary action" worry her. She gets the newspaper to find out more. Besides, she'd like to check if her ad is still in there, and if it's gotten a reply yet. She then calls the brilliant composer and apologizes for overreacting, for letting what he said about her replacement's performances on the piano upset her, for getting riled up when he told her how much progress the young conductor's latest conquest is making, and for playing the martyr when he said she was wasting her time with all the writing. It's not her fault, he tells her. All your troubles started after you were hypnotized. So you shouldn't feel responsible. She challenges him to prove it, demands that he show her the evidence. He hangs up.

Since she can't write, she goes for a walk, getting lost amid narrow, filthy alleyways she never imagined existed in the neighboring country's capital. She walks in the general direction of the city center, enters the occasional bookstore on the way, but instead of reading the beginnings of certain novels, she decides to read their endings. An interesting exercise, she thinks, reading the ending and then trying to guess everything that went before. The screenwriter has spoken to her about the step-by-step method for constructing a story. But she thinks all he's doing is trying to justify his own method by making it appear universal. She's mentioned this to him on occasion. She believes writing a novel requires a very different approach to writing a screenplay. She goes to the river and watches the boats full of tourists pass by. The same every day, she thinks, from one end of the city to the other. She then sits on the terrace of a bar and goes through some of the newspapers, looking for any articles she may not have read. She feels tired and weak, and she wonders if the whole world's conspiring to rob her of her vitality. Perhaps she's reached the end of her tether. It may not be wise, always fighting against everything and everyone, she thinks. The most reasonable thing to do, perhaps, is go home to her native city. And yet she knows her problems won't go away with a change of address. All the newspapers are still running her personal ad, but none of them feature a reply. Once back in the hotel, alone in the room, she awaits her father's return. She doesn't see the point of staying in the neighboring country's capital if she doesn't have an objective in her life. She smokes a couple of cigarettes on the balcony, watching the station, before finally deciding to go look for him. She knows it's forbidden, but she believes she should tell him about her plans to leave the city. The girl sits beside the station platforms and observes. She's not worried about being recognized. Her dyed hair and sunglasses will keep her identity under wraps. She walks up and down the main foyer, then she checks the restaurant, the café, and finally the benches where a bunch of tourists are sitting, but there isn't a sign of her father or the cousin anywhere in the station. Shouldn't one of them be on watch? she asks herself.

It's midnight, and there's no one walking the streets. The screenwriter ate a sandwich and some fruit he bought for breakfast from the hotel buffet. A car is waiting at the traffic light as he makes his way slowly to the other side of the street, limping with the help of his cane, like someone who's tired after a long day's work, or spent after a long life's living. Or perhaps it's both. He needed to get some air and have a coffee, two of the only luxuries he seems able to afford. Perhaps he's thinking about his financial situation again, or maybe his script. In contrast to the streets leading to it, the plaza is teeming with people sitting on the café terraces and around the fountain. He goes to a cigarette machine and buys a couple of boxes before sitting at one of the empty tables. On the other side of the plaza, in one of the other cafés, three guys are performing a few jazz numbers. The breeze carries the sounds of their voices and instruments toward him. Two guitars and a bass: the girl's father would enjoy that. Maybe the girl should be searching for him in the plaza. Perhaps he's sitting in a café with the college chick listening to jazz. It hasn't rained today. When the waiter arrives, he orders a coffee and a glass of water. Perhaps he needs a haircut, he thinks, while lighting a cigarette and running his other hand backward through his hair. He better not. Not until the advance is safely in the bank. He still has the same mop of hair he had when he was young. The same amount, he thinks, trying to bolster his self-image. Only the color's changed. But gray hair adds gravitas, he thinks, and his face has grown more interesting with age. It's terrible he has to remind himself of this, but no one else has bothered reassuring him up till now, and what's even more terrible, he doesn't expect anyone to. The same thoughts must cross the mind of the girl's father. And yet, the girl's father is a lot younger. Then there's the question of money. He runs his fingers through his hair again and takes a look around. The couples are all enjoying themselves as usual. He looks at the women. There isn't one with whom he could strike up a conversation, not one with whom he could have a relationship, and certainly not one who'd kindly offer to pay his bill.

He can hardly recognize her: her clothes are different—she no longer wears white jeans, a white T-shirt, and white canvas sneakers with the laces removed; her hair's different—she's cut it short and dyed it metallic blonde; and there are no more bags under her eyes, or if there are, they're hidden behind a big pair of sunglasses. The screenwriter tells her about the college chick who collects the beginnings of novels, a character he's very happy with. He quotes some of the opening lines he's collected in his notebook and asks the girl if she recognizes any of them. She finds it interesting, the way he's managed to incorporate one of her own ideas into his story, but she can't identify any of the quotes. She then gets up and takes her clothes off, puts the leather holster around her waist, setting it on the left side, unclips it so the gun's ready to be drawn, and stands completely still—her sunglasses concealing the expression in her eyes—while reading aloud a couple of passages from her novel. Perhaps, secretly, she'd like him to give her his opinion. She's sent enough chapters for him to finally be able to do so, but the screenwriter doesn't feel capable. Instead he kneels before her as she reads, kissing her inner thighs, attempting to entice them open by teasing her vulva with his tongue. He notes the stubble of pubic hair has grown back, remembers the last time he shaved her, and the photographs he took on that occasion, all of which he still has in his possession. How long has it been? Perhaps four or five weeks, yet it seems like an eternity ago. He caresses with his lips the still hairless parts of her angelic mons, then the parts with blonde or chestnut new-grown stubble. A pity about the camera; sold it for peanuts. He could be taking pictures of the girl wearing a holster and shades. She stops reading and waits silently for him to pass judgment on her work, to say whether or not she has talent, whether she possesses any style of her own, or perhaps the potential to one day develop a style of her own—anything to suggest she's on a literary path that has nothing to do with hypnosis. The screenwriter doesn't know how to tell her the truth, either about the hypnotism or the quality of her work. He is impressed by what she's written, but only because he sees himself reflected in it. He doesn't agree with the vision of the world she's given him. But at the same time, he can't stop listening to her describe that vision. The screenwriter kisses the warm pink flesh of her labia until she trembles, then he begins tonguing her clitoris slowly, deliberately, before pulling away suddenly so that she thrusts her pelvis desperately in search of him, so that he might continue licking her, and holding her labia open with his fingers, make her tremble once again, until she's struggling to stay on her feet, until she closes her book and throws it aside, until she closes her eyes and waits for this old man's rasping leathern tongue to take her to paradise. But the screenwriter stops to have a rest, uses the time to tell her, to beg her to continue writing, to not let a day go by without committing something to paper. Then he continues, and she looks down at him, at the white sheet under her feet, while biting the knuckles of one hand, grabbing the screenwriter's hair with the other—not remembering what he said, not understanding what he said, for the last thing on her mind is writing. She then draws the pistol and balances it on his forehead. He pushes his tongue as deep as he can inside her, his hands squeezing her buttocks. At the back of her mind, the girl tries to recall what she was writing about. Then the screenwriter introduces a finger into her anus, and all hope of her remembering evaporates. There was something about them running away together, or he was begging her to run away with him, or something. Somewhere far away wasn't it, where she could write and he could be her father, or was it her literary tutor? The girl looks in a mirror just in front of her, sees only the left side of her naked body reflected, moving spasmodically, the holster set beneath her left arm, as she holds the gun weakly, biting the back of her hand to muffle the moans that come whimpering out nonetheless, emitted for the relief of her body's more violent convulsions. It's as if the girl's lost all control of her body and mind. She falters, but manages to keep her balance, in part because he's holding her—because he tires, lets go, and grabs hold of her again—while licking her, and continues doing so, until she screams, until the her juices drip down her thighs and onto the sheets. She looks in the mirror again, sees ecstasy concealed behind a pair of shades. The screenwriter lays her on the bed and gently penetrates her, says something to her that she scarcely comprehends. She then cocks the pistol and sinks the barrel into his temple, parting that mop of which he's so proud, and without saying a word, fires. The short, dry crack of the gun failing to discharge resounds in the room. The screenwriter's face goes pale, his expression that of a man who should be dead but isn't. He stares at her, she says to him: do you think I've been hypnotized?

Some time goes by, perhaps minutes, perhaps hours. The girl chooses to be silent. In this respect, their rendezvouses differ very little from each other. There's always a point at which she chooses not to speak. She's forgotten the reason she came: to seek the screenwriter's approval of her writing, to tell him she's leaving the neighboring country's capital, that's she's finally decided to follow her own path in life, to say good-bye without a fuss, although, perhaps, with a little pain. She returns the pages of her novel to the envelope. It's time for her to leave, she says, while placing the envelope on the bed beside the newspapers. But she's the screenwriter's only reason for living. He has to be with her. The girl doesn't share the sentiment. Perhaps she'll write to him from their native city, send him more chapters of her novel, and keep him abreast of the voices that pronounce her name with a "ka." Not that she has any intention of keeping these promises, but she thinks it's important for him to hear them. She doesn't want to talk about love, affection, or anything like that. It will only make parting more painful. Don't go, he begs her. She looks at him. Don't leave me. The girl looks out the window into the street. She doesn't think anyone's been following her tonight, but she must always be vigilant. I won't be able to live without you, the screenwriter mumbles, who wants her to run away with him to a mythical place, a city of gold, where money isn't needed, where hardship and penury are mere states of mind. Literary talent, he says, develops slowly, by degrees; it needs time to mature—many more days, many more years in fact, than the time she's invested so far. It's the same with love. The girl disagrees. She thinks love is an uncontrollable passion— from its very beginning to its usually bitter ending. This isn't the case with literature, she says. Or if it is, it isn't the case with her. There are countries whose climates are amenable to such excesses. She remembers the words of a song she's heard: to spend all night having sex, all day writing masterpieces . . . But the misty-eyed screenwriter doesn't pay attention to her. He's dreaming about the bed in the golden city in which they'll die of exhaustion making love, the last wish of an old man who doesn't have a future to look forward to, or a past to look back on. And as he dreams, rising above the cloudy foundation on which he's promised to build them a castle, the sound of his door creaking open sends him plummeting back to Earth. He rushes to follow her out. But I'm promising you a paradise, he says, stopping her in front of the elevator. The girl takes the gun out and inserts a clip. Well, I'm promising you a bullet in the chest, she says, threatening him with it before putting it away again. After she gets in the elevator, he goes back into his room and watches her walking down the street, refusing to blink until she disappears at the point where the boulevards intersect. Does paradise exist? he wonders. And death? Then, later on, alone in his room, he reads: "5.5562 That which we know, we know purely on logical grounds. The room is empty. The female student's been opening the doors of all the rooms. So far, all have been empty, bereft of both people and furniture. The old professor cum alien hunter watches her from the kitchen doorway. Aren't you staying for a good-bye kiss? he asks her. She continues opening doors. All he has left is a bar of soap and a towel in the bathroom. Will she stay? he asks. She doesn't answer right away. He'll give her more time. In one of the rooms, all they've left behind after taking the furniture is a small pile of blankets under a sheet on the hardwood floor. The old professor feels strange taking his clothes off in an empty room, having to put some newspaper down on the floor so that there's a clean space for him to heap his clothes. And he could never lie on the floor without a blanket. It would feel like his bones were scraping up against paving stones. The girl, on the other hand, strips nonchalantly, feeling no different than she usually does, except that she believes this meeting will be their last, that it marks the end of a phase in her life. After making love on the hardwood floor, they remain there, lying next to one another, motionless. It's summer, so it's quite warm, both outside and in." There's a space separating the end of this paragraph and the beginning of the next. This, along with the girl's use of W's numerical notation, is a structural idiosyncrasy she uses

271

throughout the narrative. The screenwriter thinks the paragraphs are like a succession of scenes in a movie. Why didn't he notice this before she left? At the end of the day, style isn't everything, he says to himself, regretting not having taken better advantage of the time he had with her. "5.5563 Our problems are not abstract, but perhaps the most concrete that there are. Some time goes by, perhaps minutes, perhaps hours. The girl lies next to him on top of some blankets and sheets she found in another room, listening silently, as he whispers to her an encomium on her skin, as he tells her how much he's longed to feel its flawless texture, smooth and youthful, nary a wrinkle . . . he's never felt as drawn to something before, he says. Before, he'd have laughed at himself, but now, whenever he's within touching distance of a young woman, he's overcome with an almost uncontrollable desire. The girl stares at him. It's because I'm old, he continues. Such feelings are a symptom of decrepitude. Sometimes, in the summer, he takes the metro early in the morning, around the time young women—recently showered and perfumed, with their hair still wet—are climbing on in droves. It's like being swallowed by a wave. And he doesn't need much. A furtive brush of the finger will do. Just touching a woman's hair awakens an uncontrollable desire in him. It excites his alien hunter's instinct. If he ever touched a woman's hair on the metro, he says, he'd have to jump out of the car with her under his arm, and carry her away to his studio. He'd have to take her photograph, find her halo, and then make passionate love to her. He wouldn't be able to help himself. The female student tells him she's attracted to older men. She doesn't know whether she said it because it's true, or because she wanted to flatter him. But then she thinks to herself, it must be true; otherwise she wouldn't be lying naked beside a retired old professor. And perhaps she wouldn't have agreed to play the game if it wasn't true. A game in which she gets more and more involved each day, and in which there's a player who doesn't even know he's playing a part in it. You don't have to love me, he says. All he wants right now is to be near her, to lie next to her on the floor. He waits for her to say something. She doesn't say anything. I'll wait for you, he eventually says, hoping to ease her reluctance to speak. What time does the ship leave, she asks him, and why the City in Outer Space? But she asks only for the sake of asking. She has no intention of seeing him off on his journey. Because, he says, only there can he be free. She seems to think he'll be even busier there than here. Maybe she'll come visit him, maybe not. Her words are judicious, her tone tentative. It's more likely to be not. The old professor closes his eyes and touches her breasts. He wonders if he'll ever see her again, touch her again, if his flight into exile is futile, if it wouldn't be better to stay, to just fall on his knees and surrender to her. 5.6 The limits of language mean the limits of the No World. When he thinks about it again years later, as he wanders the empty streets of the desolate city, or languishes in the control room looking at the stars, and feels he wants to cry but knows he cannot because space has stolen his ability to cry, and he maintains an air of dignified sadness, regretting all the tears he cannot shed, the old man concludes he should have fallen on his knees, he should have surrendered to her when he had the chance." The screenwriter rereads the part about a character who's an unwilling participant in a game. He doesn't think this is plausible. It must be a literary device. What role would he have in such a game, he wonders, how would he know he wasn't breaking the rules?

It's never quiet outside the station. She's had to get used to the noise interrupting her sleep every night, until she became inured to the noise itself, and reached the point where she couldn't hear it anymore. Even so, at daybreak, as the light gradually begins streaming into the room, the sound of the cell phone ringing wakes her with a violent start. The brilliant composer has been drinking all night and is garbling his words, she can barely understand him. Still half-asleep, the girl manages to grasp the gist of his rambling—a comparison of success and failure, success depending on not taking shit from anyone. He says you don't have to do much to get shit from people, just scratching yourself is enough. He's partying with the latest conquest and some girl he met during the night. He hasn't mentioned music yet. Perhaps it got lost somewhere along the way, or perhaps the tour bus left the neighboring country's capital without it. She hangs up and gets back under the sheets. Her father hasn't gotten in yet, and she's had another bad night's sleep. Once again, she's been unable to stop thinking about the same things: aliens, hypnotism, and nothingness. She goes out to the hallway in search of Cousin McGregor, but it seems he hasn't gotten back yet either. So the girl grabs the gun and heads back to the station. Surely one of them is keeping watch. At this time in the morning there are very few people around, and hardly any cars, which combined with the dawning light gives the Grand Central Station an uncanny aspect. Perhaps it's a holiday, she thinks. Once again, there's no trace of her cousin or father. She takes out her cell phone and dials his number, but the phone's turned off and a woman's voice invites her to leave a message after the tone. When the girl gets back to the hotel room, she tries checking the other phones and the fax machine. She then goes onto the balcony to monitor the plaza. She doesn't know why, but she feels she should stick to her post on the balcony until her father finally calls. As usual, she doesn't know where he's gone, or when he'll be back. He didn't tell her, he never tells her. But she shouldn't worry about it. They really don't say much to one another at all. Are you writing? he always asks, while avoiding any of her questions. Still, she'd rather not talk about writing until she resolves the question of her hypnosis. But she knows she shouldn't be worrying about it. What should I do with the fax machine and those phones? Who's keeping watch at the station? These are now the questions that plague her. A few hours later, she phones the young conductor. He wants her to leave them alone. He wants her to stop calling him. Why is she so jealous, he asks, chuckling condescendingly, when she should be more understanding of his relationship with the new soprano? She should just accept they're not together anymore; that they don't make love anymore. Then the young conductor tells her reassuringly that, sooner or later, she'll forget all about him; time will heal her wounds. The girl would like to be able to coolly sever her association with the young conductor and brilliant composer; she'd love to be able to take a deep breath, hang up, and forget about them in that same instant. She doesn't want to wait the length of time it takes to heal a wound. So she insults him, reproaches his stupidity, his misplaced arrogance. Success often paralyzes the mind, she says, but she's never seen it happen so fast, and so thoroughly. The Sinfonietta's finished, they've been ousted from the vanguard, condemned to a future of selling out and merely parroting popular trends. The words come swift and true and from the heart. All they must do to secure musical oblivion is to keep doing what they're doing. Either way, they're stuck with the path they've chosen. It's too late for them now. She hangs up.

She still has to resolve the question of her hypnosis, and to record, as soon as possible, the *5 Pieces for piano*. She thinks about calling the sound engineer and the producer: she wants to work out the timbre and the amount of reverb needed to sustain a performance of the work at as slow tempo as as possible. She also needs the right piano, one whose hammers and pedals have been prepared exactly the way she wants. She wants to reproduce what she achieved on the piano in the hotel with the English name, whose sound she distorted using metal clips, a few pieces of her mother's jewelry, and a copy of the philosopher W's greatest work. Above all, she wants to be authentic, to be true to herself. Now a note, now another note, with an almost interminable silence in between: a surfeit of nothingness in between two ideas.

The hotel with the English name, early the next morning: the girl's mother, half hidden behind the door, her face smothered in moisturizer, peeks out to see who's there, finds her daughter, and lets her in. We hardly recognize the mother, since we've never seen her looking like this, with her hair tied back away from the creamy mask on her face, draped top-to-toe in an off-white bathrobe, almost the color of bone, pinching a cotton ball as she shuffles across the room. Once inside, the girl takes off her sunglasses. It seems to take a while for either of them to say anything; perhaps it's because the girl's visit was unexpected. Her mother's eyes dart this way and that to evade her daughter's newly dyed hair. You've changed, she says calmly, to understate the metallic blonde hue, the circles under the girl's eyes. She hasn't called to have the piano taken away yet, though the girl hasn't been practicing at all recently. She follows her mother to the bathroom and stands in the doorway, watching her bend toward her reflection in the mirror. I think I've been hypnotized, says the girl, getting straight to the point. Her mother turns to look at her momentarily before returning her attention to the mirror, as if she hadn't been listening—or if she had been, that she didn't believe her. The girl wants to know if her mother was there when she was hypnotized. It's the only reason she came. She's been checking the dates and times in her diary and she came across a particular night when her diary and novel writing suddenly became more voluble and frenetic. She gives her mother a few seconds to respond. Nonsense, she finally says, surely you don't believe in such things. She looks at her daughter in the mirror. When the scene appears onscreen, it will be as if she's looking at the camera, as if the audience is looking through the girl's eyes. Whatever, the girl says resignedly. The next setup will show both women's faces in the mirror, while the camera, of course, remains concealed. The many awkward silences will keep the tension high throughout the scene. And your father? her mother asks. I spend all day writing, he spends all day waiting, the girl replies. Waiting for what? The girl doesn't know, but she guesses her father and Cousin McGregor are waiting for something to happen in the Grand Central Station. That's why they take turns keeping watch there. And you, what do you get up to, as the piggy in the middle? Just writing, the girl says. But I do have a theory. A theory about what? The girl looks at the floor, as if having to consider something before continuing. Have you ever heard either of them talk about encounters with extraterrestrials? The woman's face, with the vizard of moisturizer now removed, seems to dry up and crack at her daughter's words. She puts her hand on the marble sink and turns to the girl, fixing her eyes on her, as if she's finally taking her seriously. Because I think it's something to do with aliens, the girl adds. Her mother wants to know whether her father told her this story or if she dreamed it up herself. There's more, says the girl, interrupting her. Then she proceeds to tell her mother all about the gravely ill astrophysicist who wears the classically-cut suit, about the person she suspects is following her, and why she felt the need to hide her identity behind a new hairdo and a pair of large sunglasses: because she might be dealing with alien hunters. She wonders if she should also tell her mother she now carries a gun. The girl moves tentatively forward with the intention of tapping her mother on the shoulder, but then she stops, hesitates, and then finally decides not to tell her. She can't think of a motive her mother would find plausible. She's not really sure herself why she carries it. Maybe she's planning to dispose of the young orchestra conductor and brilliant composer. This makes her smile. It seems a little far-fetched, even for her. All the same, she remembers she started carrying the gun after she heard the latest conquest brag on the radio about hearing voices and writing novels. Maybe her unconscious is trying to tell her something. She looks at her mother in the mirror. She can't tell if her expression denotes genuine interest, or if she's just gotten better at feigning it. Her mother turns and puts her hands on the girl's shoulders. How many hours per day do you write? she asks, looking straight into her daughter's eyes. Probably too many, she replies, looking straight back at her. You should take a break, then, her mother says. They spend a few silent moments in that awkward pose until the girl eventually breaks eye contact. Perhaps you're suffering from fatigue and you don't know it, her mother adds. Then she lists some of the girl's recent preoccupations: the sick astrophysicist, her father's strange job waiting for aliens in a train station, her suspicion that someone's following her, her suspicion that she's under hypnosis . . . and that silly new hairstyle she's adopted so people won't recognize her . . . don't you see how crazy it all is? The girl considers the list—extensive but hardly exhaustive, she thinks. What would her mother think if she knew the full list? But she doesn't want to discuss it with her. Some secrets shouldn't be shared with anyone, however close you are to them—especially a mother: perhaps the worst possible choice of confidant. The girl's mother suggests she go see a famous doctor who'll give her special vitamins. Not today, she says, she has a previous engagement, but she'll definitely go with her tomorrow. Her mother tells her to accept that she's been behaving quite strange lately: for one, she's stopped practicing piano, which is like flushing her future down the toilet; second, she's constantly fighting with the young orchestra conductor; and then there's the cousin . . . What about him? asks the girl. You know perfectly well what about him, her mother scolds, you know you never saw him, never spoke to him, just like you know all this alien business you think your father's involved in is utter nonsense. Why is she suggesting vitamins, the girl wonders, if her mother really thinks she's just crazy? But maybe she doesn't think this, maybe her mother can't talk about it because it's a secret. Of course, how naïve you've been, she says to herself, and decides not to take the matter further. The girl then thinks about the scientist in the classically-cut suit, about the link between her mother and the cousin—recalls that the first time she met him was at the reception desk of the hotel with the English name. There's no doubt in her mind that these three—four, if she includes her father—are all members of the same organization, conspirators in the same plot. She hasn't been able to add it all up yet, but she knows they're colluding. Perhaps the question of her hypnosis has been distracting her, so she hasn't been able to see what's right in front of her face. The scene continues with another awkward silence, and even more exchanges of fleeting glances. Then her mother says she's running out of time and needs to get ready for an appointment, as if this were more important than her daughter's well-being. We'll talk about it again tomorrow, she says. The girl gets the impression her mother's appointment is with the cousin. Perhaps it was a certain glint in her eye. Her mother would prefer it if the girl moved back to the hotel with the English name. It's clear her father doesn't give a damn about her. He doesn't care what you get up to, as long as you don't bother him, she says while dabbing perfume on either side of her neck. They're expecting her at the main event for the fiftieth anniversary celebrations of the liberation of the neighboring country's capital. The girl thinks her mother is a little overdressed, even for a formal ceremony. Over the past few days, she's been reading in the newspapers about all the preparations going on for the celebration, but she hasn't paid much attention, because it's for something that happened decades ago. To break another awkward silence, she asks her mother about the liberation, but then doesn't listen to her answer. She leans against the front doorpost, watching, as her mother performs a final touch-up in front of the mirror. When's the recording scheduled? she asks wearily, with an expression of slight annoyance. There won't be a recording, says the girl abruptly. Do you have any idea how long it's been since you practiced? her mother asks. Then she asks her daughter to zip up the back of her dress—a strapless black dress, half-way up her knee, very chic and very expensive. The girl reluctantly complies, and then goes to get her satchel. Maybe I've got more importance things to do right now than record the *5 Pieces for piano*, she says before exiting the hotel room, leaving her mother sitting on the edge of the bed, trying to squeeze into a pair of shoes that could very well be made of glass.

As for the recording, the specially prepared piano, and achieving that impossible sound, they can all go to hell. She hasn't the remotest chance of rising above the standard of her age with a magisterial interpretation of the *5 Pieces for piano*. It would've been the ideal music for future cities in space too. It's best to just forget about it. But how can she abandon such an ambitious project at a time like this? What if this decision, as her decision to quit music for writing, is also due to her being under hypnosis? She'd find she was living a delusion, that her life was a total lie. She'd be just a fraud. She searches in her satchel for the work of the writer who revolutionized twentieth-century literature, and tries reading some passages. But then she decides perhaps it isn't the time to engage with a work that will require all her powers of concentration. She would've liked to exorcise those spirits that keep whispering she was hypnotized, that tell her there's a conspiracy involving her parents, the scientist, and Cousin McGregor, but not even the writer who revolutionized literature can take her mind off these things, so she closes the book and puts it back in her satchel. If she isn't able to write, the waiting is going to be horrendous. She doesn't know how he does it—sitting alone in his hotel room, waiting for one of the phones to ring, or for the fax machine to kick in, or for something to happen in the Grand Central Station. She wishes she'd taken her bags with her when she left her father's hotel. She feels like she's wasting time, but she supposes time's relative when it comes to writing. Now the hours seem to drag, and every hour feels like four—four wasted hours, since she's not working on her novel. She wonders if a change of location would help. But she's so close to witnessing one of the most important events in the history of our species. She can't leave the city yet. She's been writing about the old professor, but she's hasn't fully explored the alien hunter side of his character yet, or the survivor of the great war that devastated the City in Outer Space, but she can't think of anything to write, and the little she manages to produce does nothing to galvanize her. She seems to have lost that strength, that confidence, which helped her overcome so many obstacles in her life. She seems, instead, to have become insecure, doubtful of her talent and her literary vocation. Fuck the brilliant composer, she says. She needs to go for a walk. She can't spend her life locked inside her own head, circling around the same thoughts. It's a sure way of transforming them into obsessions. Is she going mad? If so, it must be because she lives the life of a hermit, hiding away, waiting for something to happen—she doesn't know what, perhaps nothing, perhaps a call from her father to give her instructions, to tell her something, anything to dispel her uncertainty. Maybe it was too soon to give up on her idea about the cathedrals and churches. Perhaps the reason no one responded to her ad in the paper is that she didn't know how to formulate the message correctly. She takes the gun from the back of her pants. She has a lot to think about, and she's sick of doing laps in the room. The streets give her much more space to stretch her legs, although she knows there's no guarantee of the same for her mind.

He goes through every pocket twice. It's no use. He doesn't have another penny to his name. The prospect's been looming for days now but he's been simply ignoring it. He doesn't even have enough to get a croissant. It's not a good day for the screenwriter, who's been scouring half-deserted streets where most of the stores are closed, as if it were a Sunday, looking for an affordable place to eat. He decides to go back to the hotel and have breakfast. It's not only more expensive than the café on the plaza, but the waitress is hideous. At least the bill's charged to his account, though, which relieves some pressure, and gives him time to consider his options. He eats in silence, thinking. He won't be able to buy a newspaper today. He wonders if he's nearing the end of the road. Never in his life did he imagine he'd be in such dire straits. He still receives a small pension every month, but it's ridiculously small. If that was his only source of income, he'd die of starvation. He'll probably get a bigger pension when he fully retires. But then he thinks he'll probably never fully retire, that he'll more than likely croak at his writing desk. Die with his boots on, so to speak. It's too soon to be thinking about this; too early in the day for feeling sorry for oneself. With a coffee in hand, he takes out his notebook and comes up with a list of people he could petition for help. Then he performs a simple calcula- tion that lays out his current financial situation: the second advance from the producer will barely cover his debts. He'll call again. Then he thinks about calling his own son. No, not him. Maybe the girl will lend him some cash.

The producer's not answering. So he's back on the street, sit- ting on a bench, thinking about who he should turn to. He laughs at the image that pops in his head—an image of him- self, dressed in rags, sitting in a damp street corner soliciting alms. He laughs because he's unable to cry. He's never been in such a desperate situation. He gets up and makes his way slowly back to the hotel. He thinks he'd survive without one of his jackets. That's a good idea. And why not dispense with a couple of shirts as well? There's also a pair of shoes he doesn't need, a pair of trousers, and why does he need two suitcases?

He feels humiliated in front of the saleswoman. He'd have preferred to find the store closed, like so many other businesses on the day celebrating the neighboring capital's liberation. He'd have preferred to burn the clothes than be insulted with such a paltry offer. But he knows he needs the money, so he tries haggling over a few cents' difference before agreeing to the deal. Come on, it's only a few cents, he says. The offer's nonnegotiable, the saleswoman says. He has no choice but to accept. He takes the cash from her hands, trying his best to hold back the tears, and makes a promise to himself that he'll buy all his stuff back as soon as possible. He fantasizes about buying a new wardrobe once the advance arrives. Then again, he doesn't ever want to see his old shirts and jacket on the backs of strangers. No, he'll buy them back as soon as possible. Back on the street, he thinks of an old movie in which someone says you can get away with being broke when you're young, but never when you're old.

Later that night, at the hotel in front of the Grand Central Station, the girl's father still hasn't gotten back, and she's sitting beside the telephone, waiting for a call. She doesn't know from whom, although she doesn't expect the brilliant composer to call again. He was drunk as usual when he called earlier, so the girl, likewise as usual, cut the conversation short. She doesn't want to hear about him, the young conductor, or any of that riffraff. She doesn't care. As usual, she's sitting in her room doing nothing. She certainly can't write. Should she just wait around until something happens? She gets up and starts pacing up and down, growing angrier with every pace. Then she strikes the walls, again and again, before closing her eyes and gritting her teeth to hold back the tears. They're not going to make me cry, she says to herself, before repeating it again and again. Idiot, idiot, idiot! she cries. Once again, she's allowed herself to be made a fool of. To be made ridiculous. She feels like a laughingstock. She calls herself a stupid bitch for taking so long to wake up, to snap out of her fantasy, like a drunk who's finally sobered up after amusing everyone with her antics the previous night. Now they're all laughing at her. No, her mother just thinks she's crazy, and as for her father: well, he doesn't give a damn. But then there are those fuckers. She won't let them depress her. Maybe she should say good-bye to her father before going back to her native city. The girl wonders where he could be. She doesn't think there'll be any trains arriving at this hour. She presumes that neither her father nor Cousin McGregor is in the station. She wonders what would happen to the voices she hears if the aliens were to finally appear. She'd probably lose her connection with them. They've already been communicating with her for a few years now—perhaps long enough. She walks up and down the hotel room, shaking her head, gesturing nervously, with her hands in and out of her pockets. She can't seem to make a decision. Her stomach's completely empty, and it's starting to ache with all its churning, but she notes that the pain itself is killing her appetite. Like the pain of a wounded ego, she says. She's thinking about waiting for her father to get back so she can tell him she's going home. That she just can't take it anymore. He didn't tell her what time he'll be back, but she doesn't think it'll be too late. She leaves a note on his bed and goes out to a nearby restaurant. Although she's not hungry, she decides she must put something in her stomach. The night could be a long one, and she won't be able to stand the constant churning. She picks up a newspaper and flips to the ads section. Still there: "I hear voices. 1. The No World is all that is the case. Ka." Perhaps she's made a mistake, and that's why

285

she hasn't received an answer. Not that it matters to her now. Now she's finally given up hope of ever making contact. She never thought her obsession with finding out whether or not she was hypnotized would affect her so much. Now, instead of aliens, she's going in search of some elusive hypnotist. She reads that the coach of her favorite soccer team has fined the star player for his overlong vacation. She smiles, but it's soon cut short when she stumbles across a picture of the scientist in the classically-cut suit. Before she reads a single word, she knows he's dead, as if she can augur the contents of the article merely by looking at the photo, the layout of the page, the type, or something. She's surprised he was found dead in a hotel. The astrophysicist had apparently been living there for the past few years. The newspaper says nothing more about it, so the girl reads the article again and again, while eating, without relish, what she can of her meal. They could have at least given the name of the hotel. She goes back up to her father's room. Perhaps this is what's been keeping her father away from his post in the station. The girl feels a little despondent over the news. She'd been expecting it for some time, but now that it's happened, she's still taken aback. She feels as if something's suddenly changed, that nothing will be the same from this moment on. She'll wait for her father to get back so she can say good-bye, then she's going back home to try living her own life. She's mad at her mother for having colluded with her ex-colleagues. Shouldn't she just group them all together and refer to them collectively as enemies? If it weren't for them, she'd have completed her cycle of concerts and done the recording by now. What does the young conductor know about performing the *5 Pieces for piano* anyway? Neither he nor her mother seem to understand that her disposition inclines her more toward performing in a recording studio, where certain effects can be produced and experimented with, and where subtle nuances can be captured on tape, which an audience in a concert hall couldn't possibly register as they would when listening to the recording. When it comes to the business of wounding her pride, her mother's as dispassionate as a corporate executive. She'd put a lot of stock in the girl one day becoming a great pianist, and she's determined to see a return on her investment. But the girl ended up taking a different path. Besides, she's not a commodity to be traded on the market. She has ideas of her own. What did her mother expect? She didn't even know where to draw the line between parent and manager. And her father hasn't exactly been a model parent either. So when it comes to choosing between them, her dilemma is more a case of picking the better of two evils. There's still the screenwriter, she thinks. But the screenwriter's just an innocent, unwitting participant in this cruel and perverse game. Perhaps she hasn't been very honest with people generally. If something goes wrong, it's part of the game, she repeats. She's said it so many times it's become like a mantra. Perhaps looking to blame others for wrongs done to oneself is also part of the game. How are the others playing the game? Is it she, or is it everyone else that's not playing the way they should? She sits in a chair and makes a note of all the ways she plans to reproach her parents, then repeats them aloud to herself, as if rehearsing for a performance. She sets the first scene in the hotel room she's sitting in now, where she'll bid her father farewell by first incriminating him for his cold indifference, his unfeeling aloofness toward his own daughter. You damn egoist, she'll say on marching out the door, after packing her bags in front of him. Then she'll go to the hotel with the English name to spend the night, but only for the opportunity of haranguing her mother as well. Then she'll get up early in the morning to begin her journey back home. Of course, she may only be a piano starlet because of mother's connections. So she supposes it's possible she's only a commodity after all. Outside, fireworks are exploding to mark the fiftieth anniversary of the city's liberation. Her mother could be a special guest at the fireworks display. The girl's always seen her mother as an executive of sorts, but there's nothing to say she isn't a high-class hooker, rubbing shoulders with the rich and powerful. The girl is still waiting, and beginning to think it's a pointless vigil, because her father hasn't even called. She forces herself to stay awake, even going so far as to hold her eyelids open, as children do, when she feels them beginning to droop. She forces herself to stay annoyed at him, finds that rehearsing her reproaches against him help to keep her frown intact. She knows that if she falls asleep her anger will have diffused by morning, and she won't have enough fire left in her belly to really read him the riot act for all his years of neglect. But she also knows that if she falls asleep the voices will be there waiting for her on the other side, waiting in that world that overtakes us when we sleep, a world to which we all go to make our dreams a reality, and our realities a dream. When the girl eventually falls asleep, she dreams her reality is a game; that her father and Cousin McGregor are playing a game she doesn't understand; that her mother is sitting on a throne in a palace somewhere seeing everything unfolding before her. Then the Queen speaks. She says the whole world functions as a game, that the young conductor and brilliant composer aren't alone in understanding it as such. The girl pinches her arm to check if it's real, and awakens. She sees that it's dawn and that her father still hasn't gotten back. Her arm hurts like hell. She sits up to contemplate the surrounding gloom. She does what she always does when she wakes up, except this time she's fully clothed. She can never get any rest when she sleeps in her clothes. She gets up and goes to the mirror. She looks like shit, she thinks, and then notices the small bruise on her arm. First she goes to the balcony to wait, observing the traffic in front of the Grand Central Station. Then she goes back inside to continue her vigil in bed, staring at the ceiling, counting the minutes as they pass, her eyes opening and closing, sleep threatening to overtake her again until she gets up and splashes some cold water on her face, because this time she's determined to stay awake. She puts on some music, sits down with her diary, and writes that she dreamed everything was just a game. After she's done writing, she puts her earphones back on the nightstand and turns toward the balcony—toward the noise of the traffic outside, feeling reassured the world is once again on the march. After a shower and change of clothes and another futile attempt to continue her novel, she decides to just pack her bags and not wait for her father to return. She wanted him to see her pack her bags. It would've made her exit more theatrical. But she needed something to do, something to relieve all the tension. She's not as angry as she was the night before, but she still has something in her belly that will singe his hair, so she decides to wait a little longer. Before long, though, she's back in bed asleep, tossing and turning, the very picture of someone having a nightmare. The last one she had was about her mother conspiring with her father and Cousin McGregor to have her locked up in an institution. It's the only way to snap her out of her hypnotic trance, they said.

It can't be the case that everything is in fact nothing, or that it's all a dream, that we're all made of nothing but dreamstuff. So the screenwriter thinks, who's trying to discern the difference between dreams and nothingness, although he prefers the idea of a bubble, or something similar, floating around in space, in which we all dream our own individual dreams—some sad, some happy, others hellish, and just a few like paradise—but all of them together constituting a single collective dream, which is that same bubble floating around in space. And when we dream within the dream, our souls enter a region outside time and space where we find—perhaps a better word is "visit"—where we visit an event that happened either before or after the moment we fell asleep. Hence the ability to dream of something that hasn't happened yet, and who knows, maybe this would even allow for a man to dream he's shaking hands with his own departed ghost. The screenwriter returns to the previous scene, in which the girl's still waiting in her father's hotel room. Her luggage is all packed and waiting beside the front door. On the table, a few half-crumpled pages suggest a writer's unsuccessful attempts at self-resuscitation. The last thing she wrote was a kind of variation on the theme of the previous chapter. Nothing new, in other words. She thinks her inspiration has dried up, so she resorts to repetition, which gives her the illusion that she's making progress, because at least she's writing something. She counts the number of days she's been writing. She feels being hypnotized was like someone's putting a time bomb in her brain; that far from being responsible for her creativity, it ended up compromising it. She can't stomach the image of herself writing under the eyes of people who know she's been hypnotized. It's horrible. Her father has spoken to her several times about the need for both inspiration and perspiration, that it's no good having the strength to achieve something if one hasn't the will. Before leaving, she decides to give it another shot. She turns on the laptop. If she can manage even a couple of lines, she thinks, all her problems will go away. Most people are happy to do their dreaming at night, when they're asleep. They say it keeps them sane. Well, it's writing that keeps the girl sane. It's something like a drug that helps her dream by day. "5.153 In itself, a No World is neither probable nor improbable. Either a No World occurs or it does not: there is no middle way. The old professor is reading the philosopher W in one of the many dim and dank derelict buildings in the City in Outer Space. Little does he know that all his suffering, this terrible life he leads, is down to his being a hunter of aliens who doesn't know he's an alien himself." The girl then consults some notes she wrote previously, but finds nothing that galvanizes her. A couple of pages, at least! she implores, as if supplicating a deity to let some crumbs of inspiration fall from his table—or perhaps an alien from another galaxy, the same one who constantly sends her messages about Ka; either way, a being who could answer her prayer. She's read of the possibility of becoming a God oneself. It is achieved in stages—perhaps they're degrees of enlightenment—the last being the stage at which one can finally create a world of one's own. When she thinks about it, it's not much different from wanting to become a writer. The girl places the old professor in a modest room where he'll spend his days waiting for the female student to visit him. He's not sure she'll ever come, but he clings to the hope she will. The girl wonders if the professor carries any false documents. No, he's not like her father, she thinks, despite the fact that he's an alien hunter who doesn't have a license. In reality, he wouldn't even know where to get a license. Before finding a job, he'd probably take some time out to think about the future. The girl tries to decide how much time he'd have before the police came to arrest him. She wonders if it will be his wife, the director of the Academy, or one of the female student's parents who'll get the police involved. He'd probably feel safe in the City in Outer Space, since it's out of the terrestrial police's jurisdiction. They wouldn't bother chasing him into space anyway, not on the paltry charge of sleeping with one of his students. At least, that's what the girl thinks. She chronicles the arrival of the old philosophy professor at his new home, his first tentative steps of acclimation to his new environment—getting used to the false gravity, to the simulated days and nights, to the way the space colony's regulated, to the shapes of the buildings, the streets . . . She begins with the line: An alien hunter with minimal experience stands with his luggage in front of his new home, wishing he could know, or at least have a good idea, how the adventure he's begun is going to end. The girl gets up, nervously lights a cigarette, and ambles onto the balcony to smoke it. The screenwriter lights a cigarette and opens the window to aerate the room, then lifts his feet onto the sill, and leans back in his chair. More so than a writer, he feels like a detective following a variety of leads, any of which could either help or hinder his investigation. That is, trying to find ways of developing an already impossible plotline. He needs to link a series of set pieces, each belonging to a different scene, because he thinks it will help move his story along. He thinks about the screenplays that were written in the golden age, that long-since vanished epoch. What great films they became, he thinks. Nowadays, the devices he uses are considered hackneyed, perhaps even obsolete. When he's done writing, he doesn't know if he'll have the energy to finish up the dialogue with another screenwriter; and he doesn't know if he'll be able to put in all the changes the director, the producer, and the secretary who sleeps with them will want him to make. The girl's having a hard time concentrating. Even so, he thinks, at least she knows where she is, where the old professor in her story is—waiting in his modest room for a female student who may never show up. And that's all he *should* do, or that and reading the philosopher W's magnum opus. He doesn't start on page one either, but just flips through the book picking out passages at random. Such a long vigil would be purgatorial, but the screenwriter suspects the old professor would rather wait than suffer the damnation the screenwriter is already feeling, the pain in his stomach, in his heart, that never ceases. Sometimes he asks himself why he keeps on writing, but he never has an answer. There were times he resolved to quit altogether, and was quite serious about it, but within a few days, often a few hours, he found himself back at his writing desk writing. He doesn't know why. He never has an answer. It's not for the money, that's for sure. But he knows he needs the money, and this reminds him to start making headway on the producer's draft. Whatever money he gets he uses for subsistence, not luxury. So although, technically, he *does* do it for the money, it's more accurate to say he does it to survive. If he needs money, there's always the girl, who's rich, although she's also a minor, and perhaps wouldn't have the kind of disposable cash he needs at this precise moment. When he proposed they run away together, he had in mind a life in which he could easily make a living. Money worries, he says while writing, knowing that it doesn't matter what he says or thinks, money governs and directs the lives of everyone involved in the movie business, and he means everyone, both real and imaginary. He turns his attention back to the girl, leaning on the balcony railing, smoking a cigarette, her luggage still waiting for her inside, the idle laptop on the table, in its usual screensaver mode. Suddenly, the telephone rings. The agency that handled her

293

personal ad has received a reply. The girl notes it down. It's short, cryptic, just like her message. It seems to hint at a meeting that night. In all honesty, the girl doesn't believe it's genuine, but she won't ignore it after so many days' effort. Besides, it'll only require her to stay one more day in the capital. But she does wonder, why now? Why, at the precise moment she's about to grab her bags and hit the road—bam!—a reply to her message? She no longer trusts in the prospect of an alien encounter; the law of probabilities tells her it's unlikely, but it's not this that suddenly renders her a skeptic, but her recent disillusionment. If she still believes in anything, it's in the voices; the ones that tell her she's been chosen for a special mission, but she doesn't think she can figure it out all by herself, and she doesn't expect that these voices from another world, perhaps a No World, are about to start whispering any clues. But isn't she supposed to be gifted, a young woman with enormous talent, a superior being, unlike the great mass of plodding drudges that populate the Earth? And isn't this the only reason they speak to her? But how does she know they don't communicate with others? Either way, if they are communicating with her, why is she finding it so difficult to figure out her mission, her purpose in life? Like a wheel spinning in a rut, she thinks about it long and hard before eventually giving up. Still, she has other things to worry about. They may be less dramatic, but at least they're easier to deal with, she thinks. Maybe she should try resolving her problems one at a time instead of all at once. She wonders what to start with. That damn hypnosis. She needs to ask them who was present. She considers what she means by "them," and quickly comes up with a list: the young conductor, the brilliant composer, and the hypnotist herself, of course: they're the first ones that come to mind. Who else? she thinks. The people closest to

294

them: that juggler, the latest conquest, the girl's mother . . . Maybe it happened on the night the screenwriter was with them, although she's already asked the screenwriter and her mother about this. There were always a bunch of people with them when they hit the clubs, but she wouldn't have the least idea where to find most of them. She flicks her cigarette away and heads back inside, turns the computer off, and goes out for a walk. She wanders the streets without paying heed to which direction she's going in, like that character created by the writer who revolutionized twentieth-century literature, a man who wanders the streets of his city aimlessly, divagating through his conscious mind, through regions of his unconscious, dark regions from which bubble recollections of his past, the things he's read, the music he's heard, what he fears the most, what he loves the most, mingling the grand with the quotidian, walking aimlessly through the streets, and thinking aimlessly, guided only by the flux of his thoughts and feelings, joys and dejections, the systoles and diastoles that subtend a single day. As she walks the streets of the neighboring country's capital, the girl's mind bandies between thoughts of her hypnosis and her meeting with the supposed aliens. Whenever she thinks she's found a way to proceed, she immediately changes her mind, like trying to pick out a single image, idea, sensation, or association from a farrago of indistinguishable impressions flashing past her at incredible speed. It's driving her crazy. If sticking her head in a fridge would slow down her thoughts, she'd do it. By contrast, the screenwriter's story would fit into a feuilleton, the clichéd story of a man facing ruin if he can't solve his financial problems. He needs to find out if the producer sent the advance yet. He dials the number, but there's no answer. Then he calls the producer's wife, just on the off chance. If she's able to take the call, he'll ask for the contact information of old friends who live here in the neighboring country's capital. But it's useless, he thinks, a stupid plan in fact, and he hangs up. He's already thinking of other options. He needs to get a loan from somewhere before the advance comes through. He remembers the woman with whom he had a relationship forty years before. He figures it's been ten years since he last wrote to her. Not too long for an old friend. He remembers where she lived because he's been there more than once. She was always inclined to spinsterhood, so he doesn't think she'll be married. He only hopes her address will also be unchanged. He has other friends, but most are in the movie business, colleagues with whom he's worked on occasion, but most of whom he doesn't see otherwise. But if he hasn't got their contact details, there's no point in even considering them. He thinks of the box of office supplies in which he keeps all his old agendas. In his imagination he sees pages and pages of collaborative notes from back when he was somebody of note in the movie business. But he won't be able to conjure up his collaborators' addresses and phone numbers from an examination of their handwriting. He decides to visit the woman. He still thinks of her as the young woman he knew, but he knows she's no longer young. He's no longer young himself. He remembers her as she was then, as he was then: it was another time, another world; and despite their having written to each other long after that world had vanished, they haven't seen each other since. But the screenwriter never put much effort into the relationship, especially when it became strictly by correspondence, whereas she'd always write to him, always send him a card on Christmas. Walking along the street, the screenwriter asks some pedestrians for spare change, explaining that his wallet was stolen, and he needs the money to get back to his hotel. The ruse works, and he eventually has enough to grab a taxi. Once inside the building, he recalls the floor on which his friend's apartment was located, but not the apartment number. So he tries buzzing the first one. No answer. Typical, he thinks. He presses the button for the second apartment. This time a boy answers. The screenwriter asks for his friend. She's not at home, the boy says. Do you know where she is? But the boy has hung up, and the screenwriter's words are lost in the ether. He presses another button. He'll ask all her neighbors one by one if he has to. Again it's not his friend who answers, but the woman on the other end is acquainted with her, and tells the screenwriter she's gone on vacation. Great! He's just wasted time, money, and effort he simply can't afford to waste. Thanks, he says to the woman. He notes down his friend's apartment number. He finds it curious the floor still lingers in his memory. It may serve as a location to stage the girl's meeting with her friend, he thinks while heading back to the hotel, wondering who this friend will be, because, at the moment, this character doesn't even exist.

Wandering, by definition, is a going nowhere. And wandering to escape one's thoughts is as pointless as wandering to escape one's feet. It's certainly no analeptic against hypnosis. In fact, it may serve only to exacerbate it. The girl buys a newspaper and sits down to read it at a café in the city center. She reads that the star of her favorite soccer team managed to get back into shape by training alone. She reads about the celebrations for the fiftieth anniversary of the capital's liberation, about some battle in the past, part of a war that happened decades ago, in which only old geezers like the screenwriter or the philosophy professor in her novel could possibly be interested. She looks at all the pictures of the celebrations to see if her mother appears in any of them, but the only one that catches her eye is of the Little Sinfonietta after one of their performances. She's particularly struck by the latest conquest's new hairdo, which is identical to hers. The girl also notices she's holding a red clown's nose out to the crowd, and looks as if she's at the point of releasing it. She's not surprised. She reads about her tremendous success at the concerts, about her new recording contract with the same record company the girl's signed to, and about the Sinfonietta's upcoming appearance on a famous TV show. She reads all this before repeating to herself: nothing that occurs is certain, truth is only an illusion, it exists nowhere outside the mind. Nowhere outside my mind. And true enough, a little later, the girl finds herself thinking about nothing in particular. There's nothing else in the newspaper to occupy her thoughts. Nothing about the astrophysicist in the classically-cut suit, say, no more reports on his death. The reply to her comment in the classifieds matches what the agency told her word for word. Why would it be any different? The proposed meeting place is a nightclub. She supposes such places shouldn't be ruled out, although she'd rather have met at the airport or a church, even a library.

The screenwriter amuses himself juggling all these details around in his head, because at this point her story has become fully his, and he wants to explain to the director, the producer, and script editor exactly how the girl feels. He realizes that, in focusing on the girl, he's compensating for other, less complete parts of the script, because there's certainly an imbalance of sorts, every other aspect of his screenplay seeming to give way for the sake of a single character, an imbalance that will more than likely have to be corrected by someone else. But why start making excuses now? He may end up doing it himself, for when he's seen through his role as screenwriter, he'll take up the mantle of script doctor. He reads some random passages from the book about screenwriters. One day he'll start on page one and keep on going till the end. He still intends to use some examples from it to teach any potential students. One of the screenwriters confesses in an interview that only a few of the experiences he's had in his professional life were truly gratifying. In the majority of cases, almost everything that he felt was good about his work ended up on the cutting-room floor. For the screenwriter, there isn't much solace in reading this, but at least his misery has found some new company. He flips through the pages looking at all the photographs. There's only one woman among them: a blonde, leaning back in a chair, an elegant pose, wearing pearl earrings and a necklace. Behind her are shelves filled with videocassettes. Just like all the male screenwriters, she's shown at an age well past maturity, but just before gravitas has given way to dotage. All the men have gray or graying hair, wear horn-rimmed glasses, and are frequently shown posing next to the poster of a movie for which, we are led to presume, they wrote the screenplay; some others are shown looking up from a desk in an office, and others still are shown having a great time on set with actors, directors, and other film crew. The screenwriter flips through the photos and considers what films he'd liked to have collaborated on. Then he thinks he probably appreciates them more because of his aesthetic distance from them. There is a golden tint coloring them all, he thinks, but faded, as of the epoch to which they belonged. But when he reads about their points of view, what it was really like, this golden age, he wonders whether it was all that different. For there is nothing to suggest that a golden-age screenwriter had it any easier. Perhaps what he really admires, although he doesn't know it, is the success of the industry in every age, including his own, but for him, only when something has come and gone, and has become irretrievable, does it acquire an aureate aspect . . . He closes the book and puts it beside the pile of newspapers. It's best to focus on the girl, who's still wandering aimlessly around the city, whiling away her time, because she wants to postpone making a definite decision. She thinks about having to confront everyone, but then changes her mind—perhaps it's only herself she needs to confront. She goes into a music store and buys one of the first CDs she recorded. She wants to be reassured of its quality, that she's not just another flash in the pan, just another in the long line of piano prodigies who have come and gone without consequence. The biggest stars in the industry don't need to be great performers; once they attain a certain level of fame, the blinding aura of their celebrity hides many of their less obvious defects. She listens to the disc as she walks. The performance is good, but there's something missing. Perhaps, back then, her playing lacked soul. And that's the difference. If she had the opportunity to record the *5 Pieces for piano*, she'd have to bring her performance to a whole new level, a level neither she nor anyone else has yet reached. She sits on a bench by the sidewalk to write for a while. Then she closes her eyes and leans back in the sun, whiling away the hours until dusk. She thinks about visiting the bars and clubs she used to frequent with the others after the concerts. First, she has something to eat in a restaurant. The newspapers report the same news. The only difference is the local papers don't ever mention the star of her favorite soccer team. She folds it and puts it aside. She thinks of a list of bars and clubs to go to. She has plenty of time to spare before her meeting. It seems to her that aliens must have a lot of patience anyway. Meanwhile, perhaps over a drink in one of those bars, she may be able to resolve the question of her hypnosis. She's not sure if she remembers the way, but she tries to reconstruct the route she often took while barhopping with the others. Eventually, though, she gets lost walking along streets she doesn't recognize. She doesn't find even one of the bars or clubs on her mental list, and not a single member of the group of people who often joined their party over the course of a night. It's almost as if these scenes didn't occur in the same city. Even the café in front of the church looks different than it used to. She asks one of the waiters if it's still frequented by writers and musicians, as it was when she and the group went there before and after the concerts in the church. The man doesn't seem to recall this ever happening, so she goes off on a new search for all the famous cafés and restaurants she used to visit with her mother, the young conductor, and their retinue. But before long, she gets lost again, and although she asks some people for directions, none are sure of the way. It's as if the route has been erased, or that it never even existed, or that she only dreamed it. She tires of going around in circles. Then she recalls she still has some of the pills those two pricks used to give her. They should pep her up for a little while, she thinks. Minutes, perhaps hours, later, she finds herself leaning against the hood of a car in front of the nightclub, watching the entrance fixedly. She knows she may be about to have the most important first encounter of her life, indeed of anyone's life. And yet, something in her gut tells her it's too good to be true, that anyone could've replied to her message, and that the meeting might be a waste of time, which wouldn't be a surprise, since it's the running theme of the night so far, of the past few days in fact—days and nights spent wandering aimlessly through the streets, or through her mind, sitting at the laptop, not writing a line, and unable to resolve the question of her hypnosis. When she wrote the ad, she felt she could take on the world, but now she feels tired, perhaps because it's late, perhaps because she's been feeling dispirited lately; either way, she's not very enthused at the prospect of an imminent alien encounter. But might they clarify what exactly her mission is on Earth? Shadowed in the doorway, before entering the nightclub, she hides the gun in her satchel and goes to leave it in the cloakroom, her mind completely blank, like an automaton's.

She dances alone under the flashing lights, her eyes fixed, unblinking, on the shelves of bottles behind the bar. It's Friday, so there are quite a few people on the dance floor, although it isn't the busiest hour yet. The girl is moving like a zombie, hardly aware of what she's doing or where she is. She looks around the dance floor at the people around her, at the other girls in the club—both those who are dancing and the ones sitting down—biding her time, waiting for something to happen, wondering when this meeting is going to take place, a blind meeting she probably should've avoided. How will she be able to recognize him? She'll wait a while longer before leaving. She slows her dancing down until it appears she's only half-heartedly following the music's rhythm. Leaning on the bar, the cousin is watching her every movement. Perhaps he followed her because he has something important to say. She considers the possibility her father sent him to look out for her, like a guardian angel or something, but then she dismisses the thought, thinking her father would never go to such trouble for her sake. She decides to offer him a smile, but her smile quickly fades when she sees him vanish in the darkness between the flashing lights. She continues dancing. Sometimes she believes the human race has a destiny it can't even begin to imagine. A destiny she can hardly begin to imagine herself. Perhaps they're not even humans, although that's not important right now. After wasting enough time pottering around the dance floor, she collects her bag from the cloakroom and goes back outside to lean against the bonnet of a car. She should probably be getting back. She wants to plan her route precisely this time; she's sick of walking the streets using only her gut as a guide. A guy sits next to her. He smiles while taking out a hanky and wiping the sweat from his brow. She remembers having seen him on the dance floor. Light from the club's entrance is flooding the sidewalk, which is swarming with young people—some entering and exiting, some hanging around chatting and smoking. The bouncer looks at her for a moment, but he's busy dealing with the people walking in and out of the club. To one side, a group of friends are debating whether to go somewhere else. Near them, two girls are repeatedly kissing one another on the cheeks. The girl counts five kisses before deciding to leave them to it. The largest group of people seems to be waiting for someone, who finally emerges from inside the club, and after briefly checking his fly is closed, joins the rest of his party, which then swarms as a single unit down the street. This isn't the best place for dancing, says the guy who's still sitting beside the girl. He looks at her carefully and points out her striking resemblance to that famous pianist. How did he recognize her with her new clothes and hair? He tells her he went to one of her concerts, and says that her features haven't changed all that much. It seems she should start wearing her sunglasses at night, she thinks. A cap and scarf wouldn't go amiss either. She asks if he was one of the group that accompanied the musicians when they went barhopping after their concerts. He was not. The only thing he wants to talk about is the voices. He too hears voices, and that's the reason he replied to her message. What are they like? she asks, disappointed. The guy launches into his explanation, saying he often hears them call him by a different name, but when he wakes up, he can't recall what it was. Then it happens in your dreams? the girl asks. She says she hears them all the time, asleep or awake. She hears them pronounce her name with a "ka" instead of a "k" sound. He says it's probably an honest mistake. August is a horrible month. It must be even for aliens. There's nothing special about this guy, or the voices he thinks he hears. He shouldn't have bothered replying. Since he only hears voices in his dreams, maybe they should arrange to have a meeting there, because that's the only place they'd ever hit it off. August is a horrible month for everyone, whatever the city. They remain seated on the car, talking about aliens and music. He doesn't think the voices come from another galaxy, and he doesn't understand why she expects to receive any further contact, aside from him. As regards music, he knows next to nothing, so the girl ends up having to launch into a screed about twelve-tone serialism and why it's so important. She also tells him what it's like to be a so-called child prodigy, and how people try to exploit her as a brand. It's getting late, but something keeps her from going back to the hotel just yet. Maybe it's the companionship. Perhaps that's all she's been looking for. At least her head no longer feels like it's going to explode. And that's a good sign. There's a bitter wind blowing, so the girl buttons up her jacket. The guy offers to make her coffee back at his place. It's not far. She never really developed a taste for coffee, but she doesn't mind having some anyway. The pills are already keeping her wide-awake, so it'll hardly make a difference. If she were present, the girl's mother would have lost no time pointing out the fact that the guy's wearing imitation-brand clothing: a polo shirt, unbleached cotton pants, and a pair of moccasins. Casual and cheap. She grins for having thought of it. She wouldn't dare ask him what brand they're supposed to be, but she can smell an imitation from miles away, which is about the distance separating them in terms of class. It's something she inherited, in a sense, a mindset she grew up with, starting when she was an infant, to be aware of all the differences, both glaring and subtle, between people like her and people belonging to the lower classes. But she's made a promise to herself to combat this mindset and resist all thoughts proceeding from it. The guy lives in a small apartment located in a tiny square at the end of a residents-only passageway off the street. He turns on the lights and walks along a narrow corridor. The floor consists of a series of wooden planks set lengthwise under their feet. It seems strange at first, but then she considers it homey. The girl tells him she wants to be a writer, and that's the reason she gave up music, because to be a writer is all she really wants in this life. After a few minutes, or perhaps it's an hour, he's sitting with a coffee, and she a bottle of beer and what's left of a slice of cake. She was going to tell him she's at a crucial stage in her career, having discovered the source of her literary impulse in a hypnotist's swaying pendulum, but she decided against going into it. He'd like to know what it is she writes about, so she explains to him the plot of her *No World*. She tells him about an angel that isn't really an angel; about an old professor and his female student; about invisible aliens who keep watch on their charges, who either don't know they're aliens or ignore the fact. The angel isn't really an angel, but another alien who, like the others, is invisible, but invisible in the sense that it doesn't truly exist, not as something that occupies space and is made of matter exists, anyway, because it's

305

simply the creation of a single overriding consciousness. The difference being that this angel is unable to imagine the existence of other angels, and for this reason, other angels are invisible to it. She tells him about the war in the City in Outer Space, and the survivor who must face the prospect of being alone for the rest of his life, his only possessions being a tape recorder, a copy of W's magnum opus, and a gun. She's certain that her music, which he hears constantly while walking the desolate streets alone, provides some solace. She's certain it helps to calm this terrible vision he has of a universe that seems to be expanding one day and contracting the next. The constructions of the mind are the constructions of the No World. The No World is all that is the case. The guy thinks her explanation is rather like her notion of a difference between "ka" and "k," and he really doesn't know what to make of it. He's reminded of a movie in which an angel on Earth listens to other people's conversations, perhaps hearing their thoughts as well. He finds the idea interesting that nothing exists outside the mind, that everything's constructed by a single consciousness. Then he asks her what No World means. She hesitates to answer, as the idea's still a work in progress. Finally, she says the No World must be understood as a sort of game. A game that creates a reality parallel to ours, and which, in essence, is identical to ours, just seen from a different frame of reference. The No World, just like everything else, could simply be a dream. No World is simply a name for the all-encompassing thought, the thought of which all things ultimately consist. All that is the case, she adds. Then she explains that, in the beginning, there was only nothingness, and that this nothingness was all-encompassing, except for a single point of concentrated thought, too small to be seen by the naked eye, perhaps too small for an electron microscope to detect. Then, in a timeless instant, this point exploded, and in the explosion, thought began expanding outward, creating a universe that exists only within its own solitude, although it appears so real that it eventually created beings who were convinced it was real, that they were real, and so convinced were they, it was inconceivable to even admit to the possibility that all they saw around them, all they knew and loved and hated, was only a product of thought. These beings eventually thought other universes into existence, universes filled with other people, which they called unreal, fictitious, while always refusing to admit to the possibility that what they saw around them, all they loved and hated, was also unreal, fictitious; always refusing to admit to the possibility that the constantly expanding universe they lived in was just a mind that thought them into existence. The girl could tell him more about the No World, but she thinks she's said enough, and he accepts this without further comment. Then a minute goes by, perhaps more, either way, it's too late to beat around the bush, so they decide to go to bed. They have sex, but it doesn't go well, because she wants to do it fast, while he'd prefer to go at his own pace. This always happens when she pops those pills. It's nothing new to her. In any case, she acts as if there's nothing wrong. But she thinks it's strange she's now heard them whispering in another language. She tries to get some sleep, but his bed is just a mattress on the floor, and his nightstand just an upside-down fruit box. It occurs to the girl that her mother wouldn't spend a minute in this place. She doesn't know why she's suddenly thinking of her mother. At dawn, they lie in silence under the covers. The windows are open, and the girl watches the shadows of wind-stirred branches moving on the plaster molds of the ceiling. She listens to the silence outside, very different from her father's hotel room, the incessant din of the Grand Central Station. She's not looking at the guy, although she can tell he's also watching the shadows on the ceiling. When a day begins to dawn, there's a certain point at which the darkness and the light seem mixed in equal proportion. It's a magical moment, although it only lasts a few seconds—yet she's able to prolong it by closing her eyes and recalling it once it passes. In the bed, the girl closes her eyes and recalls that moment again, a moment few people ever get to see, she thinks, because they're always asleep when it happens. Then she falls asleep herself and starts dreaming about a foosball table, a formation of two defenders, five midfielders, and three strikers. She struggles to control the positions of the players and loses every game she plays. Then she's explaining to her new friend that, in her native country, the foosball tables have three defenders, three midfielders, and four strikers, and she goes wandering the streets looking for one exactly like it. A stranger approaches her and says that, in his native city, they have the best foosball tables in the world. When she awakens, they have sex a second time, with no better results than the first. While she showers, he smokes a cigarette. She asks him if she knows of any foosball tables with the three-three-four formation. He says he doesn't remember, he's not a habitual player. The girl eats breakfast quickly; she's in a hurry. She couldn't say what exactly has changed since last night, but right now she wants to be alone. He's happy to go without breakfast and has a couple of cigarettes instead. She opens her satchel, takes out the gun, and slips it between her jeans and the small of her back. Their eyes meet momentarily. I've been getting death threats, she lies. He keeps watching her, feeling a little threatened himself. There's something strange in his look. Don't worry, I'm not going to kill you, she jokes, at least not today. Before she leaves, he takes a quick

Polaroid of the two of them, reaching out his arm to snap them both, their heads tenderly touching in the same frame. The girl writes on the back of the photo the same message that brought them together. "I hear voices. 1. The No World is all that is the case." Then she writes the date and signs it "Ka." In the photo, they appear together under the door-frame, with the mattress on the floor in the background. To her relief, the guy doesn't ask for her number, nor does he ask to meet up again. So after they say their good-byes, the girl leaves. The screenwriter lifts his eyes from his typewriter, a little surprised by how dark it's become, and deduces it must be quite late. He's spent hours immersed in his writing, but before going to bed, he lights one last cigarette. He needs to relieve the strain in his neck. He turns off the light and stays seated a while, observing the windows of the building opposite. Some are still glowing with signs of life; others are stygian black. The No World is just another way of trying to replace the external world with a replica, but it's a replica that acts like a photographic negative with an image on it, but which disappears entirely once it's developed. He's hungry. When will the money arrive? he wonders.

In the morning he calls the bank from the hotel. He wants to know if they can forward him part of his next pension payment. The employee tells him there was a recent deposit made to his account. This is the advance from the producer. But then he tells the screenwriter it has to be used to cover the outstanding balance on his credit card. So he's in the black, but must be immediately put back in the red, because this employee, instead of suggesting other options, seems intent on giving him a hard time. The screenwriter can't bring him-self to write. It's not that he's drawn a blank, he just can't be bothered. He has more pressing things to worry about now. He looks down at the street from his hotel window, at the storefronts he's seen so many times before: the real-estate agency on the corner, the bakery, the shop selling women's lingerie, and the shoe and handbag store that's closed for the August vacation. His neighbor passes by her window, but now isn't the time to try getting her attention. Now isn't the time to be thinking about her. After breakfast he goes down to the lobby and reads the newspaper. On finishing, he leaves it on the table and goes out to the street, dragging his leg behind him. He gets the impression his limp has gotten worse, which would tally with the decline in his confidence, his mood, and his general psychological well-being, really. A little down the street, he stops in front of a store window, ostensibly to look at the display, but really to have a rest, and to look at his reflection in the glass. When his spirits are up, he hardly notices the limp, but now his leg is like a dead weight, and he realizes what's happening, that he's becoming depressed, and this is affecting not only his mind but his body as well, and he wonders whether it's the beginning of a slow, inexorable decline. He needs to deal with this, he thinks while waiting at the traffic light to cross the street. On arriving at the café, he takes a newspaper from one of the tables, sits down, and indicates the usual with a nod of the head. The waitress acknowledges his order. A little while later, she approaches the table with tray in hand. Have you been thinking about me? he whispers to her. The waitress gives him a sideways glance and smiles. It may be an ironic smile, and she may leave him without an answer again, but the screenwriter keeps watching her as she serves the other tables; he thinks he's made some progress at last, and that the smile indicates there's some hope for him yet. He doesn't have the inclination to write, but he starts listing, one by one, the names of people who could loan him some money: screenwriters and other people in the business, friends, distant relatives, simple acquaintances. He still has the odd telephone number written in his agenda, although most will have to be sought in the directory. All at once, the thought of obtaining the addresses and phone numbers he needs doesn't seem that difficult. What began as a terrible day hasn't turned out so badly. He thinks the day sums up his life: at times he feels capable, confident; at other times, he feels the exact opposite. I wouldn't make much of a philosopher, he thinks, smiling. Perhaps the waitress's smile is responsible for lifting his spirits, the glimmer of hope he received when she cast him a sideways glance. Perhaps that's all it is, he thinks. On getting back to his room, he sets the directory beside him on the bed and picks up the telephone.

A few hours later, the screenwriter has managed to contact some of the people on his list, mainly colleagues in the trade, people with whom he's never really been close. He asks for small sums of cash, giving the excuse that he needs to resolve a misunderstanding with the bank, and most of his relatives and close friends are on vacation, so he can't turn to them. Taking the approach of asking a lot of people for small amounts means that pretty much everyone agreed to help him out. Now the screenwriter believes he'll have enough to last until the end of the month, which is when his pension comes through. He can't rely on any more advances from the producer, and he's worried about the outstanding balance on his credit card. The conversation he had with the bank employee was pathetic, he thinks, but at this point, when everything seems to be going against him, he colors every such situation with a somber hue. He can do nothing now except wait for his friends' donations to come through. He retrieves his glasses from beside the telephone and returns to his desk, a little more hopeful than before. He rereads the last page he wrote the night before, then continues where he left off: right after the girl spent the night with the guy she met at the nightclub. He feels satisfied at having made progress on the girl's internal monologue. The universe as a great explosion of thought expanding outward. An instant before, there was nothing, and then, bang!—suddenly, thought began expanding its domain, encroaching on the void, invading everywhere, conquering its territories, bestowing sense and reason on what had no sense and reason because it didn't exist. But he still has trouble imagining nothingness, the void. He can only think of it in terms of what exists. He understands the idea of nothing existing outside of the mind, that what he sees is created by the mind in the act of thinking, but he finds the idea of nothingness itself unfathomable. Such a small detail, but crucial. Something that's accepted on faith, as received wisdom, unquestioned because impenetrable; but he wonders how, in the all-pervading nothingness, there could possibly exist a small point of concentrated thought. Where does it come from? When he tries to understand nothingness, he thinks back to the period before he conceived of even the slightest notion of what his script would be about. But there isn't any single idea in any story that slowly expands as if from a miniscule point somehow existing in the period before it was itself conceived, and which ends up growing into a fully formed screenplay. It makes no difference if the miniscule point consists of matter or thought. So thinks the girl. Although she hardly slept, she feels as if a load's been taken off her shoulders. On the street, she deliberates at a metro station before deciding to continue on foot. The hotel isn't far, but she decides to stop at a café anyway, and plan her next movements. Her writer's instinct is directing her to plan her day out properly. She orders a coffee and a glass of water, and downs another one of those pills that keep her awake and alert. But this reminds her again of those dickhead former friends of hers. She immediately dismisses the thought, because she's closed that chapter in her life: no more negative thinking, no more calling up bad memories; instead, she'll devote the next paragraph or so to her adventure with the guy she met at the nightclub. She doesn't need more than that. She finds the meeting with him was beneficial, although she can't say exactly why. Perhaps the cold night air had served as a sort of freezer, slowing down her thoughts sufficiently for her to develop her No World idea. The guy seemed interesting, but she doesn't remember his name. She'd have liked to write it in her diary. And now what? she wonders. After her failure to meet any aliens, she should probably go back to her father's hotel, get her things, and go home, just as she planned. She should also go to the hotel with the English name and say good-bye to her mother. Before leaving the café, she reads in a newspaper that the star of her favorite soccer team is training alone. It's the first time she's read anything relating to the player in one of the neighboring country's newspapers. There's other news, but the girl doesn't have it in her to concentrate on any more reading. She no longer thinks about the scientist in the classically-cut suit, and she doubts she'll find a report as to whether or not she was hypnotized in any of these newspapers. Maybe she should go see a doctor. She recalls that her mother wanted her to see quite a distinguished one. She smiles because she believes mothers never truly understand their children. Then she reconsiders going to the hotel with the English name to say good-bye. It's the first time in a while that she hasn't checked the classifieds section. In the next scene, the girl is looking out the window of a taxi, scrutinizing the faces of people walking the streets, and examining the store fronts and monuments, as if she were leaving the city forever, and is trying to record a lasting image of it. Then she opens her bag and takes out her cell phone, thinking a video would provide a better record. The taxi stops in front of the hotel with the English name. There are no such things as coincidences, the girl murmurs on seeing her mother from a distance, hand in hand with the young orchestra conductor who, for once, isn't wearing his Institute's uniform. They're strolling at a leisurely pace, as if they're just getting back from a long walk, absorbed in what looks to the girl like a private discussion. The girl tells the driver to keep the meter running while she stays in the taxi watching them, trying to read their lips, to interpret their gestures. The young conductor beams a smile at her mother, who in turn, blushes, beguiling him with a youthfulness she doesn't possess. But she suddenly catches sight of her daughter, and quickly releases his hand, before making a move toward the taxi. Here, the screenwriter intends to have a jump cut to the moment just after the girl has told the driver to put his foot on the pedal and ignore the gesticulating woman on the sidewalk, the moment just after she stops looking at her mother and fixes her eyes on the road ahead, pretending she doesn't see her, doesn't hear her calling her name. Why does everyone pronounce her name with a "ka"? she wonders, her eyes still fixed on the road ahead. It seems the young conductor's found a replacement for the maid, someone else to read passages from W while he's having sex with his latest conquest. She wonders if her mother dresses for the occasion, or whether she performs in the nude, wearing only a necklace, a pair of silk stockings, and high heels. These might throw into relief some aspect of

314

her character the conductor finds appealing, especially if she wears them while reading random passages from W's magnum opus. Then again, perhaps all that's thrown into relief is her nudity. Moments later, her cell phone rings. Why did you leave? asks her mother without preamble. I'm going home, the girl says before hanging up and returning the phone to her bag. Damn game, she mutters. Every so often, something happens to remind you of it. She thinks everything's happening according to some hidden plan, and that, one after another, she keeps falling into traps that are set for her. Why the preceding scene? If everything's a game, her mother must also be involved in it. When was this ever not the case? Where the hell have you been? asks a voice in the lobby of the hotel in front of the Grand Central Station. The girl quickly turns. It's Cousin McGregor, who's been waiting some time for her. We're leaving, he says. Let's go. We've already checked out of the rooms.

The screenwriter smiles. If he wasn't so desperate, he might even feel happy. Happy, because every step the girl takes has been fastidiously measured. She's not going anywhere, he snickers. He won't let her get away that easily. That would be running away, and he can't have the girl in his story running off on him, however jaded she might feel, however disgusted she is by what the universe is thinking into existence around her. Back in the real world, the screenwriter would also like an escape route from his own life, and although writing provides this temporarily, his problems always return once he gets up from the typewriter. He's not going anywhere either. He's tired, and his situation seems utterly hopeless. His circumstances won't allow him to get away that easily. He didn't at all like the conversation he had with the bank employee. But

he doesn't want to think about that right now. Perhaps he'll
end up going crazy and blaming himself. Desperate, hopeless,
he thinks while looking at the building across the street, at the
real estate agency on the corner, the bakery, the shop selling
women's lingerie, and the shoe and handbag store that's closed
for the August vacation. The woman in the apartment opposite looks at him for a fraction of a second. The screenwriter
somehow sensed it, and looking up, lifts his arm in greeting.
But the woman's already disappeared. It's a possibility, he
thinks. He fixes himself up in front of the bathroom mirror
and puts on his navy blue jacket, the only jacket he has left. He
takes a step backward. Not bad, he says, running his fingers
through his hair . . . he feels encouraged on remembering that
not many people his age have a full head of hair. Gray hair
suits him, and it gives him a certain gravitas. Women love running their hands through it. He crosses the street and ascends
to the floor on which the woman lives. He hardly notices his
limp. He rings the doorbell to one of the rooms and waits.
Silence. He rings again, more insistently this time. No one.
Perhaps she went out while he was in front of the mirror. He
mentally maps the layout of the hallway, in case he's picked
the wrong room. He doesn't think he has, but he'll try the
apartment next door. This time he definitely hears the sound
of footsteps coming from inside, and in an instant, the door
opens to reveal the woman he's so often gaped and wondered
at from his window across the street. She's even more beautiful up close. The screenwriter introduces himself. At first she
doesn't seem to understand, but her puzzled expression soon
changes to a look of recognition. After all this time, he says to
her, it seems rude not to come over and say hello. And since
he saw that she was in, he thought he'd take the opportunity
to make her acquaintance. She holds the door firmly without

316

loosening her grip. It's not possible to live in a hotel and not be curious about one's neighbors, he says, lifting his arm and pointing in the general direction of his room. He was thinking about inviting her to dinner, he says, trying to gain some more time. If she'd be kind enough to accept . . . Perhaps, he says, he surprised her with his visit. He then explains that he's alone in the city, and that he'd like to make a new friend, if she doesn't have any prior commitments, that is . . . the words spill one after the other from his lips, falling into his own ears as well, one after the other, sounding as awkward to him as he presumes they do to her, and he imagines that he wouldn't respond to them either. Finally, she opts for shutting the door without speaking a word. The screenwriter rings the doorbell again, but the woman doesn't answer, so he turns to make his way toward the elevator. Halfway there, though, he changes his mind, goes back, and starts thumping the door violently. You don't know what you're missing! he shouts. He strikes his cane against the floor, against the door, screaming, Bitch, you're nothing but a bitch! At the end of the hallway, a door creaks slightly open and a woman's face peeks out. Eventually, some other doors open, and some more people emerge, watching him in silence. What are you all looking at!? he demands of his audience. No one knocked on your doors and asked for your opinion! he says, raising his voice, and continuing his drumming on the woman's door. What's happening here is between me and this bitch, he says lifting his cane, so go back inside and mind your own business.

Back in his room, the screenwriter's still reeling with anger; there isn't a chance he'll write anything now, at least not until he calms himself down. He leans against the window ledge and stares at the closed blinds of her apartment window. The woman pulled them down and turned her light off, but the screenwriter can feel her eyes peeping out at him, so he keeps staring back at her, angrily, intently. Dread, fear, terror . . . he repeats to himself, his arms shaking as he holds the ledge without loosening his grip, until his rage eventually abates, and he no longer feels her eyes staring back at him. Then he goes to the telephone and calls his son. His daughter-in-law answers and they chat for a few moments. She seems a little cold, but at least she's talking to him. He's calling from the neighboring country's capital, he says. The weather's fine, although it's rained on a couple of occasions. It's sweltering over here, she says. They didn't go anywhere during the August vacation because his son's been out of work for some months now, and there don't seem to be any prospects on the horizon. The screenwriter knows where this is going, without her having to say it: so don't bother asking for any money. She puts his son on the phone. Immediately the screenwriter explains that the bank has frozen his account, and that he's in desperate need of money because he can't resolve the problem with them over the telephone. He says he'll pay his son back as soon as the producer of the film gets back from his vacation. A money order to his hotel would be the most convenient way. Before hanging up, the son inquires after his mother. Your mother didn't come with me, the screenwriter says. I'm afraid we decided to separate.

It's early, and it promises to be a beautiful day. The screenwriter sits at his desk eager to continue working, but is distracted by his mental calculations. He figures the money his son's sending will last him till the end of the month, but he may be able to get his screenplay finished before then, and once that's delivered, he could ask the producer to send him more money. He needs money orders at this point; transfers into his current account will take too long to clear. In the building opposite, his neighbor's blinds are still down. So what, it's less distracting, he thinks, returning to his work. He goes over some of the index cards and post-its strewn about the room—on his desk, his nightstand, and the other bed, on which the newspapers have been gradually piling up. It's been days since he heard from the girl. He hasn't received a single envelope, not even a paltry note. He wonders if something might have happened to her, but then he also considers the possibility that she's abandoned him, as she promised she would. Threats and promises are only wisps of breath, not realities, he says trying to allay his fears. Besides, she promised she'd keep sending him abstracts of her diary and chapters of her *No World*. Before, if she missed an appointment, she'd always dispatch a messenger with an envelope. Now, there's nothing but silence: an emptiness to which he fears he may have to grow accustomed. He misses those pages that let him know she was still alive, that reminded him he was still alive. That made him feel he somehow mattered to her. The truth is he needs the girl as much as he needs money, or even food. Isn't she the reason he came to the neighboring country's capital in the first place? It's a beautiful day outside. He looks at the sky, as if to prove himself right, then he looks down on street to observe the passersby. Sundays are strange. He'd like to go for a walk, to have breakfast at the café in the plaza, and buy his newspapers where the boulevards intersect. He wonders when his son's money will arrive, and that of the other people who agreed to give him a loan. Now that he thinks of it, he doesn't remember telling them how urgently he needs it. He goes to the phone and calls his son, but this time no one answers. So he returns to his desk, intent on getting some writing done before going down for breakfast. Once he's finished his script and cashed his check, he'll be able breathe a lot easier, he thinks. He counts the number of days it should take to complete, and reproves himself for not having written more consistently, and with greater resolution. Perhaps it's not his lack of consistency but his approach that's the problem. He might've written more had he been writing for himself instead of the producer. He has to rewrite some of the material he's sending and improve the general shape of the story. He figures he has some five or six scenes left to write until the end. During his descent, the screenwriter's impatient to leave the elevator and get something to eat. It's been too long since he's had two square meals together in one day. If he has breakfast now, it'll probably be his only decent repast, which is why he's tucking some fruit and bread into his pockets, on exiting the elevator, before sitting down to read the newspaper. He leafs randomly through the pages as if trying to decide what to read. Then the receptionist approaches: the manager would like to speak with him. He titters, reluctantly gets up, and drags his leg into an office that's as small and uncomfortable as a coffin, and completely unsuitable for accommodating two people at once, but perhaps it's the best a flophouse manager can expect. The man would like to speak in private. About what? the screenwriter says brusquely, thinking attack is the best form of defense. There's been a complaint from one of the neighbors, he says sternly, before requesting that he pay his outstanding bill. He has twenty-four hours to find another room, he adds before ending the short colloquy in a manner to suggest that the meeting has ended. Although he's been paying off some of the bill in advance, the final figure is still far too high for the screenwriter to pay. First he requests that they lower the bill for having offended him. Then he demands to check over the invoice, since he believes they're overcharging him. For a moment, he wonders who he means by "they," since he's talking about an individual with a first and last name, and although the individual he's referring to is sitting directly across from him, he can't restrain himself from referring to another by screaming, that fucking bitch! Bitch or no bitch, the manager warns, you've got twenty-four hours to find somewhere else to stay.

The screenwriter calls his wife. He'd like to confess he's tired, stressed out, but nevertheless, he must somehow muster the effort to finish his work. A titanic effort, he intones dramatically to himself, as if he were a character in one of his scripts. He'd like to confess that things have not turned out as he wanted them to, and that he feels like the world is disappearing under his feet. But he doesn't want to think about it, let alone confess it to his estranged wife, because he doesn't have a clue where he's going to find the titanic effort he needs to continue. While listening to the rings, not counting this time, but waiting until she answers, knowing she probably won't answer, he thinks about those early days when he walked with a spring in his step and champed at the bit to get back to his desk and write, when he had no trouble mustering the energy to work, the enthusiasm to press forward to the end, when he felt like a professional, someone who didn't have to teach a gaggle of excessively gifted, excessively creative, excessively annoying brats on the side, most of whom stuck their tongues out at the things he taught them, except for the girl, with whom he dreamed of escaping, of living a passionate life in some faraway paradise. So much time has passed since he left that those days seem like another age, another world. But he knows it's only been a few weeks, which may not seem like

321

much, but it's enough for the phone call to not make sense. Or perhaps it does make sense, a twisted kind of sense—warped, in just the same way as the joining in marriage of two people who aren't right for each other. The screenwriter smiles at his musings and finally hangs up the telephone. He needs to have a rest, maybe get something to eat and take a nap, because he knows he'll see things differently when he wakes up. Like the girl, he also thinks about going home, although he knows he can't. If he could start all over again . . . he reflects, but then concludes he'd more than likely make all the same mistakes. He's looking out the window again, thinking about the woman in the building opposite, imagines her watching him through a gap in her blinds. He stares fixedly at her window but resists the temptation to raise his arm. Perhaps it wasn't her, he thinks, but then figures who else could it have been? He then examines the front of the building one last time. It's strange he always refers to it as a single building when it's really composed of two: one with balconies, the other with just windows. Most of the doors leading onto the balconies have blinds and there aren't any flowers outside. He scans the storefronts along the street: the real-estate agency on the corner, the lingerie store, the bakery, and the shoe and handbag store. All are closed, except for the bakery. He already knows that Sundays are strange. He looks around, considers every detail, as if he'd like to say good-bye even to the pebbles on the ground. But it doesn't matter, what are stones, flowers, blinds—these things aren't important. If he manages to get back on his feet, perhaps he'll decide to settle in this city. It certainly is beautiful, he reflects while looking over the rooftops, as if trying to imagine what a bird would see, or perhaps an aerial photographer. He might even live out his retirement here, he thinks, however many days he has left in this world. But not in a hotel, he simply couldn't afford it. He's not like the girl's father, who's happy to stay in hotels because he's rich. Either way, in a couple of weeks, he'll have forgotten it all, as in the hours after waking from a dream. And yet, despite the futility of hoping they'll come true, of expecting that even a residue might remain beside him when he wakes up in his bed, he still likes dreaming, and perhaps that's the reason he writes screenplays. He tries calling the prostitute, but she doesn't answer. He starts talking into the receiver anyway, imagining she can hear him say he's being kicked out of the hotel, that he has until tomorrow to pack his bags and leave; imagining she asks him where he'll go, and him answering that he doesn't know. Today's Sunday, and Sundays are always strange. The prostitute asks if the producer knows about his plight, and he tells the receiver, not yet. He's almost whimpering now. He knows it's pathetic, but it doesn't matter, she doesn't know him that well, and at least she's acquainted with the ups and downs one experiences in a wayward life. Today's a strange day, he repeats, he's being kicked out of his hotel; he's got twenty-four hours to find somewhere else to stay; writing requires a titanic effort—like crossing a desert, or lifting a skyscraper, or holding up the sky itself. He's being indecisive, whereas the prostitute in his imagination speaks with assurance, confidence. Indeed, perhaps too much, for she speaks as if she's even read his script, and plays the film producer in as accomplished a way as she does his lover. It exasperates him when someone offers advice so brazenly about something they know nothing about. She offers him the same counsel as would the producer; she even imitates his voice while doing so. Take a vacation, she tells him. He doesn't think a vacation is going to help. A vacation . . . for Christ's sake! Yes, he'll go sunbathing and drink cocktails with all the employees at the bank, indeed all the staff of

323

every business that's shut for the August vacation, he thinks, including that woman who owns the bag and shoe store: in other words, people who have no mission or purpose in life. The black prostitute, he thinks, envisioning her, doesn't get to go on vacation either. The producer told him he always spent his vacation working. What's the black prostitute's mission in life? Perhaps, like him, she doesn't have one, or is deceiving herself in thinking her profession will take her somewhere. But he doesn't want her to know this, for she still trusts in their respective talents. He doesn't even know whether he's still imagining the prostitute, or if it's now the producer, or perhaps the two of them together. He imagines them embracing, and realizes he's ruined the fantasy. He hangs up the phone, turns out the lights, and lies back on the bed. He feels pathetic for having spent so long speaking to a dial tone. He does it occasionally as a form of penance, but then he always regrets having repented. He smiles at the thought. If he didn't do these kinds of things, he wouldn't be himself. He gets out of bed, turns on the light, and goes to the writing desk. There are disorganized heaps of paper everywhere. He tries to put them in order and starts gathering his things. He finds notes in the most inconspicuous corners of the room, even in the mini-kitchen that lifted his spirits on the day he arrived. He collects them all and puts them in a large plastic bag, doing so carefully, as he would his clothes when folding them into a suitcase before a long voyage. These notes have been scattered around the room for days, even weeks, and it seems almost a miracle the cleaning lady was deferential enough to leave them where they lay. He picks up an envelope from the nightstand. It contains his favorite photos of the girl, brief flashes of his happiness, which he'll take with him when he goes away. It's been so long since he's seen her, she's starting to become a memory, and while the pain of those words that struck him when she promised she would leave had left a dull ache in his chest, now that this too was fading, as everything else seems to fade in his life, as even his memory of her seems to be fading, he hopes these flashes of happiness will rekindle her memory, although without the pain. He wonders if, instead of weeks, he's spent months holed away in this room. Perhaps he's been dreaming and it's only been a few hours. Like the girl, he begins wondering if there really is nothing outside the mind. But he's starting to feel unwell again, too unwell to pursue this thought, and he considers whether he should go right to bed. He looks around for a calendar to corroborate the number of days he's stayed at the hotel, but when he picks up his bill, it's made plain: twenty-eight days in total. He leaves his typewriter and large plastic bag on the floor, next to the door, and lies back against the headboard, contemplating the room, which now looks totally bare. It's all over, he says loudly, repeatedly, closing his eyes. It's all over, it's all over . . . A minute goes by, perhaps an hour, perhaps longer than that. He finally got some rest. He's breathing more easily, and feels as if a weight's been lifted from his chest. It's all over, he remembers saying before falling asleep. He wouldn't mind listening to some music, but not that twelve-tone stuff, which he only listens to when trying to enter the mindset of his characters. For the first time since he arrived, he turns on the radio, which plays something relatively easy on the ears, a waltz. He gets up and starts dancing with his cane. There's some interference coming through the speakers, as if the sound is traveling from another galaxy, and only a fraction of the signal is managing to cover the distance. When the waltz ends, he turns the radio off, but keeps dancing anyway because he feels buoyant. It's all over, he chirps to the music of the waltz. He wants to celebrate the fact that a weight's been lifted, but he can't make his mind up who it is he'd like to be there celebrating with him. Perhaps the girl, although he doesn't imagine she'd enjoy dancing a waltz. The girl has the kind of ego that sees itself only in grim and murky plashes, a personality buoyed by the bleak and leaden aspects of life, a face whose only mirror is duplicity and guile. The screenwriter doesn't have anyone in the neighboring country's capital to dance with. Now that he's broke, even the black prostitute has left him for the producer. He sits down and riffles through the phone directory. It's not exactly true he has no one. He recalls the names of the screenwriters, directors, and assistants who agreed to send him money. All are former friends he hasn't seen in years, and it occurs to him he never told them of his return to the profession. Then again, it's probably not a good idea to call them at this hour just to invite them to a waltz and do some catching up. He better let them send the money and leave it at that.

He slept more than he needed to, and his muscles are now stiff. It's getting dark outside, and the streetlights are already on. Although it's too early for dinner, he eats the bread and fruit he's been saving in his pocket since breakfast time, and sits in the chair. There's nothing interesting on TV, not that he understands much that's being said. They need to talk more slowly; he's a foreigner after all. He turns it off and limps to the kitchen to make some coffee. He thinks about the girl and her father, but especially the girl, the would-be author. He thinks it's amazing that he should be thinking about this in light of his current situation, as if he were still in that state of grace before the girl left him, before he was kicked out of the hotel, before he was broke. He returns to the chair with his cup and lights a cigarette. Now that he's a little more relaxed, he thinks about the future. He'll probably have to start looking for a job, but he's useless at everything that doesn't involve the movies. Once again, he's considering the possibility of abandoning his career as a screenwriter, something he's done his whole life, in favor of a job for which he lacks both experience and skill. His only other option is retirement. He won't be able to teach again, that's for sure. Maybe the producer will commission another screenplay. But it's hard for him to think about writing another script when he's dwelling on all his own worst qualities. If the girl decides to come back, maybe he could start a new life with her. Perhaps she could pull him out of his financial rut. But that's a dream. She's gone. He tries calling her again, but her cell phone isn't on. Well, damn it! he says. How's he going to tell her about his imminent departure from the hotel? He's putting himself in a bad mood. He finishes his coffee and puts out his cigarette and tries taking his mind off it all. He takes a few deep breaths and thinks about something he learned from her. Perhaps if he adopted her mantra, he'd see things differently: life's a game or something like that. He says it again slowly, almost hearing her voice. It doesn't change his perception of himself as a failure. Perhaps it would be best to just accept it, try doing something else, perhaps he should enter the confessional where his conscience resides, that voice in the back of his mind that keeps telling him it's impossible to live a fulfilling life, and admit he was wrong, do penance for having believed otherwise. "I can't stop thinking that I've wasted the best years of my life," he could say, paraphrasing one of the characters in the novel by the author of lost time, except in his case, not for the sake of a woman, but because he hadn't realized any of his professional ambitions. If he was a great writer, he'd be able to write about himself, about his failures, transform them into overwhelming triumphs. The best years are the ones that are lost, the ones that are wasted in suffering, in want, for these are the years that are waiting to be retrieved, waiting to one day be written about. The tolling church bells remind him of the time. A piece of fruit, a slice of bread, a cigarette, and coffee hardly constitute a good meal, but at least he's not hungry. There's some spoiled yogurt at the back of the fridge, and the leftovers of a meal he doesn't remember having. He still has a few coins rattling in his pocket. To think, only a few hours earlier he was dancing a waltz. He sits in front of the window, lifts his feet onto the ledge, and lights a cigarette. It's hard to see the stars above the buildings, especially with all the light pollution, but at this point, he's not that fussy about the view. He's happy just to smoke his cigarette and let the evening run its course.

He could wait until midday, that's the time he has to check out of the hotel, but something's telling the screenwriter he shouldn't delay. He has to run through what's become a ritual for him now, and which he already performed after leaving his house and then his studio apartment: a ritual of renunciation. In a little over a month, he's started a new life on two occasions. From this point on, maybe he'll be doing so several times a day. He goes into the bathroom for the last time, freshens up for the last time, looks at himself in the mirror, and takes a deep breath before leaving the room for the last time. The elevator takes its time arriving. He gets the feeling he may be better off taking the stairs. He'd do it if it wasn't for his damned limp. He grips his cane impatiently and knocks it against the floor a couple of times, the strokes muted by the carpet, rendering the act meaningless. He doesn't like the muffled thud, he says to himself, because it probably unleashed a cloud of dust mites that are now colonizing his socks and the hem of his pants. He takes the elevator to the lobby. He has no clothes other than the ones he's wearing. He sold his watch and the briefcase in which he kept his screenplay and his notes. He also sold his other suitcase, the cassette player the girl gave him, his CDs, the twelve-tone book he bought in the music store, and even the book about screenwriters. All his remaining worldly belongings are stuffed in a large plastic bag on the manager's office floor, next to an old-fashioned portable typewriter. He'll collect them, along with his documentation, once he settles the bill. The money his son and old colleagues sent didn't last very long. He collects his things and leaves the manager's office with his head held high, looking straight ahead, striking his cane against the floor, which reverberates in the vicinity like a battle drum, though his army's slain, and the drummer's playing alone. His mind's a blank, he has no plans; perhaps there's no longer a place for him in this world. Then, suddenly, of all people, he sees the brilliant composer sitting in a chair in the lobby, and he has with him the soundtrack he'd promised to write. Almost identical, he assures him, to the music in that film about the angels that listen to other people's voices, not only their speech, but also their thoughts, perhaps those of everyone on Earth. The piece he composed has a melody that progresses by a series of unsettling cadences, incomplete, as though the sound of something that's approaching, but hasn't come over the horizon as yet, a veritable No World, he says. He's only been back from the tour a few days, he says, seeming apologetic about having taken so long, but he didn't just come to give him the soundtrack, which he insists was just a simple mathematical exercise for him. The exchange between the two of them is brief. Basically, the screenwriter happens to have something of interest to the brilliant composer, and the brilliant composer has money.

The screenwriter strikes the cane hard against the pavement as he walks. A pedestrian appears to challenge him with a stare, upbraid him for this cudgeling to his ears, but once the screenwriter works up the moxie to scold him back, the man's already too far away to hear the tirade. He leans against a wall directly in front of a telephone booth and has a rest, waiting for his pulse to die down. With the money the brilliant composer gave him, he managed to buy back most of the things he'd sold. Unfortunately, he must now carry them all in his large plastic bag, which, along with the typewriter, is weighing him down. He can't call his wife, but it doesn't matter, there's no way she managed to survive. It's been a month since he left her bound and gagged on the bed, and no one, not even a woman, could last that long in such a predicament. Why call her, he asks himself, if she can no longer hear the phone ring, knowing it's him taunting her, reminding her she's going to die all alone in the marriage bed, like a dog. The handles of the typewriter and the plastic bag are digging into his hands. No, he'd never do that to a dog. He puts his belongings on the ground and thinks about the black prostitute. He wouldn't mind seeking refuge in her arms and crying a little. If he wasn't practically done with his screenplay, he'd probably do so. But he feels invigorated and wants to continue his work to the end. He'd like to make a few calls, he thinks while staring at the telephone booth, but he can't. The brilliant composer gave him just enough to buy back his things, little more. Once again, he's left with just a few coins rattling in his pocket. What a rip-off. Those photographs are worth millions. As he approaches the river, he starts asking passersby for spare change. He needs something to eat, even a slice of bread will do, a single slice of bread folded around a piece of cheese, or something. He could have sold himself to the highest bidder, but he wouldn't have known how to organize the auction, and in attempting it, would have probably ended up in jail. By midday he's content at having received quite a bit of change. The cheapest food is at a place mainly frequented by indigent immigrants. He takes his meal, which is wrapped in a paper bag, and heads for the park to eat under a tree. A beggar sits down beside him. The screenwriter wonders why, with all the available seats, he chose to sit right there. The beggar would like him to share his meal in exchange for some of his wine. The screenwriter doesn't quite understand why this gesture is being made until the beggar asks him how long he's been living on the street. Then the screenwriter hands him what's left of the meal, and goes away, dragging his leg and belongings behind him, struggling to hide the fact that he's crying. He needs to find a phone to call his son. He needs to ask for more money. He doesn't even remember where he spent the money he already sent him. According to the bill, he paid for twenty-eight days at the hotel. But the sums don't add up, because he thought he'd already paid for that as well as other services. He must've spent the rest somewhere, he thinks while tearing the bill up and letting the pieces fall to the ground. He finds a phone booth and dials his son's number. He's not at home, and his daughter-in-law isn't being very helpful. In the old days he'd have barraged her with insults, but now his situation's desperate. I need to speak to my son, he whispers weakly into the phone. She keeps saying she doesn't know where he is, or when he'll be back. The woman's intractable, even the modulation in her voice is unwavering when she answers him, and the words strike the screenwriter as rehearsed. I've had to resort to begging in the streets! he says, raising his voice, before lowering it again for a final supplication, Please, I need to speak to my son. She says she needs to go, and he should try calling again later in evening. The screenwriter struggles to compose himself, but manages to concentrate his fury into a strong knock of his cane against the floor. He won't call again. His son can keep his damn money. If he does call, he says to himself, it'll be to suggest he go check on his mother; to collect the present waiting for him on the bed. His mouth waters when he imagines the look on his son's face after opening the bedroom door. The screenwriter decides to finish his script once and for all, although all this will prove is that he's able to keep a deadline, and that this is a reflection of the kind of man he is.

It is night, and he has no idea where he's going to sleep. He feels a little less agitated, having managed to collect some change, but with his mobility already hampered by a limp, the weight of the typewriter and the large plastic bag only worsens the claudication. When he was young, he'd have accepted the situation as providing a wellspring of experiences to draw on later, when he came to write about suffering—for they'd help him to do so more convincingly. But if he were young now, he wouldn't be talking about suffering at all; he'd be too busy looking for a job so he could afford a roof over his head: a means of securing himself against future suffering. Perhaps he shouldn't have stayed in a hotel, he thinks, rebuking himself, however cheap it was. He could have rented a room or an apartment. All he really needs is a desk and bed, and something to keep the rain off his head. He could've cooked his own meals instead of eating at so many restaurants. So he pursues this line of second-guessing, knowing he'd always commit the same errors again, because it's the kind of man he is. The screenwriter returns to the vicinity of the hotel, near the local church where he's often seen friars and chaplains speaking to the homeless. Maybe they'll know where he can spend the night. On arriving, however, he discovers the church is closed, and when he goes looking around the neighborhood, sees no sign of a priest, nor any of the homeless who used to roam around or sit on the church steps. He's beginning to despair, and yet he ignores the ways of the homeless, those well-established shibboleths and practices for procuring room and board. Instead, he tries pushing the door; then he tries knocking against it a few times with his cane; then he tries looking through the keyhole. Finally, he gives up, and returns to the steps to sit down. Right now, the only place he'll find any sign of life is in the plaza where he usually has a coffee. He's tired of walking around holding out one hand asking people for spare change while carrying the typewriter and large plastic bag in the other. He has a hard time getting there, and has to stop several times for a rest, but at last he finds himself exhaustedly flumping into a chair at the café in the plaza. The price of a coffee and a sandwich exhausts all his funds, and he makes them last as long as he can, until closing time, when he asks one of the waiters if he can leave his typewriter and large plastic bag in the premises until the following morning. He'll be around to collect them first thing, he says. No problem, the young waitresses have often seen him at breakfast time having his coffee, and some of the older ones also recognize him, although he rarely came in the evenings. The plaza's almost empty once he sits down beside the fountain, quite close to a miserable vagrant primped in rags. He doesn't appear conversationally inclined, for his mouth's periodically stopped by a bottle of liquor. His face is an arid landscape that's been battered by meteors, and all the dirt there makes his complexion seem darker than it is. The screenwriter stands up. If he must sleep next to a tramp, he'll do so under a bridge where the owner of the café and the waitress he likes won't see him. He'd rather they think of him as a bohemian writer who's down on his luck than a derelict hobo who begs for spare change. He thinks about the girl. All in all, wherever he ends up tonight, it won't be a good place for her to visit him.

He wakes up with his back against the wall, his jacket fully buttoned, lapels raised, and yet he's shivering with cold. It's no surprise. By the river, after midnight, the damp starts turning into ice. Sitting on some newspapers one of the tramps gave him, he listens to the loud crepitations of vehicles moving overhead, and to the bridge rumbling in resonance with them, which itself resonates with the membrane of his eardrums. He slept badly, but at least he has his cane, and he's still in one piece. He checks his top pocket to make sure no one stole his wallet, and finds some newspaper stuffed between his shirt and jacket. He reckons he must have woken up in the night and unconsciously lined his body with this insulation to keep warm. With the help of his cane, he stands up to remove the pieces of newspaper from his person and leaves them to one side. His new cohorts are fast asleep, one here, another there, two or three huddled together in a corner—he can't tell exactly, because they're almost completely covered by a cardboard box that at one time carried a fridge. His stomach is growling with hunger, and he knows he must brace up before climbing the stair and going in search of a fountain to wash himself. As his body starts coming to life, something tells him the worst is already past, that he's finally taken the crucial step. So he must finish his screenplay at last, because his mind has never been sharper, and he has the story in the palm of his hand. He knows where he's going, but he takes a detour, in case someone he knows sees him begging in the street. He asks anyone he crosses paths with, people going to work, others pulling up store shutters. And if they don't have any change, he asks for food, anything they can afford to throw away. After drinking some water at the fountain, a fruit vender offers him a peach. The screenwriter looks down and sees it's covered in bruises. Anything they can afford to throw away. Within an hour, he's collected enough change to last the day. But now he has the story in the palm of his hand, and that's all that really matters. He wonders if his sudden determination to end his script is his psyche compensating him for all he's lost. He'll ask a psychologist about it some day. In the meantime, he goes back to the café in the plaza and decides to call the girl. This time she answers. I can't write, she complains. Ever since I found out I was hypnotized, everything's gone wrong. This is all too familiar to the screenwriter, who's so dizzy with excitement to hear her voice that he asks her to just keep talking. Her voice is as necessary to him as bread and water. Perhaps he needs it to finish his script. No, in reality, he knows how it's going to end. He's only just figured it out, but he has a good idea how he wants it to end. He'd like to see her again. Perhaps they could make love in some hidden corner of the plaza, in a bar's bathroom, or under a bridge. Time is running out. Do you still believe they're following you? he asks, as the last coin drops. Not since I changed my look, she says. It's a pity he couldn't hold onto his camera. He could've photographed them making love under a bridge, and in some other strange places—places that are hidden, places no one's ever heard of, he thinks, as the line cuts out. He feels he's nearing the end, and that he could finish his work at any of the tables in the café. He collects his typewriter and takes a seat in a well-lit corner inside, thinking he'll more than likely croak at his writing desk. Die with his boots on.

It's not going to be easy. Although he knows exactly where he left off in his story, he first has to organize the potpourri of loose pages and index cards that are stuffed in the large plastic bag. Perhaps he should forget about the notes and just grab the script itself, whose pages are bound with an elastic band. After finding it near the bottom of the bag, he's soon holding the last typewritten page in his hand. Where the hell have you been? asks a voice in the lobby of the hotel in front of the Grand Central Station. The girl quickly turns. It's Cousin McGregor, who's been waiting some time for her. We're leaving, he says. Let's go. We've already checked out of our rooms. He leads her through a back door into an alleyway where a car is parked. On the way, the cousin asks about her work, but she can only repeat what she's already told him about the No World, while he, in turn, cannot see past the comparison he's already made with Leon Kowalski, the replicant. She may as well be writing his untold story, about his false, implanted memories. For the rest of the drive, both are silent. The cousin is now staying in a room in the suburbs, where her luggage and her father are waiting for her. Her father says he'd prefer if she stayed a few more days before going back home. Your mother's concerned, he tells her, before insinuating she should keep her mouth shut about whatever he and the cousin are up to. So that's it, mutters the girl, knowing deep down that she was right, but thinking they've gone right back to the beginning, to the endless waiting for someone to contact them, perhaps even the scientist in the classically-cut suit. All that's changed is the address. The screenwriter feels he's never been more in tune with his writing. The words are flowing out of him like a torrent, and he attributes this to the state of mind of someone who, having been cast out of the world, has relinquished all worldly concern. To write, then wait to die: there's nothing more for him to do. The story was once beyond his reach, just beyond the tips of his fingers, but now he has it in the palm of his hand. He looks around for the waitress and asks for another coffee. He leans back in his chair and readies his fingers on the keys of the typewriter. First, a coup d'oeil at his new office: not bad. He's never written properly in a café before, but now it seems to him the perfect place to be writing, especially when the words are flowing out of him like a torrent, meaningful words that are more than just a series of mellifluous incoherencies. He wouldn't even deign to call it a mere screenplay anymore, but that doesn't matter now. He's writing a story, and that's enough. He'd love to call his wife right now and gloat, but the poor dear must smell awful. Probably full of maggots too. You never can tell with the variable August weather. All the screenwriter has to sustain himself is coffee, water, a sandwich every now and then, and if he's lucky, a pastry. He's clinging in his mind to the old cliché that nothing can prevent progress, thinking this as his story rushes through his mind from start to finish, his fingers poised, tempted by the keys. He doesn't even need his index cards or notebooks. He knows every turn in the laby-rinth, where to introduce a new scene, where to speed the action up or slow it down, where to find the answer to some central question. He holds his script in the palm of his hand, and sees it as a bird would see it, or perhaps an aerial photog-rapher. He knows he doesn't have much time left to traverse it, but things will move along faster now that he knows exactly where he's going. Writing the screenplay no longer seems like a chore, and although it may be hard to believe, considering what's become of him, for the first time in years, he actually feels young. He even feels that things are starting to go his way. Perhaps he's finally lost his marbles. He nods his head

337

without realizing, as if unconsciously approving the possibility. Perhaps he's gone mad and doesn't know it. It's as if he's the one who was hypnotized and not the girl. But there's no way someone with his experience could be that suggestible. Besides, he doesn't remember attending any sessions with a hypnotist—neither recently nor when he was still living with his wife. But what if he was hypnotized to forget he was hypnotized? What if it was a practical joke? No, there's no way it was joke, or a vendetta either. She's dead, and dead people don't make jokes. If he had to attribute it to something, he'd say it was the fasting. Not eating has somehow purged him, distilled and strengthened his faculties enough to conclude his story. He's not thinking about it in terms of a screenplay because he knows it's a story, first and foremost, and he must write it down as it flows out of him, and not stop writing until the end. Occasionally he stops typing and wonders if he'll wake up at some point and realize it was all a hallucination, and that everything he's writing in the café is only a product of that hallucination, if he'll snap out of it and read over what he's written and see only complete gobbledygook. Fortunately, this sort of thing happens to him very rarely—seeing what he's done as worthless—and the feeling only lasts a very short time. The compulsion driving him now is something quite different. Then he cleans his glasses and keeps typing. The only other times he will allow himself to remove his fingers from the keys are to light a cigarette or to order more coffee from the waitress. He only asks for two more days, as if requesting an extension, two more days and he'll be finished. Then he can roll over and die. The waitress watches him keenly as he says these words, and he looks back at her indifferently. He knows it's too late now for there to be anything between them. "I had a farm in Africa, at the foot of the Ngong Hills," he says, and she smiles at him, a proper smile for the first time, a sincere smile. And although the screenwriter's face is haggard, piteous, he still manages to smile back at her. The clack and plink of the typewriter is unrelenting, rising above the sound of the music over the speakers or the murmurs of customers conversing, some of whom stare at him, a beggar working like a man possessed, and he knows they're watching him and think he's a beggar possessed, but he doesn't care, because he knows they're absolutely correct. He strikes the keys demonically, his two hands moving as if there were three, sounding like a trio of tap-dancing feet, or two with the help of a cane. He sees himself as if he were in a dream from which he cannot be awoken. When he eventually runs out of cigarettes, he goes to the vending machine and buys another pack. A writer works all the time, he never stops working. To think is also to work, and when he's not writing, he's thinking. And can a man stop himself from thinking?

She managed to get there by climbing a hill quite near to a plaza that was once frequented by a famous foreign writer. She's never read any of his works, but she's definitely heard of him. Even people who don't read books have heard of him. If she took the screenwriter's suggestion seriously, this would be an assignation, but there are certain things she won't do. Perhaps in thirty or forty years she'll think about it. She still avoids white clothing, her hair is still dyed, and her dark sunglasses just about conceal her features, but the screenwriter recognizes her nonetheless when she sits down in front of him in the café. She looks at him perplexedly, noting the dramatic change in his person: unclean, unshaven, in general disarray— neglect papered over by good manners and a polished accent. Something's changed in their relationship. Something the girl dare not confess, not even to herself. Do you have any cash? the screenwriter asks. How much do you need? The girl empties her pockets and slaps down some notes and coins on the table. Tell me if it's true I was hypnotized, she demands, as if her whole life depended on his answer. Do you really want to know? he asks, knowing she won't like the answer. She nods. He waits a few moments. Yes, he admits, I was there. I saw it all happen. She responds with a look of disgust and gets up to leave. Don't go, he implores her, taking her hand. The only person who could take him away from his writing is thinking about leaving him again—and just before the culmination of the plot. It's a common formula: something you'd read in a beginner's manual on storytelling. How could it be otherwise? Being hypnotized couldn't have affected her because she already had talent. All that happened was that she'd stopped believing in herself. There's another pretty obvious point. And it's as simple as that, he says. So there—it's no longer a big secret. Do you know of any dark corners nearby? he then asks, smiling suggestively. The girl smiles in turn, but it's not a happy smile, her eyes say as much, and the screenwriter even detects in them the beginnings of contempt. She brought the pages he requested. He takes them out of her hand, stealing a finger's caress. Such soft skin, he thinks, as he closes his eyes and kisses her. Everything's a game, the girl hears him say, a game of two people's shared pain. Only a game, nothing more. Do you think I'm crazy? the girl asks him, offering her hand again, as if to prove it's made of flesh and bone, as if to prove there really is a world, and that somewhere in that world there's a crusty old screenwriter sitting at a table in a café with all his worldly possessions at his side, everything he owns, stuffed into a big plastic bag, save the old-fashioned typewriter before which he sits, upon which he's trying to finish his story, having stopped momentarily to take a girl's hand, who wants to know if she's barking mad. He doesn't answer, but wants to know why she's asking. She lies and tells him there's no particular reason. Then she takes back her hand and leaves. The screenwriter stays seated, hardly budging, as he reads the pages that will guide him toward the conclusion of his story. Some people would call it the climax, but not him. Though he doesn't even remember the technical terms designating the separate parts of a story's arc. But he's not going to be teaching any classes in paradise; there'll be no more literature students, so he doesn't need to know the terminology now. But he can still invoke them instinctively, even if he doesn't know their names, and that's all that really matters in the end. All that matters, he says, bracing himself before the typewriter. Only a few pages left, he tells himself, as he considers the next scene, which is set in one of the lounges of the hotel with the English name. The girl is standing next to the piano as her mother, wearing the gravest expression she's yet shown, is handing her a large envelope. The envelope is unsealed, and the girl shows little interest as she inspects the contents: a videocassette and some photographs. She reseals the contents and leaves it on the tail of the piano. There's no need for closer scrutiny; even if she might have denied it to herself, she's always known what her destiny would be. Do you know how much damage this will do if it gets to the press? asks her mother from the other side of the piano. What's the difference? asks the girl. As long as they manage to fill a soccer stadium, it doesn't matter if a person sells their mind, their body, or their talent to do so. With the publicity these photographs will generate, combined with her skills on the piano, the girl will set the standard for the music of the future. This will be the kind of music they'll listen to in the City in Outer

Space. You better hope your father doesn't find out, warns her mother, because I don't know what he'll do! The girl continues imputing her mother's incapacity to see the bigger picture. Not what he'll do to you, adds her mother, but to that teacher of yours. The girl asks if they're demanding money, although she has a feeling the anonymous sender has already achieved his aim, and that it wasn't blackmail, but to expose her relationship with the screenwriter to her parents. Moreover, she thinks she knows exactly who the anonymous sender is. The number of possible suspects wouldn't exactly fill a soccer stadium. Her mother's called the Principal of the Scholastic Institute to alert her of the situation. But if there's no blackmail, there's no point in getting worked up, says the girl. Her mother wants to know how long the relationship's been going on. The girl says she hasn't been keeping track—a year, perhaps. They're going to fire him, her mother says, taking a few steps around the piano, thinking out loud, without looking at her daughter. He'll probably never be able to teach again. His reputation will be ruined. What I don't know is what to do with you, she says, stopping and looking back at the girl. How could you have done such a thing? A few moments go by, adding tension to the scene. If it was for money, all you had to do was ask. The girl smiles archly, but her mother keeps her eyes fixed on her. If it wasn't for money then what was it? The girl doesn't answer. What was it? her mother insists. You wouldn't understand, the girl says at last. Her mother assures her she'll do her best to understand. The girl walks away from the piano and goes to the window. The day's become misty, but she can just make out a bridge overlooking the river. It was just a game, she says. A game? With him? But he's a grown man! The girl turns to look at her mother and smiles mischievously again, because she knows it gets on her nerves. No, a game with your favorite musicians: the young conductor and brilliant composer. At night, while the screenwriter heads back to the bridge to get some sleep, he thinks about the pages the girl's been sending him. If anything, it's still a little vague in places, he thinks. She needs to make more explicit the link between the aliens and the No World. He rummages through some garbage and eats a piece of stale bread and a half-eaten apple someone else discarded. After exploring the bin to its very bottom, he manages to find a newspaper, so he goes to the nearest streetlight to sit down and read.

As he did the day before, the screenwriter walks the streets begging for change that he then spends on sandwiches and coffee. He goes to the fountain in the plaza to get a drink of water and then goes into the café to sit at his table and continue writing. The waitress occasionally pauses at his table to contemplate his furious, almost deranged expression as he types. He can't keep going like this, she warns. He only asks for two more days, as if he was requesting an extension, two more days and he'll be finished. Then he can roll over and die. To die peacefully, violently, perhaps indifferently . . . he's not sure which adjective applies. The waitress watches him closely as he says these words. She smiles at him. The screenwriter still feels quite distant from her, and yet the connection between them has never been closer, and although his face is haggard, piteous, he manages to smile back at her. He writes without stopping, until midday, when the girl pays him a visit. She's wearing a wig this time, because she once again thinks they're following her. She's carrying more pages with her. They're the last, she says. The screenwriter acknowledges to himself he's nearing the end of the script, the end of love, the end of life perhaps. Will you be back? he asks her. She says no. She'll be going back home as soon as possible. The screen-writer would have liked to start a new life with her, to have conquered every adversity with her, to have created something he's never managed to create. The girl sits on the other side of the table, of the typewriter, listening to him say these things once more. I never promised you anything, she says. Then all that's left for him to do is croak at his writing desk. Die with his boots on. He murmurs something incoherently about the time he has left, before asking her what day it is. Wednesday the thirty-first, she says, and the screenwriter gets lost in his usual reverie, imagining the two of them just barely scraping by together, but still happy since they're together, on some faraway beach, dealing with life's adversities by making love all day and all night until they expire. There are two ways to die with one's boots on, he assures her, making love or writing. Then why die on some faraway beach? she asks him, imply-ing he can die making love or writing in any old place. The screenwriter starts going over the pages she's brought him. There are only a few of them, but they're crucial, indispens-able. They mean everything, actually. Then, without looking up, he asks her to wait another day or two before abandoning him and the neighboring country's capital. Yes, they mean everything, he mumbles. They mean the story has come full circle. Are the circles concentric or spiral? Oh, what does it matter? The screenwriter's words are becoming intelligible only to himself. So the girl gets up and leaves him to his mus-ings; leaves him as she begins to doubt his sanity, turning to give him one last look before leaving the café terrace. The scene ends with a distant shot of the screenwriter sitting alone in the corner, talking to himself, although it looks like he's mouthing the words he's typing in his almost furious derange-ment on the typewriter.

It's an old discussion we revisit on occasion: "let's imagine twelve-tone music had never been invented," except now pertaining to literature. The girl's father dismisses it as a mere catchphrase of hers and her friends, something they repeat insistently, but which has little to do with any real concerns. The girl watches him from the small dining area of the apartment while he dresses at the foot of the bed. Consider, he says, the author who writes about solitude, jealousy, and the passage of time; or the writer who revolutionized twentieth-century literature. No other writers have contributed as much as these, which is why we can't describe any others with these same epithets. It's not for our sakes they became great writers, nor for the sake of the market. The girl watches him with great interest as he takes the gun from the holster that's hanging from the bedpost, clicks off the safety, and returns it to the holster again. They're important for other reasons than just being great storytellers, he continues. Perhaps neither was the best storyteller there ever was, and perhaps neither had the greatest skill as a writer, or maybe one of them did, but the point is that's not why we remember them, he says as he takes his jacket from the back of a chair and dons it before the mirror. He looks sideways at his daughter. Let me see if I can explain. The girl takes a seat. Their contribution was not necessarily different in degree, but rather in kind, to what had come before. And so considerable was their contribution, they couldn't be thought of as mere exponents of some ephemeral movement, members of a literary circle preaching some common aesthetic gospel. What they did went beyond the mere quibbling flimflam of coffeehouse cabals. Their achievement was to look farther than even the political flimflam dividing nations. The girl's father says all this standing at the door, getting ready to go. That's why they're the only two writers with these particular epithets. Then he excuses himself because he's in a hurry, and the girl's left alone with her thoughts. To write. Contribute something new. Hypnosis. She walks around the room, looks at herself in the mirror. She doesn't smoke habitually, but she lights a cigarette and looks out the window at a nondescript landscape. She certainly prefers the view from the hotel in front of the Grand Central Station. She sits in front of the laptop and resolves to write, to conquer the paralysis she believes was visited on her by the hypnotist. She still can't accept that a mere change of mindset is all she needs to break the spell. She dabbles without success with one of the scenes featuring the old philosophy professor. Perhaps she should write the ending first; she has a good idea how her story's going to end. Bad idea, she says to herself. Nothing that starts badly can be expected to end well. Perhaps she should change her approach. If she could write with the same daring, the same ingenuity she displayed at the piano . . . if her writing was different, in degree and kind, to use her father's words . . . perhaps that's what's been missing, she thinks while trying to ignore the persistent ringing of the telephone. Her mother wants to know if she's alone. She's always alone. Her father's still conducting his vigils, although she doesn't know where they are this time. Her mother wants a meeting with her old teacher. But what's the point? the girl asks. Her mother says, although unconvincingly, that she wants to come to a financial agreement with him. The girl doesn't think it will be necessary. The mother then insists, but the girl refuses to comply with her. There's no point, she says. There is a point, says her mother, and I have to see him. Why do you *have* to see him? Because he's murdered his wife, her mother confesses. He gave her a horrible death. How? the girl asks. He tied her to a bed and just left her there to die. The girl gives her mother the address of the hotel where she used to visit him. He checked out of there days ago, says her mother, or rather, was kicked out for starting a fracas with a neighbor. The old teacher's been keeping a pretty big secret, perhaps it's more than one, thinks the girl, smirking, on entering the police station with her mother. The whole world has its secrets. Some people may not even be aware of the secrets they harbor. Perhaps we're aliens without knowing it. But then that wouldn't be a true secret, she considers, for a secret is something we deliberately conceal from others. One of the police officers shows them photographs of the screenwriter's wife. There's a passport photo, but mostly shots of the crime scene. Is it possible her death was part of some game? asks the officer. As far as she knows, the game only ends once the young conductor climbs into her mother's bed, replies the girl. Her mother slaps her, humiliated. The girl looks back to the police officer. Apparently the game has already ended, she says coldly. Her mother moves away and takes a seat behind them, the shot blurring her in the background to focus on the girl and police officer. Who found her? she asks. Her son, he says. The girl is shaking when she gets back to the apartment. Her father's still out, and she resolves to write the scene. Hypnosis is no longer a concern. The only thing that has her in a trance is the knowledge that someone so close to her could be capable of something so cruel. The game continues. Indeed, perhaps there are only two people in the world who know this to be true, that the game still lacks an ending. The girl gets down to work, finally exorcised of her obsession with hypnosis, of her self-doubt, or whatever it was that paralyzed her before. As novels with various stories moving in parallel must bring them all to an end, so it is with the game, and very few players seem to realize the difficulty of dealing with so many interrelated stories that diverge from one another and get lost before finally discovering their own endings. She's now writing a scene she's been struggling with for some time: the one in which the old professor's arguing with his wife about the anonymous letter, about his relationship with the female student, with all the mutual threats, and the screaming and shouting. She thinks about the scene, not knowing how to approach it. It's not the right words she lacks, but a focus for the scene, a resolution, and nothing that comes to mind strikes her as very original. She does have a clear image of the old guy in her mind, though, sitting in front of the bed, drained, as if after a great ordeal, looking at his wife as she slowly regains consciousness. She moves her mouth to say something, but finds her words are muffled by a gag. The discovery brings her to like a splash of cold water, and her eyes become as expressive as they've ever been—darting here and there, trying to take in everything around her, to ascertain whether he's really followed through on his threats, and on discovering he has, as if trying to escape the fleshy tether binding them to the woman's sockets. He watches her to ensure she's properly secured. Then, without saying a word, gets up and goes. The girl lights a cigarette and leans out the window to smoke it. She's not looking at anything, but her mind's eye is focused on that image of the woman lying dead in the bed, for she's entranced by the notion that the old guy committed such a despicable crime. He probably justified it by convincing himself she was an alien. How else could he have eased his conscience, been able to live with himself? Then she wonders if, years later, in the City in Outer Space, while seated on a chair in the control room, looking through the windows at the stars, the old professor could deal with the return of those memories; if, between dreams, while stumbling through deserted streets, familiar to him because he sees them daily, because the ravages of war have endowed each with its own unique aspect, he'll be hoping for something to happen, something he's been waiting for years to happen, a resolution, something for which the hope becomes an end in itself to make his situation more tolerable, so he can make sense of it. The girl writes: "When the answer cannot be put into words, neither can the question be put into words. The *riddle* does not exist." This isn't the ending, but the end's right there. It's always been there. Just a few more lines.

The essence of construction, recalls the screenwriter, is for the builder to have the outcome in mind before he begins, and then to proceed upward, step by step. He feels he's only a few steps away. He's had more than enough time to read about it in the girl's *No World* and then write it down. His only regret is that he didn't figure it out a lot sooner. He's come up with the endings in the same way as someone who feels he's finally understood the rules of a game, gained control of the board. He's even read about how he's going to die, although perhaps he's always known how this would happen, he thinks, smiling. Still, he's left with a bittersweet feeling inside. A bittersweet work: that's what she's written: a mixture of flavors, though nothing to do with dodecaphony. He's not sure if her work is good or bad, for he's lost the aesthetic distance he needs to make this judgment. Neither good nor bad, just a reality that repeats itself, he says, before proceeding with his bittersweet result, a result that may not be expressible in such language, that may have nothing to do with his own language, that sounds strange, foreign, that may be better expressed in another language, the language in which masterpieces are most often written. Who better than the author of jealousy and lost time to announce at the end of a novel to those who deemed him an invalid, incapable of completing a monumental work, that the story has come full circle, closing in on itself, that the work is the place where criticism begins and ends, that the reader has assisted him, step by step, in its construction? Well, this is an idea he's stolen from the girl's father. The screenwriter needs to think of something more humble. The recovery of lost time, which is the primary goal, wouldn't be too harrowing if, in the process of writing, he also manages to recover himself—a bonus, as it were. He can't decide if either recovery is even all that important—or perhaps they're only important to him. No one else would care, and they might even prefer a different outcome altogether. Some of his colleagues in the movie business think getting to the end should take precedence over every other concern the writer might have during the writing of his story. The screenwriter takes a seat at his usual post in the back of the café and asks the waitress for his usual coffee. In front of him, a mountain of pages is begging to take its leave, his screenplay imploring to be completed and sent away—from him, from this world. Before entering the work, perhaps he needs a moment of repose to get the right perspective, the right aesthetic distance—the very things he's never bothered about, which he never thought mattered. At the end of the day, all that matters is to be in the moment. After making a last call from the café telephone, he returns to his table and lights a cigarette. "I had a farm in Africa, at the foot of the Ngong Hills," he whispers to himself. The beginning of a novel the girl's father would surely recognize. The screenwriter doesn't know why, but the words are reassuring. "I had a farm . . ." he repeats, imagining the girl's father speaking them, taking another look outside the café: at the plaza and the fountain, at the people walking back and forth, at the tables and chairs on the terrace withstanding the passage of hours and days, and he takes his first drag, long and deep, and waits a few moments before exhaling a dense lungful at the ceiling with a sigh, as though satisfying a multitude of cravings at once.

The girl hasn't written in a while. She doesn't smoke habitually, but she lights a cigarette and looks out the window at the nondescript landscape. She still prefers the view from the hotel in front of the Grand Central Station. Her father is reading, surrounded by a number of cell phones. Some things haven't changed in their environment—the phones, the fax machine, and the interminable waiting to which both of them have become inured. The girl's managed to write a few lines, but she's still not happy with them. They're about the discovery of the woman's body by her son, and the subsequent police investigation of the female student's role in the crime, or perhaps even to the philosophy professor's flight to the City in Outer Space, a city once ravaged by war, far removed from human contact, and certainly inaccessible to those pursuing him, but at the same time a prison to which he'll have condemned himself forever. But the girl finally decides most of the details are irrelevant and scraps them. Sometimes it's best to omit certain scenes, not to over-explain, let the reader connect the dots. Isn't that the way things happen in real life? Isn't it true that some things only occur in the mind and can't be shown on the page? She smokes her cigarette, observing a landscape that can only be described as very different from the view from the hotel in front of the Grand Central Station. Now and again, her father receives a call on one of his phones that he answers in a low register. The girl also receives a call she's been expecting, answers it in a low register both to imitate and mock her father, before grabbing her jacket and satchel and fixing herself up in the bathroom mirror. I'll be right back, she says. Her father lifts his eyes from his newspaper, which he rests on his knees. His face is expressionless, or perhaps it's a routine expression that could be interpreted to mean anything. Won't you be warm dressed like that? he asks. Once on the stairway, the girl hides the gun in the small of her back, behind her jeans. Then she goes outside, looks left and right to check that nobody's following her—not that anyone could possibly recognize her through her disguise—before hailing the first cab she sees, from which she alights at the corner of the boulevards. She'd prefer to walk the remaining distance, as if this was a long established ritual, to have a few more minutes to herself before confronting her destiny. While climbing the hill close to the place where the famous writer once lived, the one whose name everyone knows, even the people who no longer read his books, the girl once again gets the same feeling she's had since arriving in the neighboring country's capital, the feeling that she's being followed. She stops in front of a window and sees Cousin McGregor approaching from some meters away, barely concealing his presence. The girl decides to ignore him, and continues on her way. Perhaps he's the one who's been following her the whole time, she snickers. Perhaps he's one of those alien hunters who don't know they're aliens. When she reaches the café, she stops at the door to look for the screenwriter, who she finds sitting in the same place he's been writing, smoking, and drinking coffee the past few days. The typewriter, shifted to his left toward the edge of the table, leaves just enough space for the screenplay that rests beside it. For once, he isn't typing, and there's no paper in the carriage. The frenetic activity she saw him exhibit the last time has vanished, the determined glower has contorted into a look of serenity. He's looking through the window at the waitress moving between the tables and chairs on the terrace outside. It's only now he really feels the loss of opportunity as he sees her smiling. He thinks he could've made her happy. He lowers his eyes to count out some change on the table. He feels like calling his wife. Although he realizes it's pointless, he still likes to experience the satisfaction of vengeance. He no longer hates her, no longer resents her in any way, but he calls her out of habit, and because the feeling of revenge has to be fed. By contrast, when he thinks about the girl, he remembers only lost opportunities. The vague hope to one day run away with her, to travel the world next to that young body that so willingly surrendered to him, next to that soft, perfectly tanned skin, covered in delicate down, which he'd so like to photograph again. But he knows none of it will ever happen. The screenwriter reckons his life is coming to a sardonic sort of end, and he doesn't even know if it was worth living. Perhaps the writing made it worthwhile, because he seems to believe writing and living are equally important. He knows now that he'll never be going anywhere with the girl, that there'll be no voluntary exile, so he's learning to live his life one day at a time, something they don't teach in any school, something that isn't learned in any one place, but everywhere at once. Some people don't have enough time for it to be otherwise, he thinks. Perhaps it's just a question of focus. He'd like to know what he meant to the girl, what she was feeling when they made love, when his fingers sought relief in the touch of her skin, and every time he removed her clothes and photographed her. To know, the screenwriter murmurs, crushing his cigarette in the ashtray and raising his eyes, seeing her image appearing and moving toward him, stopping as he repeats the words, to know, as something is repeated because it's unreachable, because it's hopeless, to mark with the tip of his tongue the impossible skin of an impossible image, because his fingers cannot reach it, to know . . . three ellipsis points taking leave of his mouth at the moment she starts firing one, two, three bullets into his chest. Sometimes, time seems to stand still, he thinks. It's an absurdity, a false perception, something that cannot really be, like all those things that don't exist outside the mind, but while experiencing that false and absurd sensation of stillness, the image of the girl remains, her arms hanging loosely at her sides, the gun held weakly in one of her hands, looking at, although perhaps not seeing, the screenwriter slumped on the floor next to the table. There's a profound silence, no one in the café even budges, although some people in the plaza have heard the sound of gunfire. The waitress slowly places her tray on a table and sits down, covering her mouth with one hand, not believing what's just transpired, watching the thick dark shadow under the screenwriter's body spreading like oil spilled on the floor. Cousin McGregor then appears, as if out of nowhere, as if he were an angel from heaven, or the one in the movie the screenwriter liked to remember when he was still alive, the one who heard other people's voices, their thoughts as well, perhaps those of everyone on Earth, an angel who used to go by the name of Cousin Dedalus. He approaches in an unhurried manner, calmly, with the seamless air of a professional who's accustomed to scenes like this. Anyone would say he'd always been there, just waiting for the right opportunity. He disarms the girl and checks the screenwriter's vitals, or lack thereof. Then he stands and flashes his wallet, announcing loud and clear the word police, before taking the screenplay from the table and grabbing the girl and half-dragging her away from the scene of the crime.

Some time goes by, hours perhaps. The girl is looking through a window at the sky, blanketed by clouds, at the leaden landscape, the scarcity of verdure, at the single road in front of her, empty, and at a small beach beyond it, where black waves break in a grayer shade of white. A place well off the beaten track, it would seem. Then she sees a man walking on the sand with his dog, and by the road, a couple of nurses heading in the opposite direction. It's not long since she awoke. The last thing she remembers is her mother giving her a pill to calm her down. Then the silence, the white noise, the cosmic radiation: she has the impression that if she lets her mind go blank in a quiet place, she can hear a noise in the background that is the whisper of the cosmos. It's not the voices, the ones that pronounce her name differently, but the thought underlying them, the same thought that's been constructing itself and expanding in the surrounding nothingness over the course of eons. But right now she's not in the mood to try and formulate a theory of how an object located nowhere, that's surrounded by nothing, can be growing continually and expanding. She is sure though, that the cosmic radiation she hears in the silence vindicates any such theory. She's always attributed it to the effects of alcohol or the pills she used to take. The girl isn't experiencing any particular sensation just now, save a malaise associated with the vague memory of a dream. She's not thinking about hypnosis, but she still doesn't feel like writing. To create a parallel between her No Reality and the work she's been writing, she intended to have the old professor commit suicide. "6.4 All propositions are of equal value. 6.5 The riddle does not exist. If a No World can be framed at all, it is also possible to answer it." The girl spends some more time looking out the window before returning her attention to the room. There are various newspapers stacked on a chair, not one of which mentions the death of the screen-writer. The information still hasn't filtered through to the press. She sits on the bed. The effects of the tranquilizer are slowly wearing off, but she still feels a little sluggish. She goes into the bathroom and reacquaints herself with the now familiar image of herself with dyed hair and circles under her eyes. She splashes her face with water to wake herself up and sits on a stool, staring at the wall tiles. She's hungry. She looks at her watch. It's mid-afternoon. Then her mother enters, who's still pronouncing her name with a "ka." The girl's ready to go home, but her mother insists she wait. Wait for what? she asks, since she'd already been waiting for what seemed like an eternity in the hotel room by the Grand Central Station, and now she's waiting again in this inn in the middle of nowhere that hasn't even got a decent view. Perhaps her father, mother, and the cousin are still waiting to meet up with the aliens. You passed out; you were probably suffering from shock, her mother says before assuring her they won't be waiting much longer. See, the bags are all packed, she says, pointing to the luggage by the door. She's just waiting for a phone call and then she'll load them into the car. Meanwhile, she picks up the phone and cancels any commitments the girl may have in other capitals around the world. The girl's mind is beginning to clear. She could've sworn those commitments had already been canceled. The girl once again asks her mother about the astrophysicist in the classically-cut suit. He seemed to know her. But her mother doesn't know what she's talking about, and although the girl realizes it's a faux pas to broach the subject, she's determined to get to the bottom of the mystery. He died in the hotel in which he lived the final years of his life, says the girl, and her father must've gone to the funeral, per-haps the cousin too. There's a long silence. It doesn't seem like her mother is going to say anything. Before we go anywhere, you ought to make peace with your friends, she finally says. Her mother seems to believe the girl should reconcile with the part of her life that was real. Make peace? asks the girl. Those people are the least of her concerns right now. In fact, they're no concern at all. She hates them, and she figures they're the only ones who have nothing whatsoever to do with extraterrestrials. After a while, mother and daughter leave the room together and go down to the lobby of the inn, a small inn used mainly for rest and recuperation, located on the neighboring country's coast. Have you contacted the aliens or are you still waiting? the girl asks. Her mother looks at her, concerned. From where are you getting these obsessions? Is this how you earn your living? the girl asks, suspecting both her parents are members of the same organization. Her mother doesn't answer. She seems to be ignoring her daughter, but any member of a secret organization should have a number of answers prepared for such occasions. Just stop it! her mother demands. Then, in a nearby café, her mother hands her an envelope from the young orchestra conductor and brilliant composer. It's for you, she says. The girl takes it and puts it to one side, not bothering to open it, and continues eating her meal. There are also things the girl refuses to talk about. When she's finished eating, she picks up a newspaper and looks for any news on the star of her favorite soccer team, or perhaps something on the death of the screenwriter. Instead, she sees an article on the scientist in the classically-cut suit. She'll read it later, she thinks. She doesn't want her mother finding out. Then her mother's cell phone rings, which she answers, then pretends not to have a good signal so she can take it outside. The girl uses the opportunity to open the envelope. Inside is the photo of her standing next to the guy she met in the nightclub. It wasn't even a week ago, yet it seems like forever. I should've shot him, she says offhandedly, guessing at his ultimate fate. Along with the photo, there's a clipping of an ad by the guy in which he offers his sexual services. So that's what it was, she murmurs. On the back of the photo, there's a dedication next to the one she wrote that simply says: "a gift from your friend." Voices . . . she murmurs, remembering the game and her underdeveloped theory of the cosmos. I heard voices. The girl smirks as she tears up the photograph and clipping into several small pieces. For a nobody, the little shit has certainly upped the ante, she thinks, referring to the brilliant composer. He's an utter deviant, and whatever talent he possesses has been warped by this quality. It's evident in all his compositions. She imagines him responding to the guy's ad, meeting up with him . . . perhaps I'll kill him next time, she says aloud as her mother reenters the café. What did you say? her mother asks. Oh, nothing, the girl says, watching her mother sit down opposite her. The girl would like to know if her mother's finally made contact, but she remembers the question wasn't well received before, so she stays quiet. Perhaps her tactfulness is an effect of the tranquilizer, or that she's finally beginning to distance herself from such things. Perhaps this is another way of saying everything's a game, that life, from beginning to end, is only a game.

Numberless clouds climb over the horizon and invade the coast, imparting a leaden aspect to the day. Evening falls. On the shore, whooping seagulls are swooping overhead, while an army of Boy Scouts are marching up the road, holding their standards aloft and proud, flapping though not flagging in the eye of the wind, together out-singing the squadrons of gulls, and whistling brave defiance at the clouds. The one farthest behind, who looks less than ten years old, is wearing a bandana decked with skull and crossbones. Standing next to her mother's convertible, the girl watches them while thinking about the strange memory, as of a half-forgotten dream, adulterated by a sedative, which gives her the feeling she's waking up from something both old and new at the same time. She takes a seat in the car and starts reading the article about the scientist, while her mother oversees the transfer of their luggage. Among his documents, they discovered proof of the existence of extraterrestrial intelligence. Apparently, he dictated in his will that the news be disclosed in the event of his death. The girl recognizes the photos accompanying the text. She's seen them on more than one occasion. Another interesting detail, the scientist was found dead in the same hotel her father and the cousin were staying in, in front of the Grand Central Station. Tell me if I'm dreaming, mumbles the girl carefully, so her mother doesn't hear. She needs to be independent, to get her own place. She's a writer, if only because of hypnosis, yet it's still the only thing she wants to do in life. She doesn't know what to do with her career as a concert pianist. A career that wouldn't have been possible in the first place were it not for her mother's connections; she probably even owes her reputation as a prodigy to her mother making a few phone calls. She returns to her previous thought. Is it possible her father and the cousin now take turns staying in the scientist's room? That they moved out of the hotel in front of the Grand Central Station because they no longer had any hope of their objective being met on the station platforms? There are still a lot of questions to be answered. She drops the newspaper at her feet and tries to concentrate on ridding herself of these strange obsessions that color her whole world. She has to change her life, free herself of these burdens. She shouldn't waste another second speculating about what her parents are up to, and she doesn't want to hear another word about the young conductor or the brilliant composer. In life, in reality, she'll encounter them again under a different name, under the collective epithet, the plagiarists. It fits them like a glove. She should change the title of her novel to incorporate the word, plagiarist. They've stolen practically everything from her. Everything except money. When her mother starts the car, the girl keeps her eyes on the distance, focusing on the scouts' rucksacks, listening to the sound of their singing redoubling as they approach. The one farthest behind, who looks less than ten years old, is wearing a bandana decked with skull and crossbones. She too would whistle and sing if she could, if she was in the mood, if she could rid herself of the obsessions that have colored her reality for so long. Certain characters cross her mind, the old screenwriter, her father, the cousin, but she doesn't think they'll prove to be any different from her mother, the young conductor, or brilliant composer. Then she looks sideways at her mother, wondering if it isn't she who's really pulling all the strings, that she's only using the vague title of business executive as a front. The girl feels that she's surrounded by strange beings; she'd almost say beings from another world—remembering the phrase she heard one day in a café. Let's imagine we're talking about beings from a No World. A No World located in this one, if we must be specific: a heaven, hell, or purgatory, to which these beings have been sent, coming from other galaxies; perhaps it's a heaven for some and a hell for others, and, as such, without differentiating them, it's possible to see, living together, both the condemned being punished for their sins and the blessed being rewarded for their virtues. The girl hasn't the slightest doubt about which group she belongs to. She deserves no better for the way she's behaved. But who knows . . . Then, the girl imagines a conversation with her father, a conversation modeled after those she's had before, in which he promised her that, one day, he'd give up his rotten job and dedicate his life to writing. She isn't surprised. He'd have no problem finding things to write about. She suggests he write an autobiographical novel, a fictional account of his life. There's nothing more interesting than that. Of course, she says this thinking about the astrophysicist and the aliens, about the cousin and her mother, about the long vigil—the reason for which they're still concealing from the girl. Must there always be a reason? she wonders. Her father then suggests, sarcastically, that she should write his biography, although this would be the very opposite of what a great writer would choose to do. Better yet, she should ghostwrite his autobiography, and give it the title: *Daddy's Autobiography*. The girl would never write anything with such a title, but she stays quiet, because she doesn't see any point in contradicting him. What are you thinking about? interrupts her mother, her eyes fixed on the road ahead. The girl breaks her reverie for a fraction of a second to glance at her mother before looking straight ahead again without answering. She recalls that character of that screenwriter's, the young college chick, who went around collecting the beginnings of novels. In a similar way, one could go around collecting the endings of novels. The girl would love to find something to work with in this. She tries remembering some of the endings that have impressed her most. She remembers one in particular, by someone who, had he been a novelist instead of a gangster or a spy, might have pleased her father immensely. As for his favorite writer, the author of jealousy and solitude, she's not sure which ending her father would choose. The novel has numerous volumes, and some of the endings to those volumes are pages long, during which the author may describe a particular house, a particular street, a garden walk, the scent of a shrub, a person's gait, memories of events that took an instant to transpire, experiences that took an instant to experience, while, for the reader, unfortunately, those instants seem more like years. Cousin McGregor, on the other hand, can only offer something pitifully pithy: " . . . and his heart was going like mad and yes I said yes I will Yes." But the girl's trying to remember another ending, one her father mentioned to her before, which goes something like: ". . . it does not look to me as if you were ever going to write that autobiography. You know what I am going to do. I am going to write it for you." It's the kind of ending she'd love to have for her own novel. She smiles, thinking about the phrase, tries changing the voice: I'm certain you were never going to write your autobiography . . . The girl laughs; it reminds her of the dead screenwriter. Perhaps he actually finished his screenplay before he croaked, but that's immaterial, because at the end of the day, the only work that matters to the girl is her own. Doesn't she want to be a writer? Well, she has a good story at her fingertips: the last days of the screenwriter, with maybe a few passing references to those former friends of hers. No one will believe these things really happened, so she'll write it, but using the screenwriter's voice. The novel will be a homage to that last photo he never got to take of her, in which she's dressed in a tuxedo, or perhaps just wearing the jacket, double-breasted but unbuttoned, with a bowtie around her neck, and wearing her mother's high-heel shoes, which are clearly too big for her: a novel in which she appears ostensibly naked. In a way, it will be a continuation, the second part of the story about Cousin Dedalus she was so anxious to write, but in which he'll no longer be the protagonist. A novel that will write itself as it's being read. Whether she was hypnotized or not, she's resolute about pursuing her vocation, and for that, she has all the time in the world. The constructions of the mind are the constructions of the No World, she tells herself, as she grabs her notebook and tears out the pages of her former scribbling, one at a time, until she reaches a blank page, and inscribes her new title at the top. Perhaps she could imagine the stories succeeding one another in concentric circles, like the layers of an onion, or like those old Russian dolls, a series of stories within stories. Or perhaps she should think more along the lines of two mirrors reflecting each other, an effect that's always bothered her, but the more she thought about it, the more she imagined that this infinite regress would still take the form of a spiral, a spiral folding in on itself, for when it remains on the mirror's flat plane, this gives it the appearance of having concentric circles, although the circles grow smaller and smaller ad infinitum, but if pulled outward from that invisible, infinitesimally small center, it would assume the shape of a cone. She has yet to decide which concept will serve her best; it doesn't really matter, as long as she doesn't renew her futile obsession to write a dodecaphonic novel. But there's no rush, she can begin anytime, or choose to postpone things a little longer. It's the same as with those voices she hears calling her from the other side of the universe, pronouncing her name with a "ka." It's a secret she's not sure will ever be revealed, although she doesn't really care, because she's learned how to be patient, how to wait. When the revelation does occur, though, she expects it will be in the form of a discovery, definitive proof that there really is something outside the mind, a hypothetical reality existing somewhere in the great beyond. A single thought expanding outward, creating a nebulous galaxy without a definite shape, because it's immaterial, ethereal, something resembling God, in other words, something that doesn't physically exist, although it's capable of creating a world, a whole universe around itself, and even of envisioning a brain, something with weight and extension, in which it suspends its disbelief and imagines itself contained, a brain that can draw upon the space between stars—just as the initial thought drew upon the surrounding nothingness—to create its own universe and invent itself. She takes a look in the side-view mirror in case anyone's following her. Although perhaps it's more out of habit, as she's no longer afraid of the alien hunters. The sedative's practically worn off, and she's feeling alive again. Her mother stops at a traffic light before they enter the town center, peers beneath her sunglasses, and reads the heading written on the otherwise blank page. What was it you said the No World meant? she asks. The girl doesn't answer. She doesn't have the time to be answering stupid questions because she has the story at the tips of her fingers, and, moreover, she knows that when something's struggling to break free, she needs to give it an outlet. So she leaves a space after the title, and begins writing: "The screenwriter stands with his luggage, facing the hotel, having just gotten out of a taxi, thinking he ought to know, or at least have a good idea, how the story he intends to write is going to end . . ." Her mother suspects something's wrong. I think you should take a break, she says. All this writing can't be good for your health. "6.41 The sense of the No World must lie outside of it," the girl continues, not paying the least attention.

Barcelona, Paris, Ceret,
April 1994–July 2005

A. G. PORTA was born in Barcelona in 1954. He gained prominence in the Spanish literary world when he won the Ámbito Literario de Narrativa Prize in 1984 for a novel written with Roberto Bolaño. After a silence of over ten years—which Bolaño claimed that Porta spent reading and rereading Joyce—he began publishing novels to widespread critical acclaim.

DARREN KOOLMAN was born in 1982 on the island of Aruba, in the Netherlands Antilles. He is a poet and literary translator from Spanish, French, and Dutch. He has an M.Phil in creative writing from Trinity College Dublin.

RHETT MCNEIL has translated work by Machado de Assis, António Lobo Antunes, and Gonçalo M. Tavares.

MICHAL AJVAZ, *The Golden Age.*
   The Other City.
PIERRE ALBERT-BIROT, *Grabinoulor.*
YUZ ALESHKOVSKY, *Kangaroo.*
FELIPE ALFAU, *Chromos.*
   Locos.
IVAN ÂNGELO, *The Celebration.*
   The Tower of Glass.
ANTÓNIO LOBO ANTUNES, *Knowledge of Hell.*
   The Splendor of Portugal.
ALAIN ARIAS-MISSON, *Theatre of Incest.*
JOHN ASHBERY AND JAMES SCHUYLER,
   A Nest of Ninnies.
ROBERT ASHLEY, *Perfect Lives.*
GABRIELA AVIGUR-ROTEM, *Heatwave*
   and Crazy Birds.
DJUNA BARNES, *Ladies Almanack.*
   Ryder.
JOHN BARTH, *LETTERS.*
   Sabbatical.
DONALD BARTHELME, *The King.*
   Paradise.
SVETISLAV BASARA, *Chinese Letter.*
MIQUEL BAUÇÀ, *The Siege in the Room.*
RENÉ BELLETTO, *Dying.*
MAREK BIEŃCZYK, *Transparency.*
ANDREI BITOV, *Pushkin House.*
ANDREJ BLATNIK, *You Do Understand.*
LOUIS PAUL BOON, *Chapel Road.*
   My Little War.
   Summer in Termuren.
ROGER BOYLAN, *Killoyle.*
IGNÁCIO DE LOYOLA BRANDÃO,
   Anonymous Celebrity.
   Zero.
BONNIE BREMSER, *Troia: Mexican Memoirs.*
CHRISTINE BROOKE-ROSE, *Amalgamemnon.*
BRIGID BROPHY, *In Transit.*
GERALD L. BRUNS, *Modern Poetry and*
   the Idea of Language.
GABRIELLE BURTON, *Heartbreak Hotel.*
MICHEL BUTOR, *Degrees.*
   Mobile.
G. CABRERA INFANTE, *Infante's Inferno.*
   Three Trapped Tigers.
JULIETA CAMPOS,
   The Fear of Losing Eurydice.
ANNE CARSON, *Eros the Bittersweet.*
ORLY CASTEL-BLOOM, *Dolly City.*
LOUIS-FERDINAND CÉLINE, *Castle to Castle.*
   Conversations with Professor Y.
   London Bridge.
   Normance.
   North.
   Rigadoon.
MARIE CHAIX, *The Laurels of Lake Constance.*
HUGO CHARTERIS, *The Tide Is Right.*
ERIC CHEVILLARD, *Demolishing Nisard.*
MARC CHOLODENKO, *Mordechai Schamz.*
JOSHUA COHEN, *Witz.*
EMILY HOLMES COLEMAN, *The Shutter*
   of Snow.
ROBERT COOVER, *A Night at the Movies.*
STANLEY CRAWFORD, *Log of the S.S. The*
   Mrs Unguentine.
   Some Instructions to My Wife.
RENÉ CREVEL, *Putting My Foot in It.*
RALPH CUSACK, *Cadenza.*
NICHOLAS DELBANCO, *The Count of Concord.*
   Sherbrookes.
NIGEL DENNIS, *Cards of Identity.*

PETER DIMOCK, *A Short Rhetoric for*
   Leaving the Family.
ARIEL DORFMAN, *Konfidenz.*
COLEMAN DOWELL,
   Island People.
   Too Much Flesh and Jabez.
ARKADII DRAGOMOSHCHENKO, *Dust.*
RIKKI DUCORNET, *The Complete*
   Butcher's Tales.
   The Fountains of Neptune.
   The Jade Cabinet.
   Phosphor in Dreamland.
WILLIAM EASTLAKE, *The Bamboo Bed.*
   Castle Keep.
   Lyric of the Circle Heart.
JEAN ECHENOZ, *Chopin's Move.*
STANLEY ELKIN, *A Bad Man.*
   Criers and Kibitzers, Kibitzers
   and Criers.
   The Dick Gibson Show.
   The Franchiser.
   The Living End.
   Mrs. Ted Bliss.
FRANÇOIS EMMANUEL, *Invitation to a*
   Voyage.
SALVADOR ESPRIU, *Ariadne in the*
   Grotesque Labyrinth.
LESLIE A. FIEDLER, *Love and Death in*
   the American Novel.
JUAN FILLOY, *Op Oloop.*
ANDY FITCH, *Pop Poetics.*
GUSTAVE FLAUBERT, *Bouvard and Pécuchet.*
KASS FLEISHER, *Talking out of School.*
FORD MADOX FORD,
   The March of Literature.
JON FOSSE, *Aliss at the Fire.*
   Melancholy.
MAX FRISCH, *I'm Not Stiller.*
   Man in the Holocene.
CARLOS FUENTES, *Christopher Unborn.*
   Distant Relations.
   Terra Nostra.
   Where the Air Is Clear.
TAKEHIKO FUKUNAGA, *Flowers of Grass.*
WILLIAM GADDIS, *J R.*
   The Recognitions.
JANICE GALLOWAY, *Foreign Parts.*
   The Trick Is to Keep Breathing.
WILLIAM H. GASS, *Cartesian Sonata*
   and Other Novellas.
   Finding a Form.
   A Temple of Texts.
   The Tunnel.
   Willie Masters' Lonesome Wife.
GÉRARD GAVARRY, *Hoppla! 1 2 3.*
ETIENNE GILSON,
   The Arts of the Beautiful.
   Forms and Substances in the Arts.
C. S. GISCOMBE, *Giscome Road.*
   Here.
DOUGLAS GLOVER, *Bad News of the Heart.*
WITOLD GOMBROWICZ,
   A Kind of Testament.
PAULO EMÍLIO SALES GOMES, *P's Three*
   Women.
GEORGI GOSPODINOV, *Natural Novel.*
JUAN GOYTISOLO, *Count Julian.*
   Juan the Landless.
   Makbara.
   Marks of Identity.

FOR A FULL LIST OF PUBLICATIONS, VISIT:
www.dalkeyarchive.com

HENRY GREEN, *Back.*
Blindness.
Concluding.
Doting.
Nothing.
JACK GREEN, *Fire the Bastards!*
JIŘÍ GRUŠA, *The Questionnaire.*
MELA HARTWIG, *Am I a Redundant*
Human Being?
JOHN HAWKES, *The Passion Artist.*
Whistlejacket.
ELIZABETH HEIGHWAY, ED., *Contemporary*
Georgian Fiction.
ALEKSANDAR HEMON, ED.,
Best European Fiction.
AIDAN HIGGINS, *Balcony of Europe.*
Blind Man's Bluff
Bornholm Night-Ferry.
Flotsam and Jetsam.
Langrishe, Go Down.
Scenes from a Receding Past.
KEIZO HINO, *Isle of Dreams.*
KAZUSHI HOSAKA, *Plainsong.*
ALDOUS HUXLEY, *Antic Hay.*
Crome Yellow.
Point Counter Point.
Those Barren Leaves.
Time Must Have a Stop.
NAOYUKI II, *The Shadow of a Blue Cat.*
GERT JONKE, *The Distant Sound.*
Geometric Regional Novel.
Homage to Czerny.
The System of Vienna.
JACQUES JOUET, *Mountain R.*
Savage.
Upstaged.
MIEKO KANAI, *The Word Book.*
YORAM KANIUK, *Life on Sandpaper.*
HUGH KENNER, *Flaubert.*
Joyce and Beckett: The Stoic Comedians.
Joyce's Voices.
DANILO KIŠ, *The Attic.*
Garden, Ashes.
The Lute and the Scars
Psalm 44.
A Tomb for Boris Davidovich.
ANITA KONKKA, *A Fool's Paradise.*
GEORGE KONRÁD, *The City Builder.*
TADEUSZ KONWICKI, *A Minor Apocalypse.*
The Polish Complex.
MENIS KOUMANDAREAS, *Koula.*
ELAINE KRAF, *The Princess of 72nd Street.*
JIM KRUSOE, *Iceland.*
AYŞE KULIN, *Farewell: A Mansion in*
Occupied Istanbul.
EMILIO LASCANO TEGUI, *On Elegance*
While Sleeping.
ERIC LAURRENT, *Do Not Touch.*
VIOLETTE LEDUC, *La Bâtarde.*
EDOUARD LEVÉ, *Autoportrait.*
Suicide.
MARIO LEVI, *Istanbul Was a Fairy Tale.*
DEBORAH LEVY, *Billy and Girl.*
JOSÉ LEZAMA LIMA, *Paradiso.*
ROSA LIKSOM, *Dark Paradise.*
OSMAN LINS, *Avalovara.*
The Queen of the Prisons of Greece.
ALF MAC LOCHLAINN,
The Corpus in the Library.
Out of Focus.
RON LOEWINSOHN, *Magnetic Field(s).*
MINA LOY, *Stories and Essays of Mina Loy.*

D. KEITH MANO, *Take Five.*
MICHELINE AHARONIAN MARCOM,
The Mirror in the Well.
BEN MARCUS,
The Age of Wire and String.
WALLACE MARKFIELD,
Teitlebaum's Window.
To an Early Grave.
DAVID MARKSON, *Reader's Block.*
Wittgenstein's Mistress.
CAROLE MASO, *AVA.*
LADISLAV MATEJKA AND KRYSTYNA
POMORSKA, EDS.,
Readings in Russian Poetics:
Formalist and Structuralist Views.
HARRY MATHEWS, *Cigarettes.*
The Conversions.
The Human Country: New and
Collected Stories.
The Journalist.
My Life in CIA.
Singular Pleasures.
The Sinking of the Odradek
Stadium.
Tlooth.
JOSEPH MCELROY,
Night Soul and Other Stories.
ABDELWAHAB MEDDEB, *Talismano.*
GERHARD MEIER, *Isle of the Dead.*
HERMAN MELVILLE, *The Confidence-Man.*
AMANDA MICHALOPOULOU, *I'd Like.*
STEVEN MILLHAUSER, *The Barnum Museum.*
In the Penny Arcade.
RALPH J. MILLS, JR., *Essays on Poetry.*
MOMUS, *The Book of Jokes.*
CHRISTINE MONTALBETTI, *The Origin of Man.*
Western.
OLIVE MOORE, *Spleen.*
NICHOLAS MOSLEY, *Accident.*
Assassins.
Catastrophe Practice.
Experience and Religion.
A Garden of Trees.
Hopeful Monsters.
Imago Bird.
Impossible Object.
Inventing God.
Judith.
Look at the Dark.
Natalie Natalia.
Serpent.
Time at War.
WARREN MOTTE,
Fables of the Novel: French Fiction
since 1990.
Fiction Now: The French Novel in
the 21st Century.
Oulipo: A Primer of Potential
Literature.
GERALD MURNANE, *Barley Patch.*
Inland.
YVES NAVARRE, *Our Share of Time.*
Sweet Tooth.
DOROTHY NELSON, *In Night's City.*
Tar and Feathers.
ESHKOL NEVO, *Homesick.*
WILFRIDO D. NOLLEDO, *But for the Lovers.*
FLANN O'BRIEN, *At Swim-Two-Birds.*
The Best of Myles.
The Dalkey Archive.
The Hard Life.
The Poor Mouth.

SELECTED DALKEY ARCHIVE TITLES

SELECTED DALKEY ARCHIVE TITLES